Davon,

Thank you always
for your continued
support of my
writing. I hope you
enjoy this latest
novel and never
forget the
meaning of
home.

Nikesha

Beyond Bourbon Street

Also by Nikesha Elise Williams

Four Women
The Appeal of Ebony Jones
Love Never Fails
Adulting

Poetry

Lessons We Were Never Taught

TED Talks

Pregnancy is Inconvenient—TEDxFSU
Representation Matters—TEDxFSCJ

Beyond Bourbon Street

Nikesha Elise Williams

NEW Reads Publications | Jacksonville

Copyright © 2020 by Nikesha Elise Williams

Library of Congress Cataloging-In-Publication Data available upon request.

ISBN 978-1-7335848-6-9 (hardback)
ISBN 978-1-7335848-9-0 (ebook)

Cover Design by Gisette Gomez
Printed in the United States of America
Published by NEW Reads Publications LLC
Jacksonville, FL
newreadspub.com

First Edition: August 2020

PUBLISHER'S NOTE
This book is a work of fiction. Names, characters, places, and incidents and circumstances are the product of the author's imagination or are used fictitiously. Any resemblance to actual persons, living or dead, business establishments, events, or locales is entirely coincidental.

For Rilla Mae and Robert Ryan. I love you and I miss you. Rest well.

"The thief does not come except to steal, and to kill, and to destroy. I have come that they may have life, and that they may have it more abundantly."

John 10:10 (NKJV)

"There is no fair fight to be waged about the past."

An American Marriage, Tayari Jones

"The storm didn't discriminate, and neither will we in the recovery effort."

George W. Bush
Monday September 12, 2005

"You lie!"

Rep. "Joe" Wilson (R-South Carolina)
September 9, 2009

One

Mardi Gras—12 Weeks

"This is the type of shit I hate," Graigh says, walking through the open French doors into the Bourbon Street hotel.

"And what's that?" Joy asks, dancing a two-step behind her into the cool interior.

"All of this," Graigh waves her hand at the revelry. "The tourists; this ingratiating show for people who don't even get it."

"Graigh, it's Mardi Gras." Joy rolls her eyes. "All of this is for tourists. What's there to get? It's a party."

"Yeah, it's a party that never stops. That's what everybody thinks anyway."

"What else are they supposed to think?"

"Nothing since they don't live here. It's just that. . . This is a lie."

"Huh?"

"Don't worry about it." Graigh lags behind, letting Joy lead the way toward the bank of elevators that will take them to her floor.

Joy dances the entire way. Her body twists and shakes in time to the multitude of brass bands passing the hotel door, celebrating the PG debauchery of Fat Tuesday in the daytime. Graigh watches her friend watching herself in the reflective metal of the elevator doors. Her hands shake rhythms into the ringlets of her long Indian curls that were bagged into bundles, and then sown into the wig on her head. Her unrestrained A cups test the seams of her yellow tank top. Her booty bounces up and down then sways into a rhythmic shake. Joy is the personification of carefree. Her light twerk denotes adulting in the daytime; belying the secrets yet to come when the sun goes down, and her husband returns to their room.

The elevator dings mid-shake. Joy continues her shimmy, moving the rhythm from her ass to her shoulders. She steps onto the elevator inviting the guests getting off to dance with her. An older, beet red, and burned, couple sidle up next to her toasted peanut butter arms and join her shimmy for a beat before they head into the chaos of the Mardi Gras parades.

"Graigh, what's wrong?" Joy asks half-heartedly, once the elevator doors close. Her bounce continues in the elevator, thanks to the music piped in from the street.

"Nothing," Graigh answers, wrapping her arms across her belly.

"I know what it is," Joy says, booty dancing in front of Graigh. "You're mad you can't drink."

"Oh really?"

"Yeah. No one told you to get pregnant before Carnival in the first place. Afterwards sure, but before? Who does that? You know you want a daiquiri."

"You have all the answers, don't you?" Graigh says, stepping off the elevator onto the third floor.

"Of course, I do." Joy walks the plush carpeted hall to her hotel door, throwing her words behind her. "I mean, you can't be mad at the tourists for enjoying the delectable offerings of the Big Easy. That would mean you're mad at me. I'm a tourist, and I'm your best friend, which means you can't possibly be mad at me. That's against the bestie code."

"What are we, twelve?"

Joy ignores Graigh and slips the room key out of the tight fitted back pocket of her cutoff denim shorts and inserts it into the door. The lock clicks and she sashays into the room, letting her hips emphasize the long and short notes of the trumpets, trombones, and drums rocking the room walls from outside. The music moves Joy through the door, past the king sized bed, to the French doors leading to the balcony. Music blares from the street below. The plumage from colorful floats pass, proudly carrying krewes along the route of the twenty-four-hour party.

"I have to pee!" Graigh yells to Joy on the balcony.

"Okay!" Joy yells behind her. "Hey, Mista, throw me some beads."

A thick rope of colorful beads clatter on the wrought iron balcony railing. The clinking sound is muted by the resounding hush of the closed bathroom door.

Graigh unbuttons her jeans and eases them over her thighs. The rough, hewn fabric stutters before following her fingers guidance to slouch around her ankles. She sits on the white hotel commode. Looking at her almost flat belly she exhales. The bottle of water she drank earlier whizzes into the pipe. She sits and drips dry, trying and failing to forget the uncomfortable truth. She is pregnant. Twelve weeks pregnant with what she knows is not her first baby.

Toilet paper disintegrates against her skin. She shivers as fingers brush against her sensitivity. Jumping makes the jeans comply over her legs and butt. They remain unbuttoned and barely zipped, a comfort for her mini pooch produced by the early stages of her pregnancy. She flushes the toilet and steps up to the immaculate bowl sink, set in the granite counter. Her eyes avoid the large rectangular mirror hanging above.

Soap in hand, water running, Graigh scrubs her soiled fingers against the friction-made suds. Eyes nearly avoid contact with the mirror. Nearly, but curiosity wins. A raised brow. A lifted lid. One pupil gazes back at itself trying not to acknowledge the rest of the brown-skinned face: the other tired eye, the narrow nose flaring just a bit around the outer nostrils, preparing to spread with impending weight gain, bow-shaped lips that refuse to disappear into a straight line no matter the height of her anger, razor sharp cheek bones cutting angles into her face, the one wrinkle line in her forehead with a small white head near her hairline, and the wispy hairs of her edges raising up from their shellacked gel prison to frizz in the humidity and heat with the rest of her fluffed curls. Thirty-eight and pregnant. Graigh shakes the excess water from her hands, rubs them dry on her pants, and succumbs to her reflection. It is the first time she has seen her unobscured self in weeks.

She glares at her belly from the raised hem of her blue tee.

This time you'll live.

It is a prayer and a promise she murmurs inside herself as her gaze catches the thin pointed tips of three previously formed stretch mark lines peeking from the band of her panties, above the loosened waist of her jeans. It is the only physical evidence of what tried to grow before. What tried to live. What tried to be born. What was stolen from her. Bushy eyebrows frown in the mirror. Graigh drops her shirt and turns away from herself. She walks through the cramped room with the oversized bed, toward the brash music beckoning from the balcony.

Joy sits on one side of a wrought iron table in a matching high-backed chair, eyes closed, head bobbing to the music.

I wish my life was this simple.

Graigh takes the chair opposite Joy and tries to imitate her serene pose. Lids close over brown eyes, long lashes rest atop the thin skin covering her bony cheeks. Music encircles her, girding around her, putting a slight bop in her head and a tap in her feet. It is the exhale she's been waiting on all day. The one that alluded her in the bathroom as she sat with her thoughts, trying to forget.

"And you're telling me you don't love this. You're a liar," Joy accuses, staring at her friend.

One eye opens with a menacing look, but Graigh decides against her feeling to fight.

"It's not that I hate Mardi Gras. I love Mardi Gras. I think I just hate what Mardi Gras means in this city to people who aren't from here. It's just like everything else that people fly here for: Essence Fest, Satchmo Fest, the Bayou Classic, Jazz Fest. It's an excuse to escape, celebrate the facade of good, and forget that there's still pain. Everybody wants to laugh, and joke, eat, sing and dance away their pain at the expense of someone else. I'm that someone else. The people that live here everyday are the someone else."

"Just like the people who live in the DR or Jamaica or Haiti, or hell the Bahamas, Puerto Rico, are the someone else when we fly there for vacation. They have pain and all we experience is pleasure at their expense."

"Exactly."

"So, you're not going to vacation in the islands anymore?"

"Hell, naw . . . I'm just saying . . ."

"Just saying what? You hate everything your city is known for?"

"This carefully curated tourist experience of the French Quarter is not all New Orleans is," Graigh interrupts. "The Quarter is like Disneyland or Hollywood."

"And what's wrong with that? We all know Compton and South Central, LA exist in addition to the tourist attractions."

"But do you care?"

"If I'm going to visit California, that's not on my list of places to go."

"That's my point. You're here visiting me, but I don't live in the Quarter. I'm just showing you a good time because I know that's all you want. Hell, I even feel like a tourist and this is my home."

"Sounds like you need to go out more," Joy says.

"You don't get it. To you this is reality. For me this is a distant dream."

"Okay. And?"

Graigh huffs, "Tell me how many times you've come to visit me in the last ten years? Twice. My wedding and now. Every time we talk it's 'Girl, I gotta come down there for Essence Fest. Girl, I gotta come down there for the Classic. Girl, I'm trying to be lit for Mardi Gras.' It's never 'Graigh I just want to check on you'."

"Graigh we are both married, with careers, and families. So yes, I want to come see my bestie and get drunk and have a good time. That's not a crime. Besides, you only come see me when you're running from something. If it's not about drama, then you don't even think about crossing 10 to Tallahassee. So how about you stop trying to kill my vibe with your bitching and tell me what's really wrong with you."

"Well let me tell you what else I hate first."

Joy rolls her eyes. "What's that?"

"I love my home, but I hate the trying to be trendy. *Benjamin Button* was beautiful, and *Tremé* was necessary, even if it didn't go as deep as it should have, but everything else seems to be a reach. Performing for the sake of performing. People are only interested because of Katrina, jazz, and food."

"What about *Queen Sugar*?" Joy asks.

"I'll help out on the farm and have Ralph Angel's bail money ready anytime he needs it," Graigh says.

"That's what I thought," Joy smirks.

"Don't judge me."

"But I am. Hating everything you listed, with the exception of *Queen Sugar*, is like hating cheesesteaks and you're from Philly, or Harold's, Deep Dish, and Garret's Popcorn in Chicago, or cayenne, chicory coffee, and beignets right here."

"Beignets make me nauseous."

"So, this *is* a pregnancy rant."

"It's not the hormones. People think because they know Bourbon Street, been to one of Emeril's restaurants, went on a ghost tour for Marie Leveau, and can twerk to Big Freedia they know something. Just because you can cook Food Network's version of Cajun cuisine and texted money to the Red Cross after you saw *When the Levees Broke*, don't mean shit!" Graigh yells above the parade music.

"Who does?" Joy whispers.

"Hell, if I know," Graigh whimpers. "I feel like I don't even know myself."

Tears cascade down her face as her quiet mewling drones to uneasy silence punctuated by symbols, and snare drums from the high school band, marching in shiny polyester down the litter dirty street. Teenaged girls twirl batons and shake developed body parts. They strut in white boots, and blue and glitter gold briefs past the hotel balcony to the next tourist stop along the parade route. Graigh watches the show below and blows a dejected sigh deeper than the attachment of life growing in her womb yet to protrude from her belly.

"Graigh, you are more than twerking and a second line," Joy says offering her hand across the table. "You are more than bounce music, Master P and Cash Money taking over for the nine, nine and the two-thousand. But when people have watched shows and movies, listened to the music, and eaten the food, we believe we have a connection that makes us want to come down here, shake our ass, drink ourselves silly, and see the mystery and the magic. We want to get to know you. *I* want to know you in your element, and not just the drama you bring to my doorstep."

Graigh accepts Joy's hand without acknowledging her own shortcomings as a friend. The gesture is their apology. The exchange of energy admits what they will never say in words. What they've never had to say since they were roommates at FAMU in undergrad. Between them there has always been an understanding deeper than the blood they do not share. One touch of empathy and understanding clears the air for truth.

Breaking the embrace, Graigh stands in time to see plumes of feathers pass by the hotel on the parade route. A tribe of masked Mardi Gras Indians glide down the street following behind high schools, keeping traditions alive for the drunken foreign assembly who will never care to learn their roots.

"So, are you going to tell me what's really wrong with you?" Joy asks, coming to stand beside Graigh on the balcony rail.

"I'm pregnant." Graigh looks blankly into the crowd below.

"You are. Twelve weeks pregnant. I know you've got your appointment tomorrow afternoon. I wished I'd known you were going to get knocked up when I bought these tickets. I'd have sent the Tonys home and stayed to go with you."

"I know."

"So how do you feel?"

"I'm scared shitless."

"And your baby daddy?"

"Who knows."

Two

"Halvert," the new nurse calls from the doorway into the waiting room. "Elaine Halvert," she calls again, putting extra emphasis on the "t."

"Call me Graigh. I go by my middle name," Graigh says, approaching the nurse.

"And it's Hal-Verr," Graigh's husband, Bombei, says, exaggerating the roll of his "r" as he stands.

"Oh, I'm sorry, Dad. I just need mom right now." The nurse blocks Bombei's path. "We'll come get you when she goes back to see the doctor."

"Alright," Bombei says.

"I'll be fine," Graigh assures behind the nurse.

The door shuts and Graigh follows the nurse in lavender scrubs. Fabric swallows the legs and arms of the waif woman holding the clipboard. She leads the way to her cubicle, motioning for Graigh to set her purse down on the cloth covered chair cushion beside the cluttered laminate desk.

"Take this in the bathroom and give me a sample," the nurse says with a yawn. "Use these too."

Graigh takes the plastic cup and the packs of sanitary moist towelettes from the nurse's cold, clammy hands to the sterile bathroom just behind the three rows of cubicles. Five other women in varying stages of pregnancy sit or stand around the other office nurses, making documented small talk about the past month, or weeks, or days of their pregnancy. Graigh lingers in the bathroom doorway watching the women; some of the bigger ones stand with hands on their protruding belly, while others, apparently in the beginning of their birth journey, sit with their hands, on clenched quads.

"Is there a problem, Mrs. Halvert?" the nurse asks from her desk.

"No, I'm just catching my breath."

The bathroom door closes soundlessly. Graigh turns the small metal doorknob lock and leans against the white-gray door. Her eyes avoid the basic mirror hung above the sink. Against the door she breathes. Hands beneath her shirt, over the skin of her own belly, she pushes, prods and pokes at her pooch, waiting for a flutter that doesn't come. A sigh emanates through her gut but expels like a normal breath. She pushes the sides of her work pants, already unzipped, and unbuttoned over her hips to her ankles. The breathable wide leg fabric pools at her feet covering her pointed toe, red ballet flats.

Okay, Baby, let's see how we're doing.

Graigh fills the sample cup and sets it on a distressed, white-wood side table. She flushes, readjusts her clothes and washes her hands. When she is done, she carefully picks up her sample, walks slowly to the door, and lets herself out into nurses' bullpen.

"Just set it on the mat, over there, under your doctor's name."

The nurse's abrupt instruction startles Graigh. She meets the woman's steely brown eyes that seem to stare through her and the door to the inside of the bathroom. Breaking the gaze, Graigh tips to the counter sharing the back wall with the bathroom and sets her sample down on the marked puppy pad. She is the only sample under her physician's name. Clicking heels announce Graigh's long strides and her return to her seated nurse. Lavender fabric is collapsed where the woman's belly should rest. The material folds in on itself, never meeting the bigger body that should be there.

"How are you doing?" the nurse asks loudly, undoing the Velcro strap to take Graigh's blood pressure.

"I'm doing."

"You can answer better than that. Make a fist for me."

"I'm tired."

The nurse squeezes the pump to inflate the blood pressure band. Her eyes hawkishly watch the needle of the gauge. Graigh works to calm her rising anxiety from the standard test. She concentrates on her breath, making them even, slow, and as deep as possible without coughing for air.

"Ninety over sixty-two. That's good." She turns to the computer and asks, "Have you taken any medication besides your prenatal vitamins since you were last here?"

"No."

"Have you noticed any changes in your body? Spotting, cramping, dizziness?"

"No."

"Do you have any concerns you want to address with the doctor when you see her?"

"No."

The nurse finishes typing then stands. Graigh does the same.

"Go on out to the waiting room and grab your husband. I'll come around from the other side and take you both to the exam room."

Flat heels click down the linoleum past the bay of nurses, to the door from whence she came. Bombei stands as she enters the room. The uneven mix of mothers and the handful of fathers barely adjust their eyes as she glides around squared chairs and end tables to where he stands.

"Everything alright?" Bombei asks.

The long hairs of his full beard tickle her skin as he whispers against her forehead. His soft lips leave a kiss as he pulls her close. She doesn't answer his question, only nods her head affirmatively, that for now she is all right.

"Come on back," the nurse's voice calls from a door adjacent to the check-in counter.

Bombei takes Graigh's hand and pulls her gently behind him toward the nurse. They follow her into the office's inner sanctum, around the corners of the maze like halls, until they reach an open door to an exam room.

"Come on in. Mom, we want you to take off everything from the waist down. Dad, you can sit here," the nurse gestures to a dusty, cracked leather stool by the room's large window. "When you're finished, drape this across your waist. The doctor will be with you shortly."

Graigh waits until the wispy nurse closes the door behind her before she slides her black slacks and lace panties down her body. The sable tunic top covers her behind in the cool air-conditioned room.

"Can you hold these for me, please?" Graigh asks, with an outstretched arm toward Bombei.

He takes her hastily folded pants and underwear and sets them in his lap while she hops up on the exam table. Her butt jiggles with the bounce. A tremor of feeling ripples from a dimple down the sculpted and toned sides of her hamstrings and calves. Sitting on the exam table, Graigh pulls the ends of her shirt up from under her butt, draping the excess fabric around her hips. She pulls the paper covering the nurse handed her apart, gently peeling each corner until it is prostrate and laid against her legs.

Let's get this over with and let everything be okay.

It is another prayer she says to herself. Graigh does not look at Bombei. Her eyes are filled with her warring emotions over what's happening beneath her belly. She avoids his gaze and finds his feet perched on the bottom rungs of the stool he placed directly in front of her, as if he wanted to conduct the exam himself.

Silence settles uncomfortably around them. The tick of the small round wall clock is loud above the unspoken thoughts of husband and wife. The typical traffic noise of Canal Street is nearly muted. It only asserts itself in the chortling rumble of a semi-truck headed back to the highway.

The rays of the February sun stream through the large window at Bombei's back, immediately radiating heat on his body. Small bubbles arise on his skin and slide to his jean belted waistband beneath his thin, gray knit shirt.

Please, God, let everything be okay so she can stop stressing.

His petition repeats in his mind as the heat from the sun warms him. It will be his excuse for the sweat bubbles forming on his forehead and beneath his armpits, though he knows they began the moment Graigh disappeared with the nurse. His unanswered questions linger.

Is everything alright?

Is she okay?

What is she not telling me?

The answers are necessary to salve his own nervous energy.

"It's Doctor Marcella," a lilting voice accompanies a knock. "Are we ready?"

"Come in," Graigh calls hoarsely from the exam table.

She looks up from Bombei's feet for the first time as the doorknob turns. The doctor's white coat flutters as she steps inside the exam room, and swirls around her brown slacked legs as she presses the door closed with one hand. The loosened ends of her salt and pepper pin curls bounce around the crisply starched collar of her beige striped blouse folded on the outside of her lab coat.

"How are you guys doing today?" She asks, pushing the rolling stool between Graigh's clenched knees and Bombei's prayerful pose.

"Fine," Graigh mumbles.

"Put your feet in the stirrups, lay back, slide down, and open your knees. Any changes since I saw you last month? Any flutters?"

"Nothing. Not that I can tell," Graigh says, crooking one elbow over her head and placing a protective hand over her stomach beneath her shirt."

"That's normal. It's still early. You're only twelve weeks. Give me a deep breath. Okay a little pressure," Doctor

Marcella says, inserting a lubed finger into Graigh's vagina to check her cervix.

"Release the breath."

Graigh exhales as Doctor Marcella removes her digit. She rolls to the hulking trash can and discards the white latex gloves. Standing, she scrubs her hands wrist to fingertips over and over under the water from the sink, and then dries her hands on rough brown paper towels.

"Now we're going to get that baby's heartbeat and do an ultrasound to see how it's doing in there," Doctor Marcella says, turning around to face Graigh and Bombei. "Have you guys been trying to guess what you're having? Boy? Girl?"

"No," Graigh answers.

"Just healthy," Bombei says, lowering his praying hands from his mouth to speak.

"Well, you'll find out soon enough. This is going to be a little cold."

Doctor Marcella squeezes the ultrasound activator gel on Graigh's stomach and moves the heart monitor wand around in the goop. Left to right, up and down, from her navel to her knickers, and hip to hip, Doctor Marcella searches with a stern face, and keen ears. Graigh and Bombei both wait with bated breath. An identical prayer runs through their minds.

Beat, baby, beat.

Beat, baby, beat.

It is broken by the steady drone of what sounds like "wah, wah, wah" as the noise emerges from Graigh's uterus into the room for the gathered trio to hear.

Graigh and Bombei exhale the breaths they'd been holding since they arrived at the patient tower of University Medical Center.

Thank you.

Thank God.

Their thoughts, grateful and satisfied, give way to relaxed countenances and slight smiles as Doctor Marcella speaks.

"The heartbeat is strong. Let's take a look and see how your baby is doing in there."

She turns on the monitor to the ultrasound machine. The dark screen comes alive in shades of black, white, and gray. Warm, world rough knuckles skim Graigh's belly, gliding the wand through the gel as the makings of a baby manifests on the screen.

Graigh stares at the large pronounced head and the oval body. A head, nose, mouth, torso and the makings of feet lay serenely on her uterine wall waiting for more genetic information to stretch and grow before birth.

"It's really there."

The words escape her mouth breathily. They interrupt Bombei's own revelry. His hands drop to his sides and feet touch the ground as he sits on the edge of his stool.

"That's my boy," Bombei says. A smile slowly pierces through his closed mouth set in his bushy beard.

"Or girl," Doctor Marcella says with a smile of her own.

"Just healthy," Graigh says, sliding her fingertips through the gel of her belly to where the wand lays, projecting the image on the screen.

"It doesn't look like a Teddy Graham anymore," Bombei says.

"They grow fast," Doctor Marcella says. "In utero and in life. You two should cherish these moments."

Graigh presses gently along the places that seem to match up with the sonogram image, feeling for her baby's head and body.

"Your baby is healthy. We just want to make sure you are as well," Doctor Marcella says, rolling away from Graigh. "How's your breathing?"

"Okay if I'm moving slow," she answers still looking at the screen, feeling for where her baby is supposed to be.

"And if you're moving faster than slow?" Doctor Marcella asks, handing Graigh a damp, and warm white towel. "Use this to wipe off the gel when you're ready."

"If I'm moving faster than slow, my breaths are shorter, more measured, but not quite gasping," Graigh answers. She stares into the monitor, eyes fixed on the image of her baby, serenely sleeping waiting on God's first breath of life.

"I take it then you don't do much exercise."

"I walk," Graigh says, turning her head. "We walk the neighborhoods. The Ninth, Lakeview, the East, St. Charles Street, the Quarter, Tremé."

"How is her breath when she's walking, Dad?"

"It's fine," Graigh answers, wiping the gel and losing the image of her baby."

"I asked Mr. Halvert."

"She does alright," Bombei answers. "If we walk longer than thirty minutes though, she talks to me less than usual. That let's me know she needs to slow down."

"I suggest both of you do some meditation and work on deep breathing. Or swimming. Try to increase your lung capacity. Especially you, Mom. You're going to need it for labor if you're planning for a natural birth. Yoga could help too."

"I guess," Graigh shrugs. "What would you like me to do with this?" she asks, holding the dirty towel away from her body.

Doctor Marcella takes the towel by the corner and drops it on the sink counter.

"We'll see you guys back in a month. That's when you'll find out if it's a boy or a girl, if you like. I'll leave your chart here. Take it to reception and they'll make your next appointment. Take care of yourselves. Both of you. Especially you, Mom. You gotta carry that baby."

The doctor leaves as briskly as she came in. Her coat flutters behind her, walking shoes squeak on the linoleum as she travels down the labyrinthian hall to the next room where another patient waits.

"Feel better now?" Bombei asks, standing from his stool and handing Graigh her clothes.

"I never said I was upset."

"No, you didn't. And neither did I."

"So why are you asking if I feel better?"

"Because I can tell you do, compared to when we first arrived."

"I could say the same about you."

Graigh pulls the ends of her tunic over her unbuttoned and partially zipped pants. Clothes in place, she snatches the chart from the counter, opens the room door and marches out. Bombei catches the closing door with his hand and follows behind his stalking wife to check out.

"We'll see you back here in four weeks," an older lady with a nasally voice and green-veined hands says as she hands Graigh an appointment card.

She shoves the card into her pants pocket and flings the door open on the waiting area. Out one door and opening another, Graigh is face-to-face with her reedy nurse.

"Everything go well with Doctor Marcella?" she asks, seemingly more out of polite policy than actual concern.

"Yes. Nothing to worry about for now."

"That's good to here," the nurse says with cloying warmth. "See y'all again soon," she drawls.

The nurse waves with an Wednesday Addams smile. It is the only brightness to the woman with sunken eyes and cheeks in a uniform two sizes too big, even if it is probably an extra small.

"Thank you," Bombei says. "We'll see you next month."

He pushes the main door to the office open and waits for Graigh to pass through. She huffs by him, briskly walking down the hall and to the emergency exit door, opting instead for stairs than to wait for the elevator. Bombei also descends the steps in the dank, dust filled, musty stairwell, until he reaches the ground floor where Graigh waits beneath fluorescent lighting just outside the doorway, hand on her belly, coughing, and catching her breath.

Three

"What's wrong?" Bombei asks, turning the music down on the car stereo.

"That's the third time you've asked me that and we haven't even left the parking lot," Graigh answers, looking out the window.

"The first two times I asked you didn't answer me."

"Nothing is wrong with me. We had a good appointment. I'm just tired."

"Okay, Graigh," Bombei sighs. "Take a nap. We'll be home in a little bit."

He gives her the room to think and clear space in her mind, as he does the same. His band rehearsal schedule for his students that afternoon drifts at the periphery as he contemplates his place. His titles. Husband. Father-to-be. All to a wife who has been reluctant in each graduating step of their relationship. He's known Graigh for nearly fourteen years; his wife for ten going on eleven. She is moody and mercurial. That's made him stoic at times, empathetic at others. Always on her emotional rollercoaster. Confidence askew. She falls in and out of fits of gray just as her name suggests, and he is forced to find his way on the right side of her ups and downs. More emotional than he cares to be, her keen awareness of whatever mood she's in agitates him, because he remains unenlightened. She broods instead of talking. Retreats into herself, instead of opening up to the possibility that there are people who care enough about her to listen or help. He is forced to do the same.

Bombei turns out of the parking lot of the massive University Medical Center complex. The hulking hospital edifice, courtesy of LSU, takes up whole city blocks. It is a marked difference in comparison to the now shuttered Charity Hospital and its subsidiaries that remain defunct waiting on a new purpose.

He heads down Canal Street toward Claiborne. The sparsely leaved trees in front of the glass encased hospital cast shadows across the car in the late afternoon sun. At Claiborne, Bombei waits at the light to turn left. A half full street car passes by them at the viaduct. Left over Mardi Gras revelers hang out of the yellow windows of the electric train. Ropes of beads visible around their necks, and Go-cups filled with frozen drinks tells of a party still going, despite the new season of Lent. In the deeply Catholic city, the sight of spring breakers and the sunburned and sprightly aged hanging on to their youth, distinguish a marked difference from the folks on foot with black ashes crossed on their foreheads.

At the green light Bombei turns left on Claiborne, opting for the scenic route home instead of the highway. He turns the radio up on WWOZ. A jazz station. He catches the middle of a brass band song, one he doesn't know off hand, and nods his head to the steady beat of the music. His fingers work to keep time and tap the unfamiliar beat on the steering wheel.

The music plays as he leaves Canal Street, the gateway to the city's downtown, toward the Tremé. Fingers tap as the track changes to Louis Armstrong's "What a Wonderful World." Satchmo's husky voice fills the sedan scratching through Graigh's armor as she harmonizes an alto hum with the legendary trumpeter. Looking out the window she watches the immediate and dramatic change of scenery from new, modern construction to historic, old, and rundown. The streets narrow. The roads get bumpier; the potholes more deeply felt. The grass wild and unkempt takes over strips of concrete paths meant to be sidewalks, and spill over the curb into the street.

At Robertson and Louisa, Bombei speeds past the cemetery. The high-walled fortress looks more like a prison than a resting place. It is the only oddity, but what has always been, in a city where the dead have always lived in harmony with the living. The neighborhood appears recovered, but shells of life, the abandoned gas stations and dollar stores tell a different story. In a city that reveres the dead more than the living, mausoleums are its monuments. Both phases of life coexist as a testament to the temperance of one and the finality of the other.

Bombei sighs his censure against the reputation that New Orleans is a city of ghosts. Ghosts that aren't confined to cemeteries for people to tour, or quickly cleaned up crime scenes. As he drives, he sees ghosts everywhere. Neighborhoods, buildings, homes, razed lots, schools, and his own reflection all waiting for rest that never comes.

Across the grassy median—the neutral ground—on the other side of the street, he sees small boxy air conditioners hanging outside of the green trimmed windows of a white paneled house. The paint is dingy and peeling and in need of several coats just to sparkle. It is juxtaposed against a vacant purple home with the windows boarded up on the neighboring corner. A brick faced church, with a well-manicured lawn is behind a wrought iron fence, and another old white paneled building that was probably a corner store, remains on the fourth corner a block away. It too has white paint that is dingy and peeling covered in large graffiti, grass, and vines. The four corners are post-Katrina personified. Everywhere, on almost every corner, there are signs of death and destruction and disaster where life used to be, where life still is. Some moved home, some returned, rebuilt, and recovered, and some—many, didn't come home at all.

Bombei crosses the Industrial Canal slowing on the newly painted bridge over the murky water that claimed homes and lives. Graigh crosses herself. A habit she's had since he's known her. When they first began dating, he asked her about the cross.

"Why do you always do that?" he chuckled in jest. "Praying the water doesn't come alive and swallow you whole?"

He thought the joke would break more of her ice, but he was met with a thicker berg than he guessed. She stared at him blankly, wide set eyes sliced to slits, lips parted but no smile forming.

"I pray for the souls who were swept away in the water, for the families who survived, and for God to forgive the people who thought it was a good idea to cut a canal and sell folks land on a drained swamp below the sea."

He didn't respond to her impassioned diatribe. No head nod of agreement, no apology for his insensitivity. He let her words sit between them, storing them away to be analyzed another day; to use as a catalyst to pick her apart when she was willing. But in fourteen years she has never been willing, and he has rarely been able. She is an open book with most of her pages stuck together.

The lower Ninth Ward greets them on the other side of the bridge. The heaviness he always finds at the foot rushes into his body and threatens to strangle him, no matter how many times he's left and returned home. The chokehold loosens as he finds his way in the familiar. A sign announces their entrance into the village. A community of its own design where the waves are friendly, the food is good, and the poor Black charity case is still wanted for the crime of purporting stereotypes to desperate journalists without a second source of confirmation.

They stop at the light at Claiborne and Caffin Avenue. The campus of Doctor King Charter School is beside them. The school where their child will inevitably attend from pre-K to 12th grade buzzes with activity. Parent pick-up, members of the marching band playing random notes ahead of practice, and teens on corners talking trash to each other and into their phones. The sounds of youthful voices lift into the air and rustle through the thick foliage of old trees shrouding the school in shade. This so-called beacon of hope, which was here before, negates the neighborhood's unearned narrative. Its existence challenges the argument that to live and be black in the Ninth, is to be ignorant and poor.

Bombei races past the new fire station and makes a left three blocks later onto Charbonnet.
A house painted seafoam green and surrounded by a red fence sits on the corner blazing in the sun. It is the unofficial welcome mat to the block where empty spaces wait for their owners to come home.

This is the Lower Ninth Ward. A community where it is not uncommon to see one house recovered and renovated next to one that hasn't been touched, next to another that has been gutted, boarded up and left to rot, next to an empty lot. His block is emblematic of the above ground cemeteries he's feared since he was a boy; a memorial to what was and what used to be, forever haunted by spirits that refuse to leave.

He pulls beside Graigh's old white pickup truck in the carport of their two-story home. It's the sentry among their neighbors. The addition built on top of the original shotgun that was later squared off for more modern comforts before it was flooded with twenty-three feet of water.

"We're home," Bombei whispers above the stillness in the air.

Graigh groans awake, stretching her arms as high as they will go in the car's interior. Her jaw drops low into an elongated yawn as she arches her back and rolls her head on her neck, bringing life into her stiff joints.

"I need a nap," she proclaims from the passenger seat.

"Go inside and lay down. I've got to go back to work."

"Okay," Graigh says, reaching for the door handle.
"Wait, let me help you out."

Bombei jumps out of the running car and runs to Graigh's side. She stands in the space of the open car door. Eyes alight, her lips smirked, hands reversed on her hips, with her thumbs in the dimples he knows reside in the small of her back.

"I'm pregnant. Not handicapped. You can close the door."

It slams shut as she takes the steps up onto the high butter and beige tiled porch; restored to look like the original her grandmother picked out before she was ever an itch in her unknown daddy's pants. Graigh unlocks the white iron storm door and the heavy wooden door behind it. Still air greets her face at the threshold. Bombei stands close behind, the breath from his mouth curls circles of heat around her neck as she steps into the formal living room.

It is now as it was before the storm. White. White sofa, white love seat, white walls, mahogany and glass end tables and coffee table. Large rectangular mirrors sparkle in glittering, crystal frames. It is the room of reckoning. The room to sit in your CME Sunday clothes and take pictures on Christmas, Mother's Day, and Easter. The room of tribute and honor, a love letter to her grandmother, she wants everyone to feel welcomed in.

From the living room she passes into the dining room. The room that once shared space with a family room is now home to a wood slab, sanded down by Bombei's hand, and stained coffee black by her. It is one of the many projects they completed together, building projects that helped them build their relationship as they restored what she lost. The table set for twelve is empty save for a centerpiece of fresh fruit. It leads into the chef's kitchen. Where there was once a wall for a bedroom the space is now completely open. A wide butcher block island marks the separation point between the kitchen and dining room, with four black-leather backed bar stools on either side. The kitchen, back splashed in dove gray subway tiles, sparkles in the natural light from the French doors that break up the back wall of gray quartz countertops. The polished stainless-steel appliances gleam in the rays. The rarely used recessed lights lining the ceiling remain as unnecessary as the rectangular, tiered chandelier.

Graigh takes the stairs in the middle of the kitchen to the second floor. The stairs she demanded take the place of what used to be the home's only bathroom. Bombei fought her on the design. He wanted to keep the three-piece washroom. The bathroom he suggested be designated for guests. He thought the rounded, spiral staircase was a bit much for the modest home even with the second-floor addition, especially for the neighborhood. Graigh, was flippant in her compromise. "I got it, and I'm going to flaunt it." The final design turned the original bathroom into a half bath, and forced her to square off the stair case. She got her way in the end because the transition from floor to floor still happened in the heart of the home.

Graigh is snuggled beneath a royal blue fleece blanket when Bombei gets to the loft at the top of the stairs. Her eyes are closed but he knows she's not asleep.

"I gotta get my horn so I can meet the kids at practice," he says.

"What are you practicing for, Mardi Gras was yesterday?" Graigh asks, without opening her eyes.

"St. Joseph's Night," Bombei says, passing Graigh as he entered their master bedroom.

He picks up his trumpet case and walks back into the loft. Graigh lays uncomfortably on her side, trying to get used to the position she will be forced to sleep in once her belly gets big. Normally a stomach sleeper, her legs are adjusted for the new position. One foot sits atop her leg, knee in the air making a perfect triangle. She lays posed in passé, pretending to sleep, with the blanket up to her nose, bearding around her ears; her attempt to avoid conversation.

Bombei asks the inevitable, "What's wrong?"

"Why do you keep asking me that?"

"Because I haven't seen you like this in a long time?"

"Seen me like what? How am I today?"

"Different. Quiet. Distant. Guarded."

"I don't know why you think that. We had a good appointment. We're through the first trimester. The baby is healthy. I'm healthy. We're working. The house is done. *What* could be wrong with me?"

Her question bothers him. Maybe because it's not a question at all. It is a statement. Rhetorical; a period at the end instead of a question mark. Her tone tells him to leave. The upspeak. The inflection. She's baiting, goading him into a disagreement he will regret. When she is angry, her eyes smile, and her words cut. Her tone is her warning, a dare.

"I don't know what could be wrong with you," he begins. "I know you're different. Ever since you found out you were pregnant, you've been different. You won't let me in, you won't let me help, you won't let me . . ."

"Bombei, we've been together forever. If you don't know what to do, I don't know what I can do to help you."

"Don't shut me out, Graigh. I know your past is rushing back at you. I can see it in that glazed, glass look you have."

"What are you talking . . .?"

"You don't want to talk to me about it. Fine. But you need to talk to somebody. Especially before my baby gets here."

"Is that a threat?"

"It's not a threat. I would never threaten you, Graigh. It's a suggestion."

"One you've made repeatedly."

"Exactly. The record and the stick are broken, and the horse is dead. Talk to somebody. I haven't seen you this way since we met."

Bombei doesn't wait for her to respond. Trumpet case in hand, he jogs down the stairs, leaving Graigh behind in the same awkward position she argued from—closed eyes, knee in the air, blankets tucked around her frame. Disconnected.

He marches out of the kitchen, through the rustic dining room and to the door, avoiding the mirrors begging him to look at himself, to see the irritation, the frustration, and the defeat in his win. He had the last word, but he is no closer to what he wanted.

If she won't talk to me, she at least needs to talk to someone else. She doesn't need to be giving all her negative energy to the baby because she's harboring old shit.

On the porch he descends the singular step to the paved walk way carved between two uneven loaves of St. Augustine grass. The grass is nothing like it was when he first saw it, when he first saw her. Standing in the spot where they met, the lawn lush and sumptuous, manicured, and vibrant, he laments the marriage that has transformed into everything his home is not—unrefined, at the precipice of ruin.

He crosses the grass to the carport, rounds the still running car, and gets in on the driver's side. The jazz instrumental blares as he backs out of the carport onto the pebble rough street. He turns at the corner heading back toward the school at the corner of Caffin. He drives toward his students leaving his past behind. Leaving behind the spot where he stopped when he first came home after the storm. The spot where she stood. The spot where they met fourteen years ago.

Four

Fourteen years ago, Graigh was a blur. The first time Bombei saw her she was a brown blob awash in light colored fabric standing in spoiled topsoil. He didn't see the definition to her shape or any of her facial features. She blended in to the beige blah that he'd seen for blocks.

It was nearly one year after the storm. After the water. August 14, 2006. Bombei had been driving his car block for block through the lower Ninth Ward. He began on Jordan Avenue, starting his journey by the mysterious barge some say had never been there before the storm, that was now pushed up on the bank of the levee those same "some" believe was intentionally detonated and destroyed to purposely flood the Ninth. He rode the empty and desolate blocks of Deslonde, Tennessee, Florida Avenue, and Flood Street, mouth agape at the destruction. The rotted trees inundated with more water than they could drink. The dusty gray dirt that stood in place of carpet green lawns. Block for block he drove. Every now and again he saw families that had returned. Mothers, fathers, children, aunts, uncles, cousins, relatives, all crowded on the four wooden steps that led to the entrance of their newly erected FEMA trailers. Trailers that by comparison were smaller than the RV's some families buy for themselves to traipse across the country.

Sometimes the trailer stood in front of a concrete slab that was the foundation of a used to be house. Sometimes the trailer stood in front of a shell of a house that had been gutted and was being prepared for renovation, or rejuvenation, or whatever it is that happens to repair the despair of a house missing the element of home. Sometimes there was no trailer at all, and in its stead was a slab, or a brick, or three steps. And sometimes, most times, there was nothing at all.

It was about five-thirty in the evening. He reached the end of Lamanche, made a right turn, and began his ascent up Charbonnet toward North Claiborne Street where he would turn and merge into the midday traffic. His initial plan was to go through the Ninth until he reached Saint Bernard Parish, but with so many blocks of the same destruction he aborted his mission. Instead, he would return to the Hyatt where he had been staying indefinitely, until construction finished on his new house.

He was doing about forty miles per hour when he reached the last block of Charbonnet before Claiborne. He slowed to accommodate three children playing with a ball in the street in front of their trailer. At the end of the block he obeyed the posted stop sign but glanced in his rearview mirror before the turn. Behind him to the right he saw her standing in dead grass and dust behind a trailer. From the street she was invisible, but from his vantage point she was nearly clear. Clear enough that he decided, he was compelled, to be nosy. Bombei reversed past two lots, pulled over, parked, and got out of his car into the high heat and one hundred percent humidity.

"Good evening," he said, walking toward her.

She stood dazed but registering the greeting she blinked and shook her head quickly.

"Hello," she said.

He continued past her but stopped in front of the house beside hers. He watched. All day he had seen families or single men outside of trailers and dilapidated homes. She was a new sight. A woman, alone, standing in front of a house, with a trailer and no one else with her.

She faced him without looking at him. Appraising her appearance, he noticed she was darker than what she appeared on first glance, obvious evidence of sun kisses. Not quite milk chocolate but darker than caramel. Her eyes were big, her nose small, and her lips ripe. Her face though, was unreadable. She held her jaw tight, and her hands sat on the back of her hips at the rise of her behind. Her arms were triangles, her elbows their points. Feet firmly planted in the remnants of St. Augustine grass revealed locked legs, hyper-extended and slightly bowed on the left.

Her twisted hair was pulled tight into a bun atop her head. The honey blonde highlights glinted in the sun, especially in the stray strands hanging to her ears on either side of her sweaty and glistening face. The strand by her right ear had a cowrie shell affixed to the end. It occasionally clinked with her medium-sized gold hoop earrings.

Her face held all the fecund, nubile beauty her clothing lacked. Arched eyebrows, and glossed lips made up for the men's white tee rolled to the armpits, and the khaki cargo shorts with the belted phallus hanging in front of her. Her housework look was completed with tan canvas shoes missing the laces.

"Didn't your mama ever tell you it's rude to stare?"

The cut of her voice through the quiet air startled him.

"Naw," he shrugged. "My daddy did though, but I figured since you were so deep in thought and wasn't paying me no mind, you wouldn't notice."

"Well, I did."

"Then I apologize. I'm sorry for staring at you." He walked a little closer to her but kept his distance standing on the sidewalk in front of her. "I'm Bombei. Bombei Halvert."

"Hi."

"So, whatchu doing out here?"

"Trying to decide what I'm gon' do with this house."

"What have you decided?"

"That it's more work than the Lord allow. Who's gon' do it is a better question, because right now it's just me, by myself."

She turned away from him and stared at the house. From the outside the only tell tale signs of the storm were the markings by the national guard, and the plain plywood boards that stood over the front door and windows. A broom leaning against the faux brick facade signified the porch was recently cleaned of all the caked-up mud and debris Katrina left behind. The white iron work on the outside window frame and carport still looked to be in reasonable condition. The yard was bare save for a few strands of stubborn grass but looked as if she was about to re-sod.

"Um, miss, would you like some help with whatever your plans are for your house?"

She turned around sharply and eyed him. Her look said she was aware of his nervousness. The unease of his unplanned approach. She looked him up and down taking in his frame. Six feet tall give or take an inch, in black dickies, a plain navy-blue shirt that had seen the dryer one too many times, and a pair of white Reeboks. His hair was cut close, but his goatee was long and scraggly, yet evenly cut across the bottom. His right ear twinkled in the fading sunlight from a small earring, and he wore a silver watch on his left wrist.

"Excuse me," Bombei said again. This time louder. "Would you like some help with your house."

"Oh. I'm sorry. I didn't hear you the first time."

"If you didn't hear me the first time then you wouldn't have known I'd said it again."

She smiled, "You do construction?"

"No, but I've always been good with my hands."

"So, what do you do?"

"Music."

"Why do you want to help me with my house?"

"Because it's more work than the Lord allow, and right now it's just you, by yourself."

"Hmm. You get two points for being cute."

"So, you think I'm cute?"

She laughed. She relaxed her stance, dropped her arms from their imposed triangles and let them hang slack at her sides.

"That's not what I said, but I'll go with it."

"Well, miss . . . um . . ."

"Graigh."

"Pardon."

"My name. It's Graigh."

"Well, Miss Graigh, if you would like some help with your house I'm willing."

"That's awfully nice of you, but I don't know you."

"You could get to know me."

"Why would I want to do that?"

"Because I'm cute."

"Oh, really?"

"No," he said, chuckling. "But it seems to be just you on this block. Well, you and the family down the street; and I'm sure they have their own plans. It's rough for everyone, but if you want some help, I'm offering. That and a chance for you to get to know me before you say yes or no."

"That's nice of you to offer, Bombei, but this getting to know you sounds like your way of asking me out on a date, and not like a meeting between potential client and contractor."

"Then you're right. It is my way of asking you out. But if you don't want to call it a date then we can call it a meal, maybe dinner. It's definitely not a meeting because I'm not a contractor and I don't want you to be my client. So, Miss Graigh, what do you say?"

"Call it lunch tomorrow at the Gazebo in the Quarter and I say you have yourself a meal."

"Lunch tomorrow at the Gazebo in the Quarter. What time?"

"How 'bout two o'clock. I'll meet you there."

"Graigh, it was nice meeting you and I'll see you tomorrow for lunch."

"See you tomorrow, Bombei."

It was their beginning. He walked away from her buoyed by her charm and the ease of her friendly conversation. Casual, unpromising, yet full of the newness and realness as the Category three storm that pushed them into each other's paths. He left her that afternoon with his hope renewed after the scenery of her surroundings left him hurt.

That night, on the other side of the city in his hotel suite Bombei sat wrapped with a white towel around his waist on the edge of a lumpy bed. Out of the shower, and hungry he tried to decide between the limited food choices to make his dinner. A scowl cemented itself on his face as he looked at the menus for restaurants that were up and running again and not charging tourist prices. Nearly a year after the storm and he still had to scrounge for something decent that wouldn't make a rich man think twice.

Deciding to walk the streets until he smelled what he wanted or got turned away by the police or national guard, still holding citizens to the storm curfew, Bombei stood from the bed, opened the dresser and pulled out his clothes. In the top drawer he fished out clean boxers and an undershirt. He tossed the undergarments on the bed, then walked to the hallway near the sitting area to retrieve a pair of pants from the small closet. Jeans in tow, he walked back into the heart of the room and proceeded to get dressed.

He grabbed the remote control that laid next to his clothes on the bed and turned on the TV. The box clicked on to Cartoon Network and he didn't bother changing the channel. Dressed in everything but a real shirt, he went back to the dresser, opened a second drawer, and blindly grabbed the first T-shirt his hands touched. He threw it on over his head, stuck his arms in and pulled it down over his chest. Turning to his reflection in the mirror above the dresser, his hands smoothed the wrinkles in the rough-dried gray T-shirt. They moved slowly from his chest down to his stomach making sure the bottom hem of the shirt lay flat over his jeans. Looking at his reflection again, Bombei noticed his hands fondling the soft cotton material

She was in his thoughts, and with his body, and he'd only known her twelve hours. Their happenstance meeting was what he then considered a serendipitous accident. Now, when he passes the spot where he first noticed her, anger lives in him. Dull, dejected anger. The unrequited kind that comes from doing all he can, and knowing it's still not enough. That he still may not be enough.

The thoughts from more than a decade ago run through Bombei's head as he turns into the teacher's parking lot of Doctor King.

Sometimes I wonder if that was the best or the worst decision I've ever made.

The differences between Graigh then and Graigh now. The parts of her that he didn't understand: her distance, disquietude, her tendency to bite when barked at, her natural knack to fight instead of fleeing, even if no one fights with her. All of those traits he can identify, label, and see formulating just by the tone of her "Okay", "Yes" , "No." But he knows there is something else. The mystery emotion that makes him ask, "What's wrong?" multiple times, though he knows he will never get an answer. The unfound feasibility that makes him suggest therapy repeatedly, until she can hear the words without him ever saying them.

With his child on the way, the mystery is no longer one he wishes to unravel. It no longer pushes him to come home early so he can bask in the post-coital glow of her truth. Naked and open, raw, and real, Bombei no longer waits for the days when they can lay in tangled sheets communicating without speaking. Now, she carries his child. Son or daughter, the baby will be half hers and half his. The mystery could be passed on without him ever knowing why it exists.

She's gotta sort her shit out. Not for me. Not even for herself. For the baby.

He makes the decision for them in the middle of the school field where his young band students encircle him. His uncased trumpet is at his side as the music crushes all but one thought. His child. The child he's wanted since year two of their marriage. The child she's made him wait eight years for. Boy or girl, he knows now the mystery doesn't matter. The need to satisfy his curiosity no longer matters. All that matters is that Graigh is better than okay, no longer a prisoner to her silences, and a victim of her nebulous past.

Trumpet to his lips, Bombei blows his feelings in the air. He makes the music she used to love. The kind she used to support. The kind that's kept them together even when everything appeared to fall apart. He blows through his past the way he nearly blew through her block. Seeing only the blob that became his wife he focuses on the tangible. The pending birth of his child, instead of her intricate state of well-being. The known and yet unseen, instead of the mysterious and non-prescient past. He presses through notes, releasing what she built up, affirming his final word, and releasing Graigh's gray to the house where they reside three blocks away.

Five

The plush cushions of the turquoise chaise allow Graigh's body to melt into the cushions. She relaxes into the half-backed corner, closes her eyes, and inhales the burning sage in the room. Kicking off her shoes she exhales her breath in time to the "om" of the yoga students just beginning their practice on the floor beneath them.

"Are you comfortable?" Doctor Sophia Grace asks from her oversized black velvet sofa chair.

"I am," Graigh says, surprised by her own answer.

"Good. If the smoke gets to be too much for you, I'll put the sage out. I like to start a new relationship with clean energy."

"Thanks," Graigh says uneasily, "I appreciate that."

"What brings you to the Healing Center?"

"I don't know. My husband has been telling me to get a therapist for years, and my doctor suggested I do yoga. I saw you guys were right next to each other, so I figured two birds . . ." Graigh shrugs.

"Those are the reasons other people said you should see a therapist. I want to know why you're here."

"I'm not sure I understand what you mean," Graigh opens her eyes.

"I mean, you've come to therapy for the first time for a reason. You said your husband has suggested it for years, but from the questions you answered on the intake form, this is only your first time in a session. Why? I want to know why now, and not the other times it was suggested. You're obviously not here *for* your husband or I'd assume he'd be with you. So *why* are *you* here?"

"I don't know." Graigh awkwardly tries to sit up on the chaise.

Doctor Grace doesn't speak. She waits for Graigh to change her answer. She relaxes into her own lounge chair and closes her eyes. The vibrations from the kirtan vocalizations pierce through floor boards from the yoga studio and pour into the office space. The smoky burning sage creates a haze in the room for the music to waft.

"Is that your final answer?" Doctor Grace asks, without opening her eyes to look at Graigh.

I don't know what I'm supposed to say or what you want me to say, Graigh thinks before mumbling a paltry, "I guess."

She stares at the face before her. Doctor Sophia Grace came highly recommended from the anonymous reviews on Yelp and Google. Picked because of her picture, Graigh stares at the woman aged anywhere between forty and sixty. Sandy brown hair with light strands throughout, evidence of inevitable grays, crinkle and curl in a heart-shaped 'fro around her face. Thick cheeks press out against her hair, even without a smile on her face. Her brows, arched, shaped, and filled in are thick, brick brown bullshit stoppers. They rise and fall in Graigh's silence, imploring her to say something besides the awkwardly mumbled words that have already come out of her mouth.

Serene, even in her irritation, Doctor Grace looks at Graigh sitting uncomfortably in the corner of the chaise. Back straight, ankles hanging off the edge of the cushions, her feet are flexed, ready to plant and run out of the door. Graigh sits and waits for the Doctor, while Doctor Grace sits and waits for Graigh. They are at a draw in their game of chicken.

"Healing can only begin if you are honest. Honesty is a choice, and one you must make if you plan to have continuous sessions with me."

Doctor Grace's words land without response in the center of the room. Her syllables fall to the square tapestry laid in the middle of the floor. The thick print of the African textile absorbs the words meant for the woman still sitting, but ready to run.

"Why are you here, Graigh?" Doctor Grace asks more forcefully, though her eyes remain closed. "And before you answer, 'I don't know.' Think about what it is you have come here to tell me, a perfect stranger, that you did not want the closest people in your life to know."

Ankles relax in the cushions of the chaise instead of hanging over the edge. Shoulders meet the half-back, and Graigh's head rolls back to rest on the top cushion. Closed eyes exalt whatever is above the ceiling with a deep sigh.

Here we go.

"I am here because I'm pregnant, my marriage is shaky, and my husband and I are both concerned about my past though he won't tell me that, and I'll never admit it to him. And he has past issues of his own he won't say scares him, but I know are there. "

"Let's start with you since he's not here," Doctor Grace says. "What happened in your past?"

"That's a loaded question?"

"I can't be more specific if I don't know the back story to ask more pointed questions."

"It doesn't matter. My past isn't up for discussion right now."

"Then why are you here?"

"Because I don't know where else to go?"

"Finally, some truth."

Graigh blinks her eyes open, and slowly releases her head. Her renewed stare is met with a pleased face that smiles without smiling.

"Therapy is not easy," Doctor Grace begins. "It's not designed that way. It's work. But it's also a choice. You can either choose to do the work with me . . . or . . . take an extra yoga class and hope the asana's work out what you refuse to say."

She's a bitch.

Graigh swallows her thought and says nothing to the second threat of her relationship with Doctor Grace ending before it begins. Back and forth between relaxed and anxious her head bobs on her shoulders. She plays it off by rolling it around her neck's axis, trying again to relax. Shoulders find the chaise's half back and slouch beneath it allowing Graigh to use the full range of the vertical sofa. Lashes touch cheeks, breath expels, the clock ticks, and a chortling cough ends her moment of peace as she gasps for breath. Doctor Grace races to the ladder bookshelf behind her lounger and stubs out the sage in a conch shell.

"Are you okay? Would you like some water?"

"Yes . . . Please," Graigh manages through her gasps. "I'm sorry."

"Don't worry," Doctor Grace says producing an eight-ounce bottle of water from an inconspicuous black refrigerator beneath her dark oak desk. "I saw your chart. I should have stubbed it out a while ago."

"Yeah. If the asthma doesn't kill me first the bronchitis will. Blame Katrina."

"Katrina cough?"

"Yeah. The doctors say it's not real; but I didn't have bronchial asthma before the storm, and as you can tell it hasn't gone away."

"Where were you?" Doctor Grace asks, flopping back into the sofa chair.

"Tallahassee. I stayed with my friend Joy. Rode out the storm with her and her family. We went to FAMU together."

"Xavier. What did you study?"

"Pharmaceutical Science." Graigh drains the short bottle of water.

"But you're from here?" Doctor Grace asks, setting her notes aside.

"Born and raised. Ninth Ward."

"So why not go to Xavier?"

"I think I detect judgement."

"Yes, you absolutely do. Now answer the question. Why pass up the best for second best? *If* that."

"Don't make this rattler strike now," Graigh laughs. "I got into Xavier, but I needed to leave home. And FAM gave me more money. Tell your school to stop being cheap and maybe they can keep the best."

"Touché," Doctor Grace smiles at her HBCU rival. "What brought you back home. Most people never leave Florida."

"Tallahassee probably isn't what you're thinking of when you think of Florida. It's more like everywhere else in Georgia except Atlanta. As for why I'm here and not there . . . The past made me come home," Graigh says, losing her humor.

At least she began to open up. She's going to have to deal with the past if she wants to heal in the present.

Doctor Grace doesn't respond to Graigh's change in tone. Through the clear air of the room she watches Graigh's chest rise and fall. Her face is blank but her brow is pinched. The concentration on her breath evident, her coping mechanism on full display. Eyes closed, hands shoved deeply into the thin black jacket of her sweat suit, Doctor Grace observes as Graigh's wrists flex and release. She makes fists, and releases. Makes fists, and releases. Makes fists, then releases both her hands and her brow. She does not turn her head to catch the gaze watching her, or open her eyes to acknowledge that she is still the subject despite their moment of parity.

Pen and pad of papers in hand, Doctor Grace sketches her client's refusal to talk. Light strokes scratch the paper as Doctor Grace inks a rough outline of Graigh's body, before filling in more specific details in her face.

"You're not going to say anything?" Graigh asks anxiously.

"It wasn't my turn to speak," Doctor Grace says placing the paper and pen to the side again. "You put up a wall and you want me to either climb over it or run through it. That's not why we're here. I want you to take the wall down brick by brick."

"How am I supposed to do that?" Graigh asks, sitting all the way up on the chaise so her feet touch the floor.

"By doing the emotional work you've come here to do. That requires you to unpack your past until it no longer hurts you to think about, discuss, or analyze its effects on your present and future."

"I guess," Graigh offers standing with her hand across her belly.

"I didn't even ask," Doctor Grace says standing as well. "How far along are you?"

"I'll be four months in a few days. My next appointment is next week."

"That's about the time you find out what you're having. Are you excited? What do you want?" Doctor Grace gushes walking to her closed door.

"Just healthy," Graigh answers solemnly. "You have kids, don't you?"

"Two. A boy and a girl. And my daughter just had a daughter so that makes me a G-Mommy. How can you tell?"

"Only other mom's get this giggly over babies that aren't their own," Graigh says with a bemused smirk.

"I see your smile, but I hear pain. Are you okay?"

Doctor Grace is face-to-face with Graigh, a few inches shorter not counting the height of her hair. She stands with her hand wrapped around the door handle, arm extended, holding Graigh's departure hostage. Face-to-face, eye to eye, curls to kinks, the women watch each other both waiting for Graigh to pick her path.

"I'm fine," she says finally. "It's just this baby is kicking up a storm, and I ain't even showing yet."

You're lying.

Doctor Grace does not laugh with her. She does not move her arm, unwrap her hand, or turn the knob. She stands staring at the tall, lying woman waiting for her truth.

"Do you plan to make another appointment?" she asks.

"I'd planned to. I mean . . . if you want me . . . to," Graigh stammers.

"It's not about what I want, Graigh. It's about what you're willing to do," Doctor Grace says, turning the knob and opening the door to the small reception area.

"I'm trying to do the work," Graigh snaps. "It's my first day. I said I was going to make another appointment. You gotta give me a break."

"No, I don't," Doctor Grace says evenly. "It might be your money, but it's my time. What you won't do is waste my time. If you plan to make another appointment, then plan to try harder."

"Yep," Graigh says, gritting her teeth and stepping out of the doorway.

"Don't be dismissive. Just because you don't like what I'm saying, doesn't mean I'm wrong. Take this," Doctor Grace says, shoving the sketch into Graigh's hands.

"What's this?"

"It's you. Some doctors take notes. My sketches are my notes. I like for my clients to have them so they can see the changes in themselves as the weeks go by."

"Yeah, I guess," Graigh walks away from Doctor Grace, her eyes trained to the square sheet of paper in her hands.

"I hear your hurt. Remember, we don't always know we're hurt. Only that we're hurting others and can't figure out why?"

The words land at Graigh's back. Paused on the stairwell, she does not turn around.

"See you next week, Graigh," Doctor Grace says, closing herself back in her office.

"See you next week."

Down the stairs to the second floor, a full-bodied "om" resounds from the class just ending their practice inside the studio space for Wild Lotus Yoga. Graigh waits outside as a teacher walks over and opens the door for students to depart.

"May I help you?" a cheery faced, blonde ponytailed girl asks, inside the sweaty studio space.

"Looking to take some classes," Graigh says, hesitantly.

"First time?"

"Yes."

"Your first class is free, but you just missed our noon practice. You can come back this evening at six. That's when classes start back up here. Or if you live uptown you can go to our studio on Perrier Street. They start up again there at four."

"Okay, do you guys have a schedule?"

"It's on our website. That's the most up-to-date, just in case there are any changes."

"I'll check it out," Graigh says, walking backward toward the door.

"Hope to see you again."

"You will," Graigh promises.

She retreats to the stairs and makes her way to the first floor of The Healing Center. The complex that is four floors of self-care, and holistic practices. A center where practitioners who specialize in homeopathic conceptions, Middle Eastern medicine, yoga, therapy, art, and exercise are the norm and not the exception.

The complex boasts a free library and art gallery, a credit union and food co-op, and a bike rack rental and veterinarian. With embodiments and shrines to physical therapy gods and goddesses in the entryway, the center's unwritten mission of its commitment to the human body as it was created, before man tried to make it better, is heavily in the atmosphere.

Graigh steps outside of the brightly colored building, painted orange and teal, into the fresh afternoon air. She pulls the crumpled sketch of herself out of her pocket and looks at Doctor Grace's rendition of her. Her body suspended in mid-air in the empty white space of the square index card. Legs, waist, and chest are barely defined in the drawing. It is her face, feet, and one arm that is most pronounced. Drawn with thick, continuous straight lines, the parts of her that are well-defined are caricatured as angry angles. An angle at her elbow where her hand is shoved in her pocket. An angle at her feet where her soles flex against the air. An angle in her brows, drawn like mirroring upside down check marks, pinched together with scarcely a hair's room between them. Graigh studies what Doctor Grace says is her. Her bow lips still pronounced and present, are thinner than she knows them to be, on the chance occasion she glimpses her reflection in the mirror.

She shoves the drawing back in her jacket pocket.

My lips aren't that small. Not even when I'm pissed.

Graigh strolls the half block to her car in the newly gentrified neighborhood. Despite all the renovation and influx of "culture," this side of St. Claude Avenue can't hide what is still here. What has always been. Newness coexists with oldness in an argument each trying to win the right to be heard; trying to win the right to be the city's true narrative. It's one and only story. In the end they drown each other out and are ignored by passersby.

Graigh reaches her car parked in front of KIPP Leadership Academy. The hulking charter school building, weather beaten, but swept clean, is filled with colorful paper hanging from the inside of its windows. It casts a cool shadow across the hood of Graigh's truck. She climbs in and starts the engine. One hand on the wheel, the other on the hard wad of paper in her pocket. She flips the visor and pulls the index card out once again. Carefully unfolding herself, she studies the face and body of angles.

This don't even look like me.

Tired of looking in the fun house mirror, she casts her eyes up toward the visor mirror. Pinched check marks meet her brown-eyed gaze. She glances, comparing her real-life, angry features to the caricature on the card. The sucked in cheek bones even higher than normal, because of the hold of her mouth. Her ripe bow lips are pressed and bitten in, refusing to form a line. From the card in her lap to the mirror before her, her gaze follows the reflecting versions of herself refusing to accept what she has been seen to be.

Graigh slams the visor mirror shut then presses the button to roll the window down. The crumpled white card flies out of her hand and crunches beneath her back tire. At the corner of St. Claude and Spain Street she sees her litter— the flattened ball, stuck to the hot asphalt behind her. She makes a left onto Spain to head back home, not seeing the short, sandy-haired woman at the corner, watching her throw away her notes.

Six

March 20—16 Weeks

In a darkened room in the labyrinthian office space of UMC, Graigh and Bombei watch the fuzzy image of their baby materialize on screen, as the ultrasound technician moves her magic wand through cold goo on Graigh's slowly growing belly. Bombei holds her hand. His touch is light yet firm. Four fingers wrap around her one. His thumb slowly grazes over her knuckle. His excitement is tempered knowing she has been here before; that last time this was as far as she had gone. He strokes her hand and searches her face. It is enigmatic as she stares at the screen rapt in attention, marveling at the tiny human they've made together. The head large and round, eyes closed, arms, hands, legs, and feet floating in a cloud of protection. Their baby, without name, color, creed, or expectation, floats in Graigh's hopes and Bombei's aspirations, not knowing its parents already have goals that this child—their child—must meet. Goals unspoken until the arrival, but goals, nonetheless. Healthy and happy chief among them, successful and kind, also on the list. To live a life without racial strife, and financial struggle at the bottom of the page where goals turn into hopes, and those hopes into dreams, and those dreams into unattained fairytales never to be materialized. They stare at the screen, barely connected, but their emotions on one accord. In their silence they find the peace that eludes.

"Are we learning the sex today?" The ultrasound technician asks, breaking their trance.

"No," Graigh whispers.

"We're having a gender reveal party," Bombei explains.

"Who will keep the secret?" the woman asks from behind the screen she's turned to face her, to determine if their baby is a boy or girl.

"Put the results in an envelope. We're taking it to my brother's wife so she can plan accordingly," Graigh says.

"Will do."

The technician makes rapid clicks with her mouse with one hand, as she moves her other hand holding the wand through the goo. Point, click, sweep. She works quickly taking measurements and making notes without commentary.

"I'll print out a few copies for you guys to keep."

"Okay," Graigh says aloud, to no one in particular.

The technician hands her a towel to clean her belly. She takes the soft cloth and removes the baby activator gel from her stomach. The edges of her shirt in her fingertips, she tugs and pulls the ends down over her exposed body. The hem of the baby-tee raises just above her navel, exposing her unbuttoned and barely zipped jeans and the tip-tops of her stretch marks.

"I guess I should start buying maternity clothes."

"You look fine, Bae. Better than most women who ain't even pregnant."

"Aww. You're too kind," Graigh says, grabbing Bombei's beard and planting a kiss on his lips.

"Here are your photos," the technician says, extending the strips of black and white ultrasound images. "You won't find out from those. This has what you need for your party."

The woman's arm cuts through their closeness. She slices through their intimacy, urging them to be on their way so she can get on with her day.

Bombei and Graigh say a hasty, "Thank you," as he helps her up from her stretched out position on the cushioned exam bed.

"The nurse should be just outside the door. She'll take you back to see Doctor Marcella to finish up your appointment."

"Thank you," they say together.

Hand at her back, Bombei ushers Graigh out of the ultrasound room into the fluorescent lit hallway. The same waif nurse who took her vitals last month, waits for them outside.

"Where to?" Graigh asks, rapidly blinking her eyes to adjust to the light.

"Just around this corner," she says.

Bombei and Graigh follow the woman. His fingers are still wrapped around her one, his thumb grazes her knuckle. They walk following the nurse's red tinted brunette hair. It sticks to her scalp slick with oil. She takes them around a bend, past two doors, and into an open room that looks exactly the same as the one they were in before.

"Go ahead and hop on the table, Doctor Marcella will be with you shortly."

The door thuds closed behind the nurse. As if on cue Bombei grabs the stool and pulls it to sit front and center of the exam table. Graigh hops on top of the paper covered cushion, it crackles beneath her bottom. Eyes on her feet, and hers on the top of his head, they sit in repose, the clock marks the seconds.

In her hands she holds the ultrasounds. Eight images of her unborn baby, and a surprise in an envelope. Tiny nose, tiny mouth, tiny hands, barely recognizable toes. She thumbs threw the two sheets of images, stopping to examine each one, noting each difference in the angle of the baby's head, hands, and body.

"You're smiling," Bombei says.

"Everybody smiles when they see a baby."

"But this isn't just *a* baby. It's *our* baby."

"It is."

"Do you want to go by and see Teddy and Shandra after your appointment to give them the results?"

"Not particularly. Don't you have to go back to school for band practice?"

"Not today."

"I still don't want to go by Teddy's and Shandra's. We can do that tomorrow."

"True."

Bombei ends the conversation as quickly as he began. Two words here. One-word answers there. After more than a decade together they have learned to economize their conversation. Only saying what is necessary, never speaking in long loquacious brush strokes. Their talks are utilitarian. Even their arguments and disagreements are meticulous and pragmatic. No shouting, no excessive gesticulating, calm tones tinged with angry, sometimes four-letter words. It is as if they're baiting one another to see who will jump out of character first. Who will show the first sign of fire? The first sign of weakness. The first sign of emotional immaturity. In stoic repose, that is how they spend their days together— lounging—only saying what is necessary in the moment, but most times saying nothing at all.

"Do you want to see?" Graigh asks.

"See what?"

"Your baby." She shakes the sheets of images.

"I was waiting for you to finish."

"Here you go." Graigh extends her hand with the sonogram pictures.

He takes the photos as silence consumes the room again. The wall clock ticks. The seconds go by. They wait for Doctor Marcella to sweep into the room and bring with her a reason for them to say something, anything, even if not to each other.

"This one looks like the baby's waving," Bombei says, pointing at one image.

"Yeah, it does."

"He's going to be so handsome. Just like his daddy," Bombei says, pride swelling in his voice.

"You're so sure our baby is going to be a boy, aren't you?"

"If God is the God of miracles, blessings, favor, fairness, and answering prayers of the faithful, I am."

"Oh, really now," Graigh chuckles. "And how long have you and God been scheming against me for a boy? What if I've been praying for a girl? God's known me a lot longer than he's known you."

"Which is exactly the reason we're having a boy. God's gotta show out for me. We're still getting to know each other. You, on the other hand, know the Lord works in mysterious ways, and sometimes that mystery is just telling your ass no."

Graigh raises an eyebrow. "So, we're cursing at the Lord?"

"My bad. God know my heart."

"Don't apologize to me. Your mouth is between you and Jesus."

"Don't act like you don't cuss."

"Whatever, Mr. Halvert. Whatever," Graigh scrunches her nose and raises three fingers. "Read between the lines."

"Just because you didn't say it, doesn't mean you didn't say it," Bombei smirks.

Graigh rolls her eyes.

Three successive raps of knuckles on the exam room door announce Doctor Marcella's entrance. Audible breaths exhale as she sweeps into the room with the skinny, oily haired nurse beside her.

"How are you feeling today? And are you excited? What are we having?"

"We don't know yet," Graigh answers, trying to match Doctor Marcella's cheery lilt. "We're going to find out at a party next week."

"Then I'll wait until you guys tell me," Doctor Marcella says, slipping on her latex gloves. "I used to always ask the ultrasound tech the results to find out the same day the parents did, but over the last few years, I've ruined a lot of surprises. More and more couples opting for gender reveal parties, or to find out on delivery day. Change in the generations and technology, I guess."

Doctor Marcella straps the heart monitor to Graigh's belly, squirts the goo, and searches with the probe. The unmistakable "wah, wah, wah, wah" of impending life, blares through the silent room, drowning out the ticks of the clock, and intruding on Graigh and Bombei's singular thoughts, until they are once again connected by the child they made.

"Your baby is strong," Doctor Marcella remarks; awe-struck, as if this was her first-time hearing life in the womb, and not her fifteenth of the day.

That's right, you are. Gotta be strong to make it into this world.

Graigh smiles down at her belly, grateful for the doctor's convivial empathy; for going on their pregnancy journey with them as if she were in the relationship, and not the advisor over just this portion of their lives.

"Thank you," Graigh says softly.

Bombei stands from his stool and walks to Graigh's side, knowing the gratitude in her voice is for more than the trifle of a compliment. He knows what may have been a throwaway sentiment is affirmation for his wife. Affirmation and assurance, he long ago realized he cannot give her; especially, through this pregnancy. Every month thus far has been a milestone that's triggered her memory and made her wary of the future she hasn't lived that beckons toward both triumph and tragedy. She is constantly haunted by what happened before, and the unpredictability of what can always remain an unfortunate possibility.

"Graigh, Bombei, everything looks and sounds good; but, Mom, how are you feeling?"

I swear, I hate this question.

"I feel fine, I guess. No different than normal." Graigh shrugs.

"Are you still very tired or exhausted? How's your breathing?"

"I'm not as tired as I was in the very, very beginning, looking back on it, but I'm always down for a nap," Graigh laughs. "My breathing is fine. No attacks," she lies, not mentioning her coughing fit in Doctor Grace's office. "I even found a yoga class to try and help make my breaths longer."

"You did?" Bombei asks, looking down at his wife.

"I did. I didn't get a chance to tell you. It's downtown, Wild Lotus Yoga, and they have an uptown studio too."

"Then sounds like you're doing alright. Remember, when you're healthy, your baby is healthy. Are you feeling the baby move any?"

"I have a few flutters here and there, but nothing serious. Sometimes I don't know if it's the baby, my stomach growling, or something making me nauseous."

"It could be all three," Doctor Marcella answers. "Think more consciously about that when you feel those flutters, so we can talk about it at your next visit."

"Twenty weeks, right?" Bombei asks.

"You got it," Doctor Marcella answers. "Between now and then, you will start showing a little more, so you'll want to make sure you're sleeping on your side and you'll need to avoid supine positions because you don't want to risk cutting off anything flowing to your baby as it grows. Modify any yoga poses that don't feel good, drink lots of water, cut down on your seafood, and I'll see you guys in a month."

"Thank you," Graigh says, when the doctor finishes her scripted checklist.

The door closes behind Doctor Marcella, leaving Bombei and Graigh in the silent room, save for the ticking of the clock.

"So, how's yoga?" Bombei asks; his tone accusing.

"I don't know. I haven't been yet. I saw the studio a few days ago when I was downtown, and I stopped in. The chick told me the class had just ended, and to go look on their website," Graigh over explains, still omitting the real reason for her trip to The Healing Center.

"Oh," he replies. "What do you want to do now?" Bombei asks, as Graigh steps down from the exam table.

"Eat."

"You already have your eating pants on?" he jokes.

"All my pants are eating pants."

"Growing pants, too. What do you have a taste for?"

"Conch fritters and blackened catfish."

"What in the pregnancy craving is that?"

"You asked me what I want. That's what I want."

"To the Rum House we go."

They walk out of the exam room, their fingers wrapped around each other's, to the front desk to make the twenty-week appointment. With the sonograms in his back pocket, Bombei holds on to his present and his future, longing for more. The pad of his thumb runs across Graigh's knuckles as his hand cups the images of his soon-to-be son or daughter. He affirms for himself that both are real, as he leads Graigh out of the doctor's office, away from the hospital tower, and into the hot and humid afternoon.

Seven

Hot, white lights flash all around. They're blinding. Clear images unable to manifest in the white haze of heat. She sees nothing but feels everything. A runway padded and lined. Chairs all around. All eyes on what is not there. She feels the stares through the absence of faces. She hears the murmurs despite the absence of clear voices. It sounds like a rustling; a deep wave of crunching paper, falling rain, whispers, sighs, and sweat coalescing into one long sound that sweeps through her—leaving her washed by the omnipresent wind, shuddering from the chill, lost in her own void, shut away in her own vacuous vacuum of nothingness. The intemperate climate changes again. It is not hot or breezy. Not cold. Not clammy. The space around her is painful. White lights turn to red ones. The bulbs burning near her face are accusatory. Interrogation lamps in the color of blood. Her body reels, rejecting the atmosphere yet unable to escape it. The smell thickens around her, it is metallic and slick. The pain quickens, banging, punching, pounding at her head and her belly. And then it is gone. The red erased, replaced by darkness, stillness and a gentle stirring on her shoulder.

She is awake.

His hand is there, rocking her back and forth.

Her eyes open. They adjust to the sun streaming in through the car's windshield. They are stopped. Parked on the ferry, approaching the other side of the river.

What happened?

Graigh asks herself the question as she turns to look at Bombei's face. Concern is apparent. Questions buzz on the tip of his tongue but never escape his lips. Lines etched in his brow are long and pronounced. His sleepy eyes are full of energy; synapses firing behind them, neurons communicating what he knows, what he remembers, his own mind queries an answer so he doesn't have to ask the question.

Graigh places a hand on his cheek. Her fingers rake through his beard as her lips find his to kiss away the questions. To kiss away the pain. To erase the memory that's found them both. Lids open, electrified sleepy eyes meet wide brown ones, their lashes flutter together as their lips melt, slightly parting. A kiss of lies.

Thank you for not asking.

By the time she tells me, it won't even be an issue.

The ferry horn blares. Once. Twice. Three times, alerting riding cars their journey is over, and waiting cars that their turn is next. The wave running car carrier turns its way into its dockside parking spot. Bombei, anxious, starts the car and waits. Graigh unbuckles her seatbelt and grabs her purse off the floor between her feet. Digging through the oversized slouch bag, her hands blindly search for the long chubby stick of tinted lip gloss. She removes it, and a bottle of water, from her bag.

Graigh takes long audible gulps. Water spills down the sides of her mouth, over her throat, and rolls down her skin to her clothes. She half drains the bottle before recapping it and tossing it back in her bag. She pulls down the visor, flips up the mirror and makes quick work of applying the gloss on her lips. Lingering only for a moment to smooth an errant eyebrow hair, she flips her image away as quickly as she made it appear.

They drive off the ferry, the car bouncing along the changes in ground texture. On the other side of the river, Bombei navigates the car to her brother's house. They speed past the banks of the Mississippi, through Gretna, and into Marrero. Silence is with them the entire time. He watches the road. She looks out the window. Biting the inside of his bottom lip, he drives through neighborhoods with lush green lawns, and mature trees, chewing his thoughts until he pulls in front of a single-story home, too small for the family inside.

Fuck it. She's my wife. She oughta be able to talk to me even when she doesn't want to.

"You alright?" he asks.

"Yeah, I'm okay. I guess I fell asleep on the way. I do that a lot lately."

"You do. But that's not what I'm asking about."

"Then what are you asking about?"

She's defensive.

"Did you have a nightmare?"

"Not that I can recall."

"You sure? You were knocking your head against the window, and had your knees pulled up to your chin, with your fists pressed into your stomach."

"I was sleeping."

"You don't say."

So now she wants me to act like I don't know what I know. This shit is for the birds. She's lucky we're at her brother's house.

Bombei cuts the ignition and gets out of the car. His anger is palpable. Graigh feels the negative energy radiate around her as she opens her own door, grabs her purse, and follows behind him. The blades of grass are fragrant from the freshly cut lawn. She takes her time going up the walk to the front door, double-checking her bag for the envelope with part of her baby's identity, and the sheets of ultrasounds she promised Shandra she'd bring. At the door, Bombei is not beside her. He sits in the forest green porch swing idling side to side staring daggers at his wife. Elbows on his knees, his hands are folded into his beard as he watches her wait for him.

"I hate it when you lie to me," he says through a clenched jaw. "Ring the doorbell so we can get this over with."

He stands from the swing. The release of weight sends the country porch accoutrement circling. Its short anchor chains squeak from the motion. The doorbell resounds both inside and outside the house and is followed by the chirping bark of a dog, a fight of "I got it," and shrieks of "TeeTee."

"TeeTee, what took you so long?" comes the youngest voice, clamoring to push open the heavy wrought iron door through the handles of one of the fleur-de-lis designs.

"You have to turn the knob, dummy," comes an older, young voice.

"Don't call me dumb."

"Both of y'all get away from there. Leave the door alone. Your ainty don't wanna be bothered with you. Let her get in the house good before y'all run her away."

Shandra steps between her feuding children and turns the knob to let Bombei and Graigh inside.

"How are TeeTee's favorites?" Graigh asks, bending down in the doorway with her arms open to her niece and nephew.

"TeeTee, we can't both be your favorite. You have to pick," Quiana says.

"Okay, well you, Miss Quiana Monique, are my favorite girl, and you, Mister Kory Thomas, are my favorite boy." Graigh smiles to unappeased faces.

"I thought I was your favorite," says a deeper voice approaching.

"You are my first favorite," Graigh says, standing to hug her fourteen-year-old nephew Christian.

"But, TeeTee, you still have three favorites," Quiana whines, tugging against the seams of Graigh's pants.

"You're all my favorites in different ways. And this favorite right here needs to go take a bath. Boy, you stank," Graigh says, pulling away from Christian.

"I just cut the grass. They had me outside all morning doing stuff, while these two brats got to sit in the house watching TV."

"That's good for you, boy," Bombei says, dapping Christian's fists. "It builds character."

"I'm not a brat," Kory pouts, incensed by the insult.

"Yes, you are, brat," Christian taunts.

"If I'm a brat, yo' mama's a brat."

"Guess what, dummy? We got the same mama."

"Y'all cut it out," Shandra referees. "I just told y'all 'bout all that arguing earlier. Christian, go take a bath like your ainty said. Kory and Quiana, get away from that door and let your ainty and uncle come inside. Graigh, Bombei, y'all want something to drink?"

"Water," Graigh says, letting the door slam closed behind them.

"What you got in the cabinets, Shandra?" Bombei asks, making his way across the living room into the kitchen.

"Depends on what you want. But if you want it cold, there's some Ciroc in the freezer."

"You know you my favorite, right," Bombei says wrapping an arm around Shandra's thick waist.

"You drinkin' kinda early, don't you think?" Graigh chides.

"Not too early, since I'm not driving back," he bristles.

"Oh really."

"Yeah. I figured you'd want to drive home. Help you stay awake."

"I'm a tell y'all like I tell my chirren," Shandra begins. "Whatever y'all arguing about, I don't wanna hear it."

"It's not an argument," Graigh shuts down. "Where's my brother?"

"He in the back, in the room," Shandra says. "He just got in from the port. Trying to clean up a li'l bit since he worked all night. I'll go check on him. Tell him to hurry up. He don't need to get fancy for you. He know what you look like."

"Oh, alright."

Silence finds Graigh and Bombei standing on opposite sides of Shandra's bar, watching as she walks away, custard-colored fat rolls jiggling beneath her floral printed house dress. Even the cellulite in her legs roll as the knee-high slits in the dress leave room for the breeze she creates when she walks. Graigh's eyes follow the back of her sister-in-law's twenty-two inch sew-in, pulled together into a low ponytail, until she disappears down a hall and into a room behind closed doors.

They are left alone in the kitchen, Kory and Quiana play feet away in the living room. The wall-mounted flatscreen transmitting *Sponge Bob* in the background is unwatched.

"What is your problem?" Graigh snaps.

"I could ask you the same thing," Bombei retorts., "but you'd only lie about it."

"What are you talking about?"

"I just told you. I hate it when you lie to me."

"What lie? I was sleeping, apparently badly, and you woke me up. Where is the lie? I'm going to have a lot of bad nights and naps. I'm growing life."

"Don't blame the baby for your bullshit. I was born on a day that ends in "y," but it for damn sure wasn't yesterday."

He walks from around the bar, past the glass dining room table, to the patio door. He unlatches the sliding glass and steps outside. The doors slam together behind him. It is his warning not to follow.

Graigh sits alone at the dining room table, water glass in hand, watching his back, as he stands in one place sipping the sweet flavored vodka. Beads of sweat ball up on the back of his freshly faded hair. They will leave a ring stain of dirt on the inside line of his salmon-colored T-shirt. He broods with one hand shoved in the pockets of his khaki pants. She watches Bombei angrily gulp the last of the glass before setting it on the patio table.

Why do we have to do this now?

"Quiana and Kory, get those toys up from the middle of my floor!" Shandra yells, interrupting Graigh's thoughts.

"Shandra, you ain't gotta yell at them like that. They're just playing," Teddy says behind her.

"Just playing, my behind." Shandra steps through blocks and action figures sprawled on the living room floor. "I'm the one who cleans up behind them when they're *just playing*. So, unless you offering maid service 'round here, they need to take these toys to their room."

"Teddy, you heard your boss. Let these babies do what she says," Graigh instigates.

"Graigh, two things. For one, they're not babies, and for two, hush your mouth," Teddy says, walking over to his sister.

Graigh stands from the glass dining table and folds herself into her brother's arms. She breathes in deeply, then exhales against his chest.

"How are you?" Teddy asks, into her wind-tossed curls.

"I'm alright, I guess. I'm alright." Graigh steps back from her brother's arms.

The same brown complexion covers both of their bodies, but where Graigh's face is angular, Teddy's is completely square, and mostly clean shaven.

"You smell like soap," Graigh says, sitting back down.

"I washed my ass when I got off work. I knew company was coming," Teddy grins.

"That's the only time you wash your ass, is when you have people over? Boy, you nasty."

"All men are nasty," Shandra chimes, taking a seat beside Graigh at the round glass table.

"Where's my brother?" Teddy asks.

"Your brother-*in-law* is outside."

"Then I'm going outside. Call us if you need us."

"We will. Don't worry," Shandra promises.

Maybe you can fix his funky ass attitude, Graigh thinks, as she watches Teddy join Bombei on the patio in his extra-long black basketball shorts and T-shirt.

She watches Bombei turn from his stoic stance to greet her brother. They slap hands and embrace like old friends. A marked difference from their frosty first meeting. Back then Teddy was skeptical that Bombei, who had just begun working on Graigh's house, their family home, was going to take advantage of his sister. Bombei, unsure of why he was receiving the third degree about mulch, shingles, and dry wall, was arrogant and over confident about winning his "client's" heart, and her only remaining family. Their dapped embrace, and reference to each other as brother, is a notable improvement from their austere beginnings.

"I'm so glad they get along," Graigh exhales, still watching Bombei and Teddy outside.

"Girl, you knew your brother was going to come around," Shandra dismisses. "You know that man is just over-protective of you since you're his only sister. But I mean, damn, it's been fourteen years. He knows Bombei ain't going nowhere."

"From your lips to God's ears," Graigh whispers.

"Trouble in the Ninth Ward, because you know I can't say paradise."

"Forget you, Shandra." Graigh rolls her eyes. "Inside our house is paradise and you know it. You, Teddy, *and the kids* would be able to fit comfortably, but y'all would have to come visit on a more regular basis now, wouldn't you?"

And this is why I don't like coming across the river. Y'all got the nerve to be bougie.

"Whatever, Graigh. Your house is beautiful, but you know that man outside ain't crossing that river after dark to visit you."

"Well, y'all could come in the daytime and go home when it's dark."

"We'll see," Shandra says, deading the conversation. "Now let me see my future niece or nephew, so we can plan this party."

The party that's at my house. But y'all can't come across the river? Yeah, okay.

Graigh sighs her frustration as she picks her purse up from the floor and sets it on the table. Digging through it, she immediately pulls the loose sheets of sonogram images and slides them to Shandra. She pulls the envelope with the sex of the baby inside and holds it in her hand, while she sets her purse back on the floor.

"Oh, Graigh, look at this one. It looks like your baby is waving," Shandra marvels.

"I know," Graigh gushes. "I look at them everyday."

"You're already in baby talk mode. You've been ready. I don't know why y'all didn't have this baby years ago."

"You know why."

"Yeah, I do, but you gotta let that shit go."

"That's what everyone keeps telling me."

What they don't say, is how.

"Then it's high time you listen. Where is the picture, you're supposed to give me?" Shandra asks, leafing through the two sheets of black and white images.

"In my hands," Graigh answers.

"Hand it over so I can see if I'm having a niece or nephew."

"You act like you're having this baby."

"I might as well be, as long as you're taking to pop that thang out."

"The same amount of time it took you to have yours."

"Whatever, Graigh. Give me the damn envelope."

"Here you go." Graigh slides the envelope across the table.

"Thank you."

"Mama, can we go outside?" Quiana asks stepping up to the table.

Her tilted head makes her long pigtails drape past her shoulder, as she waits for an answer. Antsy, she rocks back and forth on her toes unable to keep still.

"Did you clean up your blocks and help Kory put away his toys?"

"I tried but he wouldn't let me in his room. He says it's for boys only," Quiana pleads.

"Go outside, girl," Shandra fusses. "In fact, we'll all go outside. Help your ainty."

"C'mon, TeeTee. I'll help you," Quiana says excitedly, coming to Graigh's side.

"Take TeeTee's purse." Graigh hands the bag over to the bubbling child.

"TeeTee, your shirt's too small. I can see your belly button. And how come your pants are open? I can almost see your panties. You're not supposed to show anybody your panties."

"Girl stop looking at me so hard and take my purse outside," Graigh says, swatting the butt of Quiana's denim dress. The flower printed ruffles at the hip ripple from her tiny legs as she scampers toward the door with Graigh's bag.

"It's time for you to get some maternity clothes," Shandra says, laughing.

"I will as soon as you buy 'em."

Graigh pulls up her pants and pulls down her too small, and too tight T-shirt. She follows Shandra through the sliding glass doors to the covered back patio.

Shandra goads, "I know what they're having," peeking into the envelope.

"Well, don't say nothing, Baby. You're going to ruin the surprise," Teddy admonishes.

"I'm not."

"Girl you know you can't hold water." Graigh laughs.

"That's why I'm going to call the bakery as soon as y'all leave and tell them, so I can feel like I'm gossiping with somebody. Quiana, slow down with all that water," Shandra yells across the patio. "You're going to be soaking wet. It ain't that hot outside. It's only March."

"But, Mama, I need the water to make the bubbles," Quiana yells back. She turns off the spigot posted on the outside corner of the house, close to the red wood fence.

"Alright, li'l girl. You get sick, you're still going to school. Don't say I didn't warn you."

"I know, Mama."

"Y'all ready for all this?" Teddy asks, sitting down on the wine-colored couch cushions of the outdoor patio set.

Is anybody ever ready?

Graigh thinks to herself as she and Shandra sit between Teddy, flanking him on either side.

"Is anybody ever ready for a baby?" Shandra gives voice to Graigh's unspoken thoughts.

"We're as ready as we can be," Graigh says.

Bombei takes one of the lone swivel chairs, sitting in front of his empty glass. An easy quiet finds the four of them. The only noise in the vicinity is Quiana's giggles from the large rectangular yard. She runs the perimeter close to the fence pulling a giant bubble ring behind her. Giant bubbles float in her wake as she runs.

"I'm ready," Bombei says, quietly staring at Quiana.

Don't have too much choice in the matter now.

He stares at the five-year-old stroking his beard wondering if his longing all these years will end up in buyer's remorse after the child arrives to the mother, he chose to commingle his DNA.

"Boy or girl. What y'all want?" Teddy asks.

"Healthy," Graigh says adamantly.

"Okay, that's you, but my man over here, I know he's gotta be itching for a boy."

"You know he is," Shandra jumps in before Bombei can answer. "Every man wants a junior to carry his name."

"I didn't," Teddy says defensively.

"Yes, you did. I just wasn't naming my baby Theodore."

"What's wrong with Theodore?" Graigh eggs on.

"Nothing's wrong with Theodore. But if y'all like it so much, why does everybody call him Teddy?"

"It's alright, Graigh," Teddy answers. "Christian still has my name."

"For a middle name," Shandra chides.

"You ready for all this, Bruh?" Teddy asks Bombei. "To fight about names, and nursery decorations, and stupid shit like that?"

"It'd be better than the stupid shit we fight about now," Bombei glowers.

"Y'all beefing?" Teddy asks.

"We're fine," Graigh covers. "Shandra what do you need me to do for this party?"

"Nothing. I'll be at your house next weekend to kick you out and set up before we find out about my niece."

"Shandra! Woman, I swear you can't hold water. You're not supposed to tell," Teddy yells.

"Or nephew," she adds, coyly. "I didn't say which and you still don't know. But I know Graigh secretly wishes she's having a girl, even if she is fronting like health is all that matters."

"Health *is* all that matters."

"Speaking of. . . How is yours?" Teddy asks.

"I'm alright. Just tired a lot. This little thing is sucking everything outta me."

"You still coughing?"

"No. Not really."

"Is it no? Or not really?"

"Not really," Graigh answers. "Unless something triggers it like smoke or something."

"So, I guess grilling is out of the question for the party then?" Shandra asks. "Seafood it is."

"You just want an excuse to have a crawfish boil."

"Graigh, it's me you're talking about. I don't ever really need an excuse for a crawfish boil. It's just, now I have one. A damn good one. Don't nobody need you hacking up a lung all over the food. I don't care if it is your party."

"Alright. Alright. Alright. What else are we going to have?" Graigh asks.

"Teddy, move so I can sit next to Graigh," Shandra fusses.

They awkwardly swap seats. Shandra rubs her rolls across Teddy as she side-steps in front of him to sit beside

Graigh. Teddy ends up in the corner of the couch, hugging the arm closest to Bombei's swivel chair.

"You alright, Bruh?" he asks Bombei as Graigh and Shandra chatter about the party beside him.

"I'm alright. As good as can be," Bombei answers cautiously.

"You don't seem alright."

"You know how your sister is." Bombei waves in Graigh's direction. "She's secretive. Doesn't like to say anything about anything. All these years, and it's like I'm still auditioning for the part of husband. Still interviewing when I've been on the job since day one."

"Yeah, but, man, she's pregnant. She's got hormones and shit raging in her body. You know she's going to be high strung, on edge, and on your nerves until that doctor places that baby in her arms. Only then, is when she's going to calm down."

"Yeah, but she was like this before we got pregnant. This shit's gotten worse."

"Just give her time," Teddy counsels.

She's had fourteen years' worth of time. Time is up.

Bombei sits back in the swivel chair without response. Hands on the cushions beside his hips, he slouches low and rests his hand against the cushioned wicker back, and swings from side to side.

"Man, I'm getting you another drink," Teddy says, swiping Bombei's glass from the table top.

He doesn't respond. Bombei sits and sways in the swivel chair. Eyes closed. Graigh and Shandra's hushed and excited voices blend into the background with Quiana's shrieks. He hears her feet scamper by, still running with the bubbles. The sliding door opens, and more feet come outside passing behind his chair.

"You can't catch me," Kory shrieks. "Christian's it. Run, Quiana!"

The boys join their sister in the yard circling the grass along the fence. Panting and out of breath, they run. Yelling and insulting each other at every turn. Their game of tag brings an inner smile to Bombei's tired mind. He sits, slouches, content with the noise of the children he's wanted for so long, even if these three are only his by proxy.

"This is a man's drink," Teddy says, setting a tumbler of brown liquid on the table in front of Bombei. "Drink up."

"Damn, man. You're trying to get me drunk. I try not to drink dark liquor before dusk."

"If you don't, drink that shit. We don't waste no alcohol around here. That's a lot better for you than that froufrou ass sweet shit you was drinking earlier."

"Baby, you didn't get us any drinks?" Shandra asks, peeking over Graigh's head.

"She can't drink."

"But I can."

"You don't need none. What have y'all decided anyway?"

"We're going to have the party at Graigh and Bombei's place next weekend around five, that way we can party hard."

"Don't you think that's kind of late?" Teddy asks.

"Boy, you act like you can't hang in the Ninth Ward one night," Graigh says defensively. "Y'all can stay the night. The only other people who are going to be at the house are Mr. Charles, Joy, Anthony, and Junior. We have plenty of room."

"That's not the point, Graigh, and you know it?"

"Don't y'all start," Shandra says loudly.

"It's nothing to start, Shandra." Graigh stands. "Even with all the work we've put into that house, he still won't come by. Our family home, he wants nothing to do with it. Like he's too good to go back to where he came from."

"It has nothing to do with me being too good to go back, Graigh, and you know it. I don't have to be there. I don't have to live there, and neither do the two of you. You choose to put yourself at risk. Hurricanes, shootings. You choose to live in the danger zone. We have three kids. We can't, and we don't have to."

"I'm not asking you to move back to the Ninth Ward. But hell, the least you could do is come visit. The only time I see you is when I come across the river to your house, on your side of town. You haven't even seen our house since we finished it. All the shit I've been through trying to restore it, build it up, and make it right, and you won't even come see. That hurts. It's where we grew up."

"Graigh, it's not about the house. I know it's beautiful. You wouldn't have anything less. But where you are, I worry about you, but you're too stubborn to move. I've made my peace with it, but that doesn't mean I have to like it or visit. I love you."

"From a distance."

"That's not fair and you know it. There have been three recovery commissions to decide what to do about the Ninth Ward, and there still ain't shit to show for it. Hell, the ULI recommendations were more than ten years ago. The levees may be stronger—and that's still up for debate—MLK may be a great school, but that doesn't change the fact that you're on low land, with few street lights, no stores, and a bunch of folk that can't afford nothing so they rob, steal, and kill just to get by."

"Sounds like you get your facts from the news, instead of the people who actually live in the neighborhood. It's their job to get on TV and tell you all the bad stuff that's happened in the city overnight and during the day. That don't mean we don't have good stuff going for us too."

"Like what?"

"We have a brand-new laundromat that just opened on Caffin and Galvez."

"You don't need a laundromat. You have a washer and dryer in the house."

"How do you know; you've never been to our house."

"Bae, that's enough," Bombei tries to interject.

"That's all you can come up with. A new laundromat. Let me know when you have a new grocery store. Or a pharmacy. You're fighting for the Ninth Ward and no one else is."

"You don't know who's fighting for what. It's not like you come down there or are doing anything."

"And what are you doing, Graigh? It's not like you used your fancy pharmacy degree to open up your own place to help the community you say you love so much."

"I live there. That's more than you will ever do."

"I don't have to, and I don't want to live there. I know our government ransomed New Orleans to the highest bidder in the name of increasing gross domestic product. Capitalism, money, greed, the get paid now; think about the consequences later, mentality…"

"You mean the American way?" Bombei chuckles.

"Now here you go on this political mess," Shandra teases.

"Naw, Baby, he's right. New Orleans was the corner boy to the government's cartel. Especially the port. When everybody was getting paid, we were an example of what other port cities should've been. Jacksonville, Savannah, Mobile, Miami. Nobody could touch the N.O. But then Katrina, and now we latent casualties not even worthy of the lie that we were good enough then, better than good enough then, to rebuild now."

"But you're working again. So that's not entirely true."

"Graigh, the only reason I'm back working at the port is because they realized they couldn't shut it down. Too much money come up and down that river that needs to go elsewhere, for them to shut it down."

"So, if the port was good enough to rebuild because of the money that means the city is worth saving. All of the city." Graigh flops back down on the couch.

"Not really," Teddy says. "That's why they haven't put much money where you are in the first place. The government knows they made this problem. Eroded the wetlands, drained the swamps, put our people in a bowl below sea level. Racism left us with nothing but the marsh to build on, and now that they see the area isn't viable, the getting is no longer good, we're left to whither, and die."

"I guess the Ninth Ward is just like an old ho," Graigh says. "Picked over, ran through, rode hard, and put away wet."

"Now you get it," Teddy says excitedly, sloshing his drink out of his glass on to his pants.

"No, I don't." Graigh says flatly.

"Bombei. Shandra. Help me out here."

"That's y'all business," Shandra says, putting both of her hands up.

"I stopped trying to convince her to leave years ago," Bombei says. "I sold both of my houses to stay in Ninth Ward. Had to go through Road Home to rebuild, and now we gotta mortgage on a house that was paid for."

"And we're not leaving," Graigh says, standing back up. "Teddy, you talk about the government this, the government that. Racism this, racism that. The truth is scientists predicted Katrina decades before it happened, and nobody gave a shit to stop developers from selling land under the sea and ruining the fucking wetlands with unnecessary water ways."

"She's mad now. You got your sister cussing," Bombei chuckles.

"Let her be mad. Don't nobody care about Graigh's hurt feelings."

"You're exactly right. Nobody cares about my hurt feelings. Just like nobody cared that the Ninth Ward is below sea level back then; so why should I give a shit now about people who have something to say about me giving a shit about this shitty-ass piece of land in the first place? It's mine come hell or high water, and the high water has already come and gone."

"You mean ours, Bae," Bombei chuckles again standing up.

"Yeah, well, whatever. You know what the hell I meant."

"This has been a wonderful discussion," Shandra cuts in before Teddy can say anything else, "but I do believe it's time to get the kids something to eat."

"Baby, they're fine. They're not even back here anymore," Teddy says, looking around.

"I know. I told them to go ride their bikes in the front while y'all were arguing."

"Then don't worry about it. When they get hungry, they'll come inside."

"And they'll be bugging me about what's for dinner. Let me just go ahead and get started now."

"Thank you for having us," Bombei says, opening the sliding doors into the dining room.

"Anytime, chile, anytime," Shandra says, stepping through.

"See y'all next weekend," Graigh says, following behind her. "Come on, Bae, let's go."

"I'll walk y'all out," Teddy says, swigging back the last of the brown liquid in his glass.

Bombei hands him his own half-filled glass and follows Graigh to the opened front door. The embellished wrought iron storm door stands between them and their parked car outside. They stand shoulder to shoulder, but not touching, silently waiting for Teddy. He drops off the glasses in the kitchen and trudges to the door.

"Okay give me a hug," he says, opening his arms to his sister.

"You get on my nerves," Graigh says, stepping into the embrace.

"I know. I just want you to be safe out there. You're all I got."

"I know."

"Bombei, take care of my sister. And make sure she's taking care of that baby. I don't want no mess come delivery day."

Me either.

"I got you, bruh," Bombei says, extending his hand.

Teddy releases Graigh and slaps Bombei to his chest. He opens the door and pushes it open and lets them both outside.

"Christian, Kory, Quiana, get out the street and get in the house. Your mama's cooking."

"Is it done?" Christian yells back.

"She just started."

"Let us know when she's done. I'll watch 'em," Christian says, circling on his bike.

"Yeah, you better." Teddy closes the storm door.

"Bye guys," Graigh yells toward her niece and nephews.

"Bye, TeeTee," they say from their bikes.

"You ready, Bae?" Bombei asks, still standing quietly beside Graigh.

"Yes."

"Here are the keys. You're driving."

"You still mad?" Graigh asks, chirping the button to unlock the car door.

Is water wet?

Bombei doesn't answer. He walks around the back of the car to the passenger door and gets in, leaving Graigh alone on the curb. She cuts through the grass and opens her own door. Pulling up her pants and pulling down her shirt, she eases her legs in the car and sits back in the seat. Starting the engine, the radio immediately comes on. R&B sounds awkwardly fill the car. Anita Baker's cover of Tyrese's *Lately*. Graigh turns down the volume of the silky crooning. She sits, Anita Baker's voice barely audible, singing about all the things that tend to slip her mind.

"So, you're still mad?" Graigh asks again.

"I'm not mad, Graigh. I told you. I hate it when you lie to me."

Eight

Graigh lays on the long chaise, relaxing into the comfortable cushions. The smell of burnt sage lingers in the room, but not as overpowering as it was before. Graigh inhales and exhales in time to the "oms" coming from the studio beneath them. Two weeks since her first appointment, she is back in Doctor Grace's den of healing. She is back to try and answer honestly the questions Doctor Grace didn't ask, but that she must ask of herself. The questions that have sent her to therapy after so many years of avoidance and coping. She lays on the turquoise cushions, body melting into the plush pillows, her feet crossed, flexed, and tapping an inaudible beat against the air.

"You're back," Doctor Grace says silkily, easing into her oversized arm chair.

"I'm back." Graigh acknowledges with a closed-eye nod.

Her hands relax across the growing bump of her belly. Today it is completely covered in one of Bombei's oversized, faded, green school T-shirts Graigh cut and tied to give her and the baby room, without self-consciously pulling at the hem of her now too-tight and too-small baby tees. She paired her new shirt with his old jeans that hang low enough off her waist that she and the baby are unbothered if they're buttoned and zipped. The tan canvas flats she took off as soon as she entered the room sit on the floor just below her jactitating feet.

Graigh breathes in time with the sighs piercing through the floorboards of the unusual counseling office, waiting for Doctor Grace's cue to say what she has come to say. To say what she has practiced in her mind the last three nights lying back-to-back with Bombei. The speech she's memorized that she doesn't want to sound like a speech because it is still the truth. Her truth.

"How are you?" Graigh asks, anxious to spill the words on her tongue.

She's ready, Doctor Grace surmises in her mind. She responds, "I'm well, and you?"

"I'm okay?"

"You sound uncertain. You're either okay or you're not. Take a moment, identify what you're feeling, and tell me what it is and why you're feeling that way. Do the work."

How am I feeling?

Graigh's feet work overtime against the air. Her toes tap an incomplete time step as she focuses on her breath, to figure out her feelings so she can describe them. Eyes closed, body in the cushions, feet tapping, she breathes in response to what she hears vibrating up through the floor, the kirtan music still a low rumble beneath the yogi's ocean of liquid movements.

"I'm restless," Graigh blurts after several breaths.

"That's obvious," Doctor Grace says without a smile. "Why are you restless?"

"I'm not sleeping well. Especially the last few days. And I'm just ready for all of this to be over. I just want to skip straight to delivery day and have my baby and be done."

"You realize once you have the baby that's just the beginning, right?"

Graigh opens her eyes to see the quizzical expression on Doctor Grace's face. The usual smile from her thick, wide cheeks is masked by hair, pressed straight and freshly clipped. It hangs forward from her face as Doctor Grace focuses on the paper in her lap, scribbling furiously, looking up only when needed to correct or add a detail in her nascent sketch.

"This session is not for you to analyze me, Graigh?"

"I know."

"Then unless the answer you're searching for is written between my brows, you may want to go back to searching inside yourself. You've started off pretty well compared to last week. Don't tense up now."

"I'm not tense."

"Don't get defensive either. It's my job to observe you and call you out on any change in character, mood, or tone. Talk."

"Bombei is mad at me because he thinks I lied to him."

"Bombei is your husband?"

"He is."

"Okay, his name never came up last week. Why does he think you lied to him?"

"Because I did." Graigh relaxes into the chaise cushions.

"What did you lie about?"

"I had a nightmare in the car on the ride to my brother's house. We were giving them the envelope with the gender of the baby so his wife can plan the gender reveal party. It was my first nightmare in at least a decade, maybe more."

"This was a very specific nightmare that you had. Not a one-off from something you ate, or saw?"

"Yes."

"What was the nightmare about?"

"Jamal."

"Who is Jamal?"

"My ex?"

"How recent of an ex is he?"

"Not recent. Nearly sixteen years ago. Bombei and I met after the storm. Two years after Jamal and I were over."

"But here we are nearly *two* decades later, and Jamal still has a hold on you."

"It's not him that has a hold on me. It's what happened."

"What happened?"

Graigh sighs.

Here we go.

She anticipated the question in bed, her back to Bombei. She prepared for the follow-ups and the answers she would give in return. But in person it is different. A different setting, time, tone, and context.

I'm not ready for this.

An answer she still doesn't want to give lingers in her cheeks, melding with the tissue of who she is; the evolved DNA of who she has become because of what happened.

"What was the nightmare about?" Doctor Grace asks, watching Graigh's hand punch the tight pockets of her oversized jeans.

"It was about our wedding, and my abortion."

"Excuse me," Doctor Grace says, sitting up against the thickest cushion of her lounger.

"The nightmare was about the day Jamal and I were supposed to get married but didn't, and the abortion I had to have after I miscarried our baby."

"When were you supposed to get married?"

"June fifteenth, two-thousand four. I was four months pregnant, but my belly was barely showing, skin had just started to stretch but with the corset I would have been fine for a day."

"But it never happened?"

"No. He broke up with me two weeks before the wedding via a Dear Graigh note. Well it didn't even say dear. It just said, *Graigh, I can't do it. I'm not ready for a ready-made family. I love you deeply, but I'm not ready. I can't.*"

"Do you still have the note he left you?"

"No. I threw it away."

"Then why do you remember it verbatim."

"I don't know. I just do. Don't you remember your rejections, even from when you were a kid?"

"No," Doctor Grace answers, assuredly.

Bullshit, Graigh sucks her teeth.

She snarks, "Then that's why I'm paying you the big bucks. I remember everything."

"Is this the only thing you've ever had nightmares about?"

"Yes. All the other bad shit that's happened . . . I sleep like a baby. This shit right here, I just can't shake."

"You have to . . ."

"Let it go. I know," Graigh finishes Doctor Grace's sentence. "You don't know how many people have been telling me those same three damn words for the last sixteen years. If I could let it go. I would. No one willingly walks around carrying all these bags of bullshit if they can help it."

"No one willingly carries B.S. around, Graigh. But if you're not dealing with your feelings or how they affect you, the B.S. piles high and the bags get heavy. You don't realize you're toting around luggage until you end up here laying on the chaise, trying to unpack it because you've finally realized it's an anchor, drowning you from your best life you refuse to live."

"So, how do I let it go?"

"Keep talking?"

"About what?"

"Tell me about the baby you lost."

How can I tell you about something I've never had?

Graigh sighs heavily again. Her hands find her belly and rest over her navel. The space where she knows the connection is immediate. The button of life that allows her to tangibly feel part of what is growing inside of her, even if she doesn't always feel the flutters she's heard will turn into kicks.

"Jamal and I found out I was pregnant in February before the wedding, but we had already been engaged four months prior. When he did his disappearing act, my plan was to keep the baby, but I couldn't. I cried nonstop. I didn't move for days. I didn't eat. I barely slept. On the day of what was supposed to be our wedding day, I started bleeding. Not spotting. Bleeding. I went to the hospital; was there for a week. When they discharged me, I packed up my Tallahassee apartment and left."

"You blame yourself for your miscarriage?" Doctor Grace asks. She sets her sketch aside and sits forward on her lounger until her bare feet hit the floor.

"Who else is there to blame? If I had taken better care of myself, my baby would be here right now. My baby would be a teenager. A little older than my nephew Christian. Who knows? If I had not been so heartbroken behind some stupid man, I wouldn't be heartbroken now about having my baby snatched from me, its remains scraped out of me, and dreams of what could have been turning into nightmares of what actually happened."

No tears. It only bothers her subconscious. She's closer to letting go than she realizes.

Doctor Grace takes mental notes of Graigh's unvarnished face as she leaves her unfiltered, hysteric-less truth in the balance between them. She stands from her lounger and grabs two bottles of water from the desk fridge. She extends one to Graigh before sitting back in her own melty cushions of comfort. Sketch notes in her lap, she takes a drink before tucking the bottle behind one of her spare pillows. Graigh's water sits on the floor. Unopened. Unwanted. Her dry eyes are closed, her hands rest on her belly, and her feet still. She lays in wait for the doctor to discover what's left of her speech.

"What did you come home to after you left?"

"My grandparents. Well, just my grandmother. My grandfather died a day or two before I got back. Those days run together, with me just getting out of the hospital and packing. I turned my phone off before I was discharged, and it was like that until I pulled in front of the house. My grandmother, my brother, his wife, and a few other people I hadn't seen in ages, were standing on the porch, almost like they were waiting for me. I knew before I got out of the truck he was gone, by just the way they were standing. My family—what family I have—we don't have family reunions.

We reunite at repasts after another person in our family has passed."

"Is your grandmother still alive?"

"No. She died February before the storm. Eight months after my grandfather. I guess she was covering up how sick she was, to take care of him. With him gone, she stopped taking care of herself. She wouldn't let me do anything for her except make soup from bouillon cubes. She gave up."

"How old were they?" Doctor Grace asks in a whisper.

"He was eighty-three. My grandmother was seventy-six."

"And how long were they married?"

"More than fifty years."

"And your parents? Where are they?"

"Not around." Graigh opens her eyes.

"Why is that?"

"Because they're not," Graigh says, anger in her voice. *I guess this wasn't among the approved topics for today.*

Doctor Grace hears the hint in Graigh's tone and backs off. She sketches in the silence of the room. The smoke from the burnt sage has cleared. The kirtan music from the yoga studio is off. The breath of the students in class is inaudible. The women lay in their respective loungers. Graigh, finished with the story she practiced, satisfied she got it out, rubs her hands back and forth across her belly, circling her navel, pulling the fabric of the washer-worn tee taut against her poking bump, to see life poke back at her. She watches her navel push at the seam of her body, where God stitched her and her baby together, not minding the watchful eyes, and sketching hands of the doctor sitting across from her.

"How often did you have the nightmares before?" Doctor Grace asks.

"On the fifteenth of every month for about two and a half years."

"When did they stop. Right before Bombei and I got married."

"When did you all get married?"

"August fifteenth, two-thousand nine. The anniversary of our first unofficial date."

"Why that date?"

"That's something you'd have to ask him. Something about taking the date of pain and giving it purpose."

"Seems like you know the answer, you just don't believe it."

"I don't believe in a lot of things."

"I know," Doctor Grace affirms. "So why did you lie to him?"

"Because I didn't want to talk about the nightmare, or Jamal, or that baby and this baby, and how I need to let go. So I lied. Kept it to myself because they'll go away just like they did before."

"Do you really want to have the same nightmares over and over again for the next two years like last time?"

"Not particularly, but people in hell want ice water and have to deal with flames. I can deal with these nightmares. It's not like I'm going to be getting much sleep when the baby comes anyway. Who cares?"

"You do. Otherwise, you wouldn't be here and we wouldn't be talking about this. You would be telling your husband, instead of a stranger."

"He already knows about Jamal, the wedding, the baby, and the nightmares. He met me in the midst of them and even triggered one. He knows."

"So why did you lie?"

"I just told you."

"Tell me again."

"I didn't want to talk about it."

"So, why talk about it now?"

Graigh opens her mouth to speak but stops. Sitting up straight against the half-backed chaise, mouth agape, hands still resting on her belly, she ponders the question. In all of her bed rehearsals, she never thought Doctor Grace would ask her why she was discussing Jamal. She knew she had to be ready to say something. She knew she needed to come in with a story. Lying beside Bombei, wide awake, together beneath the sheets, but not touching, a chasm between them, she knew she needed to fill her session with Doctor Grace with the words she was too afraid to say to him, even though he'd heard them all before.

Why talk about it now?

The unexpected question, without a prepared answer, leaves Graigh stuck staring at the doctor. The short, thick set, doctor in fitted black denim and a sleeveless red peplum top is as comfortable in the quiet as she is. Her sleek, sandy hair highlights her face of more questions than answers.

Why talk about it now?

Graigh reaches for the water bottle she set on the floor. The sweaty plastic is cold and slick in her hands as she untwists the top and brings the mouth of the bottle to her lips. The water, still cold, cascades down her throat and hits the pit of her empty stomach. She rethinks booking another session where she spends her lunch break with Doctor Grace instead of actually eating. Placing the bottle back on the floor, Graigh waits in the silence with the woman who's again gotten the best of her. The walls of the room are quiet. The ending "oms" of the yogis resounded minutes ago, followed by applause and relaxed chatter.

"I need to get back to the store," Graigh says.

"Go ahead. Just because you don't answer my questions out loud, doesn't mean you still don't need to answer them for yourself."

Graigh stands from the chaise and stretches. Arms above her head, bending back, she pulls and twists her body until it creaks and cracks with her movement. Doctor Grace watches Graigh's ministrations from her lounger with her sketch in hand. She stands when Graigh slides into her flats and grabs her white lab coat from the hook on the back of the door.

"Don't forget your water," Doctor Grace says, grabbing the bottle from the floor.

Graigh shoves it into her purse, still hanging on the back of the door, and then lifts it onto her shoulder.

"See you next week," Doctor Grace says opening her office door.

Doubt it.

"I don't know. The next few weeks are going to be busy. I'll let you know."

"Graigh, don't run."

"I'm not running. I'm coming back, just not next week."

Damnit. I guess I have to come back now. Or not.

"When you come back, at some point you need to be ready to talk about your parents as easily as you talk about everything else," Doctor Grace says. "Take these."

Doctor Grace hands Graigh the sketch from today and the one she pulled from the street two weeks ago. Graigh smiles.

"Don't throw these away. You need to see your progress."

"I won't," Graigh says.

"Don't lie to me either," Doctor Grace says, finally letting a full smile come across her face. "That's why you're here today."

"I'm not lying. I'll keep the notes." Graigh waves the crumpled, and fresh index cards in her hands.

"You better."

"I will."

"I know," Doctor Grace says, closing the door behind her client feeling the weight of one of the bags she left behind.

Nine

The warm air of the April wind blows between Bombei and Graigh as they setup tables for the party in the backyard. The air is still not warm enough to melt the frosty temperature that settled between them a week ago after their fight at Teddy and Shandra's. They work together meticulously putting two long folding tables together in the backyard. They place them perpendicular to the French doors, so that as soon as guests take the two back steps down to the ground, they know it's time to sit and eat. Graigh unfolds old Times-Picayune newspapers onto the tables, tripling the layers to keep the cleanup from the seafood shells simple. Four empty, galvanized tubs sit in the middle of the tables, ready to hold crawfish, blue crabs, shrimp, corn, smoked sausage, and potatoes.

"We need to get drinks," Bombei says stepping into the attached shed.

So much for Teddy and Shandra doing everything and coming early.

Graigh keeps the thought to herself as she watches Bombei maneuver around the shed. The space used to double as a laundry room and a salon when her grandmother was still alive, but what didn't wash away had to be replaced. The laundry was moved indoors to the second floor in the remodel. It's now a room with shelves, a laundry sorter, built-in ironing board and red front loaders, instead of the ragged shed where dirty clothes were placed on the cracked concrete ground, and a crude wooden shelf sagged in the middle from the combined weight of detergent, fabric softener, bleach and the weakening properties of washer steam, dryer heat, and New Orleans humidity.

Now the shed with its white iron door is used only for storage. Empty boxes stacked one inside the other are shoved along the back wall as if they'll need them again to move. Christmas decorations also live in the shed along with the cooler Bombei carries. They will need to fill it with ice, soda, and alcohol for their small band of merry makers who will revel in learning the sex of their baby with them.

Ten people in all. Family and close friends will celebrate and judge what life is really like in the Ninth Ward. Amongst the guests are her brother, sister in-law, and three favorites who haven't visited since she completed the construction. Bombei's father, his best friend, Joy, Anthony, and Junior arrived last night and are asleep inside. The Old Man, as Bombei refers to him, or Mr. Charles as everyone else says, took the last bedroom in the furthest corner of the house, above the kitchen overlooking the backyard. Dougie, Bombei's friend from Chicago, settled in the room across from Mr. Charles. Joy and Anthony ended up in the third and final bedroom between the master and Mr. Charles. Junior took the sofa in the loft outside of the master. The house was full and Teddy, Shandra, Christian, Kory, and Quiana had yet to arrive. The full house served as a buffer for Graigh. Even though she offered her brother and his family the option to stay, all she had left was floor space.

One of the last times he visited her was August after the storm. He needed to borrow her truck, and Christian was only a few months old. The old house was still sitting, sinking on its foundation, with the black, National Guard markings fresh and unfaded. Mounds of dirt and debris from other homes on the block lined the street. The debris from Graigh's home had been hauled away months ago. In front of her home stood a boxy FEMA trailer. It was there behind the trailer where she'd met Bombei, and later that same day it was the last time she greeted her brother. An argument about Bombei's role in her life, contractor, or lover, kept them on their respective sides of the river for the last decade, going on a second. If she didn't call, and if she didn't cross, then she didn't hear hide nor hair from him. Shandra followed his lead and Graigh kept the peace, by keeping her thoughts to herself, to see her favorites.

The afternoon would bring the winds of change. Theodore James Simone, his wife, and children would cross the river with observant eyes, and appraising mouths. Comparing and contrasting—because that's what people do, even family—what's in Marrero to what's in the Ninth. They would compare houses, street fixtures, commercial features, and even the number of potholes that had yet to be repaired after nearly fifteen years of recovery. They would compare, and they would cut with their words, not knowing that she would hurt, silently seeking approval.

Graigh stands arms akimbo, thumbs forward on her hips with her fingers resting around the dimples in her back. She's thankful for the silence as she and Bombei set up the yard, even if it is filled with tension. Looking up, in the window above her head, she sees Mr. Charles staring out at the yard. A 70-year-old, clean shaven version of Bombei stands above her in blue striped pajamas, and a white short-sleeved undershirt. The coffee cup in his hands rests against the sagging belly earned from a life well lived. He doesn't look down at her. The New Orleans native stares out over the property. The newspaper-lined tables extending from the covered porch to midway into the grassy yard just before a second standalone shed. The wrought iron fence along the back of the yard establishes property lines. Graigh watches him stare knowing he's never known what it used to look like before, or directly after the storm. She watches him until she convinces herself she sees him nod his approval. Much like his compliment last night when he arrived, "Y'all done did alright for yourselves." Graigh smiles at the small victory, knowing her brother will be a much harder pin to bowl.

They arrive in the afternoon. Quiana and Kory's bickering voices carry from Teddy's Suburban to the front door. Graigh, asleep in the bedroom, opens one eye and then another, from her latest dream turned daymare. A dream of a life not lived. She reified a day painted in pastels and scented by gardenia, magnolia, and jasmine. She dreamed of faces whose countenances were a mix of expressions; adoration and lack of faith among them. She dreamed in vivid hues of crimson contrasted with a stark white. The soundtrack accompanying the colors a cacophony of noises. She dreamed of blinding fluorescence and streetlight darkness with an internal bleating annoying and audible. She dreamed and dreamed until her memory exhausted itself, went black, and she was roused awake by the ogling words of, "Ooh, TeeTee's house is pretty." Graigh smiles to herself, thankful for Quiana's compliment.

"Your brother is here," Bombei says in the closed doorway of the room.

"I can hear them," she says, wiping cold out of her eye.

"Everybody's ready then. Just waiting on you."

"I'm getting up. Just have to put my clothes on. I showered after we finished decorating."

"How'd you sleep?"

Do I even need to answer this question?

"Alright . . . I guess."

"You're still lying," he says, opening the door and leaving the room.

But I am alright. It's not like they're real.

Flip flops slap the back of Bombei's feet as he takes the hardwood stairs down to the first floor. Graigh waits until the sounds on the second floor are no more, before she untangles her legs from the covers and stands in the thick, high carpet in just her bra, panties, belly and stretch marks. In the only full-length mirror in the house, she stands facing herself, hands on her stripes, thumbs in the navel that has yet to protrude from the life growing inside. She throws the blanket over the mirror, covering herself. Instead, she turns to her mosaic-tiled reflection that obscures her body as she pulls clothes out of the drawers. A white silk shirt, and green drawstring cargo pants tied low on her hips hang most comfortably from her body. She tugs on the hem of her shirt to adjust the tightness at her growing breasts.

Hands through her hair, she shakes loose flattened curls. Pulling, tugging, and fluffing, she situates locks and tufts around her face, creating a diagonal side part running parallel to the plane of her ear. She works by rote, standing in front of the mirror, but not seeing clearly. Not needing to see, not wanting to see, feeling instead until she looks the way she wants to. Graigh slides her feet into gold, bedazzled T-strap sandals and leaves the room. In the loft she can hear the noise of cheery voices beneath her. Low and high tones blend in laughter as she takes her time descending the stairs into the kitchen.

"It's about damn time your lazy ass woke up. We're here waiting for you. I'm ready to know what this baby is so I can shop for my god-baby."

"You keep insulting me, Joy, you won't christen this baby. You got a lot of nerve fussing at me, and you staying in my house."

"We don't have to stay here," Joy shoots back. "We could have stayed in the Quarter, where we were for Mardi Gras. We've been put out of better places than this. Ain't that right, Baby?"

"Woman, stop being mean," Anthony scolds. "You've been talking about how beautiful Graigh's house is since we hit I-10. You know good and well you won't be staying anywhere else but here, the next time you come."

"Dang, Tony, I know that, and you know that, but Graigh doesn't have to know that. She already uppity. You don't have to inflate her ego."

"I know you're not talking Miss 'I hope you have one-thousand thread count Egyptian cotton sheets, because my body breaks out if I sleep on anything less'." Graigh mimics. "Who's the uppity one?"

"Hey, hey, hey, hey, hey. Don't monopolize all the love. Graigh. Girl—come here. Pregnancy looks good on you."

"Hey, Dougie," Graigh says, walking over and falling into his embrace.

Shorter, lighter, and thinner than Bombei, Graigh is wrapped tight by his version of a bear hug, feeling his bones, and the sinews of his muscles squeeze into her with all his might.

"How're you feeling, Mama-to-be?"

"I feel alright. Good days and bad days just like anyone else." Graigh steps back from his warmth.

"Don't get too comfortable around my wife, Dougie?"

"Look a there. The boy got some bass in his voice when you get too close to his wife," Mr. Charles teases from a kitchen corner.

"Aww, Daddy, hush," Bombei ribs. "Let you tell it, you never let another man come a foot close to Mama when she was living."

"Only one that did was you, son. The only one that did was you," Mr. Charles says, regretfully. "But I love you anyway," he brightens. "And I especially love this woman here."

"And I love you, too, Mr. Charles," Graigh says, gliding to where he stands on the opposite side of the butcher block from all the commotion.

She hugs him and breathes in his clean scent. Smelling only of ivory soap from his shaved face down to his armpits, where she nuzzles in, she hugs her father-in-law deeply, enjoying the feeling she's too often missed out on."

"TeeTee, is it time to find out what kind of baby you're baking yet?" Quiana asks from the back doorway.

"I guess it is. Come on y'all, let's go outside."

Graigh and Mr. Charles lead the way out of the kitchen with Joy, Tony, Dougie, and Bombei following behind. Kory, Christian, Teddy, and Shandra, are already seated outside at one table, where Quiana joins them. Fragrant food, steaming, boiled pink and red, and hot, overflows in the tubs. A butter cream cake between the two tins says "Congratulations! It's a . . ." written in cursive frosting.

"Okay, you two stand over there behind the cake," Shandra orchestrates. "Everybody else come over here. Have your phones ready because we're only gon' do this once."

"Somebody print me out a picture then. I'm not gon' even bother with this stupid phone."

"Mr. Charles, I'll get you a copy. I'll print it out at the store when I go to work Monday," Graigh says.

She picks up the Mikasa cake cutter she and Bombei received as a wedding gift and holds the handle. He stands behind her, one hand at her waist, the other on her elbow steadying her hand.

"Please stop being mad," she whispers to him.

"Stop lying to me and I won't have anything to be mad about," he says through clenched, smiling teeth.

"Okay you two, on the count of three," Shandra prepares.

"One. Two. Three."

Graigh slices through the cake and lifts the blade revealing blue frosting.

"It's a boy!" Shandra squeals.

"Congratulations, man," Teddy yells, shaking Bombei's hand across the table.

"Man, I'm so proud of you," Dougie says, running around the table slapping Bombei on the back.

Mr. Charles nods his congratulations to Graigh with a slight tilt of his head. She mouths back thank you, with a gracious smile meant just for him.

"So, what y'all gon' name my nephew?" Shandra asks, sitting down at the table. "Everybody get your drinks and take a seat so we can eat. It's time to party."

Bottles and cans pass down the table until all the children have sodas, the men have beers, the women wine coolers, and Graigh a bottle of water and a glass of sparkling grape juice.

"Mr. Charles, won't you do us the honor of blessing the table before we dig in?" Graigh asks.

"Yes, ma'am."

Standing and clearing his throat, he prays, "Dear Heavenly Father, thank you for this food we are about to receive. We thank you for the nourishment it provides for our bodies, and the spice it will add to our lives. But most of all, Father, we thank you for the life growing in your daughter Graigh's belly. We ask that you guard and protect the life of this growing boy just like you guarded and protected the life of your son, our savior, Jesus Christ. In the name of Jesus, we all say amen."

"Let's eat," Quiana screams between Kory and Christian.

Heaps of food are spooned onto paper plates. Kory and Quiana first, then Christian and Junior, and then the adults. Graigh fixes Bombei's plate giving him more corn and crabs then shrimp, potatoes, and crawfish. She uses both hands to steady the plate handing it to him. It is another peace offering. He accepts with a mumbled "thanks."

The sound of cracking shells, licking fingers, and sniffles from the heavy spice permeate the air as the sun descends and the mosquitoes and flies hover. The lit citronella candles and tiki torches work overtime to keep the flying leeches and food hoverers away, as the motley crew of family and friends devour the basins of the Gulf's finest. The smattering food sounds are only broken by loud gulps of drinks, burps, and yawns. It is a culinary success.

"So, what y'all gon' name the baby?" Shandra asks again, breaking the silence.

"We haven't talked about it yet," Bombei says, shredding a paper napkin as he tries to remove seafood refuse from his fingers.

"But I'm sure you want a junior, right?" Tony asks.

"Baby, finish chewing your food. Don't nobody want to see all that," Joy admonishes, wiping escaped crab meat from his toffee-colored mouth.

"Thanks, Baby." He swallows, then picks up his own napkin. "But, Bombei, you do want a junior? Right?"

"Possibly," Bombei answers.

"Let that baby have his own name and his own way in life," Mr. Charles says gruffly from the head of the table. "I didn't name you after me. You don't need to name your baby after you. Let the boy have his own identity."

"He will, Daddy, he will."

"Graigh, what day are you due?" Mr. Charles asks.

"September fifth," she answers.

"Just after Katrina day," Shandra notes aloud.

"Or just before Labor Day," Graigh says quickly.

Does everything have to be talked about in reference to that damn storm?

"Well, you know babies have a mind of their own," Shandra continues. "Especially first babies. They'll come early, or they'll come late. You'll be on his time."

"I know that's right," Joy agrees.

"I guess," Graigh says.

"What do y'all plan to do to prepare for when the baby comes?" Teddy asks.

"Get the nursery together," Graigh answers. "We're going to put him in the room next to ours where Joy and Tony are."

"Oh, well you'll have to give us a tour, Graigh," Shandra says. "I wanna see."

"You sure you don't want to move?" Teddy asks, under his breath.

"Why would we move?" Graigh snaps.

The cut of her voice stops the cracking of crab legs and crawfish tails. An eerie silence falls over the table in the dusk of the sun. The coming night breeze blows through them, heightening the tension that began with Bombei and Graigh setting up the tables that morning.

"Kory, Christian, Quiana, why don't you guys go inside and wash your hands. Y'all done with your food," Shandra declares, instead of asking.

"Take Junior with you," Joy says, sensing the argument.

"No. Let them stay." Graigh's lips barely move. "Let them hear why my brother thinks I should move out my house."

"Graigh, there's nothing wrong with the house," Teddy sighs. "If it was in Lakeview, or the Parish, or over where I lived, it'd be fine. But it's not and you know it."

"So, my house is good enough for you, just not the street it's on. Teddy you grew up here, what are you talking about?"

"Are you guys really gon' do this again?" Shandra asks. "Y'all was just at it last Saturday."

Teddy ignores Shandra. "It's not like it was then and you know it. It's getting dark outside. We're in the middle of the city and you can hear crickets and frogs croaking. The middle of the city, and you hear the sounds you usually don't hear unless you're in the country. That's the problem, Graigh. Ain't nobody here. It's not even enough people here to call this a neighborhood."

"There's a whole helluva lot more here than you think. You're just not willing to see," Graigh sniffles.

"I saw the laundromat, Graigh. I saw it, the barber shop, the snowball stand, and the grocery store. But you and I both know it's not enough. I see the new fire station, MLK on the corner with the library and the rec center, and no matter how well that school is doing, you know it's not enough."

"It'll never be enough if people like you don't stop downing where you come from because of fear of another storm."

"You're crazy," Teddy says, shaking his head, trying to end the conversation.

"No, I'm not crazy!" Graigh stands from the table.

"Bae, sit down," Bombei pleads, tugging on her hand.

"No! Everybody can hear this. Wildfires, earthquakes, and mudslides in California. No one says stop building in the hills. So why should you, or anybody, tell me I can't live in an area that's supposed to be under the water, but happens to be above it?"

"Nobody is trying to tell you where you and your family can and can't live," Mr. Charles says, cautiously. "Your brother is just concerned for your safety. That's all. We all are. I left New Orleans long before Katrina because it was getting too crazy with the crime. Now it seems, after the storm, it's worse. You had 10 people shot a couple years ago, right on Bourbon street."

"I don't live on Bourbon Street."

"That's the point," Teddy says, exasperated. "I'm sure it's just a matter of time before the gunshots go off tonight."

"There's a big damn difference, Teddy, and you know it. That—not in my neighborhood—bullshit is tired. Criminals know every neighborhood, whether you live on Bourbon, Charbonnet, or Avenue G. How would you feel if I told you where you live your life, isn't worth the land it's built on? Isn't safe enough for your family? Isn't good enough for your future? It's not like the government was giving out forty acres and a tractor in the Quarter, or on St. Charles. We live where we live. You included. You didn't always live across the river. You just got there. I live where I live, and if that's not good enough for you or anybody else in the world, then fuck 'em. Excuse my language, Mr. Charles."

"No excuse needed, Graigh. I understand you loud and clear," he says, putting up his hands. "If I may?"

"Go ahead, Mr. Charles," Graigh says, sitting back down in her seat.

"Here we go," Bombei says, cutting his eyes at his father. "We don't need a history lesson, Old Man."

"Oh, boy, hush up. You just keep living."

"I intend to."

"Teddy, I don't know you very well," Mr. Charles begins, "But I think what your sister here is trying to say is valid. You grew up here in this house, in the Ninth Ward. My wife and I, and then Bombei and I, lived in the Seventh Ward. That's the land that was available to us so that's where we lived, and we didn't see nothing wrong with it before Betsy, Camille, Katrina and every other storm, before or after. So, let's play what if."

"Alright," Teddy broods, nodding his head begrudgingly.

Mr. Charles takes a swig from his green beer bottle and sets it back on the table in front of him. He wipes his hands on his gray striped shirt before beginning. The table rapt at his attention waits as he loosens his top button and pulls his collar, giving his neck more room to animate for the story telling.

"What if the levees hadn't broken all the way open? What if the water from the lake and the river hadn't bounced back and forth between their banks, rising until they swallowed everything in their paths? What if the Army Corps had heeded the warnings about hurricanes swallowing New Orleans in the sixties when they had the chance? Then you, Teddy, wouldn't be talking that shit, telling your sister not to rebuild your family home. You'd still be here. If not in this house, in the area."

"But, Mr. Charles, that's not what happened."

"That's not the point. The point is you can't tell your sister don't make her family life where she's familiar, just because you've chosen something else for your family. You're concerned for her safety here. That's fine. You're her brother, you're supposed to be concerned for her safety, no matter where she is. You're right. The city, the state, the country hasn't done right by New Orleans, especially the Ninth Ward. But that's America."

"So why live where you're not loved, Graigh?" Teddy pleads, ignoring Mr. Charles. "Why live where you're still recovering some fifteen years after the storm?"

He doesn't get it.

"Because it's still here."

"I don't get it. Just because the place still exists, because it wasn't wiped off the map, don't mean you gotta stay. I mean, everybody else who could leave left, leaving only the worst of the worst and the poorest of the poor. And then there's you."

Graigh looks in Teddy's face and sees the similarities between them. Their wide eyes and thick lips. Her nose is narrow like their mother's while his is wide, she assumes like their father's. Her brown skin is a shade lighter than his, not sure whose coloring came from whom, since the sun doesn't discriminate. In her gaze she also see's their differences, specifically their temperament. He, brazen and forthright; she moody and apoplectic. The identical current running between them—love. What makes him so fiercely protective and opposed to where she lives, is what makes her so obstinate and indignant to leave behind all she's known.

"Why do I live here when I don't have to?" Graigh repeats his question. "It's the same reason former slaves stayed in the south when they didn't have to. It's the history of Black people in America. We have to live with the decisions white people make, from slavery to the fucked-up flood protection system."

He tips his head in a nod and takes another swig from his bottle.

She continues, "We're still trying to find a way to exist, and not be seen or noticed or trampled on, or killed. We want to exist in the world, mind our business, and live our lives the same way everybody else does, without white folks taking offense that we can live without them and be happy in the process. We're here. This is where we live. This is home. We've always been here, and we're going to always be here. And for your information, look around you . . . I am recovered."

"I guess, Graigh," Teddy nods. "I guess."

"TeeTee, can we have some cake now?" Kory asks quietly, with Quiana peeking through his elbow.

"Come on, Baby, go ahead," Graigh says, weariness heavy in her voice. "Christian, Junior, y'all want some?"

"I want some," Joy chuckles.

"Bae, I'll cut you a slice," Bombei whispers in Graigh's ear.

"Thank you."

"We still need to talk."

"I know."

"And you still need to tell me the truth."

"I know."

"I love you," he sighs, and takes the cake cutter from her.

Graigh doesn't respond. She nods her love in return, sidling up closer to him on her folding chair. A line of paper plates makes its way down to them. Bombei cuts and dishes up hearty slices of cake on to each plate, careful to cut around the words "it's a . . ." on the cake. That section he saves for them, giving Graigh "it's" and himself "a . . ."

He forks a chunk of cake and offers it to her. She opens her mouth slightly as he slides the fork inside. She sucks on the moist cake until it disintegrates enough for her to swallow. He kisses her and then whispers against her lips, "It's a boy."

"We're having a boy," she says to him. "We're having a boy," she repeats, oblivious to the watching eyes looking over them as they sit, the center of their world, in the center of the backyard, of their home.

Ten

"So, what's on your agenda for today?" Joy asks over breakfast, at the kitchen island.

"We missed church," Graigh says, looking at Bombei. "So, I guess I'll go shopping once everybody leaves. See if I can find something for me and this boy."

"You would go shopping when it's time for us to go."

"Stay longer next time."

"You know she will," Tony says, reaching between them for the orange juice carafe. "Bombei are you shopping with your lady today or do you get to stay home?"

"Dougie and I are going to kick around town a little bit. Maybe set up shop on a corner in The Quarter and see if we can't rustle up some beer money."

"Graigh, Baby, when was the last time your man here has picked up that horn?"

"Dougie, he picks it up everyday going to that school. But the last time he played me something pretty I can't call it. Around here it sounds more like I'm married to Kermit Ruffins than it does Bombei Simon Halvert."

"Ooh, that girl called you by your full government name," Dougie laughs. "You better start playing for your lady. If not for her, then at least for your baby; let him know where he comes from."

"Forget all y'all. Okay," Bombei bristles. "Forget you, Graigh, for blaming me for church—you know good and well that was your fault, not mine. Forget you, Tony, for trying to say I'm soft. And most of all, forget you, Dougie, for hating on my skills. You wouldn't have never traded that alto sax for the trumpet if it wasn't for me. So, all of y'all can get out of my kitchen and stop treating my house like the free hotel."

"Um, sir, it's my house too."

"She established that last night," Tony jokes.

"That she did," Mr. Charles says, coming down the steps into the kitchen.

"Good morning, Mr. Charles." Graigh smiles.

"Good morning, Graigh. Good morning everybody."

"So, Graigh is the only one you can address directly, Old Man?" Bombei asks.

"I like her better than you, son. I thought you knew that by now."

I'd take it easier if it weren't true.

Bombei averts his gaze as he says, "That hurts, Daddy. That hurts."

"It wasn't supposed to," Mr. Charles says, pouring coffee in the same corner where he stood the night before. "It just means you chose well for yourself. Stop finding stuff to complain about. Tony's right, are you sure you going to play music, and not shopping with your lady?"

"Ha, ha, ha. Very funny y'all," Bombei steps behind Graigh's bar stool. "Bae, what's wrong? You not eating?" he asks.

"It's the eggs. They're making me nauseous. I swear for Lord this boy better not be a picky eater. Ain't nobody catering to his needs before he even gets here."

"Yes, you are." Joy laughs. "It's all about him, Boo. You didn't know? Me and Shandra can show you better than we can tell you."

"Y'all got to be bosom buddies last night," Graigh says.

"Your sister-in-law is a lot cooler than you give her credit for. And she puts up with your brother. She's damn near a saint the way he carried on last night."

"How about we don't revisit last night," Mr. Charles says loudly from the corner. "We were all here for it."

"Agreed," Bombei says. "Bae, what do you want for breakfast?"

"I'm alright," Graigh says. "I'll get something while I'm out."

"Speaking of which, Baby, we need to get going," Tony says slapping Joy's hips where she's seated beside Graigh. "Junior," he yells. "Get your stuff we gotta hit this road. You know the time changes going back."

"Mr. Charles, how long are you staying with us?" Graigh asks.

"A few more days. I'll push out of here on Tuesday, Wednesday. Makes me no mind. Baton Rouge ain't that far."

Graigh nods her agreement as Joy, Tony, and Junior bustle about the kitchen. Dishes are cleared, the island is wiped, the stove is cleaned, and the floor is swept without Graigh getting up once. She revels in the helping hands eager to do chores she would normally do alone with only the radio or a Tidal playlist to keep her company.

Dougie and Bombei head out soon after the kitchen is cleaned. Both in jeans, t-shirts, and Reeboks, with horn cases in hand. They take Graigh's truck, tossing their trumpets onto the bed before peeling out of the car port and down the street to the land of music, money, food, and women.

Joy, Anthony, and Junior leave with Graigh. Mr. Charles stands on the front porch still in his striped pajamas and undershirt, his second cup of coffee between his palms. In front of the house on the block devoid of trees, shrubbery, and any greenery save for the sod on Graigh's lawn, and a few other neighbors' homes, they say their goodbyes. Graigh hugs Joy, then Tony, and finally Junior. She lingers with him marveling in their embrace at how much he's grown. She knew him before he knew himself. When Joy called, scared, and crying that she was pregnant, not knowing Graigh was also carrying a baby. They bonded over their blessed bounty, and when tragedy struck, Graigh loved on Anthony Jr. as if he were her own. Crossing I-10 for his first birthday, and church dedication, and the wedding of his parents; she's watched him grow in the pictures Joy sent from her first ultrasounds to his yearly class picture. The baby that blossomed from a black and white gingerbread man of a fetus to a tall and lanky fifteen-year-old, reserved except for when something is really funny and his bracketed smile breaks through his lips before he covers his mouth.

"Be good, you hear me," Graigh says, letting Junior go.

"I always am, Aunty," he says stepping back from her hug.

More like sisters than friends Joy and Graigh hug again as Tony and Junior get into the car.

"Call me if you need me," Joy reassures.

"I always do."

"No, you don't, Graigh. I always call you."

"Then no need to change it up now."

"Bye, girl," Joy waves behind her as she gets into the sleek red Acura.

Graigh crosses the grass to the carport and chirps the alarm for her own car. She waves to Mr. Charles and then backs out into the street. She and the car carrying Joy, Tony, and Junior make a right onto Claiborne Avenue and head toward I-10 East. Graigh follows her friends on most of their ride as they return to Florida and she heads to Edgewater mall in Biloxi.

The ninety-minute drive along the coast reveals all that's been restored in the years since the storm. The Gulf, angelic and pristine, laps at the shore hiding its menacing violent and destructive properties beneath a calm facade. Ninety minutes away from home, Graigh turns into the Dillard's parking lot of her favorite shopping center. When she steps out of the car, she breathes in the air both familiar and not. A piece of her childhood memory she saves just for herself; shopping along the Mississippi Gulf, begging her mother to let her run across the sand, just to get her feet dirty and her toes wet. A rare smile from the elusive woman who was too hurt to hold on, too saddened to stay, and too burdened to do anything but rest.

With one hand on her belly, Graigh turns away from the water and heads into the department store bypassing eager salesclerks with spritzes of perfume and make up pallets to peddle. She steps out into the mall among the Sunday shoppers: church moms and single parents, teens, and children all liven the acoustics in the atmosphere with a crush of shrieks, laughter, and the frenetic pace of capitalism at work.

Graigh meanders through the maze of shops passing glass store front after glass store front until she arrives at The Children's Place. Wombfire greets her at the display window looking at the miniature mannequins dressed in rompers, jumpers, overalls and onesies, and bunches of tutu skirts for baby girls who will probably never grow up to be ballerinas. If she weren't already pregnant walking in the store she'd want to be.

In the boy section at the back of the store she finds onesies that say #Hug and a pack that features emojis for every day of the week. Sleepers with planets, cars, and I Love Mommy scrawled around hearts join the pile materializing on Graigh's arm.

She is in kindred company. Three women with distended bellies and another mom pushing a double running stroller round the racks delighting in agonizing over picking the perfect shirts and bottoms, socks and shoes for the boys and girls to be. The boys and girls who will poop, and pee, and spit up over everything they wear; bib and diapers be damned.

"May I take these from you and hold them at the counter while you shop?" A young clerk, no more than fifteen, asks Graigh.

"Please. Thank you," she says unloading her items into the girl's tanned arms.

Her brown ponytail swings as she bounce-walks to the register.

I wonder what it would be like to have a girl.

Graigh lets her thoughts roam as her eyes search the store for the items she hasn't looked through or picked up. She notices the selection for boys is considerably smaller than that for girls. In front of a stand of shoes, her eyes peruse over boots, sneakers and sandals made to fit precious feet that will never walk in them. The hard-bottomed white walking shoes her grandmother eventually bronzed into monuments of toddlerhood for both her and Teddy are nowhere to be found. Too old-fashioned in the store catering to millennial mothers.

Graigh grabs a pair of denim high top boots, and blue leather sandals and carries them to the clerk at the register who took her purchases.

"Will this be all for you today, ma'am?"

"Yes. Thank you."

The girl rings the items one by one removing sensors and then shoving the shoes and clothes into two plastic bags. Graigh stares out the window as people pass by, some empty handed, most not. Mostly women, many with little girls in tow.

"Where's Victoria's Secret?" Graigh asks the clerk.

"Just outside of Belk. Your total is one hundred nine dollars and ninety-five cents."

Graigh swipes her debit card and grabs her bags. She waits for the receipt before leaving the store to join the thickening crowd of shoppers in the belly of the mall. She takes the straight and curved hallways to Victoria's Secret where women walk in and out with the store's signature pink and black striped bags.

Graigh maneuvers the store until she gets to the standard "Body By Victoria" section. She picks basic colors: blacks, and beige's, and one brown bra that's almost close to her color. Choosing a half size larger than normal she adds navy blue and hunter green to the growing collection in the store's black mesh shopping bag. The bras are chosen first, nine in all, before she moves to the next table and the array of panties.

Bikini cut, briefs, high waist, boy shorts, cheekies, and thongs, Graigh rifles through them all opting for fit over style. Boy shorts for coverage, and bikini cut for belly relief, she doubles the number of panties picked for each bra checking the elastic bands to make sure they haven't already been stretched out by someone else trying them on.

Graigh passes the "Angel" collection with its whites and pastels and ends up in front of rows of gowns. She stops to feel one draping a mannequin. The deep purple, satin gown with triangle lace appliqués over the breasts, spaghetti straps, and a high waist bow gives way to long pleats that will skim and hide lumps and bumps a real woman doesn't want seen. She lingers with the flimsy gown paired with separate but matching spaghetti strap bikini cut panties. Looking ruefully from her bag to the rack where several of the gowns are bunched together behind the model display, she grabs one in a large and heads to the register.

Standing in the lanes beside items meant to be impulse purchases tailor made for women, Graigh picks through the petri dishes of lipstick and gloss, blush, and foundation, and the gift box sets of perfume. Only a clear gloss makes it into her bag. It settles on top of the purple satin fabric she snatched from the rack.

Maybe we can make up some more.

Another triple digit purchase and Graigh joins the women exiting the store. After a stop at the pretzel shop, she's back in her car, leaving the mall, facing the already warm water of the Gulf. The warm water whose gentle waves lap at ankles, allow for easy paddle boarding, and jet skiing but who's strength should never be underestimated because it is the warmth that adds speed, strength, and intensity to hurricanes.

Water. Available in three forms like God the Father, God the Son, and the Holy Spirit. Gentle to some and treacherous to others. It is both the flood of the Old Testament and the baptism of the New Testament. She circles the outer edge of the beach cleaned of debris and oil and says a prayer as she enters the highway.

Hundreds of lives were lost here too. You just can't tell anymore.

Graigh makes the ninety-minute drive along the tree lined highway in an hour. The scenery changes drastically the closer her approach to home. Biloxi's beachfront no longer wears the scars of Katrina or the oil spill. The beaches have been cleaned of tar balls, the roads repaved, the houses rebuilt, the casinos jumping, and residents, most of them, restored to their way of life as if nothing happened. Crossing the Industrial Canal into the lower Ninth Ward and swaths of blocks remain razed and empty. Entropy and graffiti are her surroundings. Desperation and poverty are written on the buildings in large bubble letters. The hand behind them claiming and reclaiming territory that belongs to no one and no one cares to find.

Everywhere where the graffiti is intentional, collages and murals, sculptures, and artwork installations, and even trash heaps made into mounds of progress, there are places where the spray-painted striations were formed in haste under the cover of night, or brazenly scribbled in the day. A declaration that whoever was behind the work was here, lived, and made purpose out of their life as they saw fit.

It is a marked difference from Biloxi or even other neighborhoods in the city. St. Bernard Parish just a few miles from Graigh's front door looks almost as if the storm never happened; the water never came. Almost, except for some empty lots. The vacancies, the places where homes used to be. The variances between the ninth in Orleans Parish and St. Bernard Parish may as well be a dividing line between war-torn Syria and a sprawling, suburban subdivision.

These are the lies the recovery tells. The tales of two New Orleans. The burgeoning city with its small enclaves of white, hipster chic suburbanites. The tech heads ready to launch their new startups finding no reason to waste a good disaster, and the newcomers who can't stand the noise of musicians—in the city that birthed jazz—and call the police on them for disturbing the peace. Then there are the natives. Some poor, mostly Black, who can't think of anywhere else to live but home, clinging to all they know in a two-armed bear hug to a city that doesn't hug back.

Graigh turns down Charbonnet and whips the black Buick LaCrosse beside the truck beneath the car port. Facing the fading markings from Katrina she purposely preserved, instead of scrubbing it away, she reads the notation. The search team arrived September 13th. More than two weeks after the storm. They made no entry.

Inside she passes through the living room and dining room. She pauses. The orange-sprayed glass windowpane that used to sit in one of the front windows now hangs above where she stands. Her Katrina cross. It denotes the search team found no bodies and no hazards inside, even though they did not go in. The cross serves as a somber reminder to all who gather at her table of what was lost, what was replaced, and what they can all be thankful for. Graigh moves from the spot shaking her head knowing Teddy has never sat at the table. He has never looked up at her cross and felt what she felt. He threw his cross away, demolished with his house and shoved in a massive metal bin, it was carted to the landfill. He trashed the very sentiment many come to find— history and modernity. A new experience that draws on their soul to stay when many of the people born and raised where their crosses lay never came back.

"Where's Dougie," Graigh says, running into Bombei coming down the stairs into the kitchen.

"He left about an hour ago. We played a little bit on Canal Street just for kicks. What did you buy?"

"Baby clothes," Graigh says with a crooked smile. "Just a few things. Some onesies, some PJ's, a couple pair of shoes."

"What does the boy need shoes for? He's not gon' walk out the womb." Bombei says.

"He still gotta have shoes so his feet don't get cold." Graigh pulls items out of the bag.

"Then why did you buy sandals?"

"You don't want his feet to sweat do you?"

"Okay," he says shaking his head. "But that's not the only bag you have."

"I know."

"What's in that bag?"

"Panties, maternity bras."

"Is that it?" He asks trying to peek through the tissue paper.

"Some lip-gloss."

"Is that it?"

"No."

"What else is in the bag, Graigh?"

He stands directly behind her, arms around her waist, his lips on her neck. Her arms are arrested at her sides; the bag barely held in her fingertips.

"Where's Mr. Charles?" she whispers through shallow breaths.

"Asleep in the room upstairs. What's in the bag, Graigh?"

"I can show you better than I can tell you."

"Then show me."

Eleven

In the dimly lit room, a candle burns blowing the scent of eucalyptus and spearmint around the room. Graigh stands in the doorway of the en suite, one arm resting on the frame, the other wrapped around her belly, facing the bed. She stands facing him, still awaiting his approval after all these years.

It begins with acknowledgement in his eyes. The brown pupils smile first. His lips follow, turning up, shielding teeth, belying seduction.

"Come here," Bombei says.

Graigh pads across the room. Her feet soundless on the thick carpet. She stops in front of him, arms by her sides, gaze to gaze, she waits for him to show her which way he wants to go. He rests his head on her slightly protruding belly. Shrouded in the purple fabric, skimming her skin, the barrier between them does nothing to slow her breathing, or stop the raised bumps of excitement from appearing on her skin. His head to her belly electrifies her senses. The response in her body is acute. Nipples raise up against the lace appliqué of the baby doll nighty. She shifts her stance from foot to foot, rubbing the fabric of the matching G-string between her slick thighs.

Her hands find the back of his head to settle her stance and slow her breath, but it is ineffective and futile. Bombei stands. With his hands at her hips he holds her in place. They are pressed body to body. Her bare thighs rub against the knot in his jeans. Back and forth her leg works against the rough hewn fabric. His hands tighten on her hips. He crumples the fabric in his hands, stretches it wide, and arrests it behind her back. His fingertips cup the spread of her cheeks. Holding her, trying to regain control, he slows his breath against her brush strokes. It, too, is ineffective and futile.

Her small, rouge manicured hands, find the edges of his gray T-shirt. She pulls it up and away from his body, until her arms are completely extended, and the shirt is coming over his head. Graigh drops it to the floor beside her feet. His hands at her back, hers to his chest she pushes gently. Bombei's body buckles at the knees against the edge of the bed and he sits. Stepping forward, one knee on opposite sides of his waist, she places her slickness on his hard belly. Rocking into his navel, her hands extend behind her grazing his jeans.

He holds. She rubs. He holds, and she rubs. In silence they are in sync. Relaxed, breathing one breath, inhaling the healing properties of the burning essential oils, exhaling the tension from the hospital, the decade old argument over their home, his hurts and stifled joy, her hurts and lies. Tangentially connected, he slides her booty back against his jeans and sits up. Releasing her waist, Bombei lays her back against his thighs. His lips find her belly beneath the gown. Skin to skin they connect. The soft flesh of his mouth against the tight and stretching skin of her stomach. He lets his kiss linger. His beard tickles. He praises and worships the miracle she's creating. He kisses his reverence into his wife, hoping his son can feel their love.

Standing with her straddled around his waist he turns and lays her gently against the exposed taupe sheets. The spread neatly folded back against the bench at the foot of the bed, Bombei lays Graigh in the middle of the king-sized expanse. On her elbows she watches him disrobe. Bombei steps out of the pool of clothing at his feet and offers his nakedness. His body above hers he kisses her forehead, and then her nose slowly lowering himself. He kisses her lips.

They meet in the middle of the suspended space. Mouth to mouth they kiss. Lips closed at first until he parts. Sliding his tongue into her mouth encouraging her to let go, he savors her taste in her compliance. Their mouths mesh, and their tongues dance finding each other once again. Tasting the other, skimming cheeks and entwining in circles. The slow burn of their kiss picks up speed. Lower lips are sucked, and bitten, left swollen and open for more. They kiss away the shelter of their marriage and allow carnality to creep in. He stiffens between her thighs. Her cloaked wetness squirms against him. Their mouths break for breath.

Sighs and pants resound in the room. She heaves against his chest. Her swollen breasts push out of the sides of the gown exposing themselves against his beard. Her nipples stand tall, hard as bullets, begging for attention. He sits up on his haunches against her. Hard and slick, he is buried beside her soaked fabric. Her hips and legs are trapped in the vice of his weight as she pushes against him to ease the building agony growing hot between her thighs.

Bombei's hands find her shoulders. His calloused fingertips slide the thin straps down her body. He follows his own motion sliding off the bed, pulling the baby doll gown over her hips, from under her ass, and to the floor. Still resting on her elbows, she watches him raise to his knees. He takes the strings at her waist and slides them off of her body, dropping it in the pile of clothing beside him.

On his knees, Bombei drags her legs forward until they hang off the bed and she can no longer peek on her elbows and see. He parts Graigh's brown thighs with praying hands letting his finger tips graze what she has to give. His lips follow the same path. Flesh to flesh, he presses against the soft and firm parts of her legs. Kneading her muscles, nibbling her skin, licking just below where she wants to be sucked, he toys with her trembling. Subtle hints of lifting hips are ignored. He takes his time, still in reverence, kissing and tickling between the thickness of her thighs. Lapping the juice that has trickled down her leg. Her body hanging forward, opened before him, he kneels at the precipice of her pleasure and leans in.

His nose finds her ball of nerves. She shudders against the steady stream of his breath. Her hips rock from side to side rolling against the air quickening the senses of her clit until his mouth covers them sopping up the sensations. She bites her bottom lip muffling a moan. Bombei adds his tongue. It licks and rolls the tiny mound, up and back, side to side, around and around. Graigh sways with his cunnilingus gymnastics. His tongue is but one aerial acrobat. He tag teams her with his mouth, licking and sopping, rolling and sucking, nibbling, and blowing, until both of her hands find his head and press more pressure into her. He lifts her limp legs to his shoulders. Her thighs immediately squeeze around his ears. Her heels dig into his back pressing his body, his head, his face, his mouth, his beard, his tongue, deeper against her.

Graigh rolls in waves against him, clenching her cheeks to keep her explosion away. Bombei feels her tension, releases the pressure, and nudges her wider to slip the tip of his gymnast into her waiting. Her outer lips and walls are wet with the nascent makings of her love. He dips into her divot and laps up what has helped to create life.

Graigh's sighs deepen to moans she no longer muffles. Her teeth are no longer clenched. Her bruised lips are parted, and panting, pleased with his expertise until he stops. Bombei stands. Her body rolls with the waves of accessed pleasure. Riding the remembrance of what he left inside, her eyes remain closed as she waits for his presence.

Bombei lays next to her. Rolling her to her side, his thigh between hers, he presses her wetness down on to his dripping stiffness and holds her there. He forces her to adjust against him. Widen for him. Deepen for him. Reach as far as she can for him. Her ass rocks in his manscaped waist. Rolling a rhythm against him, he catches her wave and moves behind her. Silent in their words, in sync in their breath, one note, one tune, one harmony, they play.

His hand slides across what they've created to find the nipples that penetrated the lace. Bombei rolls one, and then the other between his thumb and forefinger, adjusting the squeeze of his pressure as her steady body wave loses control, and her squirm turns into a bounce. He releases her breasts. One hand to her hip he pounds her into him. Up. Down. He is the drum and she is his malleable, wet stick, striking every beat.

They beat; up and down. Up and down. Her potion trickles down and around him, forcing him to hold her tighter, squeeze her closer, and push as he lands.

Bombei rolls Graigh to her belly, bracing their baby in a cup of his hands. Reared up behind her he pulls her into him. His hands palm her breasts, his teeth bite her back, his lips suck her neck.

Graigh turns her head and catches his mouth. Hers already open she kisses him with the full force and full length of her tongue, rolling every bud across his own. She tastes him to see if there is something she hasn't discovered in all the years they've been together. In all the years they've met like this. She explores with her mouth. Coming to the full height of her knees she uses the tenacity of her tongue to push him to his back.

Never breaking their kiss, she makes him her saddle and NOLA bounces along his length. With every twitch and twerk of her behind she rides him to the tip and reverberates back down. Mouth to mouth connected in essence heat rises between them. Cocoa-colored skin flushes warm in titillation. They rock.

He rocks up to seated, arms around her waist, hands on cheeks, pulling her into his pulse. Her limbs languish around his neck, crossing in the embrace, sliding against their sweat. He pulls. She pulses. Arching into him, her neck lengthens on her spine, his face finds her bosom, and he nuzzles where she will nurse. Sucking and biting the nipples he rolled, she splits her legs to the sides and slams deeply into him. He doesn't let go. Over and over he holds, and he hangs on. His nails grip into her waist. He gives her the freedom to fly them as far into her passion as she can pilot.

Bombei steers. Graigh drives. Down into him she drives. Closing her legs and wrapping them more tightly around his waist she kisses the top of his head. Graigh trails her beautiful butterfly kisses down his forehead, over the bridge of his nose to, once again, find his lips. Ripe, bruised, swollen, and flushed they ask for his attention too. His yes is the soft suck of her bottom lip into his. They are nose to nose, closed eyes to closed eyes, and mouth to mouth. She squeezes the life left in her legs around him, pulsing until her potency runs thick within their connection. Shuddering and rolling, the aftereffects force her to ride her own waves through her body. Her come down is violent. She screams the release of another orgasm, rocking it out of her until her liquid love pools between them.

Spent.

Flushed.

Physically ineffable.

Bombei lays to his back, disengages, and rolls his wife to her side while he cups their baby.

He slides back into her warmth. He is the stick and she is the drum.

He beats.

He beats until his last labored breath is wrenched from his body.

Sated and satisfied they lay together. He is the big spoon. The rising heat from their love keeps them warm atop their tousled sheets. Their breathing slows. They inhale and exhale as one, emitting the sound of the ocean.

Sleep finds them. For him it is dreamless. A sonic black. A nebulous state of bliss. Unformed and incompetent he drifts in the suspension of his resting mind. Only his hands remain active, resting around Graigh, holding their baby, feeling the unease creep back into her body. Tension stiffens her legs. The fear causes anxiety to rise on her skin.

Her sweat drips against him, rolling over the rise of her ass, and down his navel.

She is gripped in tension, shuddering and shivering. Mewling. Her body rocks against him. Her legs kick against him. Her arms press into his hands covering their baby. She is crouched in the fetal position, tense, and sweating, rocking, and protecting her baby that is still there. His hand blocks her elbows from pushing in too deep, from crunching too far forward, from succumbing to whatever information her mind tells her is real. He is her protection from herself.

Fully awake Bombei holds her steady. Both arms around her body, he presses his face into her back and breathes. He breathes into the back-beat of her heart until her shivering lessens, and her shuddering eases. He breathes in rest and reassurance until Graigh unfolds her body. But even in repose her legs are tense, her quads and hamstrings tight in their rest against his thighs. She is not a runner, but her legs are bricks.

With both arms around her waist he pulls her even closer to him. Her back is flush against his chest. He holds her firm and waits. He waits for the terrors of her mind to release her. He waits for the monsters of her imagination to subside. He waits for her to return to him.

A sigh from her mouth signals she has awakened. She has slayed the chimera of her conscience and is back, fully present in their bed. Her body warm from the heat of his wrapped embrace, she stretches in the still air. Her muscles creak as he unlooses her. She rolls to face him. Skin to skin. Eye to eye. Silence settles its subtle unease, bringing fear and doubt.

They stare at each other ignoring their nakedness. Graigh, exposed and unflinching searches the depths of his pupils for the premonition of understanding. For the privilege of empathy. In her eyes she asks for his patience.

Her eyes plead with the voice of her heart.
Please.

Bombei drops his head and stares at the rings he put on her fingers. The one and a half carat, three-stone diamond, engagement ring set between two thin bands of more diamonds. He shakes his head. Lifting her hand to his mouth he kisses her knuckles. He kisses her rings and places her palm over his heart.

They are connected again. The same but different. She feels the beat of his life blood, can count the number of pulses per minute, and can feel the quickening and slowing of his measured breaths. Breaths he takes before opening his mouth, before kissing her palm and placing it back at her side.

He asks, "When are you going to finally admit your nightmares have come back?"

Twelve

They sit in the loft outside their bedroom freshly showered. A shower taken in silence. One at a time. Bombei first, then Graigh. Not together as they normally would. They did not share the shower head and fight over who hogged all the hot water. They didn't soap each other's backs and cleanse their sexes together. They did not touch, and kiss, and giggle, and tickle one another as the tap streamed across their naked bodies now slick with more than just their love. The after routine of their post-coital coupling is broken. Innately alone they sit beside each other wrapped in robes, their most welcomed friend—silence, settling between them.

Graigh knows Bombei wants her to speak without him asking. To confide without being pressed. To trust without proof. To have faith unconditional. She knows all this, but her voice is frozen. Her capability of speaking, of offering, of giving of herself without a prompt is stunted. She sits wrapped in her robe knowing what he wants, incapable of giving him the unadulterated intimacy he craves.

If you already know, why do we have to talk about it?

Graigh sighs. "What do you want to know?" She asks looking at his face, hoping that by speaking first, she appears more open to converse than she is.

He pauses before answering. She sees disappointment color his brow and dim his eyes, as he lowers his neck, and his muted temper permeates the open space.

"I want to know how long this has been going on. And before you pretend you don't know what I'm talking about, let me be specific, how long have you been having the nightmares about Jamal and the baby?"

"You know when they started. You were there."

"Act like I don't and tell me when they began."

"In the car on the way to Teddy and Shandra's."

"So, when I asked you about it then, why couldn't you just say that?"

"Because I didn't want to talk about it."

"And now?"

"I still don't want to talk about it, but here we are. You are my husband, it's your right."

"Bullshit. You're only talking because you've been caught. Twice with me watching and now in my arms. You still don't trust me."

That's not it.

Graigh talks to herself instead of responding out loud to his words that are both observation and accusation. They disarm her. She takes the moment and searches for the truth in them. The veracity in his claim. She searches inside herself to determine if she does trust him, in everything, or only in some things. Naked beneath her robe, emotions displayed on her face, anxiety racing in her heart, her son fluttering because she is caught, she hangs her head on his truth and nods.

"It's not that I don't trust you, Bombei . . ."

"Then what is it?"

"I don't know what it is. You know everything already. Jamal, the wedding, the baby, my parents, my grandparents. You know all of it. There is nothing left to tell. That is trust. I have trusted you with myself, but that doesn't mean we have to talk about it all the time. Every time it affects me . . ."

I don't want to talk about it because I just want it all to go away.

" . . . They are my issues. Not yours," Graigh finishes.

They became my issues when I became your man. Your fiancé. Your husband.

Bombei resists the urge to stand. Hands on his bare knees, he rubs them back and forth across the thick leg hair trying hard to invite patience to meet his anger.

"Graigh, they are my issues too," he says more gently than he did in his head. "I wanted to know you when we were dating. I proposed to you knowing your problems would be our problems. My problems would be our problems. I married you wanting you to know I could be your shelter, and you mine, but you don't accept that. You reject everything I offer and for what? To suffer alone? I'm here, waiting for you to run into my love; to open up and let me help you, and you *choose* to struggle by yourself. Why?"

"I don't know?"

"After all these years, of hiding, of lying, your only excuse is, 'I don't know'?" Bombei mimics her voice.

"Because I don't know. You never have the words you need to explain feelings of hurt that are ineffable."

"We're not talking about some random person or substance in the universe, Graigh. We're talking about you."

"Okay. *I* never have the words *I* need to explain what hurt me the most. The more I want to forget. The more I try to forget . . . the more I remember. And how clear and vivid that memory is."

Bombei sighs and shakes his head.

After a long beat he says, "After all these years . . . The only thing I can come up with is . . . you might have untreated PTSD."

"How did you come to that conclusion?"

"The abortion, the breakup. Your grandfather's death. Then months later your grandmother died. Katrina was a motherfucker for all of us, especially you. You never let any of it go. When we met, I became a placebo you thought was real. You've been fooling yourself into this life for the last fourteen years and now you've realized I have no healing power at all."

"Love heals all things," Graigh says quietly.

"God's love, yes. But Baby, I'm not God."

"I never asked you to be God, Bombei. I've never asked you for anything."

"You didn't have to. I wanted to give you everything. I wanted to be all things to you, and that's where I failed. I've spent all this time trying to erase and replace Jamal. Taking all your bad memories of him, of everything, and making them good memories of me. Of us. Our meeting may have been by happenstance, but our wedding and anniversary are intentional. Even our home is another negative into a positive for you. Where *am I* in all of this. Who am I? Your husband whom you don't trust. How do you think that makes me feel?"

"I don't know."

"You've never even thought about it. Have you?"

Too wrapped up in her own damn feelings to even consider for a second, I've got my own feelings and baggage to carry on top of hers.

Graigh doesn't respond to Bombei's growing anger. The agitation puts a bounce in his legs from his raised heels to his knees. She doesn't respond to the exasperation in his voice. The exhaustion in his face. She opens her mouth but remains mute. Her eyes blink open and close still computing the same picture. Her husband. Angry. His wrath directed at her.

"My name might as well be Jamal What the Fuck Ever," he rages finally standing from the midnight blue sofa. "I'm just a surrogate for the man you say you used to love, but whom you've never gotten over."

"That's not true and you know it."

"Do I?"

"You should?"

"I don't. Sometimes I don't even know why I'm here. I for damn sure don't know what you want from me."

"What do you mean," she pleads through welling tears.

This is why I keep it to myself. You don't understand. You never have. You never will.

"I mean what do you want from me Graigh," he yells breaking through her thoughts. "What do you want from me?"

"I want you to abide with me," she yells back. "I want you to love me. Love us. Love this house. Love our life. But most importantly *love me*."

"I do love you Graigh. I've been loving you. I've loved you for the last fourteen years."

"Then keep on loving me. Love me like Darius loves Nina. Like Barack loves Michelle. Hell, like Donald Trump loves money."

"Those are the worst examples," Bombei says. "Except Barack and Michelle."

Graigh smiles at his deadpan. The ease at which he brought humor into their tension makes her chuckle. Shaking her head and wiping her eyes, she stands.

"I'm sorry," she says walking toward him. "This is just . . . It's a lot."

"What do you mean?"

Graigh loosens the belt of her robe and lets it fall open. She takes his hands and places them on her naked belly. Bombei's understanding is clear in his eyes. His hands on their growing son, their eyes locked, he nods. He kneels. He kisses her belly button. The only visible place on her body where he knows their son is connected. He kisses her navel to connect the three of them. He knows he has been sympathetic but not empathetic. Despite knowing her past, he did not and has not, considered how it's informing her present. He is open to her, but only in his own way. For his own benefit.

"I didn't want this baby," she says, grabbing the sides of his face and bringing it to meet hers. "I didn't think I could have this baby, but here I am barefoot and pregnant in the kitchen."

"We're in the loft," he jokes.

"You know what I mean," she says, smiling.

"I do. But you don't have to do it alone. Yes, you're carrying our child. But we're in this together. We're pregnant together."

"It sure as hell doesn't look like it."

"You know what I mean."

"Yeah, I do."

Graigh backs up toward the couch. Bombei follows and sits beside her. Laying against the arm of the sofa he pulls her against him. Her head on his chest, his hands resting on her open belly. They lay, splayed against one another, a comfortable silence falling between them. The setting sun casts colors and shadows through the three bay windows behind them. In the silence she sighs. Resting her eyes, clearing her mind, she concentrates on the heart beating behind her. The one that filled her with what she thought she'd never feel again. The one that made her want to try. Who made her want to start over. To love again. To touch again. To feel again. To connect—again. She lays, listening to the heart that opened hers, knowing there is more she can do. More she has to do. More she must do.

Eyes open, lips parting to speak, the words stick to the back of her throat. They clam closed in her mouth, caged by her teeth. She swallows her angst and nuzzles closer to him. Pushing her face through the space in his robe, her cheek finds the curled hairs on his chest. The warm skin beneath it resounds with the sounds of his heartbeat.

"I have a suggestion," Bombei says sleepily.

"What's that?" She mumbles.

"Counseling."

"Are you trying to say something's wrong with me?" She asks lifting her head to see him.

"No," he begins. "It would be for both of us. We didn't do it when we got married. I think we're long over due."

"We or me?" She looks at him raising an eyebrow. "You did just diagnose me with PTSD."

"I didn't diagnose you, Graigh. Calm down. I'm just saying, after the storm a lot of folks had trauma. You evacuated, but your trauma started before Katrina ever got here. And she sure as hell didn't help."

"You're right about that."

"I think it could be good for both of us."

"Because you're scared too?"

Bombei hesitates. He sighs. "Yeah. I am too."

"I don't know," she sighs.

"Think about it."

"I will."

How do I tell him I'm already going without him losing it because I didn't tell him? Another personal decision he'll think is a lie because he wasn't included in every damn thing.

A blanket of quiet covers them. Graigh closes her robe, leaving his hands on her belly. She lays back in her spot, nestled against him. The truth evaded. Her sessions with Doctor Grace denied by default because she couldn't commit to doing what he asked. Graigh holds tightly to her mess. Swimming in her mind and clouding her thoughts she wrestles her self-interests against herself. Her marriage against her mind. Her needs against her will. Connected, cheek to chest and hands to bare belly they lay together her thoughts unrevealed, words left unsaid, and the solution he suggested, she's already sought, left unspoken.

Thirteen

April 21—20 Weeks

They sit in their familiar positions waiting for Doctor Marcella. Graigh's wide legged, pregnancy work pants swish back and forth against the metal drawers of the cushioned exam table. The noise adds to the monotonous sounds of the wall clock's tick and the hum from the lights above. Swish. Tick. Hum. The sounds drone around them without anything else to drown them out. She sits, swishing her legs, phone in hand, scrolling, while Bombei's thoughts take him back to a place with high grass and even higher weeds. The tick of the clock transforms into the sound of mosquitoes buzzing around his young body. In the distance of his mind's eye, he sees the mother he never knew.

"Our baby is the size of a banana now," Graigh says.

"What's that?" Bombei asks, looking up at her.

"Baby boy. He's the size of a banana now."

"How'd you figure that?"

"My app told me."

"What else does your app say?" Bombei stands and walks beside her.

"Look. It says he's almost a pound and about half a foot tall."

"He's got some growing to do." Bombei steps in front of Graigh. "You hear that boy. You got some growing to do."

With one hand on her blouse covered belly, Bombei kisses his encouragement to the baby inside.

"You seem to be getting excited about everything."

"A little bit," Graigh says, tempering her response. "We still have a long way to go."

"We're halfway there."

"He's right. You are at the halfway point," Doctor Marcella says, stepping into the room after a cursory knock.

The waif nurse is behind her. Swathed in fabric two sizes too big for her scant body, she sways behind the doctor whose thickness is her strength. Thighs and behind dressed professionally but undeniable. Doctor Marcella's presence fills the room with brilliance and buoyance. A bubbly cheer expressing how much she loves her job. Seeing and treating women. Nurturing life before it comes into the world, and again once half of them are ready to deliver themselves.

"Doctor Marcella, how many babies have you delivered?" Graigh asks, as ultrasound gel is squeezed on her bare belly.

"About one a week for the last twenty-five years. So how many is that?"

"Fifty-two times twenty-five. Five times two is ten, carry the one. I don't know. Bae, how many is that? You're the math wiz."

"Thirteen-hundred."

"Thanks, Bae. I guess it's true what they say. Playing music does make you mathematically gifted."

The beating of their growing baby's heart enters the room interrupting their banter. The steady pulse coming through the static of the machine and the fluid of the womb is strong and clear.

"What number will he be?" Graigh asks, mesmerized.

"I have no idea." Doctor Marcella says. "That thirteen-hundred number might actually be a little higher. I've had lots of multiples on my watch, plus the number goes up if I'm on call on the weekend."

"I couldn't even imagine twins. Definitely wouldn't know what to do with triplets."

"Try quads," the Doctor deadpans.

"You've delivered quads?" Graigh asks incredulous.

"Yes ma'am. This white lady carried them a few years ago until she was about thirty-two weeks and then she was done. Too much movement, kicking, and jostling around inside. She had a scheduled C-section but I guess her babies were done too because they came on their own."

"What did she have?"

"Two girls. And two boys. A perfect split."

"That's a blessing," Graigh says, still awestruck.

"Yes, it is," Doctor Marcella grins at the memory. "But you guys have your own blessing on the way."

"That we do," Bombei says standing in the corner gazing out the window, recalling memories miles away from where he is.

"Everything looks good, Dad," Doctor Marcella explains. "Mom and baby are healthy. And as long as her breath is normal when she's asleep then there aren't any concerns on my part."

"Aside from her snoring the house down? She's normal," he jokes.

"I do not snore," Graigh says, indignant.

"How do you know? You're asleep."

"I have never snored in my life. I know I don't snore."

"Only when you're in a good deep sleep. Which you have been lately," he winks.

"Okay you two that sounds nasty. That's how you got the one you've got."

"Tell me something I don't know." Graigh smiles.

"I'll see you guys back in four weeks," Doctor Marcella says laughing on her way out.

The nurse follows behind her. Disappearing in her oversized scrubs to stand in the shadows of another appointment while the doctor gets all the praise, and she's left with dirty goop laundry.

"You're in a really good mood today," Bombei says. "What made you ask the doctor how many baby's she's delivered?"

"I wanted to make sure my baby was in good hands. Just because she's older doesn't mean she's experienced. She could be one of these newfangled folk who go back to school for something crazy after spending half their life in an unrelated field."

"You're never too old to learn."

"Whatever. I don't have time for that foolishness. I need to know all of your credentials, and they need to be lengthy."

"Don't you think you should have gotten those credentials before you got this far along?"

"I kept forgetting to ask. Blame your son here," Graigh says, sliding off the table to the floor.

"My son doesn't have anything to do with your aging memory."

"I got your aging," Graigh says, swatting Bombei on the arm. "Look it up. Pregnancy brain. It's a thing."

"Whatever, pregnancy brain. What else has got you in such a good mood?"

"Nothing really."

"You sure. You haven't been like this in months."

"Fake it 'til you make it I guess," Graigh sighs. "Let's go eat."

Good to know this is purely performance.

Shattered, Bombei follows behind her. Her not quite waddle, not quite sway carries them down the hall to the nurse's station. An exchange of papers, medical file for an appointment card, and they are done.

"We'll see you in May," the nurse waves as Graigh and Bombei walk away.

Down the hall, in and out of the elevator and the sliding glass doors of the hospital Bombei sulks to the car. Annoyed and petulant he chirps the alarm and gets in without opening her door. In silence he evaluates his overreaction.

I guess I should have been happy with her being happy and left it at that.

The opening keys of Christ Botti's "My Funny Valentine" fill the car. The sad, somber notes of the crying trumpet join in the accompaniment making the love song one of longing. One of unrequited love. Bombei turns up the instrumentation as he pulls out of the hospital lot.

"Where do you want to eat?" he mumbles under the music.

"I can't hear you," Graigh says, adjusting the volume.

"Where do you want to eat?"

"We don't have to stay downtown. We can go to Café Dauphine, near the house."

"Yup."

"What's wrong with you?"

"The better question is, wassup with you?"

"What do you mean?"

"Fake it 'til you make it," he mocks. "Where did that come from?"

I was honest.

Graigh nods her acknowledgement before her response. She computes the sudden sullenness bordering on anger. He was excited to see her excited. He was excited to be, and feel as happy as he really is about their baby without having to calm down to meet her melancholy needs. For a moment in the medical office he was able to know what it's like to have a shared plane of emotion with a mate. Oneness not derived from the physical, but the intrinsic nature of two people who have breathed the same air, shared the same experiences, and created a whole life of togetherness that their hearts beat in time with the other whether near or far. For once he felt the spiritual connectedness of intimate mutuality with his wife and she took it away.

"Does that upset you? That I'm faking my feelings. Faking my happiness for the sake of others?" She asks turning off the car stereo.

"Obviously."

"I'm sorry."

"Are you? Or are you faking that too?"

"Damn. I said I'm sorry."

You want the truth. I tell it, and you still gotta attitude. That's why I keep my feelings to myself.

"I don't know what to believe anymore," Bombei begins. "If you're faking happiness about our baby, what else are you faking? This marriage. Our whole relationship? Our life?"

"That's insecure."

"Give me a break, Graigh. Don't flip this back on me. You're the one who made the fucked-up comment."

"I'm fucked up because you can't accept my truth. That's unfair."

"Life ain't fair."

"You're exactly right. Life *isn't* fair. So, I'm fucking faking it. I'm faking happiness about the baby until I can actually *be* happy. Until I can actually know he will be okay. Until I know I will push him into this world, and he will be placed in my arms to nurse on my breasts and live on after I die. And even that shit's not a guarantee the way the police kill people. We're bringing a Black boy into America. I have all the feelings right now."

"Don't invoke the police shootings and Black Lives Matter to cover up how you're not happy about this baby."

"I'm not invoking anything. We're having a Black son. To be worried about his quality and length of life is to be a Black mother in America. The fact that I'm worried before he even gets here has as much to do with the way racism affects the infant mortality rate as it does my own past. Yours too for that matter."

"Stop with the histrionics." Bombei doubles down on his self-righteous anger ignoring her own dig at him.

"Until I know tears won't run hot down my face while my child is taken from me, until he's in my arms, I'm faking it."

"You're so damn dramatic."

"And this is the reason I don't tell you shit. When I do open up you don't want to hear about it."

"No, Graigh. It's not that I don't want to hear about it. It's that I'm tired of hearing about it. Those are two different things. All I heard about leading up to our marriage was how you were so scared. You were so nervous. You didn't want it to be like last time. And now leading up to the birth of our baby all you talk about are your fears and your nerves. You can't just be in the moment and enjoy it without that other motherfucker hanging a cloud over everything. I can't fix what he did and I'm tired of trying. I'm not him. It's about time you realize that."

"I never said you were him. I know you're not him. If it was him who I wanted, I wouldn't be here right now with you. I wouldn't be trying this hard with you. I wouldn't be faking anything at all to please you. But you don't see that shit."

"No, all I see is you having nightmares about a baby you lost damn near sixteen years ago from a man who was never worth your time."

And all I see is the fourteen years of our relationship where I didn't fake happiness about our lives.

Graigh stares out the window as Bombei takes them toward home. He takes them to St. Claude Avenue where they cross the rusty bridge over the Industrial Canal into the lower Ninth Ward. She stares out at the water as murky as her feelings. Eyes glaze over the chain link fence separating the bridge from the levers and pulleys of the flood protection system. The mural reading, "Open Your Eyes," on the side of the abandoned Naval Station building looks over the water, over the levees to the neighbors on the other side. It is a message to those living behind the mounds of grass and gravel that is supposed to protect them.

Even though the flooding wasn't as bad on this side everything that is abandoned looks abandoned. There is no hiding what happened or the lies that left lips to assuage survivors' trauma that was never followed up with any universal action. They pass a sign for St. Paul Church of God in Christ at St. Claude and Forstall, but there is no church behind the sign. Only an empty lot. Churches demolished.

Schools demolished. Government buildings. Businesses. Livelihoods. Lives.

Graigh, shut down beside him, sits quietly with angry tears rolling in long streams from the corners of her eyes. Heaviness is in her body. The heaviness she thought she'd gotten used to after so many years of being home and being with Bombei reminds her that it has never left. It is the same heaviness she has been able to ignore in her surroundings; desensitized to the signs of trauma that make up her environment. Now something inside of her has broken; has burst open.

It is rare she cries. Her typical response is anger or cutoff brooding silence. To cut from Bombei what he circumcised from her. It is the first time he's seen her real tears in months. The ones she conjured up in their loft never fell. He salved them with love before they could ever stain her face. These tears are real. They flow freely as he parks at the corner of Dauphine and Egania and cuts the engine. All that is left is the settling of the car and the silence of her sadness. Acute and piercing, he refuses to look at her. Stewing in his anger, wanting to be her comfort, but craving more, he stares at his hands on the wheel. The band on the ring finger of his left hand. The one she picked to match her set, a solid platinum ring with diamonds all around. She said she wanted everyone to know he was taken. He was all hers. She wanted the gaudiest piece of jewelry she could find for him. New Orleans in flare, but classic in construction. Platinum and diamonds—she said he was worth every one. To marry her, to take a chance on her, after everything she'd been through, everything she'd put him through, she wanted him to know he was worth it. Sitting, staring at his hands, looking at the overpriced symbol of their covenant, he wishes she would take a chance on him. That she would do her part. Instead of just him.

"I just want to feel, what I felt the first time I was pregnant, and I can't." Graigh cuts through his thoughts. "I remember how I glowed. How much joy I had no matter how my day was going. I want to get that back so badly," she sobs.

"You can't have it if you keep living in the past."

"How can I not live there? I have so many memories before you. I can't erase them. I can't get a lobotomy and remove them. I can't forget that it happened."

"What about all the memories we've been building? Where are they?"

"They're there too."

"So, call them up. We've been together longer than you and Jamal ever were, but I'm still second best. How do you think that makes me feel?"

Like shit.

She doesn't answer. With snot and sob streaming from her face, blank eyes meet her hurt eyes without comprehension or explication.

He shakes his head.

"Like I'm not good enough," Bombei answers his own question. "And never will be. Will never measure up to some other dude that couldn't even follow through on his promises."

"I never meant to make you feel like you aren't good enough. That's not how I feel. I just don't know how to replace everything that happened with everything that's happening."

"I suggested something for you to do weeks ago. Months ago. Years ago. I'm tired of suggesting."

"I'm already going," Graigh sighs.

Her admission brings stillness to the car. Her tears dry, snot crusts, and her face falls. Her fear of the truth unlocked by her greater fear of losing what she knows she loves.

"Why didn't you tell me?" He asks turning to look at her for the first time since he parked.

"I've only gone to two sessions. I was trying to work it out on my own. Wanted you to see the progress without getting sucked into the process."

"You didn't think I would be there to support you?"

"No."

"When have I not shown up for you, Graigh?"

"Always."

"So why wouldn't you want me there now?"

"Because this isn't your mess to work through. You keep saying you're tired. So why drag you into what you don't want to be a part of?"

"Because if it's for the benefit of both of us. The three of us," he says reaching over to brush her belly, "Why wouldn't I do it?"

"I don't know," she answers bereft of words.

Seeing him from a new perspective, from a new point of view, she hears his words in her heart. Listening to the love pouring from his soul she describes Doctor Sophia Grace in intricate detail. The hair. The room. The "oms" of the yoga students. The coughing fit she had on her first visit. Doctor Grace's sternness and stealth. Her force and her art.

"What are these?" Bombei asks unlocking the doors to the car.

"The notes from my session," Graigh says.

"They're pictures of you," he says staring at the drawings on the index cards. "Amazing pictures of you. Why is she drawing you?"

"So, I can physically see my progress from one session to the next," Graigh answers.

Bombei says, "You definitely look different from session one to session two. But do you feel different?"

Graigh gets out of the car first. The closed door behind her is her first answer. Undeterred Bombei follows. Stepping out of the car he comes around to her side and links himself to her arms. Together they cross the uneven street to the corner café facing a block where there are no houses missing, and most of them are lived in. Inside, soft jazz plays in the background along with a radio transmitting music from the R&B station.

"Do you feel any different?" Bombei asks inside the restaurant decked in Saints decor.

"You already know the answer to that question. It's what made you angry." Graigh wipes her face with her hands.

"I know the answer, but I want to hear it from you."

"No, I don't. But I'm trying."

"Then that's all I ask."

"Y'all can sit wherever you want," the hostess says.

Bombei takes Graigh's hand and leads her to a table in front of large windows that looks onto the street of mostly double shotguns. She rests. The lies of omission about the nightmares and therapy are out in the open. Her hand in his, she squeezes her thanks, reaffirms their connection, and returns them to their tandem orbit. Even in their anger, they exist in the other's space, the other's realm, in the persistent act of pursuit.

Fourteen

It's a sight she's seen all day. Singles and couples, straight and gay, in her aisle of eyesight buying items for fun at night. Graigh stands behind the pharmacy counter in the familiar convenience store watching the scenery she can clock by the hour.

It's not like you use your fancy pharmacy degree to open up your own place to help the community you say you love so much.

Why live where you can't even work?

Teddy's voice from a month ago comes back to her mind. In the heat of their arguments
she absorbed his comments as digs against her choice to live where they grew up. Only now does she hear it differently. Only now does she hear it as a suggestion. A possibility. An opportunity to create in her own neighborhood what she's doing somewhere else.

Graigh lets the thought roll around her mind as she slowly meanders through rows of perfectly packaged pills. On her feet, in flats, her belly rounds out the pull away fabric of her red peasant blouse showing through her open white lab coat. The pull of gravity on her belly, on her body, sends a dull ache across her lower back.

Three hours into an eight-hour day spent mostly on her feet, she stands aching, staring at a young couple remembering when that was her and Jamal. When they used to come together for condoms and lubricant, for her birth control prescription and occasionally a Plan B. When she suspected she was pregnant, she came alone. She did not insist that it become an event they share in together. At her store in Tallahassee, on her own, she bought three pregnancy tests at the end of her shift. She rang herself up, bagged her own items, and left without any of the clerks or her staff knowing. She was not ready to share in a moment she didn't know she wanted. She was not ready to share in her reality when she could barely accept it herself.

In the same way, she told Bombei she was pregnant. She took each test over the course of a day and a half with the results never wavering. Each test confirming that she was with child before the full two-minute wait time elapsed. She approached him with fear and tempered dread saying only, "I have something to show you." He followed her from the back yard where he'd been playing his trumpet—a rare occasion on its own—into the house, up the stairs, and into their bedroom then bathroom. There on his vanity she placed all three tests. One with two red lines, another with a plus sign, and the final one just said pregnant in the indicator box. His realization creeped across his face as he read every result. The joy in his eyes was unconfined, the smile on his lips spread across his cheeks into a grin. With his trumpet still in his right hand, he grabbed Graigh with his left and pulled her into him. He spun her in a circle, dipped her across his knee, and tooted a jubilee from his horn. The opening notes of the New Orleans anthem, "Oh When the Saints," blew from his cheeks into his mouthpiece, up and down through his fingers, and out of the bell. Excited and jubilant, he translated his glee into the only thing he knew. His music. He played for himself. He played for her. He played for their baby.

Her own levity displayed to appease him; to make him believe she felt what he felt. That she was as excited as he and not afraid of their intertwined future together. His music and her mindfulness got them through the first appointment with Doctor Marcella. Her fraudulent faces, faked smiles, and practiced enthusiasm made him believe what he saw until he felt the difference. Until her mind became deceptive and he witnessed her anxiety. Now, she is naked around him. The way he prefers her to be. As if they were Adam and Eve, back in the garden, walking with God, without any need to be ashamed.

Naked, with her clothes on, she watches the people coming and going from her place among the pills. Standing, she grits her teeth against the ache in her back. Shifting her weight from foot to foot she eases the sensation of her falling arches due to her constant wearing of flats. Hands on her hips, arms akimbo, she watches the latest couple troll through the family planning aisle. The young woman and man pick up one box. A pregnancy test. They approach the counter and her feet move toward them.

She is propelled from her place among the pills to the cash register at the front of the pharmacy. No one else is in line. Graigh, steps forward, leading with her belly. She plasters a thin smile on her face appearing open and inviting. As the two get closer she sees they are young. Fear hides beneath the blank stares in their eyes. He holds her hand. She leans into his shoulder, tries to disappear behind his back. Between eighteen and twenty-four at best. Old enough to know better. Old enough to be responsible, but young enough to relish in recklessness.

"Will this be all for you?" Graigh asks.

They nod and push the pregnancy test across the counter toward her as if it is diseased. Infected. That just by holding on to the box their fears will come true. Graigh picks up the package and scans the bar code. The test rings out to twenty dollars. They spared no expense on their future, opting for the most expensive test in the store. As if the small financial sacrifice will make their odds more favorable. As if their penance in payment will unpause this moment in their life, release them from this twilight of uncertainty, and usher in the relief they desperately seek.

"Do you have a rewards card?"

"No."

The answer is mumbled by the disappearing young woman. Her voice muffled behind her boyfriend's back. She shrinks herself not knowing she's accomplishing the exact opposite of what her actions wish. She is more noticeable. About five foot six with praline colored skin, a thin nose, serious almond eyes, and a thick bottom lip. In a baggy Tulane T-shirt and ripped jeans, she is the girl next door who was warned to not grow up too fast. To not be too fast. Peaking behind her cocoa powder boyfriend with tiny high top locs, a wide nose, thick mustache, and bags under his cat like eyes she is seen.

Graigh pushes the sides of her lab coat, brushing the edges of her blouse to momentarily make it taut against her belly. She exposes what she's wanted no one to see. No one to ask about. She shares what she's tried to hide from her familiar customers who believe her constant face is enough to feign friendship and pry into her personal life. Now Graigh uses it as a tool to tell her young customer that no matter where she is in her depth of emotions she is not alone. Even if it is not what she wants, not where she saw the journey of her life going, she, too, can and will do the things women were created to do, if she chooses.

It's not like you use your fancy pharmacy degree to open up your own place to help the community you say you love so much.

Teddy's statements come back to Graigh as a smile slowly creeps across the young woman's face in recognition of fertility. She steps from behind her boyfriend manifesting her full self.

She asks, "How far along are you?"

Her voice is raspy and gentle. Thin and thick at the same time she sits in the knot of her hip, her hands rest on the counter between them, eyes staring at the belly before her.

"Five months," Graigh answers.

"You're halfway there. I'm Janay," the young woman extends her hand.

"Graigh."

They shake, transferring energy, transferring stories. Janay's tense shoulders relax, and Graigh smiles. It is her first real smile of the day. The one she puts effort into despite the lies of her cheeks and the non-fold of her lips.

"This is for you," Graigh says, handing her the bag.

"Thanks."

Janay shrinks away from the counter just as quickly as she stood tall before it. Disappearing again behind the assumed boyfriend she hands him the bag.

"Congratulations," Graigh lingers.

"For what?" Janay asks, dropping her eyes. "For getting knocked up when I'm about to graduate. For throwing my life away."

"You're not throwing your life away. We're starting our lives together."

The boyfriend speaks. Firm and forceful he reaffirms the refrain Graigh can tell he's been singing for days. It is clear to her what is happening. They already know Janay is pregnant. The evidence is in their eyes. The test is for show, for insanity's sake. Taking it again, and again because she is looking for a different result. A negative result. A result that won't come.

Janay snatches the bag from his hand, turns abruptly, and walks down the aisle. The boyfriend is left behind. Hands empty. Feelings hurt.

"Thanks," he mumbles.

He follows behind Janay, dragging his feet, reconsidering his optimism; evaluating his concern for a life his partner doesn't want. He examines his own future trying to decide if her drama is worth it, if his seed is worth the time and effort it will take to convince her to let it live.

Why live where you can't even work?

Teddy's voice is again in her mind. It is no longer a suggestion, a gentle prodding. It is a question and a challenge. A direction. The beginning of instruction.

Maybe I could put my degrees to use for the people around us. Do for them what I wish someone would've done for me.

Graigh nods her head as the idea takes root in her mind. The bell rings above the door in the store. It cements her thought while also alerting everyone working someone has entered or exited. Janay and her boyfriend are gone. Graigh noticed that there were no visible signifiers to indicate engagement. Dating, and facing the reality of co-parenting. A reality that puts any woman in the position to doubt. Too many unknowns to count. Too many what ifs to answer. Too much whataboutery. But even in engagement there are no guarantees. No proven outcomes. A fact she learned the hard way.

Graigh looks at her belly. At five months, she hasn't been here before. She has nothing to compare to what she is experiencing now. The last of her comparisons ended weeks ago before she learned she was having a boy, but the persistence of her memory won't release her. Married ten years, and five months pregnant, this moment in her life is all new. She walks away from the counter realizing what Bombei has known for months. For years. She is not the same woman, and he is not the same man. He is not Jamal, and she is not the Graigh of 2004.

Back among the pills, her mind ponders new conclusions. She revisits Janay and her boyfriend seeing herself then and now in the young, scared woman, and the anxious, reassuring boyfriend. They are her metaphors and doppelgängers existing in a parallel plane to her own life. Janay's reactions were her reactions to Jamal and now to Bombei. Janay's unease is her unease despite the differences between them: age, career, position, experience. For them, for all women, pregnancy is the great equalizer. The moment in life where it no longer matters the number of degrees, the number of awards, the jobs held, or the ones still sought after. In pregnancy, personal possibilities and dreams are sacrificed for what wants to grow and breathe life. It is in this moment every woman sees herself and her child while other faces in her life become blurry.

Graigh finds her stool and sits on the black cushion. Resting her head against a row of medications that treat, heal, and sicken, her hands find her belly. Over the tightening skin and a distended navel, she taps a beat. Repeating a pattern with her fingers she taps. Across her ribs, poking her navel, pushing her side she taps.

He kicks.

Fifteen

"He kicked me," Graigh says, walking into the kitchen.

"Who kicked you?" Bombei asks turning around from the sink beneath the window.

"Your son," she says still walking toward the stairs.

She takes each step one by one without stopping, without looking behind her, knowing he will follow. At the top of the loft she continues into the bedroom, and then into the closet. Only then does she stop, but she does not turn around. Graigh sets her purse on the top shelf, slips off her flats and kicks them close to the wall. Her fingers find the bottom hem of her shirt, pull it over her head and drop it to the floor. She pulls the stretch elastic waist band of her pants below her belly. In her bra and trousers Graigh rubs her hands over her bare stomach. She circles their union over and over again, not poking, not prodding, not tapping, just telling him that she is there.

He kicks.

"He kicked," Graigh says, turning around to face Bombei in the doorway behind her.

"He did?"

"Yeah come see."

Bombei crosses the carpet to his wife and places his hands on their baby. He follows her lead and runs his hands across the skin. Together, gently, they forge their oneness that's created this moment.

He kicks.

"He kicked," Bombei says. A smile spreads across his face.

Graigh nods.

Still holding hands, Bombei drops to both knees and puts his face against the side of her stomach where his son made himself known. He listens first, and then turns his face to kiss the kick spot.

"He's in there," Graigh says reassuringly.

"I know," Bombei says standing. "And now you do too."

His hands encircle her waist and pull her closer to him. Bombei pulls Graigh's face to his and deliberately, with open eyes, kisses her mouth. He kisses her lips, her nose, and her forehead. His own reassurance to her that their son is growing.

He kicks.

"I think your son said step off his mama," Graigh jokes.

"He may have you for the next 18 years, but he'll learn. You're mine forever."

"Forever ever?"

"Forever ever," Bombei says kissing her again. "We should celebrate."

"Wait," Graigh interrupts. "I have something I want to tell you. An idea. Actually, arguing with Teddy gave me the idea."

"Really don't want to talk about your brother right now," Bombei says before kissing Graigh again.

His tongue finds her mouth and parts her lips. She is easily acquiescent. They stand and dance. Licking and lapping enjoying the movement of their mouths. His hands on her belly, her arms around his neck, they stay connected in the moment by the love running between them. The kiss that led to their creation, soft and greedy, sensual, and promising. They engage all their senses in the connected embrace that heats the skin, and arouses pleasure. Dopamine rising, they continue the kiss holding each other's faces, sucking, and biting each other's lips, giving pain and pleasure. His hands find her back and disconnects her bra straps.

She breaks the kiss.

"I told you I wanted to tell you something."

"And I told you I don't want to talk about your brother right now." Bombei pulls her back.

Graigh holds him off again, "I thought we were going to celebrate."

"We are."

Bombei leans in for another kiss. Her hand blocks him.

"So, you think I'm just going to give it up on the first kick?"

Her eyes gleam with mischief and mystery.

He plays along, "I'm sorry, Madame. Let me take you out first."

"That's more like it."

"Where would you like to go?"

"Somewhere dark?"

In a darkened corner of Kermit's Tremé Mother-in-Law Lounge Graigh and Bombei sit side by side. Empty plates of crawfish carcasses and barbecue bones are before them. He sips a tumbler of overpriced whiskey with one free hand, while she nurses a glass of cranberry juice. Right now, her hands are in his lap, his hands in hers. He flirts with the short hem of her dress, following the edge of the trimmed seamed across her thighs. His skin barely grazes her. Skimming intentionally, brushing her skin every now and again, he begins a game he plans for them to finish at home. Anticipation rises on her smooth shaved legs with every pass of his hand. With her thighs clenched and calves rubbing together she tries to still herself to his touch and fails. Up one thigh, over the rise of the other, he follows the seam deliberately dragging his short nails against her naked skin. At the intersection of her legs he detours up between both thighs to what she wants him to find. Nothing. Her tease before they left the house, she left sans panties.

His hand travels to where she clutches her courtesy. One finger inches past the thickness of her closing to what she can no longer deny. Her heat. Sticky. Hot. Wet. His index finger is lost in the moisture guiding its way by touch and memory. The dexterous digit runs slick against the apex of her pleasure. Her shudder reverberates back to him. She gulps the last of her drink and gently sets the glass on the table.

It's time to go.

"Bae, I forgot to ask you today," Bombei says beginning a benign conversation.

"Hmm," she purrs as she rocks with his stroke.

"How was your day?"

"Goooooood."

"Tell me what you wanted to tell me earlier." He breathes in her ear.

His tongue licks the outer lobe and then grazes against the sensitive part of her neck. She clamps her head to immediately dull the second sensation.

"I think . . . I think . . . I think I want to open a pharmacy," she stammers, trying to control her breath. "In the old space where my grandmother would send me."

"And that's the idea you got from your brother?"

"Yeah."

"What else happened today?"

"I can't remember."

Her voice breathy and barely audible her words float on the music blowing from the live jazz band heating up the lounge. Funk and sweat from rocking and dancing revelers will soon mask the funk and sweat emanating from the couple in the corner.

"Try," he mumbles into her shoulder.

Kisses follow his words painting the dip at her collar bone with soft petals of lust.

"I worked."

"Try harder."

"I worked hard," Graigh groans.

Bombei's fingers work diligently slipping in and out of her sanctity. Giving her inner and outer pleasure. Her thighs are parted now allowing for the full range of his hand. The full use of his four fingers and his thumb. Two slip in, stroking forward. The thumb lazily grazes across her clit. He tells her to come without saying a word. His fingers inside her speak the only language she knows. Bombei's thumb activates the ball of nerves he knows makes her want to scream even though she won't. Her mouth opens for the deafening sound that doesn't escape as he speeds up. Fingers work double time; his thumb never letting up. She receives stroke after gripping, fingered stroke. He taps on the button of her love urging her to let go of what she wants to hold on to.

"I'm going to ruin my dress," she moans against the back of his neck.

Rocking side to side to manage the pressure of pleasure she tries to disappear behind him to give his hand more leverage and her legs more room to react.

"You still didn't tell me about your day," Bombei whispers, slowing his stroke.

She breathes. Quick pants are replaced by deep inhales and exhales. She reacts to the change of her torture, sitting up, laying her head on his neck. Her hands in his lap to give back what she received.

"What do you want to know about my day?" She asks finding the bulge between his legs.

"Anything you want to tell me," he says leaning his head back.

"This young couple came in," Graigh begins letting her delicate fingers find their way to his zipper.

She opens his pants giving her own hands more room to work as his fingers remain encamped inside her, warm and wet, stroking to keep her from aching.

"Tell me," he stutters.

"Tell you what?"

She blows against his mouth but doesn't give into the kiss. Her hands maneuver inside his pants and through his boxers, until she finds her semi-hard prize. She cups the tip massaging the bead of dew with her thumb. Enticing more to flow, she uses what he produces to slick her own hand and massage his length.

"Tell you about what?" She probes again.

Up and down her hand strokes as he struggles to regain control of his words.

"The couple. That came into the store," he says sitting up.

His hand finds his glass and he knocks back the last of the brown liquid inside. Heady and overcome by his own senses he exhales the grief of her touch.

Graigh says, "They were a young couple. Her name was Janay. She's pregnant. Scared. He wants the baby. She doesn't know if she does. She reminded me of myself."

Her hands continue as he nods and absorbs her words and her presence. Up and down and over the tip. She pushes, pulls, and pulses against his vein. Against his strength.

"How did she remind you of yourself?" He asks more controlled.

"Pregnancy is a sobering moment for every woman," she whispers into his ear. "It was when I was with Jamal. It is now and I'm married to you."

She kisses his mouth but is met by his closed lips. His hand stops, fingers withdraw from her, and clamp down on her own hand in motion.

"We should go," he says zipping and buttoning his pants in his seat.

She nods her agreement not seeing the grimace on his face. The check long ago paid for, Bombei leaves a wad of singles on the table for a tip and walks away. He doesn't take her hand. He doesn't wait for her to step out of her seat, collect her purse, or readjust her dress. He walks away and waits for her in the car. Inside, the engine is running but no music is playing. The winds of change finally reach her.

She asks his infamous question, "What's wrong?"

"Nothing," he says sullenly.

"Then why'd you leave. I thought we were having a good time."

"It's nothing."

Bombei puts the gear in drive. The car lurches forward on Claiborne street. She sits back and rides in his silence. Her fingers tap restlessly on her thighs. Claiborne becomes Robertson. Her hands find his legs. His left bounces with agitation she ignores. Her fingers focus on the bulge, still stiff, pressing against his seams. She cups her hands around what's hers enticing automatic heat to arise within him.

"Stop."

His word says one thing. His actions another. He does not move her hand. He drives. Down Robertson. Over the Industrial Canal. She does not cross herself. She rolls her hand over the orb of his lingam until the contained pressure throbs against her palms. The light at the foot of the bridge turns red. Claiborne and Tennessee. He stops. She doesn't. They are nearly home. Her hands mimic her movements from the lounge finding his button first and then his zipper. The evening darkness, and the tinted windows make her bolder than she was in front of the jazz band and a cavalcade of partying people. Instead of moving inside of his clothing she unleashes her right. Long, thick, hard, and pulsing.

"What are you doing?" He asks without looking.

"Celebrating."

The light turns green. He drives. Both hands on the steering wheel, both of her hands on him. Her hands work in tandem, giving him concurrent strokes, one moves and then the other. Up, down, over. He hardens and drips across her fingers. Her own thighs stay tight, clenched, calves rubbing. She rocks in her seat focusing on her service and not on her need. Forstall. Caffin. The lights are green. Lamanche. Charbonnet. The car whips left on their block. He speeds and whips another left into the car port. The grill of the car rests inches away from the brick facade of the house.

"Get out," Bombei says forcefully cutting the engine.

She does not delay. She does not argue. Her door opens and closes. She quickly takes the steps from the walkway to the porch landing. He is behind her. Shirt untucked trying to hide what he did not put away. Under the porch light only the slick head gleams as she unlocks the doors with her keys.

Inside he slams the doors behind them and turns the two locks on the heavy front door. The only light in the house is in the kitchen. The stove light is on, but not powerful enough to reach them. The white furniture doesn't glow in front of them in the darkness. The mirrors don't reflect any light from inside, or the sparsely located street lamps outside.

"Lift up your dress."

It is not a request. It is a command.

She complies.

He palms her ass. Sliding his hand over the round, firmness of each cheek. His thumbs find her dimples and press her forward. Graigh rears back to avoid falling. Bombei walks behind her and leads her over to the armrest of the sofa. She holds on, balances. His hands find her exposed sex; still fat, and wet.

He is inside.

From the closet, to the club, to this moment, he uses his pent-up pleasure, and simmering rage in his pulse. One hand grips her shoulder, the other encircles her bump, he pulls her into his punishing stroke. It demands she let go of decorum and disrobe her demeanor.

He drills into his wife, pulling her back against him. Balls slap against her bare ass. Pants make a shuffling sound to the ground around his ankles. She does not moan, she moves. He does not grunt, he strokes. There are no sighs, and no breaths. No kisses and no extra touches outside of their connection. Their bodies speak for them. Connection is the conversation, the argument, and the reconciliation. He is urgent in his need, and she is willing to give what he takes.

One hand on the arm of the sofa, her other on top of his and their baby, she widens her stance and gives him room to give her more. She lets him move her. Allows him to punch between her walls as she pulses him from the inside. She accepts his frustration. Empathizes with his anger. And braces herself to accept more.

Bombei bucks against her. Moving by memory and not by this singular experience he forces one, then two fingers in her mouth. She sucks them dutifully. Attending to each one from the tips of his nails to the base of his hand. Her mouth gives him pressure, as he gives her sensuous pain. Holding her taut against him, he sits down on the sofa and moves her up against his length. Sprawled against the cushions he forces her down giving her access to all of him. She wiggles her hips left and right improvising against the staccato beat.

Bombei bucks again. This time he holds her belly as he pushes her to the floor. With one hand he pushes the coffee table away from them, but he doesn't let go. He holds on as he pulls her into each measured stroke. She bounces her ass up and down, twerking his dick the way she would in a club. Her movements are gluteal poetry. Vibrating, and shaking, rolling, and riding, she is fast, and slow, smooth, and rough, giving back what he has given her.

He releases the table. Both hands find her back, grip, pull, and slam. He repeats the motion over and over until he wrenches every last drop, until he has died his little death ten thousand times. He is la petite mort collapsed across her back.

Graigh rolls them both to their sides and squeezes her own death out of her epicenter. Her love and anxiety gush from her and pools sticky between them. She moves on her own wave, slipping him from inside of her, rubbing against his lingam, painting her body in their fluids. She rides the swell of her bundle of nerves to another death of one-thousand words, of one-thousand books, of one-thousand worlds.

She moves.
She moves.
She rests.

Against his chest she collapses her back. Her dress is rumpled up around her bra strap. She kicks his pants over his ankles knocking his shoes off in the process. They lay together sated and separate, half clothed, barely naked. Stewing in their cooling warmth but feeling the presence of something else. Someone else. Her words still in his mind. Her hand cradling their baby from the floor.

She asks, "Do you feel better now?"

Her question, low and sultry, sleepy with dissipating endorphins stirs the fire still simmering in him. She can't see his face to know his thoughts. She can't read his eyes and mirror his mind. She has no idea until he speaks.

Low and caustic he answers, "Fuck Jamal."

Jamal?

Jamal Michael Winston. Graigh's ex-fiancé and almost father to her lost child. The name she spoke that gave Bombei rage. In casual passing, in anything other than casual conversation, she said his name as if she were saying "trees." The man he bested but did not beat. The man whose presence is effervescent between them. There with them as they lay on the floor, getting cold but refusing to move. He is there now as he was there with them fourteen years ago.

Then, when she first welcomed him into her body inside the dark and dank FEMA trailer, he didn't know what he knows now; that they are never truly alone. Then, when Graigh's eyes pleaded, *be gentle with me*, and his begged, *just say "yes,"* he didn't know that she was extending him an invitation without releasing her other him.

Fourteen years ago, when they first moved as one, quietly loving, a whisper on a wrinkle in time, he later woke up alone. He found her sitting on the porch of her unfinished house, Rattler sweats keeping her warm in the cool October air.

There on the porch she unburdened her spirit and said the name he would come to hate. The name he had not replaced despite their years, their history, their beginning, middle and future. She told him then what he had longed to know, which is now what he's come to regret. Where once their love had been a gateway to conversation their intimacy now lacked honesty. He had craved to know all of her, to explore every piece and part of her until he had peeled back every layer. Layers he'd now like to erase, to disremember ever having been told.

The effects of the red pill he begged for never waned. He can no longer not acknowledge his role in the adjustment to his fate. Where once their intertwined souls had been the roots of their relationship, he now sees it as an inadequate salve; a BandAid on an arterial bullet wound gushing with blood. Where once their conversations flowed on the edges of every orgasm, now he knows the secrets she shared on her reconstructed steps were just phantoms of more than physical familiarity, cloaked by the ever-looming spirit of Jamal shrouded in the darkest parts of her heart.

Sixteen

In the darkened room Graigh lays on her back, feet in the air, soles flexed to the ceiling. The scent of tea tree and eucalyptus waft around the body heat darkened room as the Hare Krishna incantations play from the volume lowered stereo. She breathes normally after an hour of trying to create the sound of a conch shell with her nose. Sweat dries cold in her too-small sports bra smashing her tender breasts.

"Lower your legs to the floor gently and move into the final pose. Relax. Savasana."

She follows the prompting of the pleasant voiced yoga teacher to rest, turning into a fetal position to avoid laying on her back and putting pressure on her baby. Eyes closed, breathing in the fresh scented air, she tries to empty her mind of the thoughts she's anxious to release on Doctor Grace's turquoise chaise.

"Slowly awaken your body," the teacher says, cutting through the noise in her head. "Wiggle your toes and your fingers, and gently roll to your right side."

Graigh waits for the rest of the class to catch up. Focusing on her breath, the normal inhales and exhales that prove she is alive, her spine relaxes, and her shoulders fall away from her ears.

"Keeping your eyes closed, take one hand and push up into a seated position, half lotus, full lotus, or whatever is comfortable for you and where you are in your practice today."

Graigh wobbles into position and crosses her legs loosely. Mats and towels rustle in the room as the other students find their sit bones.

"Hands to heart center. And we'll end the class with three oms."

Graigh harmonizes with the teacher and other students, filling her lungs with air that vibrates in her chest with every breath of the one-word meditation.

"The light in me, sees and honors the light in you," the teacher says, bowing forward. "Namaste."

Graigh bows her head and whispers the Hindu valediction to herself. Her growing belly and aching lower back prevent her from lowering further. Moments pass with her in reverence before a light round of applause breaks out in the classroom full of journeying yogis. She stretches her legs in front of her and rests her arms on her back, as people pack up their towels, blocks, mats, and water bottles. The bubbly chatter in the room keeps her mind off her thoughts and her upcoming session. She hears bits and pieces of the conversation around her. Pets and children, husbands, and hobbies. Music and food. The chatter is both gritty and gentrified, gilded and transplanted.

"Did you enjoy the class?" the pale-faced teacher asks.

"It was good," Graigh says. "Different. But good. I think I stretched muscles I forgot I had."

He lowers himself to where she she rests on the mat, feet flat on the ground in the deepest of squats and asks, "Was this your first ever yoga class?"

"It was. I should probably come back when I'm not pregnant, to see what it's really about."

"You came at this time for a reason," he answers. "Honor that. Enjoy it and be thankful for it."

"I will." Graigh nods.

"Have a good one," he says, standing with the same ease as he lowered himself.

"You too."

Graigh pushes herself to her knees and rolls up the yoga mat she bought in the studio's store. Towel in hand, and rolled mat under her arm, she takes her time righting her body on her feet. With one hand on her belly, she ambles out of the studio and walks through the large complex of The Healing Center to Doctor Grace's open door.

"Are you ready for me?" Graigh asks at the threshold.

"You sound winded," Doctor Grace says, standing.

"Yoga. First time."

"Gotcha. Come on in."

Graigh saunters in the room heading directly for the chaise. Her arms are suddenly cold and her heart races. She drops her yoga mat and empty water bottle to the floor and lays on the couch, with her small hand towel wrapped around her shoulders for warmth. Doctor Grace waits for Graigh to settle, then takes her own seat, plopping down on the oversized sofa chair. The skirt of her white dress flares around her, gleaming against the dark velvet fabric. She sees Graigh's ankle bouncing against the cushions. Her hands drumming against her baby. The tight smile and faux look of relaxation pierce the picture she's trying to mask.

"How've you been?" Doctor Grace asks.

"I'm alright," Graigh begins. "Did yoga before the session. Trying to get my mind right."

"Why do you need to get your mind right?"

Because it's been a week since Bombei yelled, "Fuck, Jamal!" as if he lived in the house with us.

"Just do," Graigh says, instead of blurting the first thought that came to her mind. "This baby. We found out we're having a boy."

"Congratulations."

"Thank you."

"You don't seem excited."

"I am. I think," Graigh hesitates. "I will be when he gets here."

"How does Bombei feel about that?"

"Feel about what? Why do you want to know how he feels?"

She's defensive.

Doctor Grace eases her tone, "Because you're having a boy. All men want a junior and usually want their wives to be happy to not just be carrying their baby, but their son. So, you not being excited leads me to believe your husband must feel some kind of way about this. I know mine would."

"I didn't know you were married," Graigh says.

"I am. But right now, we're talking about your marriage. How does Bombei feel about you not being excited about your son?"

"He's pissed."

"That's what I thought."

"That's not all he's pissed about either."

"What else is there for him to be angry about?"

"As usual, Jamal. And the fact I'm going to therapy and didn't tell him about it the first time I came."

"You keep a lot of secrets," Doctor Grace says.

So, I've been told.

"I'd be quick to get pissed with you, too, if you were my husband, or I, your wife."

"Why is that?" Graigh asks, her attitude erasing whatever good vibes she conjured in yoga. "I did something he's been suggesting for years. I took his advice and followed through. Why does he get to be angry at me for doing what he asked? He should be fucking grateful."

"Why are you angry now?"

"I'm not angry," Graigh sighs. "This shit is just stupid. He's mad at me for doing what he asked me to do. That's dumb."

"I think you're looking at it the wrong way," Doctor Grace says, sketching furiously on her index card.

"How am I supposed to look at it?"

"How about he's hurt," Doctor Grace suggests. "Yes, you took his advice, and he's probably proud of you for it, but you didn't include him either. You took his advice like you were ashamed and had something to hide."

"Maybe I just wanted to keep something to myself. Have a bit of privacy. Not put myself on blast that I need help and can't control everything on my own like I used to."

"I doubt what you had before was control."

"Ouch. That hurt," Graigh says softly.

"It was supposed to. You can't keep fooling yourself into believing that things were better before. If they were you wouldn't be here. Furthermore, you're a married woman. There is no such thing as privacy. You gave up your 'I' for an 'us' the moment you said 'I do,' if not before."

Graigh relaxes in the revelation. Pulling the towel tighter around her shoulders, she leans her neck back and closes her eyes. White dresses, veils, runners, and the smell of fresh cut flowers dance beneath her lids. Chiffon, lace, and tulle are the elements of adult fairytales little girls dream about. Lessons learned from Barbie that should come with a stricter warning label. Right next to the warning about choking on small parts, there should be a warning for dreamers. In big block letters telling mothers, daughters, and motherless daughters that buying into the hype of happily ever after can only lead to heartache, and heartbreak. It's the reason Ken comes in a box sold separately. Even in plastic, forever doesn't last.

"What are you thinking about?" Doctor Grace asks, cutting through Graigh's musings.

"You know I've planned two weddings, but only walked down the aisle once."

"It makes sense."

"The wedding that wasn't was cheap. Real low budget. Like five grand in total, including my dress."

"And your actual wedding . . . The one that was. What was that like?"

"It was beautiful. Everything I never knew I wanted I had."

"What was the biggest difference between the two weddings?"

"Bombei showed up," Graigh says, opening her eyes. "He showed up. He took my hands. He said his vows. He put rings on my fingers, and a kiss on my lips."

"Then why do you keep thinking about Jamal. Why is his name never far away even after all this time?"

"Because the game of 'what if' is a motherfucker."

"Explain?" Doctor Grace demands, sketching on a second note card.

"I've planned two weddings, and this is my second pregnancy; but this is my first marriage and my first child, God willing, and the creek don't rise."

"So?" Doctor Grace looks up for elaboration with her pencil poised in the air.

"So, what if I had gotten married to Jamal? Would we still be together? Would I still live in Tallahassee? What if I had taken care of myself and I'd been able to hold on to my baby? Would that have brought Jamal back to me? Would we be good coparents? Would I have still come back to New Orleans? Would I have still met Bombei? Would he be a good stepdad? What if I had never met Bombei? Would I still be single? Would I be a single parent, somebody else's baby mama? What if the levees never broke? What if the flood never happened? Would I be thinking about opening a pharmacy if I wasn't as attached to my house, the Ninth Ward, the city? Or would I be living in Atlanta like every other Black person with some education and aspiration? Am I here because I want to be, or because I like to prove people wrong? Why am I like this? What if my mom had lived? What if I knew my father? What if . . ."

"Graigh. Stop."

"I told you. It's a motherfucker. The questions keep coming and I never have the answers to silence them."

"You don't need to silence the questions with answers," Doctor Grace says standing. "Half of them you don't need to ask at all. Deal in reality and not in fantasy. Accept your reality and stop trying to alter it into a life you will never have."

"How do you suggest I do that?"

Doctor Grace opens the small refrigerator by her desk and takes out two bottles of water. She hands one to Graigh, "Drink this."

"Thank you," Graigh says, through deep wheezing breaths.

"Graigh, the biggest challenge I see is that you spend too much time living in the past because you don't have any closure for it."

Through sips of water Graigh nods; not in agreement, not in disagreement, but for the sake of showing she's listening.

The doctor continues, "It's the reason you remember the note Jamal wrote you even though you say you no longer have it."

"You think I'm lying?" Graigh asks.

"I don't know. That's for you to confess if you are."

"I don't have it."

"Very well. Either way, you have to accept who you were with Jamal before Katrina is not the same person you are now. A breakup is traumatic. A miscarriage is traumatic. Katrina was traumatic. Who you were before all of that died the day he left, the day you lost your child, and the moment the flood consumed your home. Who are you right now?"

"I'm the sum of the death of the experiences you just named."

"If that's all you are then you might as well be dead now. It's not like you look forward to life; like you have a zeal for the future. Your obituary is written, and your epitaph is chiseled. Elaine Graigh Simone-Halvert. She died because she refused to live."

That's not true.

"I wake up every day and live and have new dreams and goals and live this life. That's not a refusal. That's a choice. A choice my . . ."

Graigh cuts her words with silence trailing in the space between them.

"A choice your who? Your what? Finish your sentence." Doctor Grace pushes as she sits beside Graigh.

"Another story, another day," Graigh laments.

"Here you go again picking and choosing what parts of your life you want help with. Which parts of your life you want to reveal. I told you if this is a game to you don't come back. Stop wasting my time."

"I'm not wasting your time. I just don't have the fucking energy to deal with Jamal, Bombei, and all the other fucked up shit in my life at once. Another story. Another damn day. Or we can call it a fucking day. How about that?"

Graigh sits up on the chaise, with her feet firmly planted on the ground. She is ready to run. To escape. To hide in flight, further than I-10 has ever carried her. She wants to hide from her dreams; her memories that surround her in the small office with Doctor Grace by her side, and the doorknob to freedom just steps away.

"I see the fire, but I never noticed the smoke," Doctor Grace says.

"What in the hell does that mean?"

"It means you compartmentalize to cope, and when that stops working one wrong word will set you off without warning. All this time you're smoking on the inside and no one ever knows. Not me. Not Bombei. Not even you. Not until you explode."

"I'm a grenade," Graigh says.

"Not even," Doctor Grace counters. "Someone has to pull the pin on a grenade. Yours is always out, and you're waiting to go off."

"I guess," Graigh says, heels bouncing on the thin carpet of the office.

"You say you wake up every day and live this life, have new dreams and goals . . ."

"I do," Graigh interrupts.

"Like what?"

"I think I want to open up my own pharmacy around the corner from me. Where my grandmother used to send me to get her prescriptions."

"Sounds like a great idea. What did Bombei say?"

"I told him, but we didn't talk about it. It wasn't really the right time. And then . . ."

"And then what?"

"I mentioned Jamal because I met this young couple in the store that reminded me of me and him when I was around their age, and Bombei lost it."

"I can imagine. Now what?"

"I don't know. I'm here. I'm trying to make it."

"Do you think making it, is living."

"I don't know. If it's not, what is?"

Doctor Grace pauses before answering Graigh's question. She looks at Graigh closely, hoping she can see her heart before she hears her words.

"That's something only you can answer. If you choose to."

"How do I do that? And don't say do the work. I'm here. I'm doing it."

Doctor Grace stands. "Yes, you're here. Physically," she gesticulates in the spacious office. "But you are a lot of places physically. Mentally, your mind is always somewhere else. Forging your life means accepting it as it is, not what it could be or could have been. No 'what if's'. Where you are right now, *this* is your only reality."

Graigh stands in front of the chaise. Water in hand, she knocks back the remaining swallows in the bottle before gathering her belongings. Doctor Grace waits by the now open door with her sketches in hand. Graigh shifts her yoga mat and empty bottle to her left and extends her right. She briefly looks at the sketches Doctor Grace places in her palm. Their eyes meet, her questions are unasked.

"The way you walked in, is not the way you're leaving," Doctor Grace says. "You walked in like the woman I met the first day. Covered, cloaked, and pretending. You're leaving angry, but a little freer. Look at your selves and decide which woman you want to be."

"Yup," Graigh dismisses stepping out of the office. "I'll see you in a few weeks."

"Only if you don't plan to waste my time."

Seventeen

May 19—24 weeks

"Come take a walk with me," Graigh says, laying her purse on the kitchen island.

"How was your massage?" Bombei asks looking up from his phone.

"It was good," Graigh answers. "Get Up. Walk. Let's go," she says pulling the back of his chair away from the counter.

"I guess it was good. You didn't have a happy ending, did you?" Bombei cuts his eyes at Graigh.

"No nasty. Get up. Let's go."

"Where are we going?"

"For a walk."

"Where."

"Up the road. Not far."

"Good. Because you know it's too early to walk the baby down." Bombei laughs.

"I know that, but if he drops a little lower, I won't be mad. His feet are all in my lungs."

"Is that even possible?"

"That's the way it feels. Now get up. Let's go."

Graigh stalks away from him, back through the dining room to the formal living room and out the front door. She leaves the doors wide open behind her for Bombei to close and lock as he takes his time coming out to the porch. She starts down the stairs as the doors close behind her. The heels of her sandals slap at her feet as she marches the short winding path between their cut front lawn to the sidewalk. On the corner stuck between a dingy gray stucco home and an empty lot she waits for him. Her thoughts drift to the faces she conjured in the midst of her massage. Her grandparents.

Her stoic grandfather she called Poppy, who never spoke much more than commands at her, and the grandmother whose thighs she used to sit between for hours. Getting her hair greased and brushed, reading, playing, if grandma was sitting, Graigh was locked in safely between the power of her thighs. Cocooned in the strength of legs that stood all day in her home salon, Graigh remembers more the feeling of security in her grandmother's presence than anything else. Trying to recall her face, to elucidate her visage is still an exercise in futility. Her nebulous memory only recalls silver hair that smelled of Sulfur 8 grease and Isoplus oil sheen.

I knew her from my birth until she took her last breath, and now I can't even remember her face.

His feet announce his presence interrupting her thoughts. Rubber soles crunch the broken sidewalk, gravel and weeds followed by his scent. His body arrives moments later, beside hers, taking her hand, and turning her face to his.

"What's so important?" He asks, eyebrows raised, lips cocked in a half smile.

"I told you a couple weeks ago before . . ." Graigh thinks better of finishing her thought. She says, "It's just something I want to share with you."

"It must be important."

"It is."

"I'm here. Let's go."

Graigh leads from the inside. Her stride one foot in front of his she pulls him along to the destination he doesn't know, even though he guards her person standing closest to the street. Bombei matches her pace ignoring the empty and overgrown lot on the right side of the street. The yard overrun by weeds as tall as saplings hides a home for sale no one wants. He focuses on the left side of the street. The side with three fresh homes, cut grass—even if it is brown and sun scorched—plants, and most of all life. Solar panels, satellite dishes, garbage cans, all signs a family has come home to stay despite the lapse of neighborhood luxuries that allow no time for leisure.

They pass four empty lots on the left, only one home is still boarded up from nearly fifteen years ago. The wood bears the marks of water. The ring where the flood settled is gone. In its place is mildew from the wet climate. It rests on the wood scarring it in another way. Bombei looks right. One house bears the boards put there either before or after the storm, the other, a shotgun, is flamingo pink, lifted the required three to six feet off the ground. Raised and left open on the bottom it is in the style of the shotgun houses before the flood, only now what used to be a crawl space for children are now gaping holes exposing pipes and wires.

Graigh's thoughts drift back to one of the earliest memories of her childhood. Then it fades. Replaced with another. One even more nascent than her grandparents. Sad eyes haunt her. Eyes that look like her own. Wide and expressive, the whites, red from tears, set in a face aged by more life than what had actually been lived. This face showed none of the youthful exuberance she as a toddler didn't know a mother should have had to give. The eyes of the woman she never knew, and let Teddy tell it, never loved. His face crowds out the eyes they both share. The feature that told people growing up who they belonged to when they nodded in their direction, then cloaked their mouths to utter whispers they almost couldn't hear.

Teddy. Her big brother. Theodore Malcolm Simone Jr. Named for a man she also didn't know. Can't ever remember having laid eyes on. A man who is among the living, but dead to her for reasons unknown. Secrets of the father, kept by the son, never to be shared with his curious daughter. One of many sore spots in their sibling relationship. Her elder by six years, Teddy hordes what she's longed to know.

Bombei watches Graigh in quiet contemplation as they walk. He on the other hand notices various levels of lift among the houses that have been restored. Most of them are only a few feet off the ground. Not the eight or ten feet some suspected in the aftermath of the water. The five-foot difference designed in the details that once again pointed the finger at the Army Corps of Engineers. If the levees hadn't failed, nobody would have gotten more than three feet of water anyway.

They pass another two-story home like theirs. This one sits eight feet in the air. Skepticism built into its construction. If there's another flood, this family will only lose their cars.

Bombei grunts, "We should have done that."

"Did what?" Graigh asks, coming out of her memories.

"Put the house on stilts like them."

"That's ugly and you know it."

"Who cares what it looks like. We don't live outside. It's safe."

"But we only needed to go up five, six feet. So that's what we did."

"What you did?"

"You poured the foundation."

Please let's not argue.

"I was only the contractor," he says raising his hands and deflecting again.

"But you're not a contractor," Graigh laughs.

Thank you, God he's not serious.

"That didn't stop you from hiring me."

"You were cute."

"I knew you thought I was cute."

"Just a little bit."

"Oh, don't start lying now."

"Whatever."

"Sixteen houses, Graigh."

"Huh?"

"Sixteen houses."

"What are you talking about?" She asks stopping again.

"In three blocks we've only seen sixteen houses including ours. And only one, maybe two other ones if you count this brick one on the corner, high enough to beat a flood."

"Six feet. Eight feet. None of it matters when you have twenty feet of water. If God is coming to collect, God is coming to collect. Noah should have told you that much."

"We ain't Noah. The flood wasn't an act of God—I don't care what the insurance company said—and everything matters."

"Yeah. Well, tell that to the people who had the two-story houses on the other side of Claiborne that still had to get rescued from their windows. What's for the Lord is for the Lord."

"If you say so."

Bombei acquiesces in silence, following the lead of his passionate wife he wished he could strangle some sense into. They turn the corner at Prieur Street and walk another two blocks. They look the same as the last. A few homes, and even that distinction is generous. Of the renovated—rehabbed relics of a Ninth Ward past—they pass another two-story home, redone in stucco, raised the minimum three feet.

They walk, she in focused determination, he in melancholy nostalgia. Before her, the mighty nine was not his neighborhood. These were not his stomping grounds. He watched the flood in 2005 with an overall pain for his city, but no pang in his heart for a neighborhood he could not claim. The tracts of low cut grass interspersed with overgrown lots, left vacant and unkempt, after homes were razed make the one time bustling village of all that was Black, and proud look like nothing more than prairie land for families too stubborn to accept they've been put out to pasture.

She's stubborn and I'm stupid. And now we're stuck.

Graigh turns the corner at Caffin Avenue and walks on the neutral ground. Bombei counts two houses on this block, not including the one with graffiti, broken windows, no doors, and weeds as tall as people.

"We're almost there." she says tugging him forward.

"Almost where?"

"You'll see."

Just tell me what this is about.

Bombei grits his teeth in his impatience and follows her lead. Past the graffitied house they pass more unkempt yards, and a couple razed plots before a church manifests before them gleaming in its cleanliness. Pressure washed red brick, glass doors and windows, a cross hanging in front, and a pitched, steeple like roof glow behind the plants, and flowers lining the lawn.

"This is the nicest building on the block."

"One of them," Graigh says solemnly.

"What's the other?"

"Your school."

He nods his head in agreement.

Graigh pulls Bombei the last few steps across the street as a name floats to the lips of her conscience. Grandma Dottie. She sees the clarity of her face that eluded her before. A picture she took before the storm, before phones had high quality cameras and you still needed a digital camera to capture the moments memories are made of. The picture stored on a memory card she last pulled out days before the funeral to send to the church to be copied onto the obituary. It showed Grandma Dottie sitting in her old rocking chair in her room. Her flannel house dress buttoned from her neck to below her knees. A grown Graigh between her knees saying, "Grandma let me take a picture of us before you set your hair."

The picture she snapped that day that captured them both was cropped for the obituary. That day, one of her last days between her grandmother's knees, she sat with her arms held high to get both of their smiling faces in the frame. The indelible imprint left in space, time, and on the camera's memory card she tucked away after retrieving the photo for the funeral. She remembers now. The smooth brown face with loose set wrinkles that folded into her forehead. A few lesson lines at the corners of her eyes and in her chin. The thin skin of her sharp angular cheeks sagging just slightly. Her lips stretched wide into a proud smile showing off her perfectly aligned dentures.

At the bottom of the picture Graigh remembers she was all smiles too. The constant sadness in her eyes over the breakup evaporated in her safe space. In the snapshot she was the girl she'd always been housed in the body of a woman, and Grandma Dottie was her haven. Her heaven on earth.

I miss you so much, Grandma.

She stops in front of a slab foundation shrouded by vegetation, and surrounded by old building posts. Behind them is a green house, that's been restored, and Burnell's. A multipurpose burgundy building established in 2014 offering neighbors barber, beauty, and laundry services, internet, and snacks. The side of the building is painted with a sign that reads, Galvez Goodies. There is life trying after the watery death, but it is behind them.

"What do you think?" Graigh asks. Her earlier eagerness is now muted and reserved.

Bombei looks at the slab. The slab her eyes have not left while she waits for his answer.

"I don't know what I'm looking at," Bombei finally answers.

"What if I said, it's my pharmacy?"

"What do you mean your pharmacy?"

"I mean," Graigh emphasizes turning to look at him. "My pharmacy in that this is where Grandma Dottie sent me all the time as a kid, and when I came back, to get her medicine and lottery tickets. But also, my pharmacy as in I want to buy the land, build the store, own it, and run it."

Her smile is thin, but turned up lips and cheeks, make her appear more hopeful than she is. One hand on her back, the other on her belly, she presses for approval, but doesn't receive her earlier kick of confirmation she felt in the car after leaving the masseuse where she cemented the idea she's had for the better part of a month. Bombei stares at the slab. She watches him stare at what is not there trying to wrap his mind around what she wants it to become. He worries this idea is one wrought by pregnancy and not passion.

"What do you think?" Graigh breaks his trance.

"I think it's a big investment and a lot of work?" Bombei answers coolly.

"Most investments are a lot of work unless it's the stock market."

She speaks to him while looking at the slab she says used to be a pharmacy. Her voice is more distant than her body, enraptured by a memory, a story he hasn't heard. A fondness he's never known. Graigh recalls Grandma Dottie going to the H&W drug store when it was on Galvez. She continued going when they moved across the street to Caffin. More like she sent Graigh to go for her. Inside they would always welcome her—the precocious child turned lanky teen —with a warm smile, a prescription filled before she had a chance to ask for it, and a lesson in the art of pharmacology. The trips to the store when she was young with Grandma Dottie began her love affair with knowing what mixtures of medicines help people heal.

Graigh leaves Bombei's side and walks between the posts onto the slab. She walks carefully as if following a pattern for a maze, as if she were reconstructing the building in her mind, and being careful to not bump into walls, a door, or the aisles of the store's interior. Bombei joins her in the middle of the slab unsure of where he's standing, or what meaning it holds.

"I wonder how much they want for it?" Graigh asks aloud.

"You can't be serious?" Bombei cuts his eyes at Graigh.

"Why can't I be?"

"We have a baby on the way?"

"And?"

"That's enough money as it is. The doctor visits for you and him once he gets here. Decorating the nursery, buying all the furniture, and daycare once you go back to work. Not to mention the bills we already have."

"You're exaggerating. You and I both know this baby's room will be ready, and if I own my own pharmacy we don't have to worry about my schedule going back to work or daycare. I am the pharmacy and the pharmacist. I can strap the baby to me, and he can come to work with me while you're at the school. I'd be closer to home, closer to you, free from the chain, and able to make my own decisions."

"Yes," Bombei agrees. "But as the pharmacy and the pharmacist everything runs off of you without assistants or techs. Hiring folks and doing payroll is not an option right now. And if you get tired, or the baby gets tired and you have to close down there's no business, there's no money, and your clients will go somewhere else if you're not reliable. Depending on if you even have clients. Fifteen houses, Graigh. Fifteen houses."

"Then I guess you better start gigging again to make the rest of these ends meet," Graigh deadpans.

The line she meant as a joke falls flat, ringing hollow and rude.

He says, "You can't be serious."

"Ugh," Graigh sighs. "It was a joke. What happened to you? You used to have so much drive. So much ambition. You built our house with a music studio, and you don't even play in it. You're content to teach, and now you want to kill my dreams?"

"Your dreams? Kill your dreams? You've had this "dream" for what a hot five minutes. Meanwhile, anything I've ever wanted to do died for the sake of loving you. Being with you. And you don't appreciate it," Bombei says angrily.

Nothing I do is good enough for you, not even the shit I do for you.

"I never said I didn't appreciate your sacrifices. Those are your words not mine," she spits nastily.

"You never said you did appreciate them either. We're here because of you and your dreams and I never said shit to stop you and *your pursuit* of *your dreams*. And now when I object to some new dream that came out of nowhere you have an issue."

"It didn't come out of nowhere," Graigh says.

"Then where did this come from. Anytime I ask you about Ms. Dottie you don't have anything to say except that she was your everything. Now you're just overflowing with memories. Which version of you am I supposed to believe?"

"The version you've always seen. I have lots of memories of Grandma Dottie they're tied to my dreams, but you don't see that."

"You've never said that."

"I thought you knew."

"How would I know unless you open your mouth and tell me, Graigh? So, what's with the pharmacy?"

"Teddy said it when we were arguing at his house before the gender reveal two months ago. I told you, but . . . Anyway, today when I was getting my massage the therapist was telling me how she got started with her own studio instead of being with some major chain. She said she wouldn't trade it for the world. I pass by this place at least once or twice a week on my way home from work. It's usually after I see you if you're out working with the band. I just take the long way down Caffin to pass the store. I've always thought of it since I came back, but now's the only time I've thought of it as being more than just a memory."

Here we go. Down another rabbit hole.

Bombei sighs shaking his head. He steps away from the slab and stands on the outside of the posts on the uneven sidewalk facing her.

He begins, "You're trying to create some fantastical version of life that doesn't exist. You're trying to recreate your childhood, or at the very least your life before the storm. Our house, this pharmacy. Graigh, look around you. We live in a dystopian wasteland. Fifteen houses in six blocks. That's what we've seen. Fifteen houses in six blocks."

"I thought it was sixteen."

"Whatever, Graigh. You know what I mean. It used to be at least fifteen houses on one side of a block. Besides the handful of new homes or renovations, everybody else you used to know who didn't die, got their money, razed the land and left."

She turns her face away from him and peers around the slab.

"You want what you used to have. Baby, that's not here. Not in this New Orleans. Not in the Ninth Ward. Not this year. Maybe not even twenty years from now. What *you* want. It's not here."

"Just because it's not here now doesn't mean it wasn't ever here. Doesn't mean it can't be here again."

"And how much longer do we have to wait before everything that used to be here gets here again. Another fifteen years?"

"I don't know."

"That's my point. To have what you want, right now, we can't be here."

"I'm not moving to Atlanta."

"Graigh, that fight is over and done with. We're in New Orleans. Fine."

"You don't seem fine," she picks at him, opening the barely healed wound of an old argument.

"I'm fine. Trust me. And even if I wasn't, this conversation is old. We've rebuilt. We're established. Now it's time to build something else." Bombei crosses the street to Burnell's.

"What's that?" She asks following behind him.

"Our family."

Bombei's long stride carries him two feet faster than Graigh's broken waddle. He crosses from Burnell's to the neutral ground to the other side of Caffin before she does.

His sneakered feet crunch the grass and kick up dirt. She's left to walk in his settling dust, dejected and angry. She looks back at the slab. The slab that used to be a pharmacy. Her pharmacy. Her heart says *see ya later* instead of goodbye. It longs for what she never knew she really wanted. Creating new dreams for her family, a yearning to serve both herself and her community.

In Bombei's wake, Graigh counts. Down Caffin, down Prieur, back to Charbonnet she counts, drifting further and further behind him.

"Forty-five," she mumbles to herself as she reaches their porch.

The number of houses she counted on her way home. All the ones she could make out along her route. All the ones she noticed where cars were parked.

"Forty-five. Not fifteen."

She takes the steps onto the elevated porch. The music reaches her as she catches her breath. Blue notes waft to her from the backyard. The flats and sharps carried on the winds of frustration travel from his breaths to her own. The blown brass wails with the tears streaming hot and steady down the sides of her face. The cascades of water fall as she goes inside the house, they've made their home. One hand on her belly, the other on her back, the definition of love kicks her from the inside out.

Eighteen

The tall oak trees on St. Charles Avenue shelter them from the sun. After a week without saying more than "Hi" and "Bye" they stand beneath old trees, in front of old houses, in a neighborhood that wreaks of old money. They are tourists in their own city, opting for an impromptu and organic walking tour of the Garden District, where the streetcar is always available when Graigh's feet give out. In front of the Belfort mansion Graigh and Bombei stand among their peers, millennials old enough to remember the sprawling estate as the site of *Real World* cast shenanigans from the early aughts. They stand beneath bends in branches before the lush grass and pristinely edged yard silent as they've been all week. Antebellum beauty is their background, feminism is their foreground. She unwilling to cede her idea to buy the pharmacy, he unwilling to see her need to rewrite history in their future. In a city where history informs the future they stand holding on to their same points of view, in the same argument, they've failed to resolve for more than ten years.

She breaks the silence first saying, "It's funny. I never really came up here as a kid."

"Why not?"

"Never had a reason to. What point is there to come and look at people who have shit you know you never could."

"Again, I ask, why not?" Bombei persists.

"I don't know. Never dreamed that big I guess."

"You're dreaming big now."

If we're gonna talk, let's talk.

"I am," she admits slowly. "But you're not?"

You never cared about my dreams. Why ask now?

He ignores the question in her voice. Bombei turns around to face the other side of the street. He looks at the houses with the lesser known history. The columns of anonymity and the iron work of the unknown. Towers to the arduous toil it took to build them. The gilded giants that make the area a top attraction for everyone but the people whose ancestors helped build these homes with their hardened hands and hardened souls from the institution of stolen labor. Only to have elders work in these same homes a century later with the hopes of owning less than half the square footage in a shotgun of their own.

Bombei asks, "Ever wonder why the people in these town houses would settle for living on top of each other when everyone else here has enough land and yard space to wall themselves off from the rest of the world."

"No. Never cared," Graigh answers. "Probably because it's cheaper and they don't have to deal with the maintenance by themselves."

"True, but if they wanted cheap and low maintenance then this is not the neighborhood. Even the street names scream rich, not frugal Freddy and nickel-saving Nancy."

"Ok, Fred what's your point?"

"My point is, just because you think you can afford to do something doesn't always mean you should if you can't do it right."

What's that supposed to mean?

"How do you know what these people can afford?" Graigh asks dodging the bait. "Who's to say the townhouse isn't right for them? Who's to say it isn't four families living in just one of these "single family" homes."

"You know what I mean Graigh?"

"I do. And my question still stands. Who's to say the pharmacy isn't right for us? Our pharmacy. Owned by us. Stocked by us. Staffed by us. Serving us. What's wrong with that?"

"Who are we serving? The healthy hipsters and do-gooder neighbors living near us as they work for Habitat for Humanity? Or the neighbors like you refusing to let go of what can't be saved because it's all they know."

"That's accusatory as fuck."

He follows behind her slow stroll. They pass more homes. Some of the old mansions have been turned into restaurants and boutique hotels. Others have become bars and law offices as well as the apartments and town houses they've already seen. But many of them, most of them remain single family homes of the rich, well-heeled, and well educated. The families inside date back to the times of King Cotton and Queen Sugar. The dilapidated domino factory in St. Bernard Parish a testament to the ease with which the elite class manage and maneuver around changing economic tides wrought by recessions, and natural disasters.

They pass the houses. Even the small homes, paupers' palaces by comparison to the grand mansions with their ornate architecture, are still heavenly steps above the boat houses, Brad Pitt's modern and futuristic constructions, and the well-renovated shotguns and double shotguns that make up their shadow of a neighborhood. Even if they aren't, they still boast an address on the Avenue. The location is a kind of currency, in itself. The currency of status, or proper positioning and placement like that of an address on Fifth Avenue, the Gold Coast, Rodeo Drive, or Beverly Hills.

The addresses where tourists flock with cameras. Phones and go pros, iPads and selfie sticks capturing the moments that they will filter for Instagram. The stoic history of stitched up war wounds patched in plaster and paneling provide beautiful backgrounds to be viewed through eyes of distortion.

"So, what if I want to save the only things I know. What's wrong with that?"

"You're not moving forward. There's no progression in your life."

"I got your progressive," Graigh smirks.

"Whatever, *Love Jones*."

The shared smile is the first in a week. In front of condos created out of an old mansion that was saved from being torn down when the area was declared a historic district, their hands find each other as they revel in a truce.

"If I'm not progressive, then what does that make you?" Graigh asks turning to look at Bombei.

A fool.

He pauses before answering. Returning her stare, he examines the arch and shape of her eyebrows. Made up and filled in, or natural, their state belies deeper meaning. She wrinkles her brows and the intensity in her eyes give insight into her true thoughts and feelings. He notices one is relaxed. The other is slightly raised, just the uppermost point of the arch. She is inquisitive and curious. Not yet defensive and feeling attacked; genuinely in the mood for knowing instead of arguing out of her own cognitive dissonance.

He says, "I'm stuck right here with you."

"What would make you progressive?" She asks more to his lips than to his face.

"Music."

The answer rushes out of him without thought or clarification. It is true, pure, and undefiled. The answer of his heart and not his head.

"But you do music."

"No," he corrects. "I teach music. To students who care more about beat machines, the best streaming services, and what they can download for free than instruments, records, and paying for art. Saying I do music is just like me saying you're a drug dealer. Both statements are true just not true to us."

"Then what would you like to do?"

"I don't know. I've never thought about it. We have a studio but we both know I don't use it. I don't even know what I would record. I practice because I teach. I play because

I feel. But it isn't a career. It isn't my career. That dream died with . . ."

The storm took more than just lives, Bombei thinks to himself cutting off his own answer.

"But you played in Chicago with Dougie after the storm," Graigh counters. "You lived that full-time musician life then."

"I did. And if I wanted to continue to do it, I should have stayed in Chicago playing at the House of Blues and wherever else. I didn't. I came back. I met you . . ."

"Katrina didn't kill your dream. I did."

"I didn't say that."

"You didn't have to."

"Graigh, I met you and I loved you from the moment I saw you. Strong, determined, defiant. You were the spirit I needed. The city needed. I conned you into letting me help you with the house and charmed you into becoming my wife. You became what music was. And now that's you and the baby. I'm here all in with you, but you're a boat unanchored ready to drift any way the wind blows."

"And what does that make you?"

"Honestly?"

"No. Lie to me," she snickers.

"I'm the anchor you're dragging along that won't hold you in place."

"You think wanting to open the pharmacy is me drifting away?"

Her eyebrows tell him proceed with caution. He answers accordingly, "Yes."

"I disagree."

"Of course, you do."

"Buying the pharmacy. Reopening the pharmacy is not drifting away. It's me digging in. My anchor beside yours. All in."

"I'll believe it when I see it."

The words escape him before he was able to think about his response. Her wide eyes are daggers. Her eyebrows checkmarks. The angles of her face are severe in her anger despite the pregnancy weight. She releases their shallow hand grip and marches ahead. Shielded by the shade of the trees her pace is quick, her anger choleric. Fused to her skin, she wears her feelings on her bare arms. One hand over her belly, the other arm swings at her side as she stomps the pavement pretending it was his face. His safe distance behind her doesn't protect him from the assault of her words. The string of expletives she whispers on every breath.

"You've got to be fucking kidding me."

She repeats the phrase over and over. Despite the pulchritudinous views around her, she focuses on the ugly. The upsetting. The untruth.

"I've been all in for a long time damnit," Graigh snaps whirling around. "If I wasn't, I wouldn't be here with you, pregnant, trying to convince you to do something I know will work. That's an all-in wife for your ass."

Her marching resumes. Faster. Her breathing is labored. Wheezy.

"Stop before you can't breathe," Bombei yells at her back.

Graigh keeps going. She keeps walking. Past the elegance of old, the renovations of new, and a relic that is as defining to the crescent city as its food and music. The streetcar rumbles past them; the quiet rolling no match for the loud, fuming, steam coming from Graigh's aura.

She drastically slows her pace, stops moving forward, and instead in circles.

"You're my wife. Yes," Bombei says catching up. "All-in? No. You say it. You may even believe it, but it's not true."

You've never been all-in. And if you were, I had to convince you first.

"If there was something or someone better out there, you'd be re-married by now. Or at the very least divorced," Graigh says.

People don't stay where they don't want to be.

Their arguments are as much about what they say as what they don't. The rhythm of their words is equal to the resounding rumbles of the thoughts they keep to themselves.

The thoughts they don't dare share in order to keep the peace. To maintain their marriage. To fight fair. But their guidelines are fading. Boundaries falling. Gloves finally coming off. After nearly fifteen years, they're finally saying all the things that have always needed to be said.

"I'm not that guy," Bombei says. "I told you the day of, I'm only doing this once. I meant that."

"So, now what?" Graigh asks.

"Now I try to get you to stop clinging to the past you can't change and cleave to me and our future and what we make of it. Not what we try to restore."

"What's wrong with restoration."

"Restoration and renovation make people think there are do overs in life. There are no do overs in life, Graigh. You only get one. *This* is our life," he says placing his palm against her belly.

He kicks.

"That boy is getting strong," Bombei marvels.

"He is. He's responding to you. To us. To this life we're going to bring him into. This place we call home. The pharmacy would be as much a part of our future as it is my past. What's wrong with that?"

"There's nothing wrong with that. I just don't believe you."

Even after all this time, he still doesn't trust me.

Graigh doesn't move from the sting of his words. She stays standing before him. His hand on her belly, his eyes trying to stare into hers, a single tear frames her cheek.

She stands before him reasoning with her mind hoping he will understand her place, her position. That he finds grace inside himself to understand her reaching back is just as much of her reaching forward. Reaching for him.

"What do you believe in?" She asks tentatively.

"I want to go to counseling with you," Bombei says ignoring the question. "I want to hear your truth. I want to see this change in you as it happens and not on some sketch card whenever you feel like telling me."

"I don't think what's happening is change, Bombei. It's an awakening of what's been asleep for so long. No hiding."

"Whatever you've been hiding I want to see. No more secrets. You want me to believe in your dreams, show them to me. Put naked on the table."

"What the hell does that mean?" Graigh asks.

"It means I want to see you naked. Your scars, your flaws, your stretch marks. Everything you don't want me to see. Everything you don't want me to know. I want in."

Graigh ponders the request.

You've gotta give to get.

Knowing she owes him the opportunity to see her as naked as she's willing to be before a stranger, she agrees without announcing her decision, and wonders if it will buy them time. Will giving him access to see her, "naked," align their souls and minds and not just their bodies. She wonders if the therapy he suggested for her was his deflection of the abandonment and rejection issues he needs to work out for himself. She wonders if their work, in tandem, will heal the rift in their marriage and get them to the river of grace to stay.

"You want to meet Doctor Grace?" Graigh asks.

"Yes," he answers. "When do you go back?"

"Tomorrow."

"I'll be there."

Nineteen

They sit side by side on the turquoise chaise. Thighs,
knees, and feet touching. Her red painted toes pop next to his
crisp white Reeboks. Their hands are beside each other, barely
touching. Doctor Grace busies herself at her desk retrieving
two cards for sketching and three miniature waters. She hands
two to Bombei and Graigh. Their "thank you's" are muffled,
said more to their toes than to her face. Doctor Grace sits
across from them in her own cushy lounger. She takes a long
swig from the bottle before setting it on the floor beside her.
Resting her back against the black cushions she situates her
note cards in her lap and tucks her pencil between curls
behind her ear. Face-to-face, four eyes stare at two not
knowing where to begin.

This ought to be interesting.

Doctor Grace breaks the silence. "Graigh you
brought a guest today."

"I did. This is Bombei. My husband."

"Pleased to meet you," Doctor Grace says scooting
forward on the sofa chair to shake Bombei's hand.

"What brings you in today?"

"He asked to come," Graigh says.

Doctor Grace nods, "I figured as much."

"How so?"

"Because in the few sessions we've had I knew that if he were to ever come it would be much later down the line if you were extending the invitation, or if I were to ask you to bring him. Seeing him here now and we've only had three sessions is surprising, which means he asked to be here. Against your wishes perhaps."

Doctor Grace lets her comment land where she intended. Their silence suffocates. The unease and tension between them is thick but she notices it only emanates from Graigh. She is the catalyst for what Bombei feels, how he acts, and how he responds.

If anything is going to change between them, it will have to begin with her.

"Perhaps." Graigh sucks her teeth.

"I am in the room." Bombei chuckles nervously.

"I'm so sorry," Doctor Grace apologizes. "What made you want to join our sessions?"

So I can know how she's really feeling when she feels it and not after she's lied to me about it.

Bombei pauses before answering. He mulls the answers he could give. The one he prepared expressly for this question and its deviation. The truth gnaws on the inside of his cheeks. He nods his head back and forth pretending to think intuitively about the answer to the question. Doctor Grace doesn't force his speech. On her time, on her watch, by her clock count she gives Bombei the same room, she gave Graigh—the first time—to speak when ready.

"I'm here because I want to know my wife," Bombei answers mixing his two prepared answers together.

"Know her in what way?"

"In all the ways a man can know a woman, maybe more. The way a twin feels the aches, the pains, even the death of their sibling."

"You want to be my twin?" Graigh scoffs.

"Why are you mocking him?" Doctor Grace asks.

"I'm not mocking him. I just think it's a bit ridiculous and impossible for my husband to want to know me like two people who shared a womb."

"Your comment is the definition of mocking," Bombei says.

"Would you prefer if the two of you kept carrying on like you've been doing hiding secrets from the other person?" Doctor Grace asks.

"She's the one with the secrets, Doc. Not me."

"I don't know you that well," Doctor Grace says pointedly. "Let me be the judge of that.

"Yes, ma'am."

"I'm not that old either. No need to be so formal."

"Okay Doctor Grace."

"Thank you. Now finish telling me more about why you're here."

"Like I said. I'm here to know my wife. To know why she can't love me the way she loved her ex. To make our marriage her reality and not what some other man threw away."

"How would you characterize your marriage?"

Trying.

It's the only word that comes to Bombei's mind, but he dares not utter it. He takes another long pause. He looks at Graigh beside him. The woman, he made his wife, who won't even meet his gaze. He stares at her profile, the angles and precision of her face disappearing into a more rounded form from the added weight of their son. Her nostrils have spread wide and flat against her cheeks, the bow of her lips are still plump and kissable despite her seething beneath the surface of her exterior.

"On the outside I wouldn't say anything is wrong or broken like grounds for divorce. But I know something's not right. She's kind of like her house was when I first met her. From the outside I barely saw the storm damage. Just the marks from the national guard that let me know something happened. It wasn't until she allowed me inside the house that I saw the damage left behind. She's the same way. On the outside I don't see anything wrong. She's beautiful . . . Goddamn gorgeous."

"Thank you," Graigh says, turning to him for the first time. He sees the water dampen the corner of her eye.

"She's strong. Intelligent. Snarky, funny, a little mean but in a playful way. But when I try to press through that, to get deep down at the purest part of who she is, I'm not allowed inside. I get shut down and that funny meanness turns into something, I want to say sinister but she's not evil. Just protective. When that's my job."

"Wow," Graigh sighs. "I didn't think you were going to say all that?"

"Why not?" Doctor Grace interrupts. "Your turn. How would you characterize your marriage?"

"I thought it was good for the most part. At least for him. I know I have issues, but I thought most of them were all in my head. That I just needed to work through my own shit, but I guess my fuckeduppedness has rubbed off on him too."

"You're not fucked up, Graigh?"

"Really? You just called me sinister and damaged. How is that not fucked up?"

"I didn't call you sinister. I just couldn't think of the right word. I think I said protective."

"After you said sinister, and evil, and damaged."

"We're all damaged . . ."

"Okay stop," Doctor Grace says raising her hands.

"Let's do it this way. Tell me everything that's right in your marriage, and not everything that's wrong."

"We can hang out," Bombei says.

"I love to hear him play his horn."

"She's sexy."

"I'm huge," Graigh says, looking at her belly. "But thanks. He's easy on the eyes too."

"The sex is good."

"Do you kiss?" Doctor Grace interrupts.

"It's a requirement," Graigh says.

"Do you talk?"

"Of course, we talk?"

"I don't mean ask each other about your day, or the weather. I mean if I were to leave this room and you presumed privacy could you carry on a conversation for the remainder of this session?

Graigh opens her mouth to answer but loses her nerve. The silence consumes the three of them. Doctor Grace tests them and gets the answer to her question simultaneously. Bombei nods his head again. Back and forth he bobs knowing the answer to the question is, "No. We don't talk." They don't talk at home, they don't talk on the phone, they barely talk during sex. In a group setting they are loquacious conversationalists, replete with old stories about how they met, the wedding, the honeymoon, work, renovating and the latest news both serious and celebrity. But he knows when it is just the two of them the economy of their words has led to a life of silence. They are together but often alone in their thoughts breaking the deafening quiet only to add a dot of color to their normal aural canvas of white noise.

"You don't talk," Doctor Grace surmises. "Bombei you can't ever know your wife unless you talk to her, and Graigh he can't know you if you don't talk back. You can't work through your issues if you don't speak. Just like I told you don't waste my time with what you won't say, you need not waste his. Same for you Bombei."

"What would you like me to say?" Graigh turns to face Bombei.

"Uh-uh," Doctor Graces says, scooting to the edge of her cushioned seat. "Don't antagonize him. That's not a question you want answered Graigh and you know it."

"It's alright, Doctor Grace. She does it all the time."

"But she shouldn't. And you shouldn't accept it."

What the fuck?

Does she think I'm weak?

"Let's take baby steps first," Bombei defends. He grabs Graigh's hands from where they rest on his legs. Her hands in his he says, "I want you to answer every question I have without getting mad. I want us to live our lives in the present and not the past. We have to be more than survivors. We just need to be us."

Graigh nods. Her held back tears fall from her balled up face. Angry at herself for breaking, she contorts her cheeks, lips, and nose, and squints her eyes to fight the flow of emotion already taking control of her body. With the back of his hands Bombei wipes her face. He dries her tears and smooths her skin until she is again recognizable.

He says, "For so long our purpose was the house. But now it's done. It is everything it once was and more. A tribute and testament to both you and Ms. Dottie. But without it to really focus on the last couple of years we've floundered. Faltered. Argued."

"We didn't argue," Graigh protests.

"Graigh we argued about having a baby until the day you told me you were pregnant. This is our purpose now. Our family. Our baby."

"You found me," she stutters. "You found me at the bottom of my brokenness. Everything you are. Everything you represent is the opposite of what I wanted when I met you. But here you are. The man who refused to go away. Who refused to stop trying. Who refused to not love me. Who refused to unlove me when I pushed him away. Here you are in therapy with me. I'm still broken Bombei. I tried to push you away to keep you from breaking too. But you're so damn persistent. So damn insistent on having what you want. And I just give it to you because to say no would be to deny the best man I've ever known."

So, you love me out of pity?

Bombei doesn't give voice to his question and the insecurity her answer wrought.

Doctor Grace intercedes handing Graigh a tissue. She says, "You are neither breaking nor broken"

Graigh wipes her face and blows her nose, wadding the tissue over and over until her swollen eyes are dry and her nose is raw.

"Bombei, what do you think after hearing your wife's characterization of your relationship?" Doctor Grace asks.

"I don't know. I am persistent, but I don't know if that means she wants me or not. It sounds like pity, not love. I don't need her to love me out of pity. To just "go with the flow," like she said the other day. Either be all in, love me, really love me, or let me go."

I don't pity you, Graigh thinks to herself. *I never said I did. Ugh. I knew this was a mistake.*

"Graigh," Doctor Grace says, opening up the room for a response.

"Oms" seep through the floor boards from the yoga class below them. Graigh joins with the class under her breath to release her anxiety in the inhale and exhale incantation. She finds her own ujjayi breath, dabs at her face again, and rubs the skin around her eyes and nose until red shows on her cocoa brown face.

"I am all in."

It doesn't sound like it.

Bombei stares at her blankly, withholding a response he knows will sound like judgement.

Graigh sighs. "I told you that the other day when we were walking down St. Charles."

Doctor Grace says, "But maybe, Graigh, that's the problem. Maybe he doesn't want you to tell him you're all in. The words are nice, but if you don't truly feel that way there's no reason for you to say them because he's not going to feel like they're true."

"How can I make him feel like I'm telling him the truth?"

"The same way you know he's dedicated to you and your family. It's in his actions. That same truth has to be in your actions as well as your words if you want him to stop questioning you."

Sipping from his water bottle, Bombei nods. Graigh mimics his movement sipping slowly from her own bottle, exhaling loudly through her own thoughts.

Actions. Actions. Actions. Actions speak louder than words.

"Let's call it a day," Doctor Grace says, scooting to the end of her over sized sofa chair. "I want to give you these."

She extends her arms; each hand holds a note card. Graigh and Bombei take them from her and flip them over. Doctor Grace studies their reactions as she sets the rest of her papers on her desk. Retrieving three more bottles of water from the refrigerator she stands by the door ready to open it and let them out.

Bombei stands first and extends his hand for Graigh. She grabs his upper arm with both her hands clinging to him. He lifts her first to her feet and then pulls her into him. Her arm is his rope. His lifeline. There in the middle of the office floor in The Healing Center Doctor Grace observes the couple in their embrace. Her pregnant body melded into his. Her arms around his neck, his arms around her waist. Her flashy toes agape between his rubber soles. They stand and let the feelings flowing through their bodies speak for them. Doctor Grace nods in the doorway letting her clients lead the next direction of conversation or lack thereof.

Unfolding from each other, Bombei takes Graigh's hand, folds her fingers in his and walks both of them to the doorway.

He says, "Thank you."

"You're quite welcome," Doctor Grace says. "What did you think?"

"I'm not sure what I think," Bombei answers. "I made my wife feel bad. She cried. And now we're going home. One burden lifted and another settling in."

"Look at your notes; especially hers. I think you'll see what happened here was worth it."

"If you say so, Doc."

"I do. She's different with you around. That I can tell, and I've only seen you two together for an hour."

"How so?" Bombei lingers.

"She's more relaxed. Not as high strung, or as mean," Doctor Grace laughs.

"Ha, ha, ha," Graigh mocks. "I'll see you soon," she says, crossing the threshold toward the stairs.

"That's right you owe me a story," Doctor Grace says.

"What story is this?" Bombei asks.

"One you already know," Graigh assures.

"All I know is that it has something to do with choosing life," Doctor Grace says.

"Uh huh," Bombei nods.

He guides her to the stairs and down, one hand on her back every step of the way. Doctor Grace watches in the doorway.

Maybe they do talk. Just not in words.

Twenty

June 5—27 Weeks

"I'm nervous. What if I don't pass?

Graigh's words fill the room. Her hands are on her belly, panic is etched into her face. Brows raised, and quizzical above her eyes; her naked face, is painted with the raw emotion of the first fear in what has been an easy, high risk pregnancy. Propped up on the exam table, Graigh waits for Doctor Marcella. Bombei is in repose on the stool before her. He brings his hands down from his beard and lets them rest in his lap.

"You'll pass," he says definitively. "How can you have gestational diabetes. You're not even big."

"Whatever. I may not be big, but this boy of yours is. I've already gained 20 pounds and I've still got another trimester to go."

"You're eating for two, Graigh. I don't see why you're being so hard on yourself about the weight. You look beautiful."

"Thank you, but I'm only supposed to gain 30 pounds to stay in a healthy range. I'm too big. I don't think I'm going to pass. Usually Doctor Marcella would be in here by now."

The high chords of her voice add intensity to her dread. She rocks back and forth on the paper covering beneath her. The sanitary separation between her still clothed body and the leather
cushion of the exam table creaks and crackles as her frustration speaks through her fidgeting. She rocks back and forth from shoulder blade to shoulder blade. The crunching paper drowns out the ticking wall clock.

Bombei stands up and goes to her side. Taking her hand, he places both of them on her belly. All three connected in one touch, he breathes beside her. Their joint inhales and exhales slow her rocking until the crackling of the paper settles.

"What is that?" Bombei asks feeling her hard belly.

"His foot. Look."

Graigh raises the hem of her yellow tank top. There beneath the fabric the skin of her belly is stretched round against their baby to be, with one alien shape poking out farther than her distended navel.

"It looks like the handle of a screwdriver," Bombei marvels.

"Touch it. It's his heel."

"How do you know?"

"He's inside of me. I know where his body parts are. We fight every day because the more comfortable he gets the more uncomfortable I get."

"You're almost there," he reassures.

"I have to pass this test first."

"Graigh. Stop worrying. This test is not what matters. It's about bringing that little boy here safely."

"I will," Graigh reassures to Bombei's unspoken fears.

The door swings wide and Doctor Marcella strides in. The thin nurse who typically comes with her is not behind her.

"How are you guys doing today?" She asks.

Bombei and Graigh mumble their answers as they await the doctor's diagnosis. She faces them with the tube of gel in hand to hear the heartbeat.

"Good your shirt is already raised. And I see you have a little gymnast in there."

"It's his foot," Graigh says.

"This is going to be a little cold."

Doctor Marcella squeezes the gel on to Graigh's belly. The heartbeat machine hums to life as the wand searches through the goo to find the sign of life to confirm what they can already see. She drags the wand down toward Graigh's navel. The sound they're all looking for comes through the speakers loud and strong. The beat of their baby's heart is quick. The *wah-wah-wah* is succinct and successive, distinguished among the uterine fluids supporting life.

"He's doing well," Doctor Marcella notes. "Now let's talk about how you're doing."

Uh oh.

The doctor hands Graigh a towel to wipe her belly. She dabs at the goo and waits for the news watching Doctor Marcella sort through her charts. Gathering papers together in a folder, the long white lab coat hides any clues that could be perceived in body language. Graigh focuses on the tilt of her head. The bone straight ends of her hair hang away from her shoulders as she studies the papers. Turning around, Doctor Marcella's face is contorted in concern.

"Despite how healthy you seem," Doctor Marcella begins. "You did not pass the glucose screening."

"I told you," Graigh says in a semi wail.

"It's not the end of the world," Doctor Marcella calms. "We just have to figure out what's going on. Did you fast long enough before the test? Are you stressed? All those factors play a role in how your body responds to the screening."

"Maybe I didn't fast long enough," Graigh relents. "I'm always hungry. So now what?"

"Now we'll set another appointment for tomorrow afternoon. Don't eat after dinner until I see you. You'll drink more of the syrup water and then we'll check to see how your body responds."

"How long will that take?" Bombei asks.

"Plan to be here about four hours or more."

"Four hours?"

"Don't worry," Graigh says. "I can get the girls to cover the pharmacy for me. You can stay at school and just come by when band practice is over. I'll still be here."

"Alright," Bombei says. "What happens after this four-hour test?"

"Well, if she passes, nothing. Everything goes back to normal and there's no need for alarm. Just keep doing what you've been doing. Walking, yoga, no drinking, no more than twelve ounces of fish or seafood a week, and no unpasteurized dairy products. You'll be in the home stretch."

"And if I don't pass?" Graigh asks panic rising in her voice.

"Then we'll deal with it." Bombei assures.

"Exactly," Doctor Marcella confirms. "If you don't pass then we'll start your weekly checkups now instead of a month from now that way we can keep a close eye on your glucose level to make sure you don't develop preeclampsia, and *if* you do we know as soon as it happens. In the meantime, you may want to change your diet for the last trimester eating lighter meals, but more frequently. Every woman is different. Relax."

"That's easy for you to say. We've come too far . . ."

Graigh's voice tapers off. She looks down at her belly, her head shaking back and forth, her body rocking back and forth, the paper beneath her crunching with every movement.

Bombei's hands find hers again. He steadies her consternation with his presence. His strength infuses her veins and soothes the anxiety she aims at herself.

"It's not your fault, Graigh."

His whispered confidence penetrates her shroud of doubt. Her face relaxes against his overtures. Her brows come down from her forehead and rest into the sultry arches above her smoldering eyes. With her jaw relaxed, her cheeks unclenched, and nostrils resting easy across the spread of her face, Doctor Marcella watches tension dissipate from Graigh.

"How are your otherwise?" Doctor Marcella asks.

"I'm okay. A little achy but that's to be expected."

"Achy yes, but if it's painful then I need to know so we can make sure everything is alright as far as the baby's growth is concerned."

"It's not painful as much as it is uncomfortable," Graigh assures. "It's mostly in my lower back, neck and shoulders."

"You may want to get a yoga ball. Laying against that for a few minutes every day will help alleviate some of those aches. Massage is also good too. Your husband should be able to help you there."

"When she lets me," Bombei says slyly.

"That's not the type of massage I meant."

"Doctor Marcella, where is your head? I was talking about rubbing her back."

"Okay you two, you don't want ladder babies, do you?"

"You never know," Bombei says cutting his eyes at Graigh.

"Let's just get this boy here first," Graigh says.

"Anything else going on?" Doctor Marcella asks. "How's your breathing."

"I don't know. I'm still alive so I guess it's okay."

"How's her breathing?" Doctor Marcella asks Bombei.

"Slow. Labored," Bombei answers.

"Yours would be too with a baby sleeping on your diaphragm," Graigh defends.

"So, why didn't you say that when I asked you the first time?" Doctor Marcella asks.

"Because I already have diabetes, and this bronchial asthma bullshit, I don't need anything else to come up wrong with me today."

"Graigh you don't have gestational diabetes. That's not confirmed. We still have to do more tests. The bronchial asthma has nothing to do with your pregnancy. Right now, there is nothing wrong with you. We want to keep it that way, and I can't do my job if you're not honest about how you're doing."

"I'm doing fine. I'm breathing. I'm alive. I'm fine."

"There's more to life than just breathing."

"I tell her that all the time," Bombei says.

"I know," Graigh sighs trying to calm herself down. "All I want right now is to keep breathing so I can hear my baby do the same."

"And you want to keep breathing afterwards? Right?" Bombei asks looking down at Graigh.

She sees the fear and pain etched into his face. She sighs, "Yes."

Her eyes speak her apology, *I'm sorry.*

I'm not my mother.

His crossed pupils settle back in place, but he doesn't look away from her. He stares at her profile trying to bore holes into her brain to discover her true thoughts. To find out if she has overcome her history or is still susceptible to the gamble of genetics. Her face answers no questions and her smile, as the doctor leaves, doesn't give rest to his mind. He is absent as he helps her off the table and through the door. His mind going the distance to an over grown field full of headstones he hasn't visited in years.

She leads them to the checkout counter. Graigh does all the talking. He stands staring, squeezing her hand to feel the pulse in his own. The pleasantries exchanged with the receptionist wash over him. He smiles and nods his greeting instead of speaking. Graigh takes a card from the receptionist and tucks it into her purse. They are on the move again. His unraveling comportment concealed in silence.

She coughs.

The rattling of her lungs breaks his trance.

He asks, "Are you okay?"

"Yeah, I'm fine. It's just a cough."

He nods his agreement and takes her hand. They walk down the hall and into the elevator as a group of people step off.

"What did you mean when you said all I want right now is to keep breathing so I can hear my baby do the same?" He asks behind the closed metal doors.

"Is that why you keep staring at me?"

"Answer the question, Graigh?"

"Why are you so worried?"

"Answer the question."

"I'm not my mother, Bombei. I'm Dottie's daughter."

"No. You're Dottie's granddaughter."

"Not according to Teddy."

"We're not talking about your brother right now."

"No, we're talking about why you're so worked up about nothing."

"It's not nothing to hear you say all I want right now is to keep breathing so I can hear my baby do the same," Bombei mimics.

She coughs.

They step out of the elevator and walk toward the sliding glass doors of University Medical Center. Their genteel gait a lie covering words they haven't said.

"All I said is that I want to get through this pregnancy and have the baby."

"That's not what you said, Graigh."

Graigh stops walking to face him. She reaches a hand to his cheek as she says, "It's what I meant. I'm going to bring him here, and I will be here."

Are you sure?

She sees the unspoken question; the concern in his visage. In the parking lot, standing face-to-face, her belly between them, she shields her eyes to see his clearly. Bombei's dark pupils sparkle beneath his hooded lids. Thick lips tucked inside his mouth present a thin line between his mustache and beard. She reaches toward the hairs of his chin and tugs them toward her.

A tight smile breaks through.

"Bombei," she says. "I want to see this baby born. I want to see this boy grow up. Why do you think I was so worried when we got here? This entire pregnancy? All I want is for him to get here. You've been so sure this entire time for me will be different, is different, why are you doubting me now?"

"I'm not."

"You are."

"I'm not doubting you. It's not you. It's . . ."

"Your mom," Graigh finishes.

"I'm good." Bombei says.

"Now *you're* lying."

He steps away from her grasp on his bearded chin. They walk to the car quiet and distanced. He opens his door. She opens her own. The heat from the closed vehicle licks their skin before they get in. It is oppressive. He turns the car on. Hot air blows through the vents leeching her breath as she sits beside him.

She coughs.

Twenty-One

The coughing started in January 2007, but Graigh didn't notice until August, when they celebrated their one-year anniversary. The coughing didn't strike Bombei as odd until the night after he proposed during their New Year's vacation in Hawaii. Then the cough was only a slight interruption. The rattle in her lungs sounded more like a deep breath, then it did a concerning hacking. But when the clear air didn't ease the intensity of her wheeze, Bombei started keeping count of how many times his soon-to-be wife lied and said she was clearing her throat when she was really catching her breath.

One night in their hotel suite off Wakiki Beach he listened to her struggle for air, coughing continuously as if she had a cold. He watched the rise and fall of her chest as she slept through her fits. The sound of phlegm loud and clear in her tracts perked his ears more than the raw power of the ocean gently subduing the earth outside the open sliding doors of their beach side retreat.

She never complained about the cough. Never mentioned it. He listened in the day and the night and watched her movements with a curious eye. He marveled at how easily she denied the deterioration of her own health when she was so adamant about everything even remotely connected to the ongoing construction of her home. What would become their home.

When they returned from vacation, construction resumed immediately to fit and frame the second story of the old house. The first floor completely finished and restructured, had no furniture and only a half bathroom for the workers to use. They slept every night in the full bed of the FEMA trailer with the air conditioning running high. Bombei listened to her breath. He watched her sleep restlessly. Her eyes were closed but her body was alive as she coughed for air. Her fists were clinched, and her arms were flexed and taut by her sides. He observed her near seizure, which was decidedly worse than what she was doing in Hawaii. The convulsions that rippled from her sternum to her navel. The tossing that sent her legs kicking the covers in search of something solid, beyond the lumpy hardness of the trailer's mattress. It was all a physical response to something happening to her he knew he could not see.

He rubbed her arm until she settled. He made contact and touched her just enough to raise the sensations that caused the fine hair to stand, and the bumpy pores of her skin to respond. Graigh awakened from the depths of her sleep to his concerned eyes staring down on her face.

"What's wrong?" She asked. "Can't sleep."

He didn't answer her question. He brought one hand to her face and pulled her toward him. Her body responded eagerly greeting him with an easy smile and an open mouth. They kissed in the slight cool of the muggy trailer in the darkened night of the ninth. Lips suckled and tongues danced. Nose breathing was a requirement of their passion. A requirement she couldn't meet. Her hand met his bare chest with force. Pressing against the curly remnants of his shaved chest hair, she pushed him away to release the itch in her throat. The cough was more violent than the last. It forced her to plant her feet on the ground beside the bed as she doubled over to find air. Head between her knees, his hand on her back, darkness shrouded his worry as he played the part of the supportive fiancé.

When her cough subsided, he pulled her into him. She snuggled on his chest neither acknowledging the broken passion or the cause of the pause. Graigh slept curved into his side, his arm snaking around her back holding her close until another cough forced him to let go. She slept. He stared; sometimes at her, sometimes out the window in the direction of the construction he could not see, but most times he just looked at the tin ceiling of the travel trailer he was convinced was slowly killing them.

The temporary solution that'd become a permanent fixture in neighborhoods across the city. The trailer that radiated heat in the summer and smelled to high heaven during the day no matter the floral disinfectant used to mask the scent. That night his olfactory glands formed his conclusion, the trailer had to go, he just had to figure out how to broach the conversation.

He waited until after breakfast; until they were on an errand together in the afternoon, where they had nothing but time to talk in a somewhat confined space.

"So, are we going to talk about what happened last night?" Bombei asked as they walked through the massive Metairie showroom of Comeaux Furniture and Appliance.

"What do you mean?" She asked half listening and unconcerned.

"I mean how you almost hacked up a lung in my mouth."

"My throat itched. Ooh look at those over there. We should definitely go stainless steel in the kitchen."

"Only women get excited over appliances."

"They're big and shiny just like everything else in this world that's amazing. Like my ring," she said waving her hand, the engagement ring sparkling on her finger.

"Whatever," he dismissed. "Don't change the subject."

"What subject?"

The question was thrown over her shoulder as she walked from the furniture pieces to the appliances shopping by feel; her hands dragged behind her.

"Last night," he said walking a step ahead of her.

"What about last night?"

Frustrated by her own disillusionment he stepped in front of her blocking her destination among the modernly designed and overly priced appliances.

"I kissed you until you coughed."

"Anybody with tongue that deep down their throat would start coughing," Graigh said.

"I'm not tripping. You're not taking me seriously."

"About what?"

"Your cough," Bombei said aggravated.

"What cough?"

"Now you're playing."

Her cough interrupted the argument in the making. Deep from her belly she doubled over between the dishwashers and the microwaves, coughing, and clearing her cloudy throat. It lasted seconds that passed like minutes. He watched the sickness trying to extricate itself from her body, as she denied it even existed. When she stood upright, her brown face was flushed and tears from exertion pooled in the corners of her eyes.

"That cough," Bombei said stepping out of her way.

"That's the first time I've coughed today," Graigh said strolling toward the refrigerators.

"It's not. It's like the fifth."

"It's allergies."

"From what. We just got around trees driving all the way out here. And there are for damn sure no flowers anywhere in sight."

"I don't know. Dust."

"Graigh, you're sick."

"From what?"

"I don't know. I'm not a damn doctor, but you cough all the time."

"No, I don't."

"Yes, you do. You cough like thirty times a day."

"Are you keeping count of how many inhales I take, and how many times I wipe my nose or my ass?"

"Don't do that."

"You're being dramatic."

"And you're being defensive."

She opened the double doors of the French door refrigerator in front of her and hid herself inside. She busied herself looking at the lighted empty shelves, counting the compartments for groceries yet to be bought, and disconnecting the contraption for ice yet to be made. Blocked from her view, he leaned against a neighboring refrigerator taming his contempt for her not seeing the obvious.

She closed the doors and stood to face him. Both clad in jeans and wife beaters, the construction dust barely wiped from their faces, her easy smile broke the tension between them. He reached for her not knowing her grin was the bedrock of the stories she told herself and others when the truth was both unfathomable and unattainable.

"I don't see what the big deal is," she said into his neck. "It's just a little cough."

"No. It's not. I don't think you realize how much, and how hard you cough for you not to have a cold or the flu."

"Maybe I'm used to it."

"Maybe," he said skepticism heavy in his voice.

"What do you think about this one?" She asked showing off the French door refrigerator a la Vanna White.

"I think it's overpriced for food storage."

"This is a wholesale store. This is almost as cheap as it gets."

"Then take me where it's cheapest." Bombei walked away from the array of tricked out ice boxes.

Graigh meandered behind him stopping to stare and touch more of the appliances. Gas stoves, and electric ranges, some with up to eight burners, and double ovens. She marveled at the variety of sizes in vents and hoods to cover the cook tops. She took mental pictures of the items she wanted for the chef's kitchen she imagined when the contractors drew up the blueprints.

Somewhere between the stackable washing machines and the colorful front loaders another inflamed itch made its way up from her lungs through her respirator and out of her mouth. She tried to muffle it in the elbow of her arm, but Bombei's pointed gaze bored into her the moment she bent her knees and dipped her head to cover up what she didn't know was so conspicuous.

He waited for her to recover. For her to dab at her eyes, wipe the corners of her mouth, and straighten her rumpled tank top before he sidled next to her to ask the question burning his lips.

With her hand in his he said, "You really don't notice every time you do that. It interrupts your entire flow. Even when you sleep."

"So, what if I did," Graigh snapped taking her hand away.

"If you noticed why don't you do something about it?"

"I never heard of anybody going to the doctor for just a cough and nothing else," Graigh said easing her tone. "I can't even believe it myself that something is wrong with me, let alone try to convince a doctor."

"It's not your job to convince them. It's their job to tell you."

"Okay, Doctor Halvert. Since you seem to have all the answers. What do you think my problem is?"

"I'm not sure. I only noticed it when I proposed. You coughed a couple times while I was on my knee, but I thought you were emotional and trying to fight back tears. But then you kept coughing the whole vacation. It wasn't as strong as it is now, but noticeable. It really gets bad at night when you're sleeping. I don't know how you get any rest."

"There you go blaming the neighborhood for everything."

"I never said anything about the neighborhood."

"You didn't have to. It's implied."

"I can't imply something I didn't intend."

"But you did."

"So, what if I did?" He demanded throwing obstinance back in her face.

"Then this conversation is dead before you even get started."

Graigh walked away declining to hear Bombei's response. She denied him a fair fight and abdicated her right to defend herself against his auspicious attack. She walked through the appliances back to the furniture side of the store. In the showrooms of bedroom furniture, she half looked, half touched the poster beds made to look like antiques, and the modern platforms in a multitude of wood colors.

"Walking away doesn't kill the conversation, Graigh." Bombei said catching up to her.

"It used to."

"Yeah. We're engaged now and will be married and living together soon. You have to face me."

Talk to me, he pleaded internally.

"Do I?"

The tone of her voice was both statement and question. Challenge and acceptance.

"Why do you think the neighborhood is to blame for my cough?" She asked.

"First of all, I didn't say that." Bombei sighed.

There's no winning with you.

Pulling on the strands of his beard he said, "You don't cough much when we're outside the house or the trailer. Which is how I know you don't have allergies. With all the dust, and mold, and whatever the hell else is in the air, you'd be worse outside then you are when we're inside, but you're not. It's the worst when you're sleeping."

"So, you're saying I'm coughing because of what?" She asked drawing out the syllables of each word.

"If I had to guess. I'd blame the trailer. I keep telling you it smells."

"Like bleach," she retorted folding her arms beneath her breasts.

"Only because I'm trying to get rid of the smell. Whatever it is, bleach can't kill it."

"Okay, so."

"So, I'm saying whatever the hell is in your trailer just might kill you."

"Here we go with the drama."

"No drama. You act like you're a prisoner of circumstance when you're not," he said with his voice rising. "If I coughed the way you coughed as often as you cough I'd have been gone to the doctor. If the place I laid my head smelled the way that piece of shit trailer does, I'd have been found somewhere else to stay. Even if that meant sleeping inside an open construction zone. All the asbestos in the world can't be as bad as the shit that's in the trailer."

"Whatever. If you didn't want to be here, you wouldn't have asked me to marry you. You knew what I was about when you got down on one knee. Hell, you knew what I was about the day you met me. Don't act brand new now. I ain't changed."

I'm not asking you to. I'm asking you to take your ass to the doctor.

"Graigh, don't do that," Bombei said exasperated. "I'm here with you because I love the shit out of your stubborn ass. But we can be here and not be in the Ninth Ward. You're a pharmacist. I teach and play music. Magazine Street, the garden district, uptown, downtown, the Parish."

"You're mad you're selling your place." She stated more than asked not relenting on her sullen and indignant attitude.

"I will make money on the house in LaPlace so no, I'm not mad. I just don't want to die young when I don't have to."

"Everything is not life or fucking death," she yells through gritted teeth.

"Yes. It is," Bombei said calmly. "If we plan to say 'til death do us part, anything that affects both of us, especially our health, is a life or death situation, and right now you're playing with fire."

Graigh rolled her eyes.

He's so damn dramatic. Everything is life or death. Hmph.

In his arms her anger began to melt. He appreciated her passion, but she knew he had a choleric temperament of his own. Against his chest she rested her head inhaling the cologne masking his musk from the work he put in cutting tile for their master bathroom. He held her. Arms around her lower back, hands gripping the supple firmness inside her back pockets. Holding her against himself, he laid against the headboard of the nearest bed beside them. He breathed. She breathed. Not looking at one another, the intensity of their argument evaporated in their intimacy. Seconds turned to minutes, internal clocks lazed, languishing in the moment of nothingness. Her eyes looked for his. He hesitated before meeting the question glowing in her gaze.

"Tell me what's on your mind," she whispered.

"Are you sure you want to know?"

"Always?"

"Even if you'll get mad?"

"Especially if I'll get mad?"

She coughed. A small one. It resounded and passed in a breath.

"I'm wondering . . ." He paused.

Her eyes urged him to go on.

"I'm wondering . . . How long you would have tried to hide what's going on if I hadn't mentioned it."

"I don't know," she answered breaking eye contact.

He lifted her chin, "If it's something this small, it makes me wonder what else you may hide?"

Twenty-Two

The rocking chair in Grandma Dottie's room barely hid her from view, but she crouched behind it anyway. Stuck against the wall behind her, she peaked out from the chair's wicker back, opening first one eye and then the other before shutting them both again. She slid down to the ground and curled under the rounded wooden swirls of the chairs gliding feet. There she waited until she heard who hunted her. The voice whispered her name in a singing lilt.

"Graigh," the voice beckoned. "Graigh. I can't find you. You're hiding too good. Give Mama a chance to win."

The voice's volume increased as it drew near. She tightened her ball below the seat of the chair and squeezed her eyes shut.

"Where could my Graigh baby be hiding. Is she in the closet?"

"Is she under the bed?"

"Did she go in the attic?"

Graigh listened to Mama muse on the hiding places she didn't choose. She listened behind the chair as her mother's voice sang her name as she searched. Graigh kept her eyes closed, and her body still, relishing in not being found.

"Well I guess I give up," Mama said flopping on the big bed.

Graigh waited to see if her mother really gave up. She opened one eye and then a second to see Mama laid out on Grandma's bed her feet flat to the ground.

"I'm right here, Mama," Graigh giggled behind the rocker.

"Who said that?" Mama asked springing her body forward.

"It's me."

"That sounds like my Graigh baby. But I don't see her."

Mama turned her head from side to side looking for Graigh.

"I'm here," Graigh said again squeezing out through the front of the chair.

"Oh, there's my Graigh baby," Mama said whirling around to watch her wiggle out of her hiding spot. "Mama would've never thought to look there. You're so smart."

"Thank you, Mama" Graigh said standing up, fists on her undeveloped hips.

"Let's play a different game. You're too good at hide and seek."

"Okay, Mama. How about the . . . tickle monster."

Graigh ran full speed into her mother's long striped dress. Her head burrowed into the fabric that buoyed her back from between her mother's open legs.

"I got you, Mama," Graigh giggled in a fit of laughter.

"Nooooo. I got you."

Mama tickle tackled Graigh to the floor until both of them fell out in front of the antique mahogany bed. They laid on their backs, staring at the ceiling fan beating the lukewarm air around the room. Their chests pumped up and down in time with one another as they tried to catch their breaths.

"Mama, why come you always beat me at tickle monster?"

"It's not why come. It's how come, Graigh."

"Sorry, Mama. How come you always beat me at tickle monster?"

"Because my fingers move faster than yours," Mama explained.

"When I get big, will my fingers move fast?"

"Yeah, but you won't beat me because I'll still be older and faster than you."

"Nuh unh. Not when you're Grandma Dottie's age and I'm old like you."

"You think Mama's old?"

"Yeah," Graigh said with a sly smile.

"I got your old," Mama said rolling on top of Graigh with her fingers tackling her in a fit of tickles.

"No, Mama no." Graigh squealed in delight.

Laughter muted any other sounds in the house. Mama's sing song chuckle and her own squeals of euphoria drowned out any other voice. Glee gurgled from Graigh's belly as she kicked her feet and rolled over onto her stomach breathing in the scent of her mother's cotton dress as it hovered over her. Cotton and magnolia. The smells from the outside line she hung some clothes on instead of putting them in the dryer.

"No, Mama, no" Graigh squealed, repeatedly.

"Do you give up?"

"Stop, Mama stop."

"Are you sure you want me to stop?"

"No."

A shrill squeal emanated out from beneath Mama's dress as Graigh refused to succumb to the dexterity of her mother's fingers. She laughed and panted. Kicked and rolled. She screamed "no" and "stop" but wasn't serious in her protest. Thrilled to be under the spell of her mother's nimble fingers she wiggled and giggled tiring herself out from all her own movements. No matter how she moved she made sure she stayed right under Mama. The loose fabric of the long dress hung low to Graigh's body. It cascaded and draped across her back and belly. Graigh wriggled side to side when the dress dropped to her face, pretending to fight the tickles, when she was really burrowing herself further into Mama's dress. The material covering her nose and mouth forced her to breathe in the familiar scent of clothing washed with a dab of rose oil and dried on the line in humid air, that carried the scent of magnolia's from the many trees planted in the front and back yards on the block.

She stayed on her back giggling, squealing, and wiggling from side to side breathing in Mama and testing her nose.

Rose oil.
She breathed.
Magnolia.
She breathed.
Wet air.
She breathed.
Mama's dried sweat.
She breathed.
She breathed.
She breathed.

Graigh gasps awake, sitting straight up from her ramp of pillows, with one hand on her belly and the other on her throat catching her breath. Cool air circulates around her calming the heat from her dream. Her body is dank. The thin material of her mint, satin night dress sticks to her lower back and thighs. She takes a deep breath creating the sound of the ocean with her nasal inhales and exhales. She mimics the ujjayi breath she found in yoga in bed. Graigh focuses on her breathing, but the dream doesn't fade. The sing song sound of a voice she scarcely remembers is alive and playing in her frontal lobe. She hums the sound she hears in her head calming her racing heart and stabilizing her body temperature. Her hands drop to her sides but feel nothing beside her.

"I thought you might want some water," Bombei says from the doorway.

"How long have you been standing there watching me?"

"Since before you woke up."

"How could you tell I was about to wake up?"

"Do you really want me to answer that question?"

"I asked it."

Bombei walks toward Graigh. He sits beside her on the tousled sheets and hands her the glass of water before saying anything else. She takes a long gulp and catches her breath, then drains the glass.

"Now, I'm going to have pee all night long."

"So, what."

"So what?" She asks raising one eyebrow in that way of hers he can never decipher. "So what, I'm going to be tired in the morning from getting up every hour, and this boy has his feet on my bladder. I swear he thinks it's a drum."

"He's just letting you know he's there," Bombei says relieved at the change of conversation.

"Thank you for the water." Graigh says quietly.

"You're welcome."

"How'd you know I'd need it."

You always do after a nightmare.

Bombei takes the glass from Graigh and sets it on the floor beside his feet. Forearms on his thighs he stares at the floor before looking back at his wife, wondering if what he heard will keep him up all night for another reason.

"Why are you staring at me like a crazy stalker?" Graigh asks.

"Because you were talking in your sleep."

"What was I saying?"

"Mostly 'no' and 'stop'," Bombei says sitting up straight. "But it wasn't like you were scared or in danger. You were laughing."

Damn. He saw the whole dream.

"I've never seen anybody laugh in their sleep. You were rolling back and forth, laughing, and smiling saying 'no' and 'stop'."

"What else did I say?"

"Mama," Bombei hesitates. "You know what you were saying?"

"I do. I just didn't know I was saying it out loud."

"So, you dream about your mother?"

"Not often. But every now and again she comes to me."

"You've never told me that. You barely talk about her."

It's not like you talk about your mother either.

Graigh decides against antagonizing Bombei. Looking away from him, her voice is forlorn when she speaks.

"I barely remember her," Graigh begins. "Even in my dreams, she's there and then she's not. I don't see her face. I hear her voice, and if I get close enough, I can smell her."

"That's when you start singing."

"Huh?"

"When you woke up, you woke up singing. Well, humming."

"It's the way she sounds."

"It's your way of trying to hold on to her."

"I guess."

"Don't brush it off, Graigh."

"I'm not."

"You are. That wall of yours is going up."

"It's not."

"Then tell me," Bombei pleads. "Tell me what she sounds like."

Graigh hears the need in Bombei's voice to connect with something he doesn't know. With something he's never had. Still, the words are caught in her throat.

She sounded like music. Like wooden and steel wind chimes blowing in a breeze from a distant front porch.

Graigh waits as the memory of her mother's voice comes back to her. She blows air through her nose until her breath takes a rhythm. She hums the sound in her head and her heart finding the notes of the sing song voice that called her Graigh baby. She hums to herself a decibel above the ticking of the downstairs wall clock. The lilting melody that was sung to her, spoken to her, laughed to her comes out in her own voice in the darkened room. The bedroom shutters are closed tight, the door to the loft and the bathroom are shut as well. They sit side by side in the darkness, he listening to the happy tinged melancholy humming on her lips.

"She had a voice like linen sheets," Graigh says, ending her song. "The kind that are best when starched, pressed, and powdered. The ones that feel better the longer you go without washing them. The kind that wrap around you and provide the right amount of balance between warmth and air. She sounded like her clothes. When I snuggled up against her softness, I could still smell the faint scent of the rose oil they were washed in and the magnolias they were dried under. That's what I remember most about her. Her voice and her smell. And those big sad eyes. She always looked like she was near tears, but they never fell."

"So, you do remember her face?"

"I just did. Most times I can't call it up."

"Don't you have a picture of her? You've put Ms. Dottie up on the wall. You should put your mom up there too."

"We both should," Graigh says, testing Bombei.

She can't see his face, but she can feel his body still next to her. His muscles go rigid against the softness of the bed. She doesn't push.

Graigh says, "Teddy has the only pictures Katrina didn't take."

"Sounds like you need to go see your brother."

"Here you go, trying to send me to him. Teddy is not the answer to everything."

Her response is annoyed. A reaction to his steeliness. Neither one of them wanting to confront the ghosts they carry. Bombei too is warned to tread lightly.

He pulls her into him. "Graigh, that's not what I'm saying. He's not the answer to everything, but for you, he is the answer to some things."

"I don't want her picture in the house anyway." Graigh wrestles out of his arms. "I don't think I could stand to see her every day. Those eyes telling what her smile wouldn't. The truth I couldn't understand behind her laughter. Behind her song."

"I don't know what to say."

"Maybe that was her problem," Graigh continues not hearing his vapid summary. "Everything was bottled in until she let herself out. She loosed herself."

"Sounds to me like you do the same thing."

"I'm nothing like my mother."

"How do you know? She didn't live long enough for you to know her, and you said it yourself, you barely remember her."

"I know because I'm still here. I'm already older than she ever lived to be. That's how I know. I'm nothing like her."

"There's that wall again."

"As long as we focus on mine, we don't have to focus on yours, right?"

"Graigh, that's not what I was . . ."

"No. It's fine. We can talk about me because it's simple. I'm nothing like my mother. She quit. I didn't."

"But you've wanted to."

"I've never said that."

"Graigh, some things you don't have to say. The way you don't let go of your past, how you don't forget some things, and only remember parts of other things. You're a jigsaw puzzle without all the pieces and it drives you crazy, but instead of talking about it you keep it all to yourself. All bottled up inside."

"So, you're afraid I'm going to let myself out. Loose myself like Mama did?" Graigh asks.

"Sometimes I am," Bombei answers.

"Only sometimes?"

"Don't screw your face up at me. You asked the questions that started us down this worm hole."

"Answer the question, Bombei."

"Yes," he says letting the word linger before he continues. "Only sometimes do I worry about you. It's not sadness that subsumes you. I think it's anger and loss. Those missing pieces, even the pieces taken from you, yes, they hurt, but you're more mad than anything else. That's why you go from zero to a hundred anytime we talk. It's your way of plugging in the pieces, but you're finding out they don't fit. Your replacement pieces aren't as good as the others."

"Maybe I should have hired you instead of Doctor Grace."

"You don't want to talk to me."

"Damn."

"It's true."

"But you think I should talk to my brother?"

"About some things. I do. He still doesn't know why you came back here from Florida and that was almost twenty years ago. You both need to know some things."

"And what about you?" Graigh asks.

"What do you mean?"

Graigh feels the rigidness return to his body beside her. She feels his own wall going up higher and stronger around him. The emotional fortress he doesn't want her to break down. The gated and guarded parts of himself he doesn't want her to have access to. In the darkness of their room his inhales are inaudible as he tries to brace himself for a potential interrogation he's never had to face.

"We're always working on me," Graigh says. "I get it, I'm carrying the baby and you're concerned. But when are you going to admit your concern is fear? When are you going to start talking?"

"To who, Graigh?" Bombei asks. "Who can I talk to?"

"Mr. Charles."

"He don't talk to me."

"He don't, or he won't?"

"What difference does it make, the conversation is not happening."

Bombei rolls over to his side of the bed, turns his back to Graigh and lays down. She follows his movements and lays behind him. She becomes the big spoon, despite how awkward due to the bump of her belly. With her head on his shoulder, and her breasts in his back she breathes into him the calm he's always trying to give her. Their breaths and their heartbeats sync and align. Tension dissipates from his body. Graigh kisses the back of Bombei's neck.

Closing her eyes, she says, "I'll go see my brother . . ."

Bombei hears the unfinished half of her sentence. In his heart he hears her voice engraving in love, *as long as you talk to your dad.*

They fall asleep in the roaring silence surrounded by the resurrected ghosts of their mothers and the residue of sorrows sowed into their souls.

Twenty-Three

"Where are my sunglasses? Bae, have you seen my sunglasses?" Graigh asks rummaging through the kitchen cabinets.

"I told you no the last eight times you asked me," Bombei smirks.

"Well, help me find them," Graigh snaps.

"You just told me to sit my ass down because I wasn't helping you."

"And now I'm asking you to help me."

"Graigh, stop stalling."

"Stalling?" She says whipping around slapping her face with her own curly hair.

"Yes. You're stalling. You don't need sunglasses to go see your brother."

"They're not for me to go see my brother. They're so I'm not driving half blind on the way there. The sun is ferocious out there."

"Then pull the front visor down," Bombei says grabbing her hand and walking toward the front door.

"You have an answer for everything don't you?"

"If it'll get you to go talk to Teddy, then, yes."

Graigh rolls her eyes making sure he sees the imbalance in what he's asking her to do.

"Thank you." Bombei says grateful for Graigh holding her tongue.

"I don't like you." Graigh says petulantly.

"But you love me." Bombei grins from ear to ear.

"Only on Monday's, Wednesday's and Friday's."

"That's cold."

"Nope. That's Saturday."

"You'll be fine, Bae," he says palming the swollen apples of her cheeks.

He kisses her forehead and turns her around in his arms. Against his chest she lays, pretending to be helpless. With one arm wrapped around her chest, he uses his other hand to open the doors and walk her out to the car. Down the steps, through the grass, and to the drivers side door, he holds her tight, guiding her on her journey from behind.

"Do I have to go?" She pouts looking up at him.

"Yes, you do. And I . . . I may give my old man a call."

"Do more than think about it."

Bombei doesn't answer in the affirmative or negative about his plans to reach out to his father to tackle his own ghosts. Instead he takes the keys from Graigh's gripped hands and chirps the remote to unlock the door. He gently, nudges her inside. Her body acquiesces, but her lips purse in protest. Bombei kisses her mouth and closes the door behind her. She turns the key, then stretches her arms against the car's ceiling. The sunglasses she thought she lost are in the overhead compartment behind the built-in garage door opener. She pulls the frames on her face, puts the car in reverse and backs out of the carport onto the street without turning to look at Bombei's smirking face. At the corner stop sign she text's Teddy:

I'm on my way.

Graigh pulls up to Teddy and Shandra's suburban house with dread growing in her already swollen belly. She presses her navel in and palms the stretching skin.

He kicks.

Reassured, she gets out of the car with the makings of a smile.

"TeeTee, TeeTee, TeeTee," is shouted from inside the house door.

Kory and Quiana clamor to open the screen door first. They both manage to force the glass door open as Graigh steps onto the porch.

"Come in, TeeTee," Kory says, holding the door open for her.

"Thank you, Kory. You're such a gentleman."

"I know."

"Now that was rude."

"That's because he ain't no gentleman," Quiana quips.

"I am a gentleman. I just don't like you."

"That's enough you two. Go find you some business and go play."

The voice belongs to Teddy. He shoos Quiana and Kory away from the door.

"Girl you getting big," he says pulling Graigh into him.

They hug as best they can. She breaks the embrace first and steps away from her brother.

"Where's Shandra?"

"She and Christian went to the store."

"Oh."

"What's going on with yah, Girl?" Teddy asks.

"Nothing much. I'm hanging in there. Just stopped by for a minute."

"Bombei text me right after you did. He said you had something to talk to me about."

"I swear that man has more loyalty to you than me," Graigh mutters.

"Brothers gotta look out for brothers."

"Reminder, you wouldn't have a brother if it wasn't for me."

"Why you gotta focus on the details? We know how we became brothers."

"Then y'all better act like it."

"Whatever. You want something to drink?"

"Cranberry juice, please."

"Alright. I'll get it. Go on outside and we can talk on the patio. I'll bring it out there."

Graigh follows her brother's instructions and glides from the front door to the back door. She slides the glass that opens onto the patio and steps out onto the brick pavers. She chooses the chair with the matching footrest and eases down onto the cushions. Sunglasses still on her face, Graigh props up her feet, puts one hand behind her head, and the other across her belly. She waits for Teddy to join her.

He kicks.

Graigh closes her eyes beneath the frames and lets her mind take her to the dream that brought her to her brother. The dream of her mother. The woman with a voice as soft as sheets, and eyes as sad as Mary in mourning. The silky song of a voice calling her name. The woman who called her "Graigh baby" and never by her given name, Elaine. Her voice is in stereo, and her eyes are loud and in technicolor. The rest of her face is a fuzzy mystery.

Graigh squeezes her closed eyes to sharpen the image but it dissipates. The sad eyes turn away from her, the lilting voice is muzzled. She can't even call up her scent. Rose oil and magnolias elude her. The familiar smells refuse to penetrate the yard of steaming mulch. She sighs her frustration and waits; clearing her mind thinking of nothing.

"I brought some juice, some crackers, and some turkey. I didn't know what you wanted, but I figured you'd be hungry," Teddy says coming out of the house with a tray of food and juice poured into wine glasses.

"Aren't you a regular Chef Boy-R-Teddy."

"I does what I can when my wife ain't around."

"Then I'm a have to tell Shandra she needs to go out more."

"Don't come 'round here ruining my good thing now. I'll send you home."

"Shut up, Teddy."

He lays the spread before them. A sleeve of salted wheat crackers round the outermost circle of the tray, cheese is immediately inside of it, followed by an assortment of smoked and peppered turkey. Teddy places one glass in front of Graigh and the other in front of the outdoor sofa where he takes a seat.

"Help yourself," he says with a flourish of his hands.

"Thank you."

Graigh drops her feet to the ground and scoots forward on her seat. She makes a sandwich with the crackers, cheese, and meat, taking small bites as she eats, stalling the inevitable. She sips the juice between bites and develops a rhythm of eating to keep from talking. Make a sandwich, bite, bite, drink repeat. Teddy watches Graigh tear through the tray with just three crackers in his own hand. He sets them back down within her reach. Her hands gather them up as she consumes her emotions and eats her feelings.

"What you have to say to me is that bad?"

Graigh stops mid swig and swallows the mouthful of food. It takes her two swallows before everything goes down, and another gulp of juice before her mouth is clear, and her throat moistened enough to speak.

"No, I'm sorry. Just hungry," she lies without caring if he believes her. "You know. The baby," she points to her belly.

"I remember." Teddy nods. "Went through it three times with Shandra. She said she wanted another one, but my wallet can't handle a fourth baby."

"At least you know what you can and can't afford."

"That's one of the keys to life. What is it Grandma Dottie used to say, "Pick one, Boy, you can't serve greed and God.""

"She used to always catch you stealing quarters out her purse." Graigh laughs.

"I thought she wouldn't miss the quarters since she always had so many singles."

"She did always have a wallet full o' money."

"If I knew then, what I know now, I'd a thought Grandma was at the strip club."

"Don't you talk about Dottie like that." Graigh swats at Teddy.

"I'm just saying. She had a lot of singles."

"You know it was to give to the other kids in Sunday school. Bribing them to learn a new bible verse, or at the very least not fall asleep in class."

"Grandma was funny like that. Bribing the kids to learn and stay awake, then teach the story of how Jesus cleared the temple of the den of robbers, to make all the kids give their money in tithes."

"She called it . . ."

"The power of persuasion," they say together.

Laughter holds off the familial tension. The fond memory temporarily closes the schism between them. The one they both know is always there but forgotten until one of them falls in and they find themselves trying to argue their way back to brotherly and sisterly love. The smiles they exchange now are kind. They acknowledge that they lead separate lives but are still bound by blood.

"So, what brings you by, Graigh baby?"

"Wow," Graigh says, dropping her mouth in disbelief.

"Wow, what?" Teddy asks.

"I can't believe you said that."

"Said what?"

"Graigh baby."

"Oh. That's what we all called you when you were being good."

"You never called me that. And neither did Grandma Dottie. Only Mama called me that."

"Oh . . . Well . . . I guess . . . Whatever . . . What's the big deal?"

"Nothing," Graigh says, trying to close the conversation she didn't intend to open.

"What is it, Graigh?" Teddy says, more forcefully. "You're here for a reason. I love you, and I'm happy to see you, but you're here for a reason."

Sounds like you already know why I'm here.

Graigh holds the thought that would start an argument. Instead she says, "It's nothing. It's just . . . I dreamed of her last night."

"Dreamed of who?"

"Mama."

"And?"

"Well," Graigh hesitates. She sighs heavily, "I'm in therapy. Bombei has come too. The doctor keeps wanting me to dig deep, and do the work, and be open and honest. And on top of being pregnant, and what happened the last time, I just have a lot of questions."

"What do you mean the last time?"

Shit.

Graigh sighs for an answer. She buys her time breathing. Inhaling and exhaling deeply in the fresh outside air of the yard. She took off her sunglasses when Teddy stepped outside and now wishes she hadn't removed them. She knows he can see her face as her eyes roll towards heaven and she turns her head toward the back fence.

"What do you mean, last time?" He repeats.

"Here we go," she mutters. "I was pregnant before."

"When?" Teddy demands.

"Before I came home for good."

"When you were with that guy. What was his name?" Teddy snaps his fingers trying to remember.

"Jamal."

"Yeah. That's him. That's the clown you were supposed to marry."

"Yeah."

"I'm sure you're glad you dodged that bullet."

"If you say so."

"What do you mean if I say so?"

"He left because I was pregnant, and he wasn't prepared to be a husband and a daddy, so he bounced."

"Damn, Graigh."

"I know."

"What happened to the baby?" Teddy asks softly.

"I had planned to keep it, but I guess God had other plans. I lost it . . . we hadn't even learned the gender yet."

"I'm so sorry."

"It's nothing for you to be sorry about. You didn't do it," Graigh pushes through. "I had a miscarriage on the day we were supposed to get married. I went to the doctor and they had to do an abortion because my body wasn't pushing the baby out like it was supposed to. After that I packed my shit and I came back home. When I got here Poppy was gone and I didn't tell anybody."

"You told Shandra," Teddy says quietly.

"You've known this whole time?" Graigh asks incredulous.

"How could you tell my wife, and not tell your own brother?"

He's got a point.

Graigh sighs and looks away. She wants to stand, but she stays seated. She puts her feet on the footrest, then takes them down. She puts her feet up again and crosses her ankles. She uncrosses her ankles. She's stuck, unable to reach for the meat, cheese, and crackers on the tray, unable to reach her wine glass of juice. She rests in her discomfort. Ill at ease she focuses on her breath. The air comes in broken, gasping waves, before it smooths out into long drags her lungs can process.

"I didn't think you cared." Graigh says, settling her heart.

"Why wouldn't I care?" Teddy exclaims. "You're my little sister. I'm gon' always care."

"Sometimes," Graigh says. "Most times I think you hate me."

"Why would I hate you?"

"Because of Mama."

"I was a kid."

"So was I."

"I didn't hate you."

"That's not what you said."

"What else was I supposed to say. We were at her funeral. She was gone. You didn't even cry."

"I was six. I didn't know I was supposed to cry."

"How could you not know?" Teddy coughs away his tears. "She was our mom."

"I don't know. I was with Grandma Dottie, and she said everything was gon' be fine and I believed her."

"You were always with Grandma. Even when you were a baby. It was like you never wanted to be around Mama. You rejected her."

"How am I responsible for my actions as an infant. I don't even remember," Graigh shrieks.

"That's not the point, Graigh. Once you were big enough to know better, you still rejected her. Always bothering Grandma while she was doing hair, couldn't even be bothered to play with me and Mama. She tried so hard to get you to come to her, and when you finally did, we'd have to shoo Grandma away, so you'd stay with Mama."

"Teddy, I didn't know. I was a baby, a kid. How can you blame me for her depression?"

"She was only depressed because of you."

"Are you sure about that?" Graigh challenges.

"Well, you and Daddy."

"You didn't even want to say it," Graigh yells. "Trying to make everything seem like it's my fault. I didn't reject her. He did. I went to the arms of the one who held me, who fed me, who loved me. I loved Mama, but can you say she felt the same about me."

"She loved you, Graigh. You were her Graigh baby."

"When it was convenient."

"Well, it's certainly convenient for you to start dreaming of her now."

"Maybe, because I'm concerned about how I'm going to be as a mother. If I'm going to get depressed and push my baby away, and then take my own life."

"Then that's something you and your doctor need to work through don't you think." Teddy stands.

"That's why I'm here now, Theodore." Graigh stands as well. "I can't work through shit if I don't have the whole fucking story."

"What do you mean? Seems like you got it pretty worked out for yourself. I don't see why you're in therapy in the first place. You ain't crazy. Just mean as hell."

"You know what I mean," Graigh says pressing through the anger emanating from both of them. "I don't have the whole story and you know it."

"Oh. You came over here to ask about Mama and Daddy together."

"You knew him, and you're the only one alive left to tell me about him, so start talking." Graigh sits back down in her chair and props up her feet.

"There's nothing to tell. He was a musician like your husband. Played the trombone. He took off after you were born because he couldn't stand no crying baby."

"There you go blaming me for things I can't be responsible for. I was an infant. What part of that don't you understand."

"I'm not blaming you for Daddy taking off or for Mama committing suicide. It just all happened once you got in the world."

"That sounds like blame to me," Graigh says.

"Call it whatever you want. It happened and it's over." Teddy sighs.

"But it's not."

"What do you mean?" Teddy asks. "Neither one of them is around. It's over."

"The sins of the mother always carry over to the daughter."

"You could say the same thing about the sins of the father, but I'm nothing like our deserting ass daddy. I married my wife, and I take care of my kids no matter how much they cry, fuss, or fight."

"Congratulations to you. We're talking about me."

"Okay, Graigh. What about you?"

"Don't be mean."

"Why not. It's your natural disposition."

"I told Bombei this was a bad idea."

"No, it's only a bad idea because you don't want to be bothered with the truth. You're not getting what you want and could give a damn about how anyone else feels."

"Oh really."

"Yeah, really. That's why I'm sure Jamal left. He probably tried to tell you he didn't want a baby and you just wouldn't fucking listen. You never do."

"Fuck you, Teddy. That was uncalled for."

Graigh stands up. She knocks the footstool out of the way as she stumbles over her feet. She catches the back of the chair she had been sitting in for balance. It rocks backwards, but her weight pushes it forward.

"Are you alright?" Teddy asks scrambling to her side.

"I'm fine," she says pushing him away. "Don't touch me."

"Graigh. I'm sorry."

"No, you're not. Don't apologize for shit you're not sorry for."

"What I said was unnecessary."

"It was, but it just reminded me why I don't tell you shit and why I don't ask you shit. I'm taking my ass home. I'll figure this out on my own."

"Graigh," Teddy yells.

She storms in front of him through the sliding glass doors and the living room to the front door.

"Graigh," Teddy yells jogging to catch up with her.

"What. Theodore. What."

"I didn't mean to upset you. It's just that. I'm sensitive about mama."

"Yeah, well I'm sensitive about a lot of shit too."

"I know. What I said about Jamal. It was wrong."

"But you meant it. I'm surprised you kept it in this long."

"I figured if you wanted me to know you'd eventually tell me."

"Yeah. Well, I bet you I won't tell you shit else," Graigh says through her tears.

"Don't be like that," Teddy says pulling her toward him.

"Get off of me."

"No."

"Teddy, I'm not playing. Let me go."

"No."

"You're squishing me and the baby."

He relents, releasing her body. She wipes her eyes and nose on the shoulder of his shirt before she steps out of his space.

"Really, Graigh? Now I gotta take this off and wash it."

"That's what you get for being mean to me. Don't you ever tell me I deserved to be deserted and have a miscarriage. That's fucked up."

"I said I was sorry. Why do you think I gave Bombei such a hard time when you started dating him and he was supposed to be your contractor?"

"Yeah, I guess," Graigh sighs in discontent.

"I didn't want the same thing to happen to you twice. He just turned out to be a good dude, even if he is a so-called musician."

"Yeah he did," Graigh agrees. "Too good."

"Go home, Graigh."

"I am."

Teddy pulls her in again and hugs her. His arms around her neck, hers at her sides, she accepts the love but doesn't offer any back.

"I'm sorry," Teddy says in her ear. "For what I said about you, the other baby, what happened. I'm sorry."

"So was Jamal," Graigh says, pulling away.

Jamal was always sorry until he wasn't.

She steps out of the storm door and closes the door on her brother and his apology.

"For real, Graigh. I'm sorry." He says as the door slams behind her.

"So was Jamal," she says under her breath walking down the path back to her car.

Twenty-Four

The suburban houses blow past her in a blur. The bright colored paneling, red bricks, and manicured lawns of Marrero all blend into the background as Graigh drives the long route home. Over the bridge into highway traffic, the cars weave in and out from lane to lane in front, behind, and beside her. They disappear from her periphery as her mind's eye takes over her present day. The heavy traffic flowing across the Westbank Expressway dissolves into just two cars parked on her street nearly fifteen years ago. They hide her shell of a house and FEMA trailer from neighbors who had yet to return.

Graigh's truck and Bombei's car blocked their view of the street. The vehicles blocked their view of damage and destruction. Debris as fresh as the retired storm piled high in a house thrown off of its foundation, twisted catty corner, and left a mangled mess of itself. That was her view. Damage, debris, and destruction. She sat alone on the steps of what she was trying to rebuild, looking out over what someone else had lost.

Inside the trailer, Bombei awoke alone in their cold and sticky stained sheets. He rolled over to his right side and looked at the clock on her nightstand. The digital numbers read 4:00 a.m. He called Graigh's, name but she didn't answer.

He listened to the trailer for sounds of her movement. There was none. He grabbed his clothes from the floor, dressed, and walked out of the bedroom, toward the front door and stepped outside. There she was sitting on the yellow and cream tile steps of the front porch wrapped in a burgundy blanket. He could barely see her. The only light was from a utility pole; one of necessity. It powered the block with electricity. Bombei walked over and sat beside her. Graigh didn't say anything; she didn't glance up as he walked over, or even acknowledge he was there. It was up to him to break the silence, to initiate the conversation.

"Why are you outside at this time of night?" Bombei asked into the darkness.

"Do you remember when you asked me why I smile and shake my head at you when you swirl your drinks around in your glass?"

Her question threw him off guard. He wasn't prepared for an interrogation of his behavior and her response to it. The response she'd had since their very first meeting about her house at the Gazebo in the French Quarter when he was still feigning to be her contractor just to get to know her better. She arrived late and made her way to the patio table where he'd been seated. Ice water with a lemon wedge was set before him and her empty chair. As she walked up, he took a sip, and she smiled and shook her head before taking her seat. Any time he drank something with ice be it water, a snowball, or a daiquiri, she gave the same nostalgic, goofy grin, and then chased away the memory, replacing her temporal merriment for melancholy.

He answered her slowly, "Yes."

"You remind me of him," Graigh said quietly gazing at the wreckage in front of her.

"Him who?" Bombei asked unsure of the direction of their conversation, and the doppelgänger he was being compared to.

She ignored his tone and continued, "I was supposed to get married on June fifteenth two years ago. You remind me of him when you swirl your drinks and the ice clinks. I was supposed to be Mrs. Jamal Winston."

"But you came back here at the end of June," Bombei said not following the disjointed information.

"I got back June thirtieth."

He met her silence with a disquietude of his own. Bombei processed what Graigh told him in three short sentences. She was supposed to be married. Celebrating her two-year anniversary with the love of her life. Glowing on the fifteenth of every month instead of hiding away from it. Bombei blinked back his understanding and asked a question for his own clarity.

"Is he the reason you act so strange on the fifteenth? The reason you jumped and cringed when I scraped the chair against the ground at The Gazebo?"

"You did a lot that triggered memories of him when we first met. The fifteenth is bigger than just Jamal. It was the beginning of this hell I'm living now."

Back then, Bombei didn't prod. He didn't challenge her silences. He saw them as introspective moments of reflection and not the deliberate censorship of herself he now knows them to be. Back then, on that porch step in the cool October air, fourteen months after the storm he gave Graigh the space to take her time. He basked in her calm agitation poised to know the woman he fell for the moment he reversed his car into her dead grass. He relished this culmination of their three months together, the coronation of their courtship, and being allowed the chance to uncover the woman who stood behind the guarded Graigh. The Graigh she withdrew into when she was overwhelmed and under pressure. Jamal was an opening. A revelation he didn't know to keep secret. A jack he could never push back into the box.

She blurted, "I was pregnant. Four months."

Graigh turned to look at his face for a reaction. The reaction a woman knows she will receive from a man any time a pending life is mentioned, whether she's talking to the child's father or not. She looked at him and through him knowing he was trying to still his brow, and make the pupils and the whites of his eyes emotionless. He didn't know what she saw, and she didn't say. She gazed at him through the slits of her almond eyes, their vivid intensity piercing through to his soul.

"What . . . What happened to the baby?" He stuttered into her stare.

"I had a miscarriage," Graigh answered, breaking her glare. "Then an involuntary abortion. When I walked up at the restaurant and you were swirling your glass, I thought, *here we go again*. Then when you and your chivalry scraped my chair against the concrete I thought, *Fuck. Here we go again*. I smiled because of the fondness and jumped because of the frankness. Love and loss reside in tandem. Feelings so visceral they can only be outwardly, and awkwardly expressed."

Bombei didn't respond. He waited in the darkness for her to finish speaking, wanting to hear more about her fifteenth phantoms. The silence surrounding them was deafening; filled with the chatter of ghosts from the city. It seemed to him as if the lost souls, the abandoned buildings, and the drowned bodies all spoke at once. As if they were all trying to tell their story, daring him to listen. He only wanted to listen to her. Her phantoms. Her ghosts. Her stories.

As their three months turned into four, and four into five he would treat her with kid gloves as the date approached. Doting on her continually, checking on her well-being, sending flowers to remind her of him and make her forget what would never leave her. The sting may have gone away, but the dull ache of her painful memories never dissipated.

Graigh drives through residential traffic remembering how he looked at her then. The two of them sitting side by side on the porch. She wrapped in the burgundy blanket, the skin of her face glowing. Her eyes rimmed with the sadness that shown before he stirred her from the inside. "I got pregnant in February before the wedding," she said to him then. "But Jamal and I had been engaged four months prior."

Her qualification served two purposes. The first, that she wasn't setting a trap. The second that her decisions thereafter were focused on family.

"The wedding was always supposed to be in June," she said staring through him once again. "But two weeks before we were supposed to walk down the aisle, he wrote me a letter that said, *Graigh, I can't do it. I'm not ready for a ready-made family. I love you deeply but I'm not ready. I can't.*"

Bombei watched Graigh say the words of the letter as if she held it in her hands and was reading it to him. Her voice was stale and cold, laced with the sting of rejection of not just her but also of her baby. Their baby. The baby she would eventually lose.

"What did you do?" He asked in a whisper above the breeze.

"I planned to keep the baby even though the wedding was off, but I cried non-stop. I didn't move for days. I didn't eat. I barely slept. On the day that was supposed to be my wedding I started bleeding. I went to the doctor pregnant. I left the hospital a week later 10 pounds lighter and single. I went home to my apartment packed my shit, and left, only to arrive home to more loss. More death."

He nodded his head and kept the conversation going with another question.

"Why'd you come here?"

"It's all I know. I couldn't stay in Tallahassee. This is home, no matter how fucked up my relationship is with it, it's where I belong."

Graigh exhaled. She blew out her breath to keep from crying. She stared straight ahead at the destruction in front of her. She didn't want to look and see pity in Bombei's eyes. She didn't want to see any more sadness; not in him. Not in herself. It's the reason she stopped looking in the mirror, unless she absolutely had to. The reason they remained covered with blankets, and only reflect her image when she can't see it. When she is sleeping.

Graigh exhaled and shuddered beneath the blanket thinking about the trauma, the hurt, the misunderstandings, and the want of something different that sent her away to school. Those same pangs brought her home. Water sent her away, and it's brought her back again.

Where you've been. What you've gone through. It all informs your return. It's all a cycle.

Bombei interrupted her thoughts. "Is this house, the building thing, really what this is all about now? Home? Home away from Jamal. Or . . ."

"That's what it's always been about."

Graigh remembers her answer in the present. The strength of her voice, despite the subject matter. That answer was the first time she looked at him that night. He nodded and moved closer signaling the end of her confession. Sidled together, Bombei took the blanket from her and wrapped it around them both. She folded herself into his lap. He stroked her kinky hair and traced his fingers freely along the length of her twists. She surrendered into him and he relished her voluntary closeness, her confession, her trust. As she laid in his lap, he fondled the cowrie shells affixed to the single strands on the ends of her hair. She stared at the immense destruction caused by wind and water while he rubbed her body stroking her with comfort and understanding. Entwined with each other until the first rays of daybreak they sat on the construction site of what has now become their marital home basking in the beginning of her truth.

That's why Jamal left. He probably tried to tell you he didn't want a baby and you just wouldn't fucking listen. You never do.

Teddy's words sting her subconscious as she turns onto her street. She pulls beside her truck in the carport, and stares at the preserved wounds of the old house, that have been healed. Bombei is inside, but Jamal still lives inside her mind. After all these years her comebacks to the blow back of his decision still don't measure equally to the purposeful intention of his inflicted pain.

Graigh cuts the engine. Her present senses take over from her past as she sits, her hands on her belly, knowing her retort to Teddy was cut short.

Jamal was sorry, but he was never sorry.

Twenty-Five

"How was your visit with your brother?" Bombei asks Graigh as she steps inside the front door.

"What're you doing sitting up here for? You busy door popping waiting for me to get back?"

"Okay, old lady? You were definitely raised by old people."

"For one, tell me something I don't know. And for two, don't come for my Grandma Dottie like that. She didn't do nothing to you. Never met you. And she don't visit you in your sleep. Leave my Dottie alone."

"So, the visit with your brother didn't go well?" Bombei asks chuckling.

"What do you think? I had no business going across the river to spill my guts to Theodore."

"So, he's Theodore now?" Bombei asks standing from the white sofa.

"That's his name?"

"And your name is Elaine. What's the difference?"

"Damn, can I lock the door before we start to arguing please?"

Graigh turns the key in the ornate storm door and then the large wooden door behind her. She feels his nearness before his touch. His aura before his hands on her waist turn her around to face him.

"I'm sorry," he apologizes placing a kiss on her nose.

"You should be," she pouts refusing to look up at him. "It's your fault I went over there anyway. What did you do all day?"

Bombei ignores the subtext of her question and refuses to answer. He says, "I take it your brother didn't tell you anything about your parents."

"I need a drink to talk about this."

Graigh uses her belly to bulldoze past Bombei. She shakes out of his grasp as he tries to catch hold of her fingers and walks through the dining room into the kitchen. He follows closely on her heels, stopping behind her as she removes a bottle of red wine from the back of the refrigerator and sets it on the island. Around the counter tops to the back wall, Graigh fishes out a long-stemmed goblet from one of the custom wood and glass paneled cabinets. She pours until the wine licks the rim.

"Go ahead and say what you want to say, instead of staring at me like that," Graigh demands carefully picking up the nearly overflowing glass.

"I don't have anything to say. I'll watch you drink that whole glass and put my son in danger of fetal alcohol syndrome. Go ahead. You've already lost one baby."

"That was a fucked up thing to say."

"Look at what you're about to do. Your actions are fucked up."

"Did you talk to Mr. Charles about your mom?"

Graigh's eyes bore holes into Bombei's face daring him to say something else that will continue the descent of their conversation from decency. From his wrinkled brows, to his scrunched nosed, and scowled lips she blazons the face burnished in her brain and takes a single sip from the wine. His eyes challenge her actions. His hands ball into angry fists at his sides. One knocks his thigh. The other knocks the back of the bar stool. He waits to see what choice she makes.

She tests the limits of their relationship with a second sip. A sip that noticeably moves the contents of the glass lower. Bombei walks away from her, head down, shaking, mumbling. His feet echo on the stairs as he takes them two at a time. She stares at her still more than half filled glass.

He kicks.

Graigh takes the glass and pours the rest of the contents in the sink beside the refrigerator. She leaves it on the counter, one droplet of wine left in the bottom poised to dry and leave a red tattoo in the center where the stem and base of the goblet meet. A deep inhale in, a longer exhale out. She breathes. Graigh faces the stairs and ascends behind her husband.

She pauses on the landing before taking the second flight. Winded. Her hands on the carpeted stairs in front of her, she is doubled over catching her breath. A cough escapes despite her best efforts to muffle the sound. The dry hack causes her ears to itch, and her nose to run. She lifts her body only slightly, nowhere near close to righting herself. With her index finger she brings relief to her adenoids.

Another cough looses itself from her inflamed lungs. It is the salve she is looking for. She coughs again and then stands up straight. Swollen ankles and tired feet cause her knees to buckle. Graigh grips the banister with one hand. By the time equilibrium find her again, the knuckles of her balancing hand are red.

She takes the steps one by one like a toddler just learning how to maneuver stairs without the use of their hands. At the top she sees Bombei sprawled across the couch with the TV up loud, ESPN giving him the facts and figures on Zion Williamson. Graigh takes the sofa chair beside him and kicks off her cargo, and canvas flats. Her feet find the clock faced coffee table as she rests her head against the back of the chair. She closes her eyes and counts her breaths. The first sixty calm her racing heart from her exertion on the stairs. The second sixty clear the formations of the headache from her first taste of alcohol in more than six months. The third sixty are a personal challenge to see if she can really find the meditative zone she's urged to seek in yoga. The space where her mind blanks and all her energy from the twisted ends of her curls to her pedicured callouses focus on the sole purpose of peace. She begins the fourth sixty and stops herself fifteen ujjayi inhales in.

"I poured it out." Graigh breathes.

"Good for you," Bombei says without timbre or inflection. "It's nice of you to think of someone other than yourself."

"And here we go again. I've been thinking of everyone but myself this entire pregnancy."

"And what about the fourteen and a half years before that? Who were you thinking about then?"

"What does this have to do with anything?"

"You tell me. You're the one who tried to empty a bottle of wine into my son."

"Because I needed it after my day with my brother. The day you insisted I take to visit him, clear the air, and find out more about my parents, when you for damn sure didn't do the same. And for your information, Doctor Marcella says I can have a glass of red wine once a week. I just choose not to."

"No, that's where you're wrong," Bombei says sitting up from the plush suede sofa. "We decided together you wouldn't drink because you're already high-risk and *we* didn't want any unnecessary complications. Don't act like you're doing me any favors."

"Again, I ask, what does this have to do with anything?"

"I don't know, Graigh. You're the one who came in the door pissed off with an attitude. I know that's how you get when you get all worked up, and you got pregnancy hormones and shit, but you're being extra ridiculous today."

"And yet you still haven't addressed the fact that you *did not* talk to your dad like we agreed."

"I'll talk to him when I get ready."

"Whatever."

"Yeah. Whatever."

Graigh mutters, "All this drama because I poured myself a drink?"

Graigh takes her feet down from the table. They both sit on the edge of their respective cushions; legs spread and square, elbows on their arms. They're seated in fighting position. If they stand up, they'll be squared off, ready to throw verbal jabs in place of the physical ones denoted in the precepts of their postures.

"Graigh, it's not about the drink and you know it."

"No, I don't. If it's not about the drink, then what are you so pissy about?"

"You. Your whole demeanor. I was sitting in the front waiting for you to get back because I figured you'd be pretty pissed because you and Teddy can never have a regular conversation."

"That's his fault not mine," Graigh deflects.

"It doesn't matter whose fault it is. He's my brother-in-law and you're my wife, but in the end I always choose your side. That's what I was doing when I was sitting there waiting for you. Choosing your side. Giving you the space to work out your feelings and tell me what happened other than keeping it to yourself with all the shit that goes on in your head."

"And what about the shit that goes on in your head. What about your fears? I've given you plenty of space to talk, to work it out—with or without me—and you refuse to even acknowledge that your shit exists."

"We're not talking about me right now. We're talking about you."

"Well, thank you for being so gracious. Such a gentleman," she sneers. "I was ready to tell you about all the *shit* going on in my head when you flipped out about me having two sips of wine."

"Two sips, two glasses, or two bottles. *We* agreed you wouldn't drink to ensure a healthy delivery of *our* child."

"I know what we agreed to, but right now I'm in sensory overload so I need something else, *besides you* to help me chill the fuck out. Is that enough truth for you? Do you have enough space to receive that? You're always treating me like I'm some basket case. Yeah, I got issues. But newsflash Bae, we all got issues. Including your ass."

"I never said I didn't. I'm not afraid to confront my shit and address it?"

"Oh really!" Graigh exclaims an octave higher than normal.

"Really."

"So, when was the last time you talked to Mr. Charles about your own damn mama, you so worried about mine."

"There's nothing to talk about. He loved me and resented me at the same time. He's told me that enough and without having to take a drink to do so. He blamed me for her death, but then raised me to remember her because he says I look like her. In the end he made his peace. Have you?"

"I can't make peace with what I barely remember. I remember her voice and her smell and sometimes her eyes. The rest of her face is a blur."

"Why didn't you ask Teddy for a picture of her so you could put it up beside Mrs. Dottie."

"I never got that far. He blames me for mama's death and for daddy leaving when I was a baby. He said he doesn't, but he does. Then he blamed me for Jamal leaving me, and me losing my own baby so I left."

"I'm sorry," Bombei says, dropping his arms for the first time since their argument began.

"There's nothing for you to be sorry about you didn't know."

"I still feel bad. I didn't know it got that bad. I thought he just said stuff you didn't want to hear."

"He said a lot of things I didn't want to hear. Then I got home and you said the same shit because I had a drink."

He sighs his frustration at her singular point of contention.

"So, no I didn't get to ask for a picture or find out more about mama."

"What about your dad?" Bombei asks quietly.

"I learned he was a musician like you. He played the trombone. He left because he couldn't stand no crying baby."

"That's it."

"Yeah. Which explains why Teddy didn't like you at first."

"Because all musicians are irresponsible?" Bombei asks.

"No, because the only other musician he knew was irresponsible."

"So now what?"

"I don't know."

"Are you going to tell Doctor Grace?"

"Tell her what, there's nothing to tell."

"There is," Bombei insists.

Graigh audibly blows the air out of her mouth. A sigh of exasperation. The sigh of all the ideations of her ineffable emotions summed up in the expelling of air. She plants her heels back on the clock face of the coffee table and lays her head against the back cushion of the chair. She takes the space she's given and counts her breaths to sixty to calm her heart. She counts the next sixty to slow the racing thoughts in her head.

Why can't it all just go away.

The muscles of her outstretched legs shake in her gray leggings. Her hands fidget with the hem of her navy peasant top. She plays with her clothing knowing Bombei is right but refusing to admit it.

"When do you go back to therapy?" Bombei interrupts.

"Tomorrow."

"I'm going with you."

"Why?"

"Not to talk about us. To support you," he says.

"When are you going to talk about you?"

"I'm good." Bombei says, iron in his voice.

Graigh rolls her eyes heavenward. She doesn't push because she doesn't want to fight. Incapable of another petty argument she nods her reticence and leans back against the matching blue suede chair. His response is his presence. He lifts her dead weight from the chair and guides her into their adjacent bedroom. On top of the spread they lay, her back to his front. His arm around her belly, his hand fondling the connection at her navel. Their argument wanes as their tested love remains unwavering.

Sleep finds them both. Dark, dreamless rest. The soundtrack is a hummed lullaby neither of them knows the words to. The scent of magnolias and rose oil perfumes Graigh's dream and fills Bombei's nose as he nuzzles the neck of his wife, he doesn't know smells just like her mother.

Twenty-Six

The smell of burnt sage lingers in the small office room. The air is hazy between Doctor Grace's oversized lounger and where Graigh and Bombei sit. They watch her busy herself, gathering three bottles of water, index cards, and black charcoal pencils to take her notes. They focus on her body movements, her jostling, as she ignores them. Working to still her own mind and refocus her energy from the surprise she received when she saw Graigh being accompanied up the stairs. Unprepared for the unexpected, Doctor Grace checks and double checks her materials before she sits down to face them.

She asks, "Why are you here today?"

Cautiously, Graigh looks at Bombei before answering, "To tell you about my mother."

She squeezes his hand and presses her stiff body into the enveloping cushions of the chaise. Her heels hammer out the commotion of her nerves. They beat out the lies she wants to tell to avoid the truth she has rarely spoken.

"Just your mother?" Doctor Grace questions briefly looking from her sketch pad to observe Graigh's strained face.

"And her father," Bombei says.

"I still don't know much about my father to tell." Graigh responds to Doctor Grace but looks at Bombei.

Her eyes plead with his to let her go at her own pace. To unbury her burdens one at a time. To unlock her skeletons fleshless cadaver, by fleshless cadaver. Her eyes—known to blaze fire, shoot daggers, and slide into corners of accusation —open to their full potential, rounded and sad, big and wide, begging for freedom to find her own way into her family history, and out of it as well. She stares into his face, making her case, in wordless arguments, in persuasive prose that only requires body language instead of audible nouns and verbs. Side by side they sit, thighs touching, fingertips grazing, demeanors zipped and locked in protective cloaks that have done them more harm than good.

Doctor Grace sketches them together. She notices Bombei affects her mood as much as her swallowed memories. She brushes the strokes of their bodies in their silence refusing to rush the work she demanded they do. Arced lines form Bombei's knees inclined inward toward Graigh though her's remain straight ahead. His body is a massive bulwark shielding his wife and unborn son from the obscene words and works of the world. Doctor Grace creates a series of ovals to form his head tilted toward his wife, so that the fuzzy outer layers of her curls just barely brush his cheek. She draws their connection in places she knows they don't consciously intend to be connected.

"Why don't you start by speaking about the parent you knew the least?" Doctor Grace offers engrossed in her sketched graphics.

"That would be my father." Graigh sighs.

"What about him?"

Doctor Grace stops her sketching and calms her pencil to catch her patient praying to the god of her husband's patience for permission to articulate the incomparable. To diffuse the difficult in her mind and make it defenseless against her healing.

"I visited my brother yesterday," Graigh begins taking her hand away from Bombei and placing it in the warmth of her own lap. "I went to ask him about our Mama and Daddy, but we didn't get that far."

"What did he tell you about your father?" Doctor Grace asks.

"He told me my daddy was a musician. He played the trombone. Bombei plays the trumpet. Anyway, he said Daddy left Mama because he couldn't stand no crying baby. I was that crying baby."

"What else did your brother say?"

"About what?" Graigh snaps.

Her conspicuous candor is cloaked again. Doctor Grace sketches furiously catching the harsh line of Graigh's set jaw despite the pregnancy weight threatening to drown her features. The arched eyebrows pointed in their poise ready to fight off any answer to the question posed. The jerk of her hands from her lap to her swelling belly suggesting her motherly defenses for her child are both innate and reflexive when faced with what she doesn't like. The straight back, the stilled feet, the tentative arms ready to swing even though she's still seated. Doctor Grace captures it all in the strokes of her pencil allowing the new silence to show she's backing off, if only slightly, from the sensitive line of questioning.

"I meant about your father," Doctor Grace clarifies. "You don't have to run down your whole conversation with your brother for me, unless he's one of your original issues that brought you to me three months ago."

"Teddy and I have issues but he's not the reason I came to see you."

"So, tell me anything else there is to know about your father."

"I can't. I don't know him. Wouldn't even be able to pick him out in a line up."

"What is his name?"

"Theodore Malcolm Simone. I guess. Teddy's a junior."

"Since you know his name have you ever tried to look him up?"

"No. Never had a longing to."

"Tell me about your mother," Doctor Grace says.

"Mama smelled good, but was always sad, and if I remember correctly, I think she could sing."

"What makes you think that?"

"She had a way of singing my name," Graigh says distantly.

Transported on the arms of time she draws up her dream to explain. "She used to call for me saying 'Graigh Baby. Oh, Graigh Baby. Where oh where is my Graigh Baby.' When she sang for me like that I would always come, even if I was with Grandma Dottie. When she sang for me, I knew she really wanted me."

"What do you mean 'when she *really* wanted you?' She was your mother and you were a young child, why wouldn't she want you?"

Doctor Grace's question is more genuine than professional. Not the traditional follow up. She is perplexed as a mother, empathetic as a therapist, and confused as a daughter. Her human nature asks for an explanation more than her degrees hanging on the smoky gray walls clouded with the residue of cleansing sage. Doctor Grace sets her sketch cards aside and bores into Graigh, singling her out in her vision, forgetting Bombei is beside her. They have a conversation with their eyes.

I told you when you came back to be ready.

I thought I was. I'm trying.

Try harder.

Graigh begins, "My earliest memories are all of Grandma Dottie. Being in her arms to fall asleep. Laying between her and Poppy at night. She fed me, bathed me, took me to church, took me to school, showed me how to do my hair. At every age I can remember, I remember her, not Mama, but now Mama's the one visiting me in my dreams."

"Explain?"

"The other night we were playing hide and seek in Grandma Dottie's room in the old house. Well, the way it used to look. She sang for me to come out, but I stayed hidden. When she pretended not to find me, I came out and surprised her. Then she tickled me until I coughed myself awake."

"How did you feel in the dream?"

"Loved."

"How did you feel when you woke up?"

"Abandoned."

"How did you feel as a child?"

"Loved. At all times. Grandma Dottie made sure of it. She was love."

"And your mother?"

"She was a friend and sometimes she was love. But she wasn't constant. She wasn't consistent. She wasn't there enough for me to remember to miss her when she decided to leave."

"Where did she go?"

"She died. Suicide," Graigh pauses.

Bombei holds her hand dutifully though anger burns inside of him. Envy fueled rage makes him run hot and cold as he listens to details, some he's never been told, with the Doctor they barely know. He is both spectator and support system. Learning when he's already supposed to be a master of his wife's moods; her memories. He holds her hand because it is what he is supposed to do. Even though it's not what he wants to do. He is angry that she can't tell the difference. The arrogance of her ignorance layers mad on top of mad, but he sits listening to learn more about her that he may never be told on his own.

For fourteen and a half years I've been wanting, asking, begging, for the full story. And she goes to therapy and gives it all up.

Resentful, Bombei wants to stand, wants to rise and walk out to illustrate that it is he who should be sought when she wants to unburden her soul's secrets and not some random lady found on Yelp!.

"She was six when her mama died," Bombei says to contribute to the conversation that has nothing to do with him. "Pills and a creole potion of something left her dead in the bed to be discovered by her own son before he went to school."

Bombei fills in the story in Graigh's choked silence. The memories she thought she never formed flood her as if the past were right now and the present a forgotten future.

"She argued with her brother yesterday when she went to ask him more about their parents. I suggested she go; I just didn't think it would turn out like it did."

"How did it turn out?" Doctor Grace asks looking at them both.

Graigh sniffs and taps the back of his hand for Bombei to continue. Rendered mute by her own emotions she breathes as Bombei adds context to the rest of her character.

"Her brother blamed her for their father leaving, their mother's suicide, and then blamed her for her own miscarriage when she was engaged before. By the time she got home, we got into it over the same thing before she told me what happened with Teddy."

"It seems to me like she has you to thank for all this self-exploration she's doing."

"I doubt she's grateful," Bombei says spitefully. "She likes to keep everything to herself and just move on, but she doesn't know how."

"I'm still sitting here you know," Graigh ekes out in a croaky voice.

"Are you grateful for digging up all this pain?" Doctor Grace asks looking only at Graigh.

"I'm still here, aren't I? I'm still coming to see you. What does it matter if I'm grateful or not? I'm here."

Ungrateful is what she is.

"That's how she goes through life," Bombei says not even trying to mask the bitterness in his voice. "She just exists. She's never present. Unless it was with her Grandma Dottie."

"That's unfair and judgmental," Doctor Grace admonishes. "It seems to me in the short time I've been seeing *your* wife, and now you, everything she does is because *you* suggested it. Even if she doesn't want to. Everything she does, she does for you."

"I don't see it?"

"Blind men rarely do."

"Then break it down for me, Doc."

"She came to therapy because you told her she needed to. She went to see her brother yesterday to find out more about her parents at your suggestion."

"I married him because he asked," Graigh adds finding the strength of her voice. "I'm having this baby because he wanted a child. The only thing I haven't compromised on is our house."

"Yet we don't do anything until you say it's okay," Bombei says turning to her. "What you're doing for me you're doing for you because everything is still on Graigh's terms?"

"Bombei, there's no need to point blame," Doctor Grace intercedes. "My only point is that she's trying for you and it seems to not be enough."

"I've been trying for her since we met and it's still not enough because my name ain't Jamal."

"This has nothing to do with Jamal," Graigh snaps. "I don't bring him up, you do. I don't say his name, you do. You feeling inadequate over someone who left me is not my problem, it's yours. Own your shit like you always tell me to do. Your shortcomings and insecurities and the lies you tell yourself are your issues. Not mine."

"That's where you're wrong Graigh," Doctor Grace says holding up her hand. "When you marry your issues become his issues, just as his issues become your issues. The same as your money becomes his money, and his money becomes your money. In a marriage you each inherit the other's wealth, responsibilities, emotions, problems, baggage, and even medical history. You are a union. All of your strengths and weaknesses are united by your relationship, and now you're doing your best to untangle it and figure out how to live and love above the kinks of fallible human nature."

"What the hell does that mean?" Bombei snaps.

"It means you're each trying to please the other person working on half the information because you're not being open with each other about your issues. It's not just

Graigh that needs to be here right now. It's you too. She's not the only one who needs to do the work. So, what are you going to do?"

I doubt you come back.

Doctor Grace keeps her thought to herself as she stands up from her lounger to let her words sink in. She removes herself as a stationary object for them to forge their anger against and forces them to look inward. They sit side by side no longer caressing, no longer touching, no longer inclined toward one another. Their separation is deliberate and rigid. A migrating ant colony could trail the space between their shoulder blades against the chaise, down the middle lengths of their arms, through the thin parting of their thighs, over the hump between their knees and down to the floor past their feet without either one of them ever knowing. They sit side by side in their own worlds. They share space but not life. They are individuals in a couple, singles who decided to get married, parts greater than the combined whole.

Doctor Grace retrieves three more miniature water bottles from the desk refrigerator. She hands one to each of them, before twisting the cap of her own and flopping back on her lounger. They nod their thanks, words still too much to utter as they try to code and decipher their jumble of feelings amidst the psychoanalytical chastisement.

"So, why are you here today?" Doctor Grace asks picking up her sketch cards, ignoring the countenances scowling at her.

"I already answered this question," Graigh huffs.

"Then you should have no problem answering it again."

"To tell you about my mother and father. That's the work you wanted me to do. That's the story you demanded I have the next time I came to see you."

"Okay, so now you've told me. How do you feel? Are you cured?"

"I feel worse than I did the first time I came in here."

"Good. What about you?" Doctor Grace asks Bombei.

"I'm good." He answers dismissively.

"When you're ready to stop lying come back and see me."

"What did you say?" Bombei asks snapping his head toward Graigh.

"She didn't say anything," Doctor Grace calms, trying to assuage his anger. "This is what I do. Read people. Today, I got a read on you. When you're ready to stop lying to yourself come back and see me. Anyway, Graigh, look at you in this sketch. You look better than you did the first time you breached my doors, and it's not all the pregnancy glow."

Doctor Grace hands over her sketch card. Filled in mostly at the beginning of their appointment. The hard lines of Bombei's face are in direct contrast to the serene tranquility resting on hers, roughly sketched in black and white, on the index card.

"I look happier," Graigh says, puzzled by the illustration.

"Perhaps you are."

"I guess."

"So, why are you here today?" Doctor Grace asks for the third time.

"To tell you that I'm scared I'm going to be like my mother when I have this baby, and there's no Grandma Dottie around to pick up the slack when I fail."

"That's what I'm for," Bombei says, hurt evident in his voice.

"I know but it's not the same," Graigh dismisses. "You're going to go back to work. You have your students. Hell, your mom didn't commit suicide when you were six and leave you wandering as an adult if something is mentally wrong with you. You won't have postpartum depression because there's nothing growing inside you that will depart and leave you as alone as we are when we come into this world."

Her words flood out until they become unintelligible between her gasps for breath. The tears hot, heavy, and wet sting her face, roll down her fattening cheeks to her neck and pool in her collar bone. Snot sob clouds her nose and cupids bow. In Bombei's hardened chest she composes herself. He is, once again, her refuge out of duty and empathy. Her defense so she can be vulnerable. He swallows his anger at the stranger who has pried open his wife and revels in the fact that she is at least open and turning to him for solace.

"Graigh postpartum depression is not a given and mental illness manifests itself in many forms," Doctor Grace says. "Your concern for your son now shows you will have concern for him later whether you connect with him in those first few months or not. Even if you feel disjointed you probably won't hurt him."

"You said probably. How can I be sure?" Graigh asks, needing absolutes and not speculation.

"Because I'm here," Bombei answers, kissing through her curls to the top of her head.

His answer is enough that Doctor Grace doesn't respond. She allows them their moment, sliding off the side of her lounger to stand by the office door. Doctor Grace watches Bombei rock Graigh in their embrace. Her eyes are closed; sated and assured in him. His remain open, darting, glancing, glaring at everything except the woman holding on to him. Fire rims his pupils, and desire burns his belly. Doctor Grace observes the familiar twitch in a man's thigh. Bombei shakes his foot to loosen the hold of his masculinity overwhelming the predominantly estrogen energy. She sees the sexual submission he wants to inflict as a fix, and the full surrender already happening that will never allow him to have his way.

Doctor Grace grabs her charcoal and another index card from her desk and sketches furiously in the opened doorway to her office. Straight and curved lines create wild eyes, a pensive forehead, cinched cheeks, and a scraggly beard. She sketches his posture in jeans and a T-shirt; the relaxed wears juxtaposed against his troubled demeanor.

Captured in her notes she emblazons the confusion residing in his body: desire and anger, envy, and agitation. Locked in their embrace they are passion personified without enough compassion to temper their choleric coupling.

"You ready?" Bombei whispers in Graigh's ear.

Graigh nods as she stands shaking herself loose from his grasp realizing she is before an audience and not alone. She walks forward, eyes ahead, sipping her water.

She mumbles, "See you next time," noncommittal to a date.

"Thanks," Bombei mumbles as well.

"This is for you," Doctor Grace says handing him the index card of the two them where he is the central focus.

"Why do I need notes?" He asks still standing inside the door towering over the doctor.

Doctor Grace doesn't answer, "When you're ready to stop lying to yourself come back and see me."

"What am I lying about? I love my wife, and I'm here to support her even when she pisses me off," Bombei says, looking toward Graigh for personal confirmation.

"Like I said, when you're ready to stop lying to yourself come back and see me. Not before. I don't like people wasting my time."

"What am I lying about? You're saying I don't love and support my wife?"

"I'm not saying that at all," Doctor Grace says taking hold of the door handle. "I'm saying come back and see me when you want to tell yourself the truth, the way your wife is doing now."

Twenty-Seven

The bell rings inside the Canal street store announcing another customer. Most people who enter hang in the front of the store rifling through tourist traps set just for them. If it's raining and they didn't expect it, they go for the umbrellas. If it's sunny, humid, and hot, they go for the water, and if they're drunk, they find their way to the beads and plastic masks. It's always Mardi Gras in the Quarter, which means it's always Mardi Gras in Graigh's store in the heart of the city's ancestral revelry and new age debauchery.

Her customers are mostly those looking for quick over the counter prescriptions; an antibiotic for a twenty-four hour itch, a cream to cover a night of less than deadly disappointment, or an emergency shot or serum for a screaming baby or elderly parent on a family trip who didn't plan well for pleasure, pain, and unpredictability. There are some regulars, but they are few and far between. Restaurant owners and employees who find it easier to pick up whatever meds they need at the pharmacy they pass daily, and spend most of their time around, rather than the one that is nearest to their neighborhood.

This time the bell announced a new regular. One whose trips to the Quarter are part of her hidden life that won't remain disclosed for much longer. The candy brown face, and serious eyes whose expression of indecision and doubt was only relieved by finding a kindred circumstance behind the register. Graigh finds her prescription before she asks for it and sets it on the counter as she reaches it, with both hands on her hips and her wristlet dangling beside her.

"How you doing today?"

"Hanging in there, Miss Graigh. Just hanging in there," Janay says.

"Prenatal vitamins only?"

"It's the only thing I need."

"How far along are you now?" Graigh asks scanning the prescription pills.

"Eighteen weeks."

"Congratulations. Did you find out what you're having yet?"

"We're having a little girl."

"That's exciting."

"I guess," Janay says turning her head.

"Janay, you'll be alright. You're not the first woman in the world to get pregnant and have a baby under less than ideal circumstances."

"That's easy for you to say, Miss Graigh. You're married."

And that doesn't make my circumstances ideal.

Graigh says, "Hand me your rewards card please."

She scans the card and bags the pills without a word. She watches Janay follow the commands on the screen of the debit reader. Graigh knows her own silence is abrupt and unwarranted fueled by her present pregnancy, and the ever-present memories of the baby she didn't have.

"Have a good day," Graigh says, once Janay's transaction is complete.

"Is something wrong?" Janay asks. Her eagle eyes implore for answers.

"Nothing. Let's just say I've been where you are more than you know."

In a way, I'm there now.

Janay doesn't respond to the distant answer. She nods her head, places the plastic bag holding her meds around her other wrist, and sits in the knot of her hip, expecting more of an answer from the woman who's given her hope every month just by her pregnant presence behind the counter.

"What name are you thinking about?" Graigh asks stepping over to the pharmacy consultation window.

She opens the latch, steps outside of her sequestered library of prescriptions, and sits in one of the waiting chairs.

"I can't stand all day," Graigh explains. "I'm not supposed to be on my feet that much now, and this boy is killing my back, my ankles and everything else."

Janay sits tentatively beside her.

"Aasha," she answers. "I like Aasha."

"And your boyfriend."

"He's just happy I picked a name."

"That's good. I never got to that point," Graigh says quietly.

"What do you mean? Y'all haven't picked a name yet. Miss Graigh you gotta get on it you're about to pop."

"I mean I was pregnant once before."

"Oh."

Janay's swift and sudden understanding plunges them into an all-encompassing silence. The hum of the overpowering store air conditioner resounds around them. The internal radio blasting jazz, zydeco, top forty, and store promos is loud and obnoxious. Graigh's labored breath is short on intakes. A succinct and successive gasp. Staccato and stubborn she catches air because she knows she has to.

"I was in a similar situation as you," Graigh continues after a few unsuccessful deep breaths. "Finishing school. Engaged. Planning a wedding and then I found out I was pregnant. We were going to keep the baby. I was nervous. He was confident. At least he lied and said he was. Wedding day approaches. I get a Dear Graigh letter with a bullshit explanation from a ghost of a man I thought I knew. Depressed, I lost the baby never knowing what he or she could've ever become."

"I'm so sorry." Janay explodes in condolences. "I didn't know."

"You weren't supposed to know. Do what you need to do to get Aasha here. Take care of yourself, and your body, no matter what."

"Don't blame yourself."

"I've got more than a decade of blame heaped up on this body. But this boy right here might change that," Graigh says pointing at her belly.

"What do you mean?"

Graigh sighs before answering. Her eyes meet Janay's. Spreading nose to wide nose. Fattened face to fattening face. Cocoa to caramel candy skin. Curly bun to silky ponytail. She examines herself from her other life in the past, showing up again in the future in someone else's body. She looks at the woman before her, sent to her by the world to teach her a lesson she did not learn. The universe's way of making sure she does not make the same mistakes and moves on from her history.

"Truth be told, I didn't want this baby," Graigh says. "I wasn't ready for this baby. In some ways, I'm still not. Still not comfortable carrying him. But the bigger I get, the stronger he gets, the more determined his kicks get for me to keep opening my heart, the more everything else melts away. Now I just want him here, in my arms, lying next to me."

"What does your husband say?"

"Sometimes he resents me for how I feel but he will never tell me that. He tries to be supportive as I work through my shit, but you know he's a man and his ego is fragile. He doesn't like feeling threatened by someone he's never met."

"Jeff resents me because he doesn't think I care about the baby."

"Do you care?"

"I care. I love her, but this was not the plan."

"Does anything in life ever go according to our plans?"

"No, but you know what I mean."

"I do. You won't ever have the chance to do you without thinking about your daughter."

"Exactly," Janay agrees. "His life is not going to change. His job options, how much he makes, none of that will change. But all of that will change for me."

"I understand."

"So, like I said, this was not the plan."

"Then have the baby and you and Jeff can make a new plan. Together. One that doesn't feel like you're making all the sacrifices."

"And what about you?" Janay asks.

"I'm having the baby in ten weeks; more or less. Any plans after that are to be determined. I have an idea right now, but my husband is against it."

"Your life is already together," Janay assesses. "We're just starting."

"But if you're starting together, why worry?"

"It'd be different if we were engaged or married. We're not. Right now, I'm just going to be his baby mama. That shit ain't cute."

And being engaged or a wife offers no more guarantees or securities.

Graigh doesn't oppose Janay's logic. She doesn't dispute her truth. It is the same way she felt with Jamal. They had more commitment at the time than Janay does now, and still the relationship ended with her destined to be a baby mama until she was welcomed into the club of mothers who miscarry. She nods to herself knowingly, understanding that children born out of wedlock are assumed to be destined to be a scourge on the Black race; diagnosed as a problem at their birth. Yet no one talks about the disease that produces these problem children. Love with no strings attached. Love without commitment. Fucking without love. No one talks about the disease of wanting to be needed, wanted, adored, cherished, remembered, and honored. Nobody talks about wanting to be loved so badly, that desperately, that leads to rash decisions, stolen moments, and problem children ten months later. Graigh nods knowingly, knowing that everyone

—mothers, grandmothers, momos, other baby mamas, and never to be mother-in-laws—criticize the diagnosis, determined to get a second opinion, while no one ever addresses the disease.

"Do you want more?" Graigh asks.

"I don't know. I just want to graduate without a baby gnawing at my nipples when I cross the stage. Now I have to take double the load of classes this summer and next semester so I can finish early, get my degree, have my baby, and be a stay at home baby mama while I look for my first job."

"But you have a plan. You just don't like it. I'm a tell you something Janay that people have been telling me for years. Get over it. This is life."

"That shit's easier said than done."

"You're preaching to the choir," Graigh commiserates.

"I gotta get going," Janay stands. "I can't read my books by osmosis, and Lord knows every time I open one this little girl is like 'Mommy, let's take a nap.'"

"That's going to get worse before it gets better. I need a nap right now. Be careful out there in that heat."

"I didn't park too far away."

Janay steps away from the makeshift waiting area leaving Graigh seated outside the counter. Away from her pills, isolated in her thoughts, she hums a song Bombei used to play. She taps the rhythm on her belly to her baby boy growing beneath it.

He kicks.

She rubs the spot and pokes back.

He kicks.

Graigh holds the back cushion of the waiting area chair. She uses it as leverage to get to her feet. One hand on the chair, the other on her belly, she pushes him away from her ribs, and to the other side of her body.

He kicks and moves back to where he was.

"Stop now. That hurts," Graigh says to her jostling stomach.

He kicks.

The store bell dings. Graigh waddles back behind her counter to the back of her shelves of pills and potions that heal ailments and sometimes even cure disease. All but one. At her fingertips she has the remedy for viral infections, the temporary reprieve from terminal illness, and concoctions marketed as proven cures for the common cold. Between her shelves as tall as walls she can hold in her hand respite for the sick and weary, relief for the worried, and health for those who need healing. She has at her disposal almost every bottleable cure known to man; except one. There is no pill for the lovesick, there is no potion for the heartbroken, there is no concoction for the head over heels, and there is no rest for the loveless or love lost. For that disease she has no answer to bottle and instruct as she hands it over to waiting patients. All she can offer, all anyone can offer, is an autopsy of what went wrong, a diagnosis for when it is over, or a cautionary smile when it moves to a different level. For love can transform from death to life, from what you can't live with, to what you refuse to live without. A disease that goes from attacking your body to cooperating with it; love is a cure without a concoction.

He kicks.

The store bell dings.

The air conditioner hums.

The radio promo ends. Music comes on. A woman's voice belts about her disease. She sings her diagnosis and her remedy. Her reprieve is to lose, her plan to win again, all after she experienced the side effects of an unknown him.

"I'm here to pick up my prescription," a customer says leaning over the counter.

Graigh walks toward the customer humming along with the radio. She taps the beat on her belly for her baby to hear too.

He kicks.

"How may I help you?" she asks.

The man slides the prescription paper across the counter as if he can't stand to touch it. She picks up the note and reads the doctor's instructions.

"One moment," she says turning to her shelves. "I have to get it out of the back."

Graigh rummages through potent panaceas to find the latest elixir for the most common disease that ends in many different diagnoses.

"Follow the directions on the label," Graigh says approaching the customer at the counter again.

"Okay," he says gruffly. "How long will it take?"

Graigh scans the bottle. "You should feel a lot better in three to five days. A week at most."

Twenty-Eight

July 1—30 Weeks

"Girl I thought the week would never end," Joy exclaims, inside the exam room.

"Oh yeah, why is that?" Graigh asks, laid out on the cushioned table.

"Because I had to make sure I got here to see your pregnant ass."

"My pregnant ass is not the only reason you're here *this* weekend."

"What's your point?" Joy deadpans. "Essence Fest *just happened* to coincide with your doctor's appointment. Two birds."

Graigh rolls her eyes, "Whatever. That's what I thought."

"Anyway, I'm just happy I get to see this belly in person. The only pictures you post on FaceBook and Instagram are selfies and memes. Nobody can tell you're pregnant from that."

"Nobody needs to know I'm pregnant."

"I do."

"You know me in real life?"

"I do, and you have yet to send me a bumpie?"

"What the hell is a bumpie?"

"Chile, check your app. That's when you take a picture of your baby bump to keep up with the growing process."

"I thought people only did that as part of a photo shoot," Graigh says.

"Sometimes," Joy says.

"I saw pictures of a white couple at the gas station. He filled her up until she exploded a baby."

"I saw that one too. I guess it went viral."

"Me and my baby don't ever need to be viral."

"Okay pharmacist. It's not that kind of viral."

"I know, but it still sounds nasty as hell. Who wants to be viral?"

"Kylie Jenner."

"Knock, knock," Doctor Marcella says sweeping into the room.

"Graigh this is your doctor?" Joy asks astounded by the statuesque, graying woman in the white lab coat. "Why didn't you tell me she was so fly."

"It's kind of hard to say how fabulous my doctor is when she's looking at places, I don't even let my husband see."

"You let him see most of it, or you wouldn't be here now," Doctor Marcella quips.

"And she's shady. I like you," Joy says.

"I like you too," Doctor Marcella says right back. "You've got this lady here laughing instead of looking tense and anxious like she usually does when she's up on my table. You should come with her to every appointment."

"I wish I could but I'm visiting from Tallahassee."

"Got it."

"She was my first bundle of Joy," Graigh jokes.

"Joy Matthews," she says extending her hand to Doctor Marcella.

"Marcella Jean-Pierre."

"How've you been doing since the last time I saw you?" Doctor Marcella asks Graigh.

"My feet hurt. My back hurts. I can't sleep. It's hot outside. I'm hot inside. I sweat everywhere, and when I'm stank, I'm too tired to get in the shower, and I have no patience to sit in the tub only to need help getting up when I'm done."

"Aah, you're at that place every pregnant woman reaches. You're ready to be done."

"Been ready," Graigh emphasizes.

"Seven more weeks and your little boy will be here. Give or take."

"Are you sure we can't make it three."

"Graigh, there's no reason to induce you early. You just barely missed gestational diabetes. Let's not rock the boat trying to induce you and create more problems than you want. We don't want your anxiety to elevate to high blood pressure, or preeclampsia. He'll be here on his time."

"So, that's a no?"

"Sounds like a 'hell no' to me," Joy giggles.

"Was anybody even talking to you?" Graigh snaps.

"Don't get mad at me because you can't have your way."

"Hush, Joy."

Girlish laughter resounds in the room of women. The ease of their camaraderie is cemented in banter. Joy sits back in the corner chair, beside the window and gives Doctor Marcella room to work. Graigh's appointment routine begins. Baby listening gel is squirted on her protruding belly. The sonic wand begins its fishing expedition. Silence encompasses the room. Each woman holds her breath until the sounds of life break through the skin. The steady staccato rhythm of the baby's heartbeat penetrates the sterile space followed by a collective sigh of relief. Graigh's sigh and then cough is the loudest. It overtakes the steady "wah, wah, wah" of the baby living inside of her as chortles of phlegm rattle along her throat, clouding the words that can't escape her vocal cords. The corners of her eyes tear as she struggles to sit up and and breathe. The wand drops from her belly and away from Doctor Marcella's hand. She and Joy grab each one of

Graigh's arms and pull her forward. They prop her upright. Joy's hand rests on Graigh's lower back, Doctor Marcella's hand rests at her mid back. They rub circular motions on her bare skin sending their calm energy into her body until the coughing spell passes, her inflamed lungs rest, and her breath returns to normal.

Joy and Doctor Marcella step away from her tentatively. Cautious steps. The steps you take when you're unsure of whether you should stay or go, if you're needed or not.

"Thank you," Graigh mutters laying back on the table.

Her brown face is flushed red, her undertones overtake her cocoa complexion. She dabs at her eyes with the pads of her fingers. Graigh dries away the dampness and pulls apart her lashes as she plays with her face to avoid facing her friend and doctor. She ignores the stares boring into her hands that are really meant for her eyes. Her fingers sweep across her brows, then her closed lids and the corners of her eyes until she can't wipe anymore; until her eyes are itchy from her own irritation and not the tears she coughed out in distress.

Doctor Marcella breaks the turgid air. "Your feet hurt, your back hurts, you can't sleep, you're hot, and sweaty, and too drained to bathe. Nowhere in there did you mention you can barely breathe."

"Because there's nothing else you can do for me about that, just like you can't induce me early and take this baby out so I can go back to breathing normally."

"So, the baby's to blame for why she almost died?" Joy asks.

"She didn't almost die," Doctor Marcella cautions. "And the baby is not exactly to blame."

"Not exactly means partially." Joy says flatly.

"Joy, just listen. Damn!" Graigh snaps.

"She speaks."

"How are you feeling?" Doctor Marcella asks Graigh.

"I'm fine now."

"Are you?"

"Yeah, just add sighing to the list of things that trigger coughing fits. It joins deep breaths, laughing too much, too long, or too hard, and snoring."

"Damn, Graigh you can't do shit."

"Shut. Up. Joy."

"Your breathing may be heavier while pregnant," Doctor Marcella begins. "Especially in this last trimester. But that doesn't mean it should necessarily be harder. Or that you should slip into convulsions every time you feel a tickle in your throat."

"I know," Graigh admits. "I tried yoga to help with the breathing."

"Oh really," Doctor Marcella perks. "How did it go?"

"It's easiest when I'm sitting still and doing nothing. But trying to combine the way they breathe in class while doing half the poses is too much."

"Well, keep trying since you refuse to take the inhaler. Though it would help since it seems like everything around you causes you to cough," Doctor Marcella says gently.

"She's stubborn, Doc, I thought you knew that by now," Joy says.

"Ignore her," Graigh says.

Doctor Marcella continues, "It's most likely the added weight from the baby. You've already gained the recommended 30 pounds for the entire pregnancy. These next ten weeks will be a challenge for you, especially in the heat. As much as I recommend walking to stay active, I'm considering that you may need to be on bed rest, or at the very least, stay off your feet for the majority of the day."

"That means you need to stop working," Joy says plainly.

"I have a stool at work."

"But I'm sure you only use it once you're already tired, not to keep you from getting tired."

"Stop acting like you know me."

"But it seems like she does," Doctor Marcella interjects. "You need to do whatever is necessary to take care of yourself or you're not going to just stress yourself, but your baby."

"Listen to the doctor, Graigh."

"I'm listening, Joy."

"You may have also developed allergies since being pregnant. I don't want you to take anything for it just yet but try and limit your time outside as well."

"So much for Essence Fest this weekend," Graigh says.

"Graigh, we can still hang," Joy says. "We just need to be inside."

"Inside, outside, Essence Fest is everywhere." Graigh snickers.

"But you know good and well you don't want to be around a bunch of people outside."

"You're right I don't, but since Bombei is playing in the super lounge tomorrow night I was prepared to be out and about until I fall out."

"Let's have none of that," Doctor Marcella cuts in. "Take care of yourself and I'll see you in three weeks."

Doctor Marcella sweeps out of the room. Her African print circle skirt and white lab coat flow behind her as she goes. The back of her mules slap her feet as she walks down the linoleum lined hallway. The door closes snugly walling off the sound of walking. Its finality leaves an enduring silence, Joy's accusing stare, and Graigh's sullen non-verbal response.

She towels off the baby heartbeat gel from her belly and the tops of her pants, then pulls down her green peplum pregnancy top. The fabric pulls away and flows over her belly, even though the expandable elastic of her maternity cutoffs lay right on her skin.

"Help me up," Graigh demands.

"So, we not gon' talk about what just happened? We're just going to get up and walk out like you didn't almost die in the doctor's office?"

"Joy, I didn't die. I wasn't even close to death. Doctor Marcella said the same thing. Stop overreacting. I just couldn't breathe."

"The last person who publicly declared he couldn't breathe is dead."

"Yeah, but I'm not being choked to death by the police."

"Breathing is the only way you live."

"Which is exactly what I'm doing now. Now help me up and quit asking me questions before I start coughing again."

"You're lucky you're pregnant?"

"Why is that?"

"Because otherwise I'd beat you up."

"Joy, hush and help me off this damn table please."

"What do you do when Bombei's not here?" Joy asks getting out of her chair and walking toward Graigh.

"He's always here. Every appointment. Sitting in that chair once he gets kicked off the doctor's stool."

"Your ass is spoiled."

"No," Graigh says, stepping down to the ground. "Just loved."

"Whatever."

"Don't be jealous."

"Girl, ain't nobody jealous of you and Bombei. Tony and Junior treat me just fine."

"Then why did your voice go up an octave?"

"Look who's talking in musical terms. I guess you finally learned something from your man."

"And now you're changing the subject."

"You know what, I can't stand you."

"Back at you, Boo. Now let's go."

"We can leave, but we're still going to talk about you almost dying."

Graigh turns her face and rolls her eyes at Joy. The gesture is returned. Graigh heaps her purse on her shoulder from the exam table, pulls the door handle and walks the rectangular halls of the medical office until she reaches the receptionist.

"Three weeks," Graigh says, handing over her chart.

"We'll see you back July twenty-fourth. Is this same time okay?"

"That works," Graigh says, typing the appointment reminder in her phone. "See you then."

Graigh leads the way out of the office and toward the elevator. She and Joy stand in silence waiting for their ride. Inside the elevator, they are shoulder to shoulder facing the doors. Graigh fidgets—sunglasses on her face, gum in her mouth, lip gloss applied to her lips, keys in her hand—to block Joy's interrogation.

They reach the main floor of the hospital complex and walk out together. Even with Graigh's slower pace, their strides match, and their steps are in sync. Joy makes the intentional adjustment to stay with Graigh. Their walk is one of friends who've known each other since freshman year at FAM. Friends who climbed the campus' hills in sneakers, sandals, and heels once they mastered the pits, and potholes of the grass and pavement. From sharing a dorm, to a college apartment, to guest rooms when one is in town visiting the other, their synchronicity is indicative of friends who've swapped stories of failed tests, first loves, bad sex, great sex, bad breakups and pre-wedding jitters.

They walk across the parking lot to their awaiting cars. Joy is parked behind Graigh. She arrived in the city, dropped Tony and the luggage off with Bombei, and kept on rolling to the hospital to be with her friend. With their strides identical, thoughts intuitive, and feelings empathic they get into their cars without more words, without discussions, or even acknowledging the conversation they know they're going to have as Graigh leads the way to her home.

The phone ringing inside Graigh's truck does not surprise her. It is anticipated. So is her begrudging, "Hello."

"What's with the cough?" Joy asks.

"Blame Katrina."

"You can't blame Katrina for everything."

"Yes, I can, and this time, it's really her fault."

"How's that."

"Storm, flood, debris, toxins. Trailer, heat, humidity, formaldehyde equals hashtag Katrina cough, or bronchial asthma."

"For true, Graigh?"

"Are you practicing your New Orleans accent?"

"When in Rome."

"Yes, it's true. They've tried to get me to take an inhaler, but this is the first time it's been this bad. I swear this boy is determined to sap everything out of me including my air."

"Don't blame the baby, you're the one who got knocked up," Joy jokes.

"I know you're not talking, asking me all the time when I'm going to have a baby. Between you and Bombei I didn't know whose pressure was worst."

"Whatever. I'm not the one who got you pregnant so you can't put that on me."

"Anyway . . . I've been walking and doing yoga to increase my lung capacity, but if I have allergies now, then I have no choice but to stay inside and get fat."

"You're not fat, Graigh, you're pregnant."

"The baby is only like five pounds which means those other twenty-five pounds are all me and I still have seven weeks to go. You heard the doctor. She didn't say it, but she meant it. I'm fat and I need to slow down but all I want to do is sleep and eat, and I can't even sleep because I'm either getting kicked all night, or I'm up coughing and wheezing all night, with Bombei staring at me like I'm about to die."

Joy lets Graigh rant and calm down without commentary. She follows behind her friend over the Industrial Canal into the lower Ninth Ward. They are silent on the phone. Their breaths speak for them. What's not being said speaks the loudest. They blow through the green lights passing the sights along Claiborne street, the fire station, the school, until Graigh turns on Charbonnet. She pulls in behind

Bombei and Joy parks on the street in front of the house. Their call is ended without a goodbye.

Joy gets out first and quickly makes her way to Graigh's door. She wants to be there to see her friend's face when she steps out of her cocoon to face the world. The first thing she notices are the tear streaked stains dried on thickening cheeks. Eyes wiped red to hide the truth.

"Come here," Joy says enfolding Graigh in a hug.

"I'm fine, Joy."

"No, you're not. You don't have to lie to me."

"I'm not."

"Graigh, just let me hug you. Damn."

She relents and falls into her friend's arms. Baby belly to mommy pooch they embrace. Arms around each other's backs they stand their holding, listening to nothing but breath, air, and the occasional bird. Graigh sighs and shrugs letting the imaginary weight on her shoulders, the invisible pressure she carries, be lifted by her other half. Her sister-friend. Her kindred spirit. Her soulmate.

"How do you feel?" Joy asks.

"I'm still scared shitless."

"And Bombei? What does he say?"

"If I tell him that he gets pissed. One day I told him I was faking it until I make it. Just because most days I worry .. . Worry about if we're all going to make it until the due date. But we didn't get that far before he lost his shit and made it about Jamal."

"Was it about Jamal?" Joy asks unburying her head to look at Graigh's face.

"No. And just like I told him, everything ain't about Jamal."

"I'm asking, not accusing."

"I appreciate you for it, but I finally took Bombei's advice to go to therapy and do what you've been telling me to do for years, let it go."

"And you've been keeping that from me for how long?"

"Don't act like you're hurt poking your lip out at me. I ain't Tony."

"Whatever. You should've told me."

"There's nothing to tell. I see this lady when I need to. She's bitchy and straight to the point which is probably what I need. She forces me to be honest and keep things in perspective."

"What does she say?"

"She tells me I have to do the work to understand and deal with my feelings instead of stuffing them."

"And what are you doing?"

"I'm trying to do that, but with him it's so damn difficult."

"Did you think it was going to be easy?"

"I don't know what I thought."

"Is that why you're scared."

"Maybe. What's the point of us having this baby if we're not going to make it as a couple?"

"Who said anything about divorce?"

"No one."

"So how did your mind get there?"

Because no one gets everything.

Graigh doesn't answer. She lets Joy go, shrugs her shoulders, adjusts the hem of her green top, and walks away. Joy follows leaving a comma in the conversation she knows they will resume. Graigh unlocks the door and pushes her way inside the cool air of the old, but new house. Jovial men's voices fill the entire space. Tony and Bombei laughing and joking in the kitchen carries to them in the white room. The one nearly identical to what Grandma Dottie had before Katrina came to kill, steal, and destroy.

"They sound like they're having a good time," Graigh says.

"Probably talking about us." Joy says adjusting her clothes in the mirror beside Graigh.

She fusses with the strapless top of her blue maxi dress, tucking in the hanger strings, and lifting her strapless bra back into a suitable position.

"Ooh, Girl that heat just makes you want to get naked."

"Just wait until tonight for that. I put y'all in the last room, so I don't have to hear you two going at it."

"Well, at least you know." Joy giggles.

"Yeah I do." Graigh smiles. "It works both ways. The nursery in the middle is the buffer for both of us."

"Ooh, Graigh. Are you still doing the nasty?"

"I said I'm scared shitless. That doesn't have anything to do with sex. Most times it's the only time my mind isn't on anything and everything else."

"Do tell."

"Rough, angry, fun, slow, it doesn't matter. He gives it, I take it, give it back."

"So, you do love your husband."

"Never said I didn't."

"Then how did you get to things not working out."

"In my experiences, not much does?"

"Graigh, look at me. You're thirty weeks pregnant. That beautiful baby boy will be here before you know it. You and Bombei are going to love on him and dote on him through the smiles, the giggles, the screams, the shitty diapers, the terrible twos, threes, fours, and the surly teens. And you're going to love each other more through it. You've won Graigh. You've got to accept that you've won. You're in this big beautiful house where you've always wanted to be, your husband is by your side, and you're starting a family of your own. You've won."

"But it doesn't feel like it."

"Look at yourself in the mirror Graigh. I know you don't like to but look at yourself. You're not the same woman who ran out of Tallahassee with your feelings on your forehead. Hell, you're not the same woman who came back home after the storm determined to rebuild. You've done it all and are finally reaping the rewards. Why can't you settle in your own happiness?"

"Maybe, I'm afraid of that too. Afraid that once I do, the other shoe will drop, and everything will be taken away."

No one gets everything.

"Do you hear that man in there? He ain't going nowhere. Allow yourself to be happy."

I'll try.

Graigh nods her head while looking at herself through the mosaic mirrors. Beside Joy she sees both the women they were and the women they've become. From fighting the last phase of pubescent acne, to learning how to apply makeup, buying clothes meant for their shape, and walking in heels no matter how much their feet hurt. Their friendship is more of a sisterhood. Graigh leans her head on Joy trying to release the weight and pressure she feels. Shoulder to shoulder, kinky twists to jumbo box braids, they look in the mirror.

"We've come a long way," Graigh says.

"Girl . . . Yes. We. Have. And guess what?"

"What's that best friend?"

"We've won."

"I guess we did."

"You've gotta believe that."

"I will."

I'll try.

Joy nods her head in acceptance knowing the slight admission, the tiny mention of trying, is good enough for now. She grabs Graigh's hand and leads her through her own house. Through the dining room, past the Katrina cross and into the kitchen where they thought the men were. Their noise is coming from the backyard. Bombei and Tony stand over the grill, beers in one hand, tongs, and a spatula in the other tag teaming dinner. Joy leads Graigh outside.

"Hey," Bombei and Tony say together.

"What, y'all doing out here." Joy asks.

"Dinner," Tony says. He kisses Joy on the nose.

"How was the appointment?" Bombei asks, walking to Graigh who stands just below the back door.

"The baby is fine, but I may have allergies now."

"Why's that?"

"I had a fit in the doctor's office."

"Damn, Bae, I'm sorry."

"Joy was there and so was Doctor Marcella. I'm okay. Just need to stay inside and off my feet."

"Then go inside away from the smoke, I'll bring you a plate."

Bombei kisses Graigh's forehead and returns to the grill.

"I'll come with you," Joy says pecking Tony's lips. "Alright y'all, don't enjoy this bro-fest too much."

"Go in the house," Tony yells from the grill.

"Don't start showing out just because Bombei is here."

"Whatever woman."

"Whatever man."

Graigh follows Joy inside. She grabs two glasses out of the cabinet and the pitcher from the refrigerator. She pours water for herself and Joy, and then takes a seat at the island. They sit and sip watching Bombei and Tony through the doors.

"I told you, you won," Joy says taking another sip. "Tony ain't even all that funny, and Bombei's out there cracking up."

"You laugh at his jokes."

"I'm his wife. I'm supposed to. Bombei doesn't have to and he's still laughing. That's a winner right there."

"Maybe he is. Maybe I'll keep him around for a little while longer."

"Like forever?"

"Maybe."

"Girl, stop. Just say it. You won."

"Perhaps we both did."

Twenty-Nine

Music ricochets from concrete wall to concrete wall inside the Super Dome. Dim lights in the hallways do nothing to dim the shine of the different shades of brown people who are oiled up, moisturized, and buttered down. From créme brûlée custard to deep cocoa, every hue and tone of skin-folk is in view. Legs, arms, thighs, backs, breasts, toes, bellies, and more are all dressed up and displayed like acrylic on canvas. Body glitter and gold dust flakes shimmer and shine on bronze skin. Eyeshadows in all the colors of all the palettes are mixed with muddy contours, and drastic highlights, feathers for lashes, and crowns made of hair. African prints are tucked and wrapped, tied, and hiked, zipped, and buttoned across busts, around heads, over butts, patched on pockets, stitched from seam to seam, and adorned as dresses, rompers, skirts, and shirts. Bangles jangle from arms, hefty earrings pull heavy loads on dangling lobes, and rings right themselves on every finger wrapping around the base to the knuckles, and some nearly reaching the nails. Hair is worn in every permutation from bone straight to 4c kinks, Sisquo blonde to rainbow highlights, up dos, down dos, lobs, bobs, wigs, and weaves. Inside the Dome it is a classy carnival made of mostly women. The multi-degreed, heavily pedigreed Essence veterans, to the first-time summer breakers hoping to aspire to the #lifegoals and #blackgirlmagic of the executives being unexecutive for the one weekend they wait and plan for. The girls' trip of all girls' trips. Inside the Dome, Graigh, Joy, and Tony maneuver their way through the organized chaos. They walk the perimeter surrounding the main stage to the superlounge where Dougie and Bombei will play on stage.

"I don't think I can hear myself think in here," Joy says loudly.

"You wanted to do Essence. This is Essence," Graigh says.

"Has it always been like this?"

"The last time I came I was a kid tagging along with Grandma Dottie. Patti Labelle started offstage with her shoes on the piano and Frankie Beverly and Maze closed with the whole arena walking out singing Joy & Pain. And even then, it was loud. The women were a little more conservative but not by much."

"Now it's 'bye-bye, Patti Labelle' and 'hello, Beyoncé'."

"Not really. Chaka Khan. Diana Ross. The divas still come, and everybody gets it in together. And everybody loves Beyoncé."

"I know that's right."

"And why am I here?" Tony asks.

"Because you're here to support your brothers in bromance who happen to be performing in the band."

"Hashtag gigging," Graigh says, rolling her eyes.

"Don't be like that, Graigh. You know you're proud."

"I'm proud, I just wish my big ass wasn't pregnant, walking around this Dome. I'm tired."

"Girl come on. We're here now. Just enjoy it. The set shouldn't be that long."

"Tell Bombei to forgive me if I fall asleep."

"You will not fall asleep with all this noise."

"I did with Dottie. No reason to change it up now."

"You ladies want anything to drink?" Tony asks after they situate themselves at a reserved table.

"Cranberry juice for me," Graigh says.

"I'll take the same. But put some vodka in mine."

"What kind?"

"Ciroc; peach if they have it."

"Got it," Tony says taking the drink order to the bar behind them.

Graigh and Joy sit at the table that is high above the main floor crowd pressed up against the black tarp barriers to separate the people from the stars. She pushes her chair back to comfortably accommodate her belly, then dabs at the perspiration accumulated on her top lip from the walk around the Dome. Graigh folds the cocktail napkin in half and uses it as a fan. Her face and pits receive the first of the self-created air to no avail. She sets the shredded paper back on the table and drums her fingers against the hard top. Joy watches Graigh's ministrations as she adjusts the tie of her royal blue tunic dress and moves her twists, adorned with cowrie shells and braid cuffs, from half up and half down to a high puff ponytail.

"I got your drinks ladies," Tony says setting their glasses on the table.

"Thanks, Love," Joy says, kissing his mouth.

He bends his wiry frame into the open seat beside his wife. Low haircut, clean shaven, tan linen pants, and a white linen shirt, lay against his sepia skin. The swaths of fabric are distinctly cool and chic as if he were dressed for the desert in Dubai and not the swampy heat of what was once one of America's largest slave ports. Ever the academic, his black, half rimmed glasses sit close to his face. He wears his life's work on his sleeve, from cultural anthropology student to professor, he is the definition of the venerable and gracefully aging man.

"What are you ladies talking about?" Tony asks.

"Nothing," Joy says quickly. "Just watching Graigh go through the motions of being an uncomfortable pregnant lady."

"That wasn't very nice," Tony chides.

"Thank you, Tony." Graigh says. "At least somebody has some manners around here."

"Manners my ass. You are uncomfortable. And the way you keep pulling at your clothes, and your hair, and fanning and carrying on is making me uncomfortable too. I might as well get naked for you because that's where you're headed."

Joy's words are accompanied with a dramatic imitation of Graigh's motions. She shrugs her shoulders, pulls at her emerald, jade, and black floral romper, and tosses her braids from side to side. When she's done, she knocks back her drink and dramatically slams the glass on the table.

"I didn't do all that," Graigh says, rolling her eyes.

"You might as well have."

"Why are you two friends again?" Tony smirks.

"You know, I sometimes wonder the same thing," Graigh nods.

"We're friends because who else would have been your maid of honor, and who else is going to plan your baby shower?"

"Uh, ma'am, I did the exact same thing for you. So, don't trip."

"I know. Payback's a bitch," Joy cackles.

"Don't get any ideas," Graigh admonishes. "I'm not playing too many stupid games, and you can forget about people coming up to rub my belly for good luck, or measure me and see how fat I've gotten. It's too hot for all that."

"Do you two ever agree on anything?" Tony asks jokingly.

"More than you know, Love," Joy says reassuringly. "More than you know?"

"Like what?"

"We agreed that Graigh should have gone out with Bombei. We agreed that she married the *right* one. We agreed she's going to be the best mother in the world to this big behind boy. And we agree that I'm the bestest best friend ever."

"You were doing so well until then." Graigh laughs, then sips her cranberry juice.

"Speaking of the one," Tony says. "Graigh I have something to tell you when we get out of here."

"No, he doesn't." Joy elbows his arm.

"Yes, I do. It's not like it's going to matter."

"Then I'll tell her."

"Tell me what?" Graigh asks puzzled.

"Don't worry about it, it's not important right now," Joy dismisses. "Let's enjoy the show."

"Let's," Graigh says, turning toward the stage.

The music starts in the darkness. The trumpets roar loud and clear. The house lights go black and the stage lights come up. Bombei and Dougie play under a spotlight. In time together, their fingers moving furiously, and their cheeks expand like blow fish and contract just as quickly. Their advanced two step takes them upstage and downstage, and side to side. They crisscross each other swinging in their upper bodies from high to low, their trumpets moving and producing sounds to electrify the crowds. They transition from "Jock-a-Mo" to "Bouncing Back" as the rest of the band backs them up through the set that includes traditional New Orleans music to Cash Money and Big Freedia to bring out the artist who will perform in front of the mic-stand set at center stage.

Graigh stands to her bejeweled sandaled feet to applaud Bombei and Dougie's duet as they walk the soloist to the mic. She shrieks at the top of her lungs for the trumpeters while the rest of the audience welcomes the singer who glows under the advance adoration. The sounds of the band drop low as the music from the backing track comes up higher, the audience below remains standing. Graigh sits back down.

"You're pretty proud," Joy says smugly.

"Of course, I am. This is Essence Fest and my man is on the freaking stage. Who wouldn't be proud?"

"Just thought you were tired, sleepy, uncomfortable, too hot, and too pregnant to be here."

"I am. But I'm still here."

"I guess he won too," Joy says, sipping the morsels of liquid remaining in her glass.

"We both did," Graigh smiles, pleased with herself.

"Did you guys enjoy the show?" Bombei asks, back in their bedroom.

"Of course. It's good to see you in your element outside of a school function," Graigh says, untying the belted string of her dress.

"Let me get that."

He takes Graigh's hands and puts them at her side. His fingers travel from the skin beneath the hem of her dress, over her rounded cheeks to the middle of her back. They crawl around to the front of her dress and loosen the knot cinching her pregnant shape. Bombei lets the long string drop to the floor at their feet. He takes her hands in his and kisses the back of each.

"I saw you cheering," he says.

"You were good. It was a good set. We all were hooting and hollering for you."

"Joy and Tony liked it too?"

"Yeah," Graigh says, letting her voice trail.

"Why'd you say it like that?" Bombei asks.

"They were acting strange tonight."

"How so?"

"Tony said he had to tell me something, and Joy shut him down. I don't think I've ever seen that happen?"

"Is she pregnant?"

"Naw. She would've told me that before tonight. It's something else."

"What did they say?"

"Nothing. She said it wasn't important, and that she'd tell me later."

"Then it's not important, and she'll tell you later."

"I just think it is," Graigh muses.

"Don't worry about it," Bombei says reaching for Graigh.

He grabs the hem of her dress, takes a handful of fabric in each grasp and lifts. The dress grazes her skin as it's removed, skimming her hips, the backs of her arms, and the sides of her face. He drops it to the floor, beside the ribbon for a belt. A royal blue G-string and matching bra leave little for his imagination. Barefoot and heavily pregnant Graigh sashays to the door of the closet. Reaching her hands behind her back, she unclasps her bra, and throws it toward the pile on the floor.

She hits the switch controlling the light on the wall and walks in darkness toward the bed. The white numbers of the iHome clock illuminate the time. Three a.m. The time when the only things open are Waffle House, legs, and mouths. The only necessary sounds are moans and the occasional siren drowned out by whines and wails from bedrooms, hotels, and motels citywide.

"Play me," Graigh says.

He obliges her request, leads them to the bed, and lays down behind her. Playing her like he played his trumpet, Bombei presses his fingers up and down her body. The fingers of his right hand play her thighs, then her hips. Grooving in the dimples above her butt, he plays the flats across her smooth back, then comes down to find the rhythms in her arm and elbow. His fingers write a song without notes, scale the octaves without keys, and turn her body into an instrument of song.

Together they are a two-man band writing their own rhymes in the writhes of their bodies. They create their own cadence in the contortion of their limbs and generate their own genre by the gesticulation of their voices. They are frenetic points of energy; kinetic and crazed, firing synapses, transmitting passion and pleasure between their own orifices of light. Their rhythm is off the scales and departed from any clef. They are freestyle. They are improv. They are jazz. They are love.

When he leaves her elysium breath returns to them, fast and deep, before smoothing out with still regularity. She rests against his back, blowing out air as her skin cools, her fantasies fade, and lucidity returns. His heartbeat plays on against her back. His hands twirl in her twists, following the extension of one tendril over the smooth back of the cowrie shell at the end, up the soft strands of hair, to the thick roots of her scalp. He plays in the mass of curly follicles, massaging the top of her head with experienced hands.

"How was that?" Bombei asks after the wail of a siren passes by.

"Better than your show."

"The encore was only for you."

"As it should be," Graigh says, slouching deeply against him.

He pulls her body up against his, then lays them both down on the opposite side of the bed. In his arms, his hands on her belly she lays against him, eyes open to the wall. He kisses the back of her neck and buries his head on the pillow. Graigh does not rest against him. He feels agitation in her body.

He asks, "What's wrong?"

"Nothing. Just something's off with Joy. She's hiding something."

"It's not important," he says intuitively. "Go to sleep, Bae. She'll tell you another day."

"I know. It's just . . . something's not right."

Graigh closes her eyes and drifts into her tormented dreams of rocking chairs, sad eyes, rose oil, magnolias and white sheets. Two nightmares combined into one are backed by the beating heart of her present life. Every time she opens her eyes in fright, she closes them again assured that her dreams are not as real as the reality lying beside her.

Thirty

The beat of the bass drum pouring out of the soundbar in the house blasts moveable music all around the tables of food and people gathered in the backyard. Rebirth Brass Band's "Move Your Body" sends a shimmy and shake between Graigh and Bombei, a tooted up twerk between Joy and Tony, and a round of frenzied buckjumps, hops, skips, runs, and twirls between Junior, Quiana, Kory, and Christian. Teddy and Shandra show off their footwork taking a lap around the grill where Dougie mans the meat being smoked to perfection. The atmosphere is convivial between family and friends despite the tension still remaining between Teddy and Graigh. He arrived with open arms that she fell into, even though she didn't want to. She refused to hug him back or say more than what could easily be communicated through a head nod and a bat of her lashes.

The smoke rises high into the air from the charcoal grill. Traditional Fourth of July hotdogs and hamburgers share space with slabs of ribs, chicken breasts, wingettes, drumettes, and turkey legs. Flames lap the food as the men each take a turn of basting, checking, and talking shit to each other about who's the grill master amongst them. Amidst the obnoxiously loud and infectious music they all second line around the yard. Hips roll and booties shake. Graigh leads the line around the perimeter of the yard carefully avoiding the smoking grill in the middle that might set off a coughing spell. With an inhaler begrudgingly in the pocket of her red maxi dress, she thrusts and dips her body forward and back, one hand on her hip, one hand holding the hem of her dress and her belly as she spins and drops, then pretends to have trouble coming back up to standing, before waggling her walk forward to keep the line going. Behind her Bombei grabs her hips and ass and holds on as she sways, gyrates, and becomes one with the music. He follows her lead, bumping the beat against her butt with his pelvis, and trying some footwork of his own. The song ends and transitions into another just like it. Just as up tempo, just as swinging, just as wild, demanding the second line continue. The children oblige. Quiana leads the way, her little body in a black and white striped sundress jumping, twirling, and whirling around, waggling her imagination, and thrusting her dreams as best she can to emulate the rounded curves of her mother, the pregnant graces of her aunt, and the rolling gyrations of Joy. Junior and Christian bring up the back with Christian showing Junior step for intricate step the footwork associated with celebration, and the sounds of this part of the dirty south.

The adults are back at their stations. The men around the grill, the women under the patio awning swatting at files, checking plastic wrap, and foil covers to prevent the outside from contaminating what's inside.

"Baby, get me a pan?" Teddy yells from the grill. "Some of this meat is ready to come off."

"I'll get it," Graigh says before Shandra can respond. "I need to get out of this heat anyway."

"We all do," Joy seconds.

She and Shandra follow behind Graigh through the French doors and into the kitchen. Graigh rummages through the lower cabinets beneath the sink pulling out throwaway aluminum pans of varying sizes. She picks the two largest pans, deep and rectangular, and places the smaller, more shallow square pans, back in their rightful places.

"I got 'em," Graigh says, walking slowly along the sink and counters back to the door.

"You alright?" Shandra asks, concern apparent in her voice.

"My feet and ankles hurt. Too much second lining."

"You forgot your big ass was pregnant, didn't you?" Joy asks.

"Shut up, Joy."

"Out there dancing and shaking like you're not about to be somebody's mama."

"Correct me if I'm wrong heifer, but you were out there doing that and then some. Both of you were." Graigh glares between Shandra and Joy.

"Yeah, but we aren't the ones getting ready to pop a baby."

"Don't remind me," Graigh grimaces. "I am not prepared."

"Don't worry, neither were we," Shandra says. "No woman is ever ready to have a baby."

"Until they put that baby in your arms," Joy adds.

"And even then, you don't know what you're doing those first days and weeks."

"Try months."

"I know that's right," Shandra says, slapping Joy five.

"Y'all better bring that pan before this meat burn," Teddy yells from the grill.

"Go on and give it to him," Graigh says, handing the two aluminum pans to Shandra.

"Y'all still not talking?"

"Nope. But I'm glad you guys could come even if my brother is a stubborn asshole."

"You're just as stubborn," Shandra says, stepping out the back door. "Phone calls go both ways."

"Not when he needs to apologize."

Shandra doesn't respond to the escalating jab. She shakes her head and walks off Graigh's obstinance. Her blue-black, blunt cut, bob wig shakes with the motion, as does the rest of her body covered in a purple camisole and red shorts with gold accents that match her thin strapped sandals. Graigh watches from the doorway as Shandra approaches Teddy from behind and hands him the pans by wrapping her arms around his waist. He turns around, lifts the brim of his Saints hat and plants a kiss on her lips. Her hands cross tightly behind his back resting on the crease between his white T-shirt and dark denim jeans.

"She really loves your brother," Joy observes from one of the barstools at the island inside.

"Loves his dirty drawls," Graigh says wistfully.

"Obviously."

"Y'all gon' make out, or you gon' to take the food off the grill? Don't nobody want no burnt meat?" Bombei yells outside.

"What's up with your man?" Joy asks.

"I don't know. Hangry probably."

"Oh. I was going to say blue balls."

"You're so damn nasty," Graigh humphs, coming back to the island beside Joy. "It's definitely not blue balls. He got some last night and this morning."

"Good for you. All Tony had was his hand once I got as pregnant as you are."

"These days all I want is to do is eat, sleep, and have sex. This baby has my libido through the roof. It's not even right."

"At least the two of you are finally on the same page. What's going on with you and your brother?"

"I went to see him last month after I kept having dreams of mama to find out more about her and my daddy, and let's just say he wasn't happy with my questions. Hell, he didn't even let me get to my questions. Blamed me for mama's suicide saying I neglected her for Grandma Dottie. I told him about Jamal, and somehow, he blamed me for that too. He said he was sorry, but I wasn't and I'm not in the mood to accept fake ass apologies."

"You'll never get a real apology if you always think he's insincere," Joy says.

"I'll know when he's sincere."

"You mean like now? He's at your house. He's helping your husband cook. If that's not sincerity, then I don't know what is."

"I guess."

"You just like being mad at folks."

Graigh leaves the accusation unanswered.

She asks a question of her own, "What was Tony trying to tell me yesterday?"

"When?" Joy's braided hair swishes against her bare back in her orange lace romper as she whips around.

"When we were at the concert."

"Girl, I don't know."

"Then why did you say you'd tell me later?"

"Was I drinking?"

"Don't deflect."

"I'm not. You know as well as I do that I'm not responsible for my words and most of my actions when I'm drinking."

"Isn't that convenient."

"Y'all coming outside to eat, or are you staying in the air while the rest of us endure this heat?" Bombei asks, peaking his head inside the door.

"We're coming," Graigh says, wobbling off the stool. "My feet were hurting."

"Joy, what's your excuse?" Bombei asks.

"Duh. Best friend support."

"Open the door, Bae," Graigh says, pushing his head out the door. "Baby, coming through."

"You ain't that damn big." He steps aside to open the door wide for Graigh and Joy.

"Did y'all bless the food?" Graigh asks.

"We blessed it when we bought it."

"That's trifling. What do you want to eat?" She grabs a paper plate from the edge of the first table on the patio.

"Don't worry about me. Get yours."

Bombei comes behind Graigh and kisses the back of her neck, then grabs his own plate, napkin, and plastic silverware. She leads the way down the line of tables packed with food. Macaroni and cheese, potato salad, baked beans, a hamburger, a hotdog, a couple ribs, and a boiled crab from the ice chest of seafood, along with a few potatoes and a piece of corn. The line follows slowly behind her as everyone piles their plates high with all the food displayed. Graigh grabs a bottle of water from the chest of drinks in front of the shed and sits on the concrete step in front of the back doors. Bombei joins her, Joy and Tony lean against the shed balancing their bodies and plates, while Teddy, Shandra, and Dougie sit in the few folding chairs scattered around the yard. Junior and Christian stand along the back fence while Kory and Quiana sit and fight on a blanket spread across the grass. Silence descends on the group as the sound of smacking jaws joins in chorus with Trombone Shorty pulling the bluesy beat out of his sliding horn on "Do to Me."

Dougie taps his foot in time to the song, and wipes his brow and says, "Damn how much pepper did you put in?"

"Sounds like you haven't had properly seasoned food since you left," Bombei ribs.

"Lightweight." Graigh laughs.

"Whatever pregnant lady."

"Looks like it's about to rain," Tony says looking up from his chair.

"Wouldn't surprise me," Teddy says shrugging.

"You guys ready for hurricane season?" Dougie asks.

"Define ready," Shandra challenges.

"Batteries, flashlights, generators, an evacuation plan. Ready," Dougie says wiping his mouth and hands.

"Boy you've been in Chicago too long," Teddy guffaws. "It's only July. Storm season just getting started and ain't nobody buying a thing for a storm that may not come our way. We had our once in a generation storm."

"So, you forgot Katrina even happened?"

Teddy mutters, "Look around you, we can't forget."

Graigh glares.

Shandra yells an incredulous, "Hell naw. All that water. We ain't never gon' forget. We just don't let that bitch run our lives."

"That bitch, huh?"

"That's what she was," Graigh says lowly. "She was one of the enslaved people who refused to be captured.

"Come again?" Dougie asks perplexed.

Graigh smirks as she stares him down. She assesses his appearance: high top sponge curls, baby blue polo, khaki shorts, and canvas boat shoes.

She says, "Hurricanes are the spirits of our enslaved ancestors thrown overboard for insurance money, sickness, death, insurrection, and those who intentionally drowned themselves all coming together in the present to wreak havoc on the world."

"And what was Katrina's issue?"

"She was tired of being disrespected just like every other Black woman in history." Shandra cackles.

"I know that's right!" Joy jumps from against the wall to slap her new sister friend five.

"So, what were Andrew, Charley, Sandy, Matthew, Maria, Harvey and Dorian's problems?" Tony asks.

Graigh says, "Same problem. Tired of disrespect. Tired of the bullshit, just plain ol' tired."

"Say it like that and it sounds like Katrina was, and is, and is to come." Dougie jokes.

"Like Jesus," Shandra says.

"Amen." Joy laughs.

Graigh rolls her eyes.

Dougie sees her displeasure. He says, "Okay, Graigh, school me."

"Please, don't get my wife started," Bombei says.

"As long as she's not talking about this damn house, I think we're good." Teddy adds.

"Oh, trust me, I'm getting to my house," Graigh says, pushing her body weight off the step.

"New Orleans has always been a divided city. Divided by race, class, caste or color."

"Quadroon and octoroon balls, anyone," Shandra church shouts.

"Even today white people mostly live in the west, and black people in the east. White people on high ground and black people on low ground."

"Graigh there's damage everywhere if you pay attention," Tony says.

If you pay attention.

Graigh rolls her eyes as she watches Tony walk his plate over to the trash can. A different pair of linen pants swish as he goes. He comes back to sit beside Joy.

He says, "When we've been in the quarter and even downtown, if you're high up you can look out a window and see abandoned, boarded up buildings caved in and dilapidated. And I'm not just talking about the Hard Rock."

"True," Graigh admits. "It'll be fifteen years in a month and the black neighborhoods still look like the hurricane just came through. The people who came back to rebuild like me were hassled by the insurance people, and Road Home . . ."

"That's because it was designed for Black folks to be fleeced out of what they had into having nothing to survive," Bombei interrupts.

Graigh continues, "Plus the ever changing, incompetent lawyers losing papers. Some folks didn't have clear ownership or line of succession. It's a mess. Hell, I had papers proving this is my house and it still took us years to get our claim settled and enough money to renovate right and we still didn't have enough. Now we're underwater on a house, I used to own outright, and the housing market collapse took the last little value we had."

Dougie says, "But, Graigh, you know how it goes. The government—city, state, and federal—bail out banks, itself, and other countries, and only sometimes its people."

"And usually only white people," Teddy says.

"Exactly," Graigh says. "The first thing them people said after the storm was, they were gon' rebuild a smaller, taller New Orleans. Which means white. They can't come right out and say it, but basically abandoning Black people who never asked to be here in the first place."

Bombei adds, "There are states' rights, federal rights, and white people's rights. You know the Bill of Rights don't apply to us, since we didn't even become people to them until one-hundred fifty years after it was written. Then it took another one hundred years after that when the Civil Rights Act, Voting Rights act, and Brown gave white folks less choice."

"Y'all gotta stop watching all that Black righteous shit on Netflix," Dougie chides.

"I keep telling you *13th* and *Black Panthers: Vanguard of the Revolution* are a must see."

"Don't forget *I'm Not Your Negro* and *When They See Us*," Joy chimes in.

"They don't never see us," Dougie says. "And my Daddy and them lived through all that shit. I'm good."

"Anyway," Graigh interrupts. "My point is racism is as second nature to this city as a second line."

"Chile, there's racism everywhere," Shandra adds.

"So why stay if it's so bad?" Dougie asks.

"A few reasons." Bombei holds his arm in front of Graigh's twitching legs. "First of all, the Great Recession stifled reconstruction in New Orleans the same way the KKK and the Hayes Bargain stymied Reconstruction after The Civil War. White America gets sick, the rest of the world gets pneumonia, and Black people damn near die. That's first of all. Secondly, you right. We don't have to be here. None of us sitting here have to be. We're here because we want to be here, because we choose to be here. Ain't no need to let other folk, the government or otherwise, run us out of our home."

"Damn, Graigh, he defends being here more than you do," Teddy says.

"My wife doesn't have to fight her battles alone."

"Thank you, Baby," Graigh says, sitting down beside him.

On the stoop she sidles closer to him, her wide hips pressed next to his narrow ones. Their knees touch, hands clasp, and fingers interlocked. Her head rests against his temple. Her silent satisfaction forces joy to creep across her unassuming face. The widened cheeks and bow lips smile beyond their natural resting point. She glows beyond the halo aura of her pregnancy from the inside out. Pride of both place and mate calm her beating heart and rest her anxious nerves. She releases the inhaler in her pocket she's gripped most of the day, and breathes deeply through her nose, constricting the back of her throat creating the sound of the ocean. Graigh takes several yoga breaths as she listens to the contemporary sounds of home rocking and rolling through the outdoor speakers piped from the sound bar in the house.

Bombei lifts Graigh's hand to his lips and kisses her knuckles.

He continues, "We came back to rebuild and that's what we did. We just want our city fixed and for the process to be fair."

"Y'all know for damn sure it ain't fair," Teddy says. "Y'all got white neighbors now. I ain't never seen white people living 'round here when I was little."

"They're taking the opportunity in the tragedy," Graigh says. "They see the advantage of disaster and destruction. Some of 'em live here, some rent here. All of 'em in it for the money . . . whenever it flows this way."

"Until a better opportunity comes along," Bombei sneers.

"This shit is depressing," Teddy laments. "I swear I'm a stop coming over here."

Graigh narrows her eyes at her brother. "It's not like you come over here a lot now," she snaps.

"What for?" Teddy snaps back. "Ain't shit over here —besides you—everything else is fucked up and people making money off of it left and right hand over fist."

"We saw the bike tour riding down the block when we pulled up," Shandra explains.

"The bike tour?" Dougie asks, puzzled.

"Another iteration of America's favorite past time," Bombei says.

"What's that?"

"Making money off of Black people; generally speaking. Making money off of Black people's pain and suffering specifically speaking. The tourists . . ."

"White people," Shandra says.

"The tourists, most of them white people," Bombei clarifies, "go on tours of the damaged areas from Katrina snapping pictures and shit."

"Just the next version of the minstrel show," Teddy says.

"Well, I ain't shucking and cooning for no one." Graigh says.

"No, you just up here crying at the same thing. Black pain as trauma porn. You hate to watch but can't turn away."

"It ain't my fault they fucked up what God made?" Graigh says, her voice getting caught in her throat.

"What are you talking about?" Teddy asks.

"Six bodies of water surround the city. Three made by God. Three made by man. And they all are drowning us. "

Dougie asks, "Again, why stay?"

"Where you want us to go?" Bombei asks.

"The country is big. Go anywhere. Hell, that's how the people that ain't come back got out in the first place. One-way tickets to some elsewhere."

Teddy says, "They called us refugees during Katrina. Said it was better to sleep on the floor of the Astrodome then in our own house, in our own bed. You think somewhere else in this country is gon' welcome us now?"

"Us?" Graigh raises her eyebrow.

"All you gotta do is look at what's happening on the border to know the rest of America ain't too keen on brown people moving out of where they're supposed to be," Shandra says.

Her comment cools the tension between brother and sister. She supports Teddy without calling him on his wavering position about the future of the neighborhood he used to call home but is reluctant to visit. With looks between brother and sister, husband, and sister-in-law Shandra pleads with her eyes for them to remain civil as everyone tries to discuss and dissect a problem that has yet to reveal a solution.

"I just don't understand," Dougie says. "If y'all gon' stay why not march or band together, complain, elect a new councilman, something."

"We just got a new mayor." Graigh says. "Let the sis work and see what she can do."

"Naw, Dougie's right," Teddy says. "Y'all down here everyday with only a few streetlights, grass as high as people, and potholes as big as craters. Whatever *sis* is doing ain't enough."

"If the city ain't got time to come fix the street, you think they got time to cut grass?" Bombei asks incredulous.

"That's my point. Y'all down here everyday. Some of this property that's all blighted the city owns. But what are they doing with it?"

"Nothing," Shandra says.

"Yet they got time to pass a noise ordinance in the Tremé," Dougie says. "It's the Tremé. It's supposed to be noisy."

"It's no different than New York featuring white people advertising for homes in Harlem and Brooklyn," Joy says.

"One word. Gentrification," Graigh says.

"For all its faults New Orleans most closely resembles the melting pot America pretends to be," Bombei takes over for Graigh. "Yes, we were a bustling slave port. But we were also home to one of the largest concentrations of free Black folk outside of Haiti. We were free folk before George Martin ever thought of a wildling."

"Winter is over." Teddy says.

"Still the best series ever," Tony adds.

"Behind *The Wire*," Dougie and Bombei say together.

"My man," Bombei says reaching over to slap Dougie's hand. "Your taste in TV ain't half bad, but the stupid box is making you forget your history."

"If it wasn't about music, I wasn't paying attention."

"Then you better read a book."

"Whatever man. History is just what it is. History. The shit ain't changing."

The conversation meanders from reviving the neighborhood, to race and politics, to history and back again. The eating has ceased, the drinking has yet to commence, and the gathering of adults all speak not only to be heard, but to be understood."

Bombei says, "Revisionist history is real. You don't know what these MAGA loving Trumpians will put in textbooks."

"So, what are you doing about it?" Dougie asks "You teach."

"Half the day I spend my time telling these kids the truth and not the lies they read that slaves were indentured servants or workers who came voluntarily to build a country on a continent that didn't belong to them in the first place."

"You can blame Ben Carson and Betsy DeVos for the perpetuation of those lies."

"The whole damn administration!"

"Hell yeah," Joy agrees. "Betsy DeVos ass talking about HBCU's are bastions for school choice. Bitch please. And then they had the nerve to invite her to speak at BCU's commencement."

"BCU not FAMU," Graigh says slyly. "Wouldn't have been a graduation they pulled that stunt at FAM."

"It was barely a graduation at Bethune."

"I know. I saw," Graigh says.

"Either way," Tony jumps in. "I think the point of this convoluted history lesson is to one, know your history, and two, no y'all don't have a hurricane plan."

"Basically," Bombei laughs. "Pass me a beer out the cooler please."

"We'll get a hurricane plan when the fish at the aquarium get one," Graigh laughs.

"What do you mean?" Tony asks scrunching his nose.

"The power was out so long most of the fish at the aquarium died because the air pumps for the tanks weren't working," Dougie says.

"So, you remember that?" Bombei asks incredulous.

"Hell yeah. That shit was crazy. Fish dying in a flood."

"They didn't die in the flood," Graigh corrects.

"Well, as a result of the flood. Same difference."

"Damn," Tony says. "I don't remember that story."

"There were so many stories coming out it was hard to keep track," Joy says.

Nods of agreement circle the group as Kermit Ruffins's sings about how he's so New Orleans, roll calling his favorite musicians.

"Well, speaking of stories," Tony interjects. "Graigh I've got a story for you."

"What's that?" Graigh asks through closed eyes laying against Bombei.

"I saw Jamal before we got on the road to come here. You know he's getting married and has a baby on the way. His lady is about as big as you are. She kind of looks like you too."

"Hell, no, she didn't," Joy snaps, giving Tony the evil eye.

"That's some story," Graigh says coolly. "Why'd you think I needed to know that."

"He wasn't thinking," Joy jumps in. "You're happy. You're married to the most patient man in the history of the world. He's kind of cute too. And you're about to have his baby. You didn't *need* to know anything about Jamal's trifling ass."

"TeeTee, who's Jamal?" Quiana asks Graigh, walking up to the adults.

"Nobody, Baby. Nobody at all."

Thirty-One

"That was an interesting conversation," Bombei says as he and Graigh load the dishes into the dishwasher.

"What do you mean?" Graigh asks knowingly.

"Why did Tony feel like he had to tell you that?"

"That's a better question for Tony than for me."

"No matter what, it's never just us," Bombei mutters running a damp towel across the counter tops.

His arms sweep in big circular motions wiping away water, and other liquid condensation. Crumbs fall to the floor. He wipes from the counter tops kissing the edges of the French doors, to the stove on the next wall, making sure not to miss polishing the overhead microwave.

"He always finds his way in our business, and I don't even know this motherfucker," Bombei murmurs.

His mouth moves hurling insults and curses as his arms work, wiping, shining, polishing, and waxing until there's a brilliant sheen over everything. Graigh stands still at the sink where he left her with the broom from the pantry.

"Maybe he didn't think I'd care. Which I don't," she offers stroking the floor with long motions.

"If he didn't think you'd care then he wouldn't have brought it up."

"But if I don't care it doesn't matter who or what he brings up. The opposite of love is not hate, it's indifference."

"So now you're indifferent to Jamal?"

"Bae, it's been a long time. Why wouldn't I be?"

"Then why didn't you answer the question?" He asks squared up at the kitchen island. "You shouldn't be doing that, you know," he gently admonishes.

"I do it any other time," Graigh says, rounding the island to where he is.

"Yeah, but any other time you weren't pregnant."

"I'm fine. The baby's fine. He's kicking right now. Do you want me to lift up my dress to show you this alien invasion happening inside me or can you just take my word for it?"

"It's not that I can't take your word. I just don't want anything to happen. You know that sweeping motion . . . it's not good for him."

"Yeah? Who told you that?"

"My old man," Bombei says releasing some of his hushed fear over his palpable anger.

So y'all finally talked?

Graigh keeps her question to herself as she bumps her back into his shoulder and relinquishes the broom. He takes the handle from her and finishes her trip around the island. Graigh sits on one of the bar stools with her feet up on another. In silence she watches Bombei retrace her steps around the island. This time he uses the edge of the bristles to dip into the tight corners where the stove and refrigerator are wedged between cabinets. He sweeps still muttering to himself; complaining aloud. She listens to him murmur unsure of where to jump in to reassure him of their love. In this moment Graigh is as confused as Bombei as to why Tony felt the need to insight drama into their already tenuous relationship, and why Joy allowed it knowing Jamal had always been a sore spot for them both, especially Bombei.

"Sometimes I swear I'm not sure if I did the right thing," Bombei gripes.

"What do you mean?" Graigh asks.

"It's nothing."

"If it's nothing, say what it is."

What did you do wrong?

Come back?

Get married?

Get me pregnant?

What did you do wrong?

"It's been damn near fifteen years, Graigh. It's nothing."

"What's nothing?" She takes her feet down from the bar stool.

She's ready to run. To lunge. To attack and hide. She's perched on the edge of her seat, her belly warm and heavy in her lap, her eyes are narrowed as they gaze in his face where he sits atop the counter, the broom tucked back in its place in the pantry.

"It's nothing Graigh," he says taking his head to his hands. "I just sometimes wonder if . . ."

"If. What?"

"If . . . If I did the right thing."

If any of this was supposed to be my life.

"What the hell does that mean?"

Her agitation is palpable. His frustration mounts. Her hands drum the butcher block island. His leg bounces atop the smooth quartz countertops. Head still in his hands, he massages his temples raising his gaze to meet her stare. Brown eyes to darker brown eyes, the deep line in her forehead tells him he can't take back what he's said, and he can't not finish what he's saying. His unease mutes his throat, her desire to know emboldens her own voice.

"What. Does. That. Mean?"

"It means, I've always wondered if I did the right thing marrying you. Loving you. Helping you. Hell, stopping to meet you. Or should I have just drove on by like I did when I passed everybody else trying to put this shit show of their lives back together."

"So, our entire lives are a mistake to you now?"

Here we go again, Bombei thinks as his frustrations admonish him for the argument he incited.

"Wow," Graigh says.

She catastrophizes in her mind. Unamazed and unexcited she scoots her butt backwards to the crease of the stool cushion and seat back. Her arms stretch long against the counter. She yawns. Releasing the tension of her facial muscles she sighs her own feelings into the ether of emotions that can't be taken back. His words that can't be reneged or recalled.

"Then why are we here?" She asks tentatively.

"Lately, it's a question I've asked myself every day. Why are we here? How did we get here? Why are we married? Why did you say yes? I know why I asked, but why did you say yes? That's more my question than anything else."

"Because it was the right thing to do," she blurts.

Shit.

Graigh covers her mouth trying to hold in more words she can't take back. Bombei nods his head in response to her excited utterance. The Freudian slip she couldn't control. The unbridled, unadulterated truth from the center of her soul.

"That's fucked up," he says quietly hopping down from the counter.

"No, it's reality," Graigh defends. "Who else was going to the love me the way you love me. Who else was going to hold me the way you hold me? Who else was going to deal with my crazy the way you patiently deal with my crazy to this day? Saying yes to you was the right thing to do. Marrying you was the right thing to do."

"I don't want to be the runner up in your life. I don't want to be your sloppy seconds because you couldn't keep your first-place prize. I ain't no fucking charity case. Not in life; and I for damn sure don't need to be one in love."

"Who says you were sloppy seconds? Me saying yes to you had nothing to do with you and everything to do with me. My mental, my psych, my state of mind. After all this time, you think that I think that I should have married him instead? The truth is I never wanted to get married at all. I wished I hadn't gotten married at all. But what woman doesn't say yes to a man who would do anything for her? What woman doesn't say yes to a man who loves her through what he doesn't understand? What woman doesn't say yes to a man who gives up a music career, a house on high ground in the suburbs, settles for teaching in a Ninth Ward school that hadn't reopened yet, and living in a house so destitute he had to build it from the ground up to make it inhabitable? Who doesn't say yes to that?"

"Then Graigh, I could have been anybody. Any fucking body."

"But you aren't just anybody. You're the man I couldn't say no to. The man I still can't say no to. So, I took your hand. I took your name. I accepted marriage praying if I just love him harder, devote myself to him more, tell him everything, even what scares me then I won't be scared, I won't be holding back. But as hard as I try, I never get there. You still love me more than I love you."

"Whoever loves the hardest has the least power," Bombei resigns.

Graigh doesn't answer. She lets the truth stand alone. Unquestioned. Unmitigated by remarks to the contrary. In the fast fading light of the sun the kitchen darkens his features. His back to the casting shadows, his countenance is steady, set in his jaw, heavy in his brokenhearted fury. The scars she caused cut wet lines from his eyes across his face. He pushes himself away from the counter and makes his way toward the steps. Burdened feet trudge on the thick carpet with the weight of their reality. He pulls off his powder blue polo and carries it up the stairs across his shoulders, silently making his way toward their room in another part of the home he helped build.

She sits at the table in her own stewing silence. Boiling in her own emotions; a gumbo of grief; absolved of the lies she's told herself after finally telling the truth, feeling worse than she expected, but better than she deserves.

He kicks.

The pipes come alive with the water pressure from the shower. In the quiet house she can hear his movements; accurately imagine his motions as she sits a floor below him knowing his nighttime routine when he's angry, hurt, or happy. The steaming water cascades over his body, dampening his faded head and dripping from his long beard to his chest. He holds the wall in front of him letting the water rinse over his back. She knows he stays like this for more than a moment, letting whatever healing properties come from the flat rain shower head fall over him. In this house the bathroom is his sanctuary, his Gilead, and the water from their shower is his balm. She knows once he's sufficiently soaked his stance changes. His head raises. His arms hug in, as he balls his fists. He jabs, he upper cuts, he throws combinations. In the shower, in his hurt and anger, he fights off the creeping aggression, the nagging feeling of feelings that are not and will never be facts. Beneath the water, bobbing and weaving away from no one, Bombei boxes in the shadows of the shower.

On the stairs she hears him grunt. Successively. Consecutively.

The green workout band that stays coiled in the shower caddy is now in his hands. His feet stand on the rope and his fingers are coiled around the rubber hand grips as he curls his arms working his biceps. She knows he will do ten sets of twenty or until the water runs cold. If it's cold he will wash. If it's lukewarm he will flip his hands, change his stance, slightly bend his knees, and continue his workout with butterflies. In the shower, the water wastefully running, he works out his anger on his own body. Boxing it away. Curling it away. Another ten sets of twenty. Grunts mark every rep of every set.

Graigh slides her underwear off from beneath her maxi dress and removes her bra. She tosses the bed blanket over the full-length mirror and pulls the covers to lay on her side of the bed. She wraps herself around the body pillow that's supposed to ease her aches and soothe her pains. She hugs the cushion, though it does nothing for the headache throbbing from the crown of her twists down the spine of her back. Hugging tightly to the intangible, she listens to the self-evident in the bathroom beside her. The water is finally turned off, and she hears him slam the shower door closed. He is all sounds. Wet feet cross the tiled floor, the rustle and shimmy of the oversized bath towel dries across his body. He coughs. The light clicks. The door to their bedroom opens. Darkness surrounds them. He is naked only for a moment. In underwear and pajama pants Bombei pulls back his side of the bed and lays down. They are side by side with a mile between them. A cozy queen bed where they each snuggle up to their respective edge. They go to sleep together, each in the bed, in the room, alone.

Thirty-Two

Alone, Bombei climbs the stairs to the second-floor office of The Healing Center. Doctor Grace's words from a month ago echo in his head.

Come back and see me when you're ready to stop lying to yourself.

The therapy session he went to with Graigh for support where he was turned into a target is magnified by his own admitted insecurities. The bomb Tony dropped and left in the middle of their back yard, that he carried into their kitchen and master suite where they slept back to back, neither wanting to look to see when the emotional grenade would detonate.

Come back and see me when you're ready to stop lying to yourself.

Doctor Grace said it to him twice. Her second iteration came with a challenge, to return to her chaise to tell himself the truth. He dismissed her analysis as an attempt to garner more business, to keep people in a constant state of dis-ease, to fatten her coffers, keep her coins rolling in and stay employed. But whether her motive was purely for financial gain or for his excelled mental health, he can't shake the thought that maybe he is lying to himself. Maybe he is shielding the truth from his inner being to keep up the facade of a mostly happy home; a mostly happy husband, a mostly happy man.

We bicker, but what couple doesn't. She gives up the booty and gives good head, so what if she's difficult and mean as hell.

So why didn't we even acknowledge each other last night if everything is okay?

He knows he's equally difficult. He leaves the toilet seat up. Sometimes on purpose now that she's pregnant just to see if she'll notice on her nightly voyages to the bathroom. He asks her questions he knows she won't want to answer and blocks her path anytime she seems to fall back into habits from her past. Jamal, Teddy, Dottie, and her grand idea of re-opening a Katrina shuttered pharmacy. He knows he is her doorstop to her life before, barring entry into the known world before him. A blockade, a barricade before what doesn't include him.

But is this life a lie?
Did I make a mistake?
Should I have just kept driving?
Is she holding both of us back?

The question forms before he can dismiss it. Before he can forget the words that formed his suspicion.

Is she holding both of us back?

He asks of himself what he cannot answer. What he doesn't want to answer, because if the answer is, "yes," it means he's wasted his time trying to make a marriage work for more than a decade when they should have remained friends and parted ways when her house work involved outside contractors and no longer required his brand of neighborhood handy man services. If the answer to his question is, "yes," then it means she was a waste of a stop in the Ninth Ward in 2006. A waste of a ring. A waste of selling his brand new, never lived in home in LaPlace. If the answer to his question is, "yes," then it means she is a waste of his talent; of his life. Yet there it remains mulling around in his head with Doctor Grace's own challenge.

Is she holding both of us back?

Come back and see me when you're ready to stop lying to yourself. Come back and see me when you want to tell yourself the truth.

The door to Doctor Grace's office is open when he reaches the top of the steps. She waits for him with an unreadable expression plastered across her spectacled face hidden by the enormity of her curly hair. Doctor Sophia Grace's stance is wide, her feet firmly planted in her chunky, black leather sandals, matching her black work shorts, and sleeveless black peplum top with leather appliqués. Only her skin breaks up her brooding ensemble. Her legs were his only view for most of his climb up the stairs. Her butter cream casing, from the thigh meat exposed just above her kneecap to the heels of her backless sandals, is even in complexion. Smooth and subtle in the thickness testing the seams of the pressed shorts, belying the weight of the load she carries behind her.

"Good afternoon," he says.

"Good afternoon," Doctor Grace says once his gaze catches up to her face. "I must say I was surprised to get your call. Come on in."

"You're the one who suggested I come back," he says taking a seat on the chaise the color of the shallowest part of the ocean.

The door closes behind them and the door lock clicks. Doctor Grace grabs a clip board and a stack of note cards from the top of her desk. She opens the refrigerator and retrieves two water bottles.

Handing one to Bombei she says, "I said only come back, by yourself that is, when you're ready to stop lying to yourself. When you're ready to tell the truth."

"I'm here," he says noncommittally.

"But are you ready to tell the truth. Otherwise you can leave, and I can find something else better to do to with my time for the next hour."

"You don't mince words do you. I can see why my wife likes you. You're just as mean as she is."

"First of all, your wife is not mean, and neither am I. Secondly, time is money. Neither one of us has either to waste. As the saying goes talk is cheap, and BS runs the marathon."

"Never heard that one before," he laughs uneasily.

"It's a saying in my house. My husband's to be exact."

"Got it."

"So why are you here?" Doctor Grace asks staring down at her note cards scribbling with the coal pencil.

"To tell the truth," Bombei says.

"About what?"

"I don't know. About why my relationship with my wife is so fucked up right now. We're having a baby, and now I'm wondering if me pressuring her to start our family, was the right thing to do in the first place."

"You're here to talk." Doctor Grace says scribbling.

She brushes the outline of the tall man sitting on her couch with one knee raised. The one that bounces. The one that tells of his agitation. Quick strokes bring his body to fruition, the rough-dried wrinkles of his khaki work pants, and short sleeved white polo, to the form of his feet in his canvas flip flops. Every detail of the shape of his body comes to life on the small three by five index card save for the slide of his eyes, the curve of his mouth, and the grip of his hands. Those details she will fill in last. The coal rests between her dirtied fingers. Her gaze lifts to meet his and their eyes lock. Inquisitive to curious, their expressions conceal their thoughts that are locked behind tongue, lips, and teeth.

Bombei blinks first, breaking the stare. Doctor Grace lifts her entire head and leans back into the plush cushion of her sofa chair. With her feet outstretched in front of her, relaxed, and nearly reclined she watches his eyes bounce from the brightly colored print on the floor, to the smoke rising in circles behind her from the burning sage. His eyes scan the shelves behind her head. The back wall of books she's read or been recommended to read. His eyes bounce to the framed degrees on the wall shared with the door, back to the floor print, and then to his hands in his lap. They are cupped, one on top of the other, one beating a steady rhythm into the other.

He looks back at the floor print, voice unsteady, "Aren't you going to ask me something?"

"You came to talk to me. Talk."

"About what?"

"About why you're here."

"I just told you."

"The synopsis yes. I want the whole book, not the Cliff's Notes version."

"We had a fight."

"That's a start. About what?"

"Jamal. Her ex-boyfriend. Almost baby-daddy."

"Almost husband."

"She's talked about him here?"

"You know I'm not allowed to disclose that."

"You just did."

"You're wasting my time."

"Whatever. We fought about Jamal."

"Why?"

"Because her best friend and her husband were in town for Essence. My friend was down because we performed in the super lounge with one of the acts. We had a cookout the other day when her best friend's husband just decides to say in front of everybody that Jamal is getting married and has a baby on the way, and that his old lady looks like my wife."

"And what did your wife say?"

"She didn't say anything, told Quiana he was nobody."

"Who is Quiana?"

"Our niece. Her niece. Her brother and sister-in-law's daughter."

"Why do you feel the need to distance yourself from her family, as if they aren't also your family."

"I'm not. I didn't."

"You did."

Bombei ends the tête-à-tête shutting down and shutting out Doctor Grace from the budding conversation.

He shakes his head and broods, resisting the urge to stand, walk out of the door, down the steps and deal with his life on his own.

"How old is she?" Doctor Grace redirects. "Quiana?"

"Five."

"You don't believe Graigh when she called Jamal a 'nobody?'"

"No."

"Why not?"

"Because I don't have all of her," Bombei says dropping his cupped hands between his open legs. "Every time we seem to be okay. To be happy. To be moving forward with our lives, and our futures, this random motherfucker I don't even know pops back up in her mind and I'm left holding the bag of her bullshit."

"So why are you still together? Why are you having a baby if you don't want to be bothered with her 'bullshit?'" Doctor Grace asks air quoting the word.

"I don't know. Life happens. Ten years married, fourteen years together. She said yes. I don't fucking know."

"Yes, you do. You just said it. She said yes. She said yes to marrying you, she said yes to having your baby, even though it scares her. She's said yes to anything you've ever asked her."

"Not everything."

"What did she say no to?"

"To moving. That was her non-negotiable."

"Well good. You don't want a doormat, do you?"

"No, I don't want a door mat. But I don't want to constantly have to fight somebody either. I want her to fight with me."

"Who are you to say she's not fighting with you? Not fighting for you? For your relationship? You just don't like the way that she does it."

"Now you're taking her side," Bombei says standing.

Doctor Grace looks at him from her seat as he stands. Arms akimbo, he paces back and forth across the edge of the African print rug closest to the chaise. He stops when he hears the noise from the yoga studio come through the floorboards. The three "oms" of the full afternoon class vibrate through the walls; low, guttural, and distinct. The sound waves from the chakra cleansing sounds of vocal cords in discordant harmony stop Bombei in his tracks. He sits back down on the couch and smooths his hands from the thighs to the knees of his pants.

"I knew this was a mistake," he mutters.

"Don't get secretive now," Doctor Grace challenges. "You wanted to tell the truth. You should expect that I tell you the truth back."

"How can you say what the truth is? With all due respect you don't even know us."

"People only say 'with all due respect' before they say something disrespectful. And no, I don't know you well, but I've known your wife, of you, and now you long enough to know that I'm not taking her side by saying that she's trying to work out her own issues to make you happy, and you're still not satisfied."

"Is that right?"

"Your issues are with you. If she said Jamal is nobody then he's nobody, or don't you have other women in your past who used to hold a prominent position who are now known as nobody."

"I do, but . . ."

"No buts. Everyone has a past."

"Yes, but my past isn't informing my future the way hers is."

"Yes, it is. You just haven't admitted to it yet. It's easier to see the speck in your wife's eye than it is to see the plank in your own."

"Then what's my plank, Doc? Diagnose me."

Doctor Grace leaves the flippant comment where it lays, with Bombei still grimacing at her instead of at himself. She looks down to her sketch card and puts coal to cheap card stock. She sketches in lines around his eyes and mouth and flares his nose wide across his narrow face. Quick, straight lines cut the cheekbones of her creation and the stern hold of his jaw line. The slit for eyes, shrinking pupils and heavily hooded lids further add to his simmering furor. Her pencil touches up his long scraggly beard before moving to his hands. She emphasizes the veins in his hands and fingers as she illustrates the hold of one fist inside a palm. Paper covering rock, the amenable beating the unreasonable.

"I've done everything for her," Bombei blurts filling the uncomfortable silence.

"Mm-hm," Doctor Grace acknowledges.

"I built her a house I didn't want; in a neighborhood I don't want to live in. I sold both of my homes that I loved, one out of necessity and one for her. I gave up my musicianship to teach in a city that made me believe I could be bigger than Louis Armstrong. I've done everything for her. Through Katrina. Helping her recover from the storm. Jamal. Given her new purpose. And she shits on me for some man who left her for a fucking look-a-like."

"And what are her sacrifices?"

"I don't know."

"Exactly."

"What does that mean?"

"You're keeping count in love and she's not. You want to be rewarded for loving your wife the best way you know how, and I'm sorry to say there are no prizes in love. There are no elections to win when it comes to whom the heart votes for. You do because you love, not because you expect to be paid back. You're keeping count of all you've done and I bet she couldn't even name one thing, because for her it's not about who does what, it's just about loving and being with you, making you happy, even if she compromises the small parts of herself that make up the big parts of who she is."

"I guess."

"Don't accept something I've said if you don't believe it. If you think I'm a crock say that. But you keep saying what you've done that's been so hard, yet you're still in it. You're still married to her even though you're in a house you built in a neighborhood you don't like."

"You don't understand. We were forged after Katrina. It was just us and God. And I guess Jamal."

"Don't do that. Jamal is not your ghost."

"One she shared with me."

"To be honest with you. To be vulnerable with you. To show you that she was unafraid to show you she was broken but mending. Unafraid to give you her mended pieces for safe keeping."

"Is that right?"

"That's right," Doctor Grace says sipping from the miniature water bottle she placed at her feet. "You made a man you don't know your mortal enemy when he should be a non-factor. Or as your wife said, nobody."

Bombei doesn't respond. The silence subsumes the small distance between them as the heavy panting of unified breaths at work seep into the room. The call of asanas accompanies the breathing in the quiet room smelling of burnt sage. Doctor Grace stands first. Her chunky heels clip-clop to the door, and her hands tap Bombei's note against the skin of her knee. He follows behind her, a steady of stream of breath blowing from his body; his exhale exaggerated and unsatisfactory.

"This is for you," she says opening the door for him.

"Thanks," he says taking the index card without looking at it. "So that's it?"

"Well, our time is up. You can come back again if you like, but only if you're ready to talk truth and solution and not play the blame game. It's entirely up to you."

"Yup."

I won't be back here.

Bombei steps across the threshold and casually takes the stairs to the bottom floor. His flip flops slap the back of his heels with every step of his wide gait. Outside in the fresh air of St. Claude Avenue he looks at the index card he received from Doctor Grace. He examines his hardened features in awe. The roughness of his countenance from his beard to his eyes, the worry wrinkles at his brow, around his eyes and mouth, and the hardened grip of his hands. Every detail of his body is in black and white. He studies how she captured the uneven cuffs in his pants, and the crispness of his shirt juxtaposed against his scrunched toes in his sandals, along with his smooth haircut and slight waves. Going back to his face he stares at the reflection of what Doctor Grace saw before releasing the card to the breeze.

"You might want to pick that up and hold on to it before your next session," Graigh says, quietly leaning against the building.

"What are you doing here?" Bombei asks startled.

"I was coming to take the yoga class, but I saw your car. I waited to see which way you would come out from. Pick up your note," she urges with her chin.

"Are you mad?" Bombei asks bending down to pick up the index card.

Not that you would have a right to be.

"Why would I be mad? You're the one who stopped speaking to me last night."

She's definitely mad.

He hears the subtext of the context she didn't provide.

He says, "I'm sorry. I just can't shake the Jamal shit Tony pulled."

"Then be mad at them, not me."

"But he's your ex."

"Exactly," Graigh says, still leaning against the building. "Ex. You are my present, and my future." She cradles their baby.

"You sure about that?" Bombei asks.

Graigh steps off the wall toward him. Her long, red, sleeveless, summer sweater blows behind her. In gray yoga pants with sheer, triangle cut outs, and a white maternity sport top she approaches him belly first. Their baby leading the way.

"I've never been more sure about anything else in my life."

"Really?"

"You're like the sunflowers we used to see in people's yards right after the storm. They stood up so big and pretty and tall. Golden and defiant sucking up the toxicity still in the ground, taking away the death and leaving behind something beautiful."

"It was crazy to see the sunflowers in front of shambles for homes, standing in patches of dirt with no grass, and barely a bird or bee in the air to pollinate them."

"Too much science Mr. Teacher, but I get it," Graigh ribs. "How was your session?"

"She's mean as hell, but it was alright."

"Yeah. She's effective. You coming back?"

"With you? Yes. By myself? I don't know."

"What do you want to do now?" She asks stepping into his person.

"Go home," he says wrapping his arms around her waist. "Go swimming. In you."

Thirty-Three

July 24—33 weeks

Bombei swims in his own thoughts while he waits. Memories of his motherless childhood flash before his eyes. Sitting in the chair of the medical office exam room waiting with Graigh for Doctor Marcella, he tries to imagine the mother he never knew. The face he wants to see doesn't materialize. Instead, it morphs into Doctor Grace. The recalcitrant therapist whose only focus in her practice is time, money, and telling the truth.

Why are you having a baby if you don't want to be bothered with her bullshit?

She's said yes to anything you've ever asked her.

She's trying to work out her own issues to make you happy, and you're still not satisfied.

His recall of her words to him come with an extra caustic layer of attitude. A healthy skepticism from what he sees as the supposedly neutral party taking sides.

She's supposed to be Switzerland, but I should have known she'd act just like the woman she is and take Graigh's side.

Bombei shakes his head trying to dismiss the final thought that came to him. A questioning of his own rationalization.

But is she right?

Bombei looks over at Graigh laid back on the exam table, eyes closed, slightly snoring. Nodding off at the most inopportune times, at the most inconvenient of places has become her specialty as of late. If there's a wait she's resting her eyes as she calls it, storing up her strength and sleep for when their son arrives. She rests. He thinks.

Bombei massages his fingers against his temples. His eyes return to her body sleeping on the table. Her belly bulging with the life of their son. She wears one of his school T-shirts. It's already rolled up beneath her breast allowing the doctor easy access to check the baby's heartbeat whenever she decides to stroll into the exam room. Bombei watches Graigh sleep. Her chest rises and falls with her labored breath. Her belly rolls backward and forward with the frantic movements of their son quickly filling up a confined space. He watches the show poking through Graigh's skin, trying to make out if he sees a fist or an elbow, the bottom of a foot or a heel, the back of his baby's head or the boy's butt. Life goes on inside of Graigh as life moves ahead around her.

"Knock, Knock. It's Doctor Marcella."

The voice and swinging door interrupt the war of words in his head. The doctor waltzes in with authority. Dressed in white from collar to bleached camel hair mules the swing in her step is exacerbated by the swirl of her lab coat. She bristles about the confines of the room turning from nurse, to sink, to stool, to standing over Graigh and her naked belly.

"I guess we'll let mom sleep, and just check on this baby, who from the looks of things is doing quite well," Doctor Marcella grins looking at Bombei.

"I'm up," Graigh croaks with her eyes closed.

"It's okay if you're not. In the home stretch I slept everywhere. Restaurants while waiting for a table, on the streetcar. I even fell asleep at ESSENCE Fest in the Dome. Mama was tired."

Doctor Marcella chuckles easily at her own memory as she squirts the baby sounding gel on Graigh's belly. Bombei nods his head wistfully. Envious.

Someone who appreciates their past but is not trying to stay in it.

Jealousy slowly fills his body as he waits with bated breath to hear the familiar bleating noise that assures everyone there is life in the womb. That the waiting is still worth it.

"I can't get a hold of him," Doctor Marcella says to Graigh's distended stomach. "I see you moving little boy. Mom, I think your son is running away from me."

"Try towards the bottom near my pants."

"That's where I was going next."

Graigh sits up on her haunches and watches Doctor Marcella swoop the wand in the goo of her belly before descending to her hemline. Three passes below her navel and the nascent sounds of life blare in the silent room. Their sighs reverberate from the walls covering the ticking of the clock.

"I feared the worse there for a minute," Bombei says, exhaustion in his voice.

"I don't know why," Graigh reassures. "I told you he was up, and you saw him moving."

"I know. I know. I just did."

"I didn't," she says to Doctor Marcella.

"That's because you can feel him moving," The doctor says handing Graigh a towel to dry herself off.

"That's for damn sure." Graigh snorts in a chuckle.

The throaty noise turns into a cough.

She muffles it; tries to constrict the back of her throat to swallow the lung rattling wave rolling up from her chest cavity and threatening to exit her mouth with the force of a butterfly tremor that causes catastrophic earthquakes halfway around the world. Her face contorts to regain control. She holds her breath and then slowly wheezes air back into her inflamed lungs. Graigh smiles victoriously when the wave passes without her breaking her posture and being possessed by her body's internal, involuntary responses.

"His feet stay in my chest and my ribs," she says picking up her part of the conversation. "Some days it feels like he's going to push off the walls of my body and swim his way out. No pushing necessary."

"It may feel like that but let me tell you now that's not going to happen," Doctor Marcella says hovering over Graigh. "What I do want to talk about is what just happened there. The coughing seems to be worse, not stable or any better."

"It is worse," Bombei says from his chair. "She just doesn't like to talk about it."

"It's not that I don't like to talk about it," Graigh lies. "I just expect it to get worse the bigger I get. It's par for the pregnancy."

His eye roll at his wife who's not facing him is his only response. He reserves any other comments behind his teeth, knowing she doesn't want him airing her medical dirty laundry before she's ready. He slouches back against the flattened cushions of the forest green office chair listing to himself all her shortcomings.

Secretive.
Selfish.
Stubborn.
Sly.
Ungrateful.
Inconsiderate.
A liar.
Stuck in the past.
Maybe she is holding both of us back.

Bombei's own voice in his head is interrupted by the owl eyed Doctor who demanded he forgo keeping score. That he stop counting the wins and the losses and just love. He presses harder into his temples; thinking, clearing his mind, trying desperately to shake his thought.

Is she holding both of us back?

"Aside from the coughing, you and baby are doing great," Bombei hears Doctor Marcella say, bringing his attention back into the room with them.

She says, "I think he's about all out of room inside of there."

"You don't say." Graigh side-eyes the Doctor.

"You're almost there. Just a few more weeks," Bombei says. His voice is flat despite his attempt to participate in the conversation.

Graigh asks, "Are you sure you can't take him today?"

Her eyes plead with the doctor fanning herself in her long white lab coat. Doctor Marcella's sleeveless camel linen dress does nothing to keep her cool despite the air-conditioned medical tower.

"I'm sure. You're not even thirty-six weeks yet. And you're not super high risk that we need to induce you then either. If he's not coming on his own, then it's not time. Three to seven or eight weeks, give or take, and you two will be parents."

"What do you mean give or take, Doc?" Bombei asks.

"I mean your son is nearly fully formed and you're about to be on the clock. First babies come when they want to. They're forging a path all their own. There has been no other baby before them. He can come two weeks early. He may come two weeks late, though we wouldn't let him wait that long. The placenta stops being viable after about 41 and a half weeks. But like I said, we're on his time."

"Baby, please come early?" Graigh begs to her belly.

"Are you ready for that?" Doctor Marcella asks eyeing Graigh.

"I'm ready for this to be over. I'm ready for me to have my body, and for him to have his. I'm ready to sleep and not smell every damn thing."

"Oh, Baby," Doctor Marcella smirks. "It's going to get worse before it gets any better. You might have your body back, but it will never be the same. Don't plan on sleeping much those first three to six months, and as far as smell, it may go back to normal, it may not. Your body after a baby, including your senses are never truly your own again."

Tell me about it.

A deep resigned sigh is Graigh's only response. She blows disgruntled air through her nose in short bursts and puffs as she pushes herself upright on the reclined exam table. One hand in the middle of the padded cushion, the other gripping the edge, Graigh balances her body until she is steady, then stands on the spotted white linoleum. She uses her hands to hike the elastic of her jean shorts from beneath her belly over her distended stomach. Unrolling Bombei's T-shirt down to meet her shorts, she pulls the fabric forward creating air within herself to get rid of the sticky, humid, and hot.

"Well, if the two of you don't have any more questions," Doctor Marcella says catching Graigh's eye, then I will leave you with your chart and I'll see you in three weeks.

"See you then," Bombei says standing.

Doctor Marcella's sandals slide across the floor as she crosses the threshold and walks the hallway back to her office where she will wait for the nurses to tell her, her next patient is ready. The door lock clicks behind her, leaving Bombei with a hot, irritable, pregnant wife and a ticking clock. Each second marks off the flapping of Graigh's arms as she continuously pulls the fabric of her shirt away from her body. The pulling arm mimics a bird ascending into the sky, beating against the stale air of the room. Bombei grabs her hand to stop her motion and stills them at her side.

Graigh leans into him. Against the collar of his royal blue button down, paired with rough hewn dark denim jeans, her body presses next to his as she sinks her head into his neck. Warm breath against his skin, she rests in her nuzzle. He backs them up against a wall to support her lean and his stand. Hands around her waist he pulls her as close as physically possible.

This is not a lie.

His mind works to reestablish the veracity of the statement while his soul remains unsettled.

This is not a lie.

He wants the decree to validate their union, and the fidelity of their relationship. He wants a guarantee that their chance meeting was more than happenstance, his bold approach more than bravado, her reluctant yes more than whimsy, and her persistent company more than comfort.

With her body laid against his, surrendered into him, he wants the truth Doctor Grace urged him to focus on so that he may fall back inside the double locked abyss of his subconscious.

Bombei clings tight to her body knowing she is his religion and he's trying not to become a disenchanted disciple. He holds her as she fans herself hoping she feels the love blowing back into her. He nods his head and resolves to love her patiently, kindly, compassionately, fiercely, and protectively without envy or jealousy. She is his god and he prays that she remains more than a wizard who wasn't, a deity he should have never deigned to serve.

"C'mon, it's time to go," Bombei says gently into her ear.

"Ugh," she sighs. "I just want to go somewhere, get naked, lay down, and not move."

"I know some places where that's an option."

"You missed the part about me not moving."

"Get your head out of the gutter. I have restraint. I wasn't even talking about that."

"I'm just making sure. Let's go."

He holds the door open allowing her to pass through and lead the way. He follows as they round the corners to the receptionist. The soles of his fresh white Converse squeak against the floor. Leaning on the counter, he pulls her back against his chest. She pushes her body away and fans her face with her hand.

"Three weeks," Graigh says to the receptionist.

"Is August fourteenth good for you?" The thick voiced woman asks not looking up from her computer.

"I'll be here."

"Can you come in the morning? 10 a.m.?"

"See you then," Graigh says.

Graigh walks away fanning herself as they move through the office doors and into the hallway.

"Are you really that hot?" Bombei asks.

"I told you, yes," Graigh answers.

"But how? They have the AC on blast. You're just tired."

"Tired of being pregnant," Graigh says, opening the emergency exit doors to the stairwell.

"Why are you taking the stairs?" he asks, staring at her from the top.

"I don't know, I feel like walking."

Bombei watches Graigh stomp down the steps, using more energy than necessary to reach the bottom. He jogs down at a rhythmic pace keeping time with the beat in his head. He whistles, creating patterns with his wind and the echo of the hollow concrete stair well. She is waiting for him at the very bottom when he comes running up behind her, still keeping time, still whistling. Her foot taps to the beat of his music, irritated but entertained. Bombei holds out his hand for her as he pushes the door open onto the bottom floor of the office building. Graigh takes it, reluctantly, shortening her steps and walking beside him as his mouth hums his whistle, out of the hospital doors and to the car.

He opens his doors and starts the engine and AC before going around to her side and helping her settle into the low seat. Inside her hands find the controls for all the vents to make sure they're opened completely. She even checks the console vent that's supposed to keep the back seat cool, making sure it too is circulating inside the small confines of the car. She presses the sync button on the control panel and turns the air to its lowest temperature. Fifty-eight degrees of cold, man-made air flows into the car. Graigh reclines her seat rendering the shoulder strap of her seatbelt ineffective. Laid back, she once again exposes her belly. She sighs. Relieved and grateful. With her eyes closed, she pulls her knees into the fetal position, and turns her body toward Bombei in the driver's seat.

"Are you good now?"

"I'm better."

He reverses the car out of the parking space and maneuvers the parking lot until he's out and facing Canal street. The tenor of Harry Connick Jr.'s voice croons through the stereo, singing in Spanish, asking the woman of his affection to kiss him much. Harry's is the only voice from Canal to Claiborne to North Robertson. Somewhere between her crossing her body as they crossed the canal and home, he asks the question that's been burning his tongue since they left the doctor's office.

"Are you really that hot, or are you just being a brat?"

One eye opens first peering at him driving the residential speed limit as they near their home. Graigh pushes her body up in the seat and then lifts the lever to bring the seat back to meet her. With her heels beneath her butt, and her knees angled toward him, her posture is open and welcoming even if her heart is not. He doesn't look her way. He doesn't see her own subconscious at work as his was during the appointment. He doesn't let his bewildered eyes and puzzled face from his new resolution to love without counting wins and losses give way to regret.

He focuses on what he can see and says, "For once, tell me how you really feel without us arguing first, or are you going to keep pretending you can't stand the heat when you've lived here all of your life."

"Not all of my life."

"Excuse me? Your time in Tallahassee not included."

"There's nothing wrong. It's just hot."

"It's New Orleans. It's always hot. Try again."

"I'm not sure what you want me to say. You want me to feel something I don't. Say something I can't."

"Okay, let's try it this way. Are you scared?"

"I've been scared this whole time. That's not new. Now my fear is less about him not making it here, then it is about what the hell we're going to do to keep him here."

"What do you mean? He's going to make it. You've got a few more weeks."

"I know that," Graigh snaps. "Everybody keeps telling me how much longer, how much I'm going to be in love when he gets here, how everything is going to be when we bring him home. Why can't everybody just let me feel what I feel?"

"Present company included."

"Yes."

"It'd be one thing if you actually allowed yourself to feel your feelings. That I could deal with, but you run from yourself. So, what am I supposed to do then?"

That's hypocritical.

Bombei pulls into the carport uneasy with his own accusation even if it is honest. He puts the engine in park but keeps the car on, the air running. Fifty-eight degrees of truth serum coats both of their tongues creating a space for the conversation they've never wanted to have.

Graigh says, "Let me keep running and hiding until I'm ready to come out from my rock, unbury my head from the sand, and face my future."

"That's no way to live."

"That's the way I've been living."

"And that's the reason you're in therapy now."

"Says the man who told me I needed to go."

"As a way to get you to face your shit before you pass it on to our son."

"Is that why you went by yourself? To do the same?"

"Don't use sarcasm to get out of this. We're talking. Talk."

"About what. You already know I'm scared. The only way to not be scared is to keep on living. That's what I'm doing. Is that not good enough for you?"

"Don't do that. Don't pick a fight. We're good at that."

"I'm well aware."

"Sometimes damnit, I just want to shake the shit out of you."

"I bet you do," Graigh says not being able to hold a straight face.

In his frustration she finds laughter. In his mounting anger she finds humor. The giggles are her act of contrition. Her apology for being contrary even if she is being honest. In this moment she is more honest than him about the indecision of her emotions, the uncertainty of her feelings, and the ambiguity of her consciousness. Laughter is the salve that sustains their marriage. As a couple it is their salvation when prayer urges action.

"Besides scared, what else are you feeling?" Bombei asks after the laughter has subsided.

"I don't know. Unprepared. The baby's room isn't finished. The baby shower isn't finalized. I don't know what they're going to do at work while I'm gone, if they're going to move someone else into my store and give it to them permanently and find somewhere else for me or not. You still don't want to talk about the store around the corner."

"It's not feasible for us right now, Graigh."

"Yes. It is. You just don't want to do it."

"No, I don't want to do it. It's a lot of money on an idea you don't know will work."

"Because this community doesn't need a pharmacy? You've got to be kidding me."

"We need a pharmacy, but that doesn't mean you have to open one."

"If not me, then who?"

"If the guys who owned it originally didn't reopen after the storm, then something should tell you that there's something either wrong with the property, the location, or both."

"Something we will never know if we don't at least talk to a realtor about the location."

"How did we even get on this crazy ass idea of yours."

"Why does it have to be crazy? Because you don't agree?" Graigh challenges.

"And here we are arguing." Bombei says.

"You started it. I'm going inside."

"And there you go running again?"

What else do you want me to do.

Graigh gives voice to her exasperation, "What else am I supposed to do? You want to talk about what you want to talk about. I give in and talk to you, and when I bring up something that you don't want to talk about, you run just as much as I do."

"How am I running. I'm right here. I'm not threatening to go inside. You are."

"Just because you don't walk away or don't leave the space we share doesn't mean you're not running. Where were you during our appointment with Doctor Marcella?"

His blank face is his only answer to her observation. It steeps her anger, charging the air around them with electrons ready to attack.

Graigh continues, "When you shut down uncomfortable conversations, that's you running. When you stop talking and go shadow box in the shower, that's you running. When we have angry sex, that's you running. And when you go talk to Doctor Grace, my therapist, without me, that's you running. So yeah, I want to open the pharmacy around the corner. I'm scared about the baby coming, because nothing is ready, and this world is crazy. That's my truth but what the hell is yours? You spend all your time trying to analyze and deduce me. Stop holding up a mirror and turn that shit on yourself."

"Whatever," Bombei says, failing to steel himself against the legitimacy of her attack.

"You know I'm right. You wanna talk about me. About my feelings. Let's talk about yours."

"I'm fine."

"No, you're not. You're just as scared as I am."

"What reason do I have to be scared?" Bombei asks.

"You know why," Graigh says. "You want to talk about my past and my issues so much, let's talk about yours. I saw how you looked at Mr. Charles when he was here."

"What are you talking about?"

Bombei shifts in the driver's seat. He uses the switch to push it back even further away from the steering wheel. His hands pull at his cargo shorts, creating more room in the legs that barely skim the sides of his thighs. His hands smooth the wrinkles of his plum T-shirt. They tug at his beard and smooth the deep waves of his hair.

He picks at himself remembering the comment from months ago that was meant to be a joke. *I like her better than you. I thought you knew that by now.* What was said in jest was received as a reminder of neglect by the child of a grieving father.

"So, are you ready to talk about the real reason you don't want me to do anything?" Graigh asks.

"You're pregnant."

"Pregnant, not handicapped. I can open my own doors . . ."

"I'm a gentleman."

"I can put away groceries . . ."

"You always complain about your feet and your back hurting, so I try to take the load off of you."

"You don't let me sweep, or mop . . ."

"You may strangle the baby."

"But you're not just worried about the baby, like I'm worried about the baby."

"What are you trying to say, Graigh?"

"I'm not trying to say anything. I'm saying you're scared."

"Of what?" Bombei says indignantly.

"For me."

So, what if I am. That's my pain. Just like your pain is your pain.

Bombei doesn't respond. His mind hurtles him backwards in time out of the city, to somewhere called the country, where he can remember standing in a thicket, the remnants of a felled stand all around him, his dad, Mr. Charles, standing in front of him shielding his eyes from everything except the tears falling down his face.

Thirty-Four

Bombei blocked his young face from the sun. The rays shone brightly between the sparsely populated branches. Thirsty limbs from the once vibrant trees crackled beneath his feet. They were twigs. Ashen, gray and fragile instead of their once rich brown bark; strong and flexible. Any time he moved a foot, or an arm the sound of the popping tree debris gave away his position. He couldn't hide, not even in his silence, against the backdrop of dead trees, and the peeling whitewash of sinking headstones. Death surrounded him and his father who looked closer to going over to the other side of the ground every year they came to lay flowers and pay tribute to the mother he never met.

Shirley Ryan Halvert. Bombei mouthed his mom's name as he watched his father kneel down to place the three bouquets of flowers in front of her grave. A bouquet of calla lilies he was told were her favorites. A bouquet of roses from his dad, and a bouquet of sunflower's he'd picked out himself. His eyes traveled back and forth across his father's hands as he watched him arrange the three vases they'd bought against the headstone. He poured the flower food from the open bouquets into each of the vases, and then water from the gallon jug they'd bought from a gas station along the way. Bombei's father worked meticulously, pulling a utility knife from his pocket to clip the stems on a diagonal before placing one of each flower into all three vases. Red, yellow, and white petals mixed and mingled as they all vied for attention in the triangular arrangement of the vases. The flowers looked like a starburst of color by the time his father finished. He couldn't tell where the roses began or the sunflowers ended, nor from which stem the calla lilies came. The flowers appeared as if they'd all grown together, from the same seed, and shared the same root. They bloomed boldly in front of the epitaph:

Shirley Ryan Halvert

Sunrise May 19, 1956—Sunset January 10, 1980

Greatest and Most Loving Wife and Mother

His dad stood to his feet, his face wet and his hands full with the plastic wrappers and stems from the bouquets in his left, and the half-filled jug of water in his right. Sweat and tears poured down his face in the sun. They always came to see her on her birthday, his dad choosing to remember her the way she lived and not on the day she died. For him, that day did not exist, even if it was his only son's birthday. Bombei was celebrated on the ninth or the eleventh if the date of his actual birthday landed on a Saturday, or any day he chose so long as it was not the tenth. For the last two years he chose to celebrate his half birthday instead. July tenth. After the Halvert house day of mourning, and after her birthday. It was a day all to himself that had no meaning, no significance, and no extra weight or baggage he didn't know whether he was supposed to carry.

This year, he was ten. He was looking forward to a hotel party where he and his friends planned to play in the pool, eat po'boys, and get a sugar high from SnoBalls in red, blue, purple, and orange. But first he had to get through this day. That morning he sat with his dad as he flipped through their wedding album. Every year he noticed something different about her; he paid more attention to the woman enshrined in the image. This year it was her hair. He focused on her curls. He could still see the luster of her dark hair in the sepia picture. Her netted wedding veil shrouded her face, but it didn't hide all her hair. Thick and straight with a tight under curl on the end, he noticed a rhinestoned bobby pin kept it and the veil in place. On the next page of the album her veil was up showing off her face. Her skin was almost the same color as the tint of the photograph. He knew she was a fair brown. He studied the way her hair hit her collar bone in her off-the-shoulder wedding dress. In one picture taken from the back, she laid her head against his dad's. They leaned in toward one another. His short afro flattened against the crown of her head, her hair hanging down to just above where her bra strap would be. He noticed the ends of the back of her hair hung straight in the image, probably a late reception picture when sweat from dancing had begun to melt off the makeup and caused pressed hair to revert to its natural state.

As he sat by his father looking at his mother he imagined the music they danced to that made her lose her curls in the back of her hair.

He asked, "Daddy, what song did you and Mama dance to?"

"You Are the Sunshine of My Life," his father answered somberly.

"By Stevie Wonder?"

"It had just come out and was the song playing in the restaurant when we went out on our first date. We were sixteen."

The brief story was the most his father had ever said to him on her day since he could remember. Usually he was just told "come on, let's go." He followed, making sure he stayed quiet, didn't ask to many questions, and didn't ask for anything for himself; nothing to eat, and nothing to drink until after they left the cemetery.

That's what he was waiting on. His stomach growled, his feet hurt, and his arms were tired from shielding his eyes from the sun as he stood in the dead brush, waiting for his turn. They would say her favorite Bible verse, tell her goodbye, and walk hand in hand between the sunken tombstones to get back in the car that waited for them at the side of the road. But none of that would happen until his dad dried his face in his elbows.

Bombei found a spot in the crush of branches that no longer made noise with the shifting of his weight. The twigs beneath his feet were all snapped into bits. The branches by his arms were diminutive shrubs whose tips barely touched him, barely scratched. He stood still in the thicket. The standing trees far behind him worked hard to lean toward the sun and provide shade, but there was no cover, and the trees and shrubs beneath him provided no rest for his tired feet. He watched from his hand hooded eyes as his father raised one arm to his face then the other. He never dropped a stem or a plastic wrapper from the flowers. The jug of water never slipped his grip. His arms lifted in succession, he wiped his face on his elbows, but the river from his eyes never stopped flowing. The growing ocean around the collar of his T-shirt never stopped deepening.

He watched, noticing the sprinkling of gray hairs in his father's beard. They'd only recently begun to show, just like the gray patch in the back of his low faded head. Aged beyond his years, only the elasticity of his skin showed he was still in his youth. Bombei watched his father's arms lift, one by one, over and over again, until they finally settled by his side. Bombei waited in his thicket. He waited until he was called, until he was summoned before approaching his mother.

A look and a tip of the head was all he needed to move. He carefully stepped through the crackling branches and approached the gravestone. He stood beside his father. His head reaching the upper part of his arm. He waited again until his Dad cleared his throat.

Together they said, "They that wait on the Lord shall renew their strength. They shall mount up on wings like an eagle. They shall run and not grow weary. They shall walk and not grow faint."

"Your momma said that while she was in labor with you," his dad said after a beat. "She repeated it over and over in the room where we thought she was going to give birth. It was the last thing I heard her say when they wheeled her out to go to the operating room to handle *complications*."

Bombei nodded in response not sure if he should ask the question burning his tongue. "What complications?" Or should he wait in repose because he wasn't so much being told a story, as he was hearing a man's buried memory.

His father continued, "They asked me in case of emergency who should they save first. I don't remember answering the question, and to this day I'm not sure if I regret my panic that made me silent when she needed me to speak up for her most."

Bombei stayed quiet to the story he'd only recently learned. Every year he learned more and more about the unfortunate circumstances of his birth. He listened with his eyes closed, and his ears open, imagining the woman from the picture saying the words he just said as she tried to make them two from one.

"Your momma was some kind of special, Boy," his dad continued. "She was some kind of special. She was my Shirley-girl. That's what I called her."

Bombei watched as his Dad stood beside her tombstone. Leaning against it, one arm atop it as if he were holding on to her instead of formed cement, with a brief inscription of her brief contributions to the world.

"Bye, Baby," his father said walking away from the grave. "I'll see you again, Shirley-girl."

His goodbye was thrown over his shoulder as if she was standing waiting to catch it. Waiting to say it back. It's the way he always said goodbye. Like he knew she could hear him. As if he could hear her voice.

Bombei waited until his dad cleared half of the small cemetery before he closed in on his mother's grave. He waited until he could barely hear him hum the old gospel hymn whose words he never sang. When the tenor sound of the music was just barely audible, Bombei approached the flowers, knelt down before them, and inhaled. He smelled the scent of the three of them together. He imprinted it into his mind to remind him that the three of them do all share something together. That it's not just his mom, or dad's Shirley-girl, that they are still family, even if everything they do is separate.

He felt the eyes on his back telling him to hurry up; to come on. That even though her day wasn't over, it was still time to go. The memory too much. The reminders too real. The grief too great to handle.

"Bye, Mama," Bombei said walking away from the grave.

He walked quickly toward the waiting car. The old, forest green, Camry was already running. His dad waited inside smoking a cigarette. He didn't smoke except twice a year; on the Halvert house day of mourning, and on Shirley-girl's special day. He smoked when he didn't want to cry and was trying to forget. The hazy curlicues hovered above his face and head when Bombei got in the car. He rolled down his window and leaned his head out of the car blowing smoke into the atmosphere. He finished his cigarette facing her grave, accepting his reality, that his Shirley-girl was gone until he came to see her again. His father dropped the butt, shifted the car in gear, and slowly rolled to the stop sign at the entrance of the small cemetery on the side of the road.

"What you say to your momma that took you so long?"

"Just saying bye, that's all."

"You didn't say nothing bad about me, did you?"

Bombei noticed he asked the question with a smile, but his tone was not a joke. He didn't want his Shirley-girl to know anything bad about him. He didn't want her to think he wasn't doing right by their son. He didn't want her to know about the long bouts of silence between them, and the unanswered questions about her. He didn't want her to know about the time when he was five when he'd gotten spanked because he insisted on asking for something to eat before they arrived at the cemetery, or last year when he wet himself on her grave because they'd been standing there for so long and he didn't want to get a beating. He could see behind his father's smiling face, and serious soul, that he didn't want his Shirley-girl to know that he needed help but was too proud to ask for it, and too heartbroken to seek it from somewhere else, from somebody else.

"I just told her bye," Bombei muttered looking out his window.

"That was a long goodbye."

"I guess I miss her."

"You can't miss what you ain't never had."

Bombei didn't respond to the falsehood he was supposed to accept as truth. He knew to leave the alternative fact where it landed, between them, never to be acknowledged again.

"I got you something for your birthday?" His dad said reaching beneath his seat, barely keeping the wheel straight.

Looking at the road he handed Bombei a bound book wrapped in a blue receiving blanket.

"She was making it for you. To remember all your moments."

"What is it?"

"It's your baby book."

Bombei nodded his head to the confession more intrigued by the new images of the woman who gave him life. The images were in full color at varying stages of her pregnancy. Her hair as long and as thick as he could tell from her wedding photo hung nearly to her butt in a low ponytail. She stood in green grass with her hands on her hips supporting her arching back and round stomach. Black shorts showed off her legs, and a white men's T-shirt covered her belly. The sleeves were cut off to accommodate for the heat.

The caption below the picture was dated September 10, 1979. She was six months pregnant then.

Bombei flipped to another page in the bound book. This time she was seated. Her hair curled around her shoulders, smiling, holding up a fan of money for the camera to see. The caption notated that it was her baby shower, December 20, 1979. It was the last picture in the book, the last captured memory before she departed. Bombei turned the page expecting to see blank paper, but was surprised to find a letter dated January 10, 1980, 6 a.m.

"Read it," his dad said watching from his periphery. "She refused to go to the operating room until she was done with her letter."

My dearest baby boy Bombei,

I can't wait to meet you. I can't wait to hold you in my arms. I can't wait to see you, to smell your baby smell, to see your hair change from womb straight to thick and curly. I have to make this quick because the nurses and your Daddy are rushing me to go to make sure we get you here. It's been a long night. You've been taking your time to come into this world and teaching me the true meaning of the word labor. I can tell you that it's nothing like what I've been doing at the school. Teaching music class and chorus. I know you've been hearing the students sing to you while you've been in there, and me too. Your daddy sometimes too. Anyway, that's work. This labor thing is completely different. They say I've been laboring too long and now you're making me a little sick. I think they're just tired of seeing me sweating, and walking, and moaning, and groaning, and screaming Charity down. But you're worth it. And you're worth the wait. I see the nurses and the doctors whispering and talking to your Daddy. I just want you to always know I love you more than this life itself. You're worth every bead of sweat, every step I take, every moan, every groan, and every ounce of blood it takes for me to get you here. I have so much planned for us to do. And your Daddy knows. I told him all my plans for you. The zoo, the aquarium, beignets when you get some teeth, sucking the head of the crawfish, opening your own crabs, fishing, playing under the bridge by the lake, masking Indian at least once. You've got to be somebody's spy boy. And Mardi Gras. I want you to dance, or sing, or play, in at least one of the parades. I gotta go now so we can get you here. I can't wait to kiss your face and tell you I love you. No matter what happens I want you to always know that I love you and God loves you. Remember, "They that wait on the Lord, shall renew their strength, they shall mount up and soar on wings like eagles. They shall run and not grow weary; they shall walk and not grow faint." I've been waiting ten long months to meet you. I'm not weary and I'm not faint from labor because the plans of the diligent will surely lead to prosperity. You will be prosperous, you will be loved, you will be successful, you will be happy, you will have joy, and you will leave a legacy that will outlive both me, you, and your daddy. I gotta go now. See you soon.

Love Mama.

The tears flowed freely from his eyes as he closed the baby book. The drops of water disappeared into the plastic wrapping overlaid on top of the brown cover. He didn't lift his elbows to his face to hide his running emotions. He faced forward and cried. He watched the road leaving the country taking them back to the city. Taking them back to the house she never got to share with them; with him.

"Daddy, what time was I born?" Bombei croaked through his tears.

"Open the book. Your birth certificate is in there, but I believe it was 7:34 a.m."

"What time did she die?"

"8:46."

"Did she ever get to hold me?"

"I wasn't in there, but the Doctors told me that she did see you, and I could tell she got close to you because there was blood and stuff on her lips, nose, and cheek before they cleaned her body, but I don't know if she held you. They had to get you cleaned up and take care of her at the same time."

Bombei nodded stoically re-opening the baby book in his lap. He opened it back to her letter. Back to her steady, cursive handwriting. The loops and flourishes from her own hand looked more like calligraphy than standard cursive. He studied the feminine curve of her handwriting discerning what she must have been like. Assuming that she was girly, obsessed with beauty both in herself and manifested in her surroundings. He knew it was because of her they had peach curtains in their living room, and mint walls in the kitchen. He knew it was because of her that marigold curtains hung in Daddy's bedroom even though he rarely wore any color at all. He knew it was because of her that their home was decorated with mirrors, cheap photo prints of famous paintings, and wicker baskets stuck in corners to hold whatever knick knacks accumulated in each room. He knew she was the reason Daddy cleaned with lavender and lemon.

Turning the page, he found another handwritten note. This one written in all caps. Rough and straight edged.

"You don't have to read that one," his dad said glancing over to see what he was looking at.

"It's from you, Daddy."

"Read it later."

Bombei turned the page. It was filled with pictures of him. Days one through seven. Weeks two, three, and four. Months one through twelve. Years one through five. His baby book was completed. Every memory captured. All of his doctor appointments documented. His first teeth captured in photos, and the ones that had fallen out contained in a baggie taped to the page. The pictures celebrating his milestones of his first year were all snapped on either the ninth of the month or the eleventh. None of them were dated the tenth. His birthday pictures were the same from two to five.

Bombei closed the book and lifted the receiving blanket it was wrapped into his face. He inhaled a scent he didn't recognize; one he could not place as having ever smelled before. It didn't smell like her calla lilies, or the lavender Daddy cleaned the house with. It didn't smell like roses. He left the blanket laid over his face allowing it to transport him back in time to his earliest memory. He was hoping to get back to the day of his birth when for a moment she put her face against his and breathed the last of her life into him.

"It's her perfume," his dad said looking straight ahead at the highway in front of them.

"What kind did she wear?"

"They don't make it anymore. I first got it for her when we graduated high school and she wore it every day she lived. I guess the blanket trapped her smell when she put it and everything else into the box."

"What else is in the box?"

"You can see for yourself when we get back home."

"Thanks, Daddy," Bombei mumbled holding back another round of his tears. "This is a good birthday gift."

"I know it's a little early. Or well I guess it's a little late. But I wanted you to have it on her day. I think you're old enough now."

Bombei nodded beneath the blanket still covering his face. He did his best to limit his tears, so he didn't ruin the last of her with himself, so he didn't take the last of what she left him and cannibalize her essence. His face covered; he didn't see his dad's tears falling freely. He didn't see the streaked cheeks, unwiped and unashamed. They cried together each wracked with their own grief, their own mourning, their own heartache. It was the first time Bombei had cried about his mother. It was the first time he felt anything other than contempt and the occasional curiosity for the woman who stole all the attention from his dad that should have been his. He cried because he didn't know, because now he would never know more about Mama, about Shirley-girl; the woman who gave her life for his. He cried quietly, beneath the blanket that still smelled like her discontinued perfume. They were the first of many tears to fall over the many years he would grow to the miss the mama he'd met in passing between the land of the living.

By the time Bombei pulled the blanket from his face they were driving past downtown headed home. His stomach grumbled reminding him that he hadn't eaten. Now it was a pressing need whereas in the cemetery, amid his pain, the physical pangs of life didn't matter.

His dad asked with a knowing smile, "What do you say we go by Dooky Chase and get some gumbo?"

"Was it her favorite?" Bombei asked raising his arm to his face, to dry the last drops from the well of tears in his eyes.

"You damn straight it was," his Dad chuckled at an unshared memory. "You damn straight."

Thirty-Five

"Baby, are you almost dressed, everyone is waiting for you down stairs?" Bombei asks coming into their bedroom.

"I'm dressed I just can't fasten my shoe straps," Graigh says stepping into the hallway between their bedroom and bathroom.

"You look amazing," he says.

"I look huge."

"That's my wife you're talking about."

"Ha, ha, and thank you. Now are you going to fasten these shoes or not?"

"They're kind of high don't you think."

"I gotta show off these legs since the rest of me has been overtaken by your son."

"You don't have to show that much."

"Thick thighs save lives."

"How many other lives you trying to save besides mine?"

"Boy, just fasten my shoes please," Graigh says holding one foot up in the air.

Bombei walks over to where she hangs in the hallway and sits on the floor beneath her. At thirty-five weeks she radiates in the pronouncement of her pregnancy. Seeing her glow touches him internally, arouses his love, and increases his desire. Bombei places her dainty foot in his lap and threads the rose gold strap through the golden buckle. His hand lingers on the heel of her foot as he places it back to the floor. It traipses to her other foot lifting it off the ground, placing it in his lap, and following the same steps. He takes his time, focusing on the thin strap, placing the stem of the buckle in the same position as he did for her other foot, and then secures it in place. He places her foot on the floor in front of him but doesn't release it. His hand travels from her soft heels, up the back of her bare leg, over her taught calves, shaped from standing and reaching all day in the pharmacy, to the meat of her inner thigh just above her knee. He looks up from the work of his hands to her face staring inquisitive daggers into the top of his forehead.

Don't start.

Graigh smirks, "Didn't you just tell me to hurry up because everyone is waiting?"

Bombei studies the hang of her twists to her shoulders. She has them twisted back on the right and swept over on the left. Cowrie shells, gold hair cuffs, and rose gold braid thread are affixed throughout adorning her crown. It is the hairstyle he most loved on her. The style she wore the day he made them meet, now recreated to mimic the exact hang she had when she says they went on their first official date. When they had their first argument about Katrina. When she left him standing on the porch of her FEMA trailer without a kiss or a goodbye, concupiscent, aroused, and alone. He looks at her glowing in the backlight from their illuminated bathroom, his hand flat against the thinnest part of her thigh, his finger almost at the point where her legs meet daring her to say everything but stop. Graigh steps back from temptation and adjusts the hem of her hot pink dress stretched over her distended belly.

Don't start.

Her warning reverberates through her body, as she steels her flesh to his touch.

"We don't have enough time," Graigh says, removing her foot from his lap.

"I'll be quick," Bombei pleads looking up at her.

"For one, no, you won't. You never are. And for two, brevity is never a good thing."

"But you've considered . . ."

"We're going to be late, My Love." Graigh cuts him off and steps around him to the door leading them both out of the bedroom.

"We can't be late if the party's in our own home."

"Let's go."

Bombei stands and adjusts the waist of his navy-blue dress pants. He shakes his left and right legs and meets her in the doorway. Graigh loops her arm through the crook of his extended elbow and follows his lead through the loft, down the steps, through the kitchen and dining room and into the living room meant only for special occasions.

Scattered amongst the stark white furniture and the sparkling rectangular mirrors are their friends and family. Mr. Charles and Dougie and the women they brought with them, Joy and Tony, Shandra and Teddy, Janay, and her boyfriend, a few of Bombei's coworkers from the school, and the two pharmacy techs who work the closest with Graigh. Some sit, most stand in a semi-circle formed around a high back, white leather chair, with mocha wood arms and feet. Bombei leads Graigh to the chair and helps her ease into the low seat.

"Don't cross your legs like that, you're showing too much." He drags his hand across her exposed thigh before stepping away.

Graigh adjusts her legs, crosses her ankles, and tugs at the hem of her dress to no avail.

"Shall we begin with games?" Joy asks stepping into the center of the room where the coffee table used to be.

"Depends on what we're playing," Graigh cuts her eyes at Joy.

"Well our mommy-to-be, is a bit of a control freak, so we only have a few games to get through before we can just chill and eat. Let's start with pregnant *Taboo*. The men versus the women."

"I'll keep score," Graigh says from behind Joy.

"No, you have to play too. Let's go, men first."

Through five rounds of *Taboo*, a word scramble, and several guessing games, Graigh and Bombei converse without words. Their eyes speak as do their body movements. Their hearts' desire longing to be alone, instead of at the center of attention in their packed house for their baby shower. Across the room their gazes catch and Graigh stares at him as he stares back at her. He licks his lips. She shakes her head.

Not now.

Soon.

His eyes simmer and Bombei steels his jaw in an effort to find patience as the last game comes to an end.

With one hand on her belly, Graigh leads the line of people to the buffet of food Shandra prepared. She lingers at each foil pan deciding what she has a taste for. Red beans and rice and ribs make it on to her plate along with more than a couple slices of cornbread. She balances the hefty load on the flimsy, baby shower themed plate as she attempts to grab a bottle of water.

"Let me get that for you," Janay says grabbing the bottle just out of Graigh's reach.

"Thank you. I'd be pissed if I dropped this plate."

"I know you would," Janay says touching her own protruding belly. "These kids gotta eat."

"And so, do we," Graigh laughs.

"Excuse me, but do you mind if I borrow my wife for a minute," Bombei says.

He pulls Graigh into the kitchen out of earshot of the people circling their dining room table, piling food on their plates.

"That was abrupt." Graigh sets her plate down on the island.

"I need you to myself," Bombei says.

"You have me to yourself all the time. And everyone will be leaving soon enough anyway."

"It doesn't seem like it," he says letting his hands travel up the back of her neck to the nape of her hairline. His fingers linger in the new growth, and gently pull at the tightly coiled curls of her kitchen. He pulls the curls apart until his finger rests on a bare piece of the bottom of her scalp. Going around and around in a circular motion he massages the space noticing the subtle changes in her body. Graigh drops what's left of the rib and sucks her fingers cleans as Bombei's hands move their massage from the nape of her neck to the middle of her head. He massages her scalp through the thickness of her new growth and twists. Graigh relaxes her head into his capable hands and enjoys the connection between them. His fingers and her sighs of appreciation pick up their wordless conversation.

I need more.

Not yet.

Bombei increases the intensity in his fingers to express his need elsewhere. Graigh's sighs deepen into low, guttural growls as pressure and tension build on her scalp from the earnestness of his motions rubbing and massaging circles, she wished she could rub and massage on him.

"What y'all doing in here?" Joy asks stepping into the kitchen.

"She had a headache," Bombei lies. "I was helping her out. You alright, Bae?"

Graigh nods her head beneath his grip, opens her eyes and winces. Slowly Bombei removes his hands from her head as they come back to normal under Joy's knowing gaze.

"I'm going upstairs," Bombei says walking toward the staircase.

Graigh watches him walk away, their wordless tête-à-tête continues in their stare.

Come with me.

Not yet.

"That was intense," Joy says with a smile creeping across her face.

"Not yet it wasn't," Graigh says coolly.

"I was coming to tell you we can wrap up with you opening your gifts, but it seems like you two are in a hurry."

"Perhaps," Graigh shrugs.

"Don't perhaps me, Heifer. This is not a headache face. This is an I'm about to get some face. That man is ready to jump your pregnant bones and will do it right here in the middle of this kitchen where I have to eat breakfast in the morning?"

"Because this is about you?" Graigh asks raising an eyebrow. "Who said you were invited to breakfast?"

"I did, since we're staying here. You better be making me breakfast," Joy says.

"We may be busy at breakfast."

"You mean you'll be getting busy as his breakfast."

"Either way, we'll be busy."

"I guess you're ready to wrap this party up?"

"If it's done, it's done," Graigh says, getting up from the island. "I'll be back."

"Go on drain your man dry. We'll wait."

"Don't be obscene."

"Tony and I haven't been together all these years to not know what phantom headaches, and a quick trip upstairs means."

Graigh rolls her eyes and smooths out her waddle as she takes the stairs one by one. Her high heeled feet press into the carpet of the steps. Pressure mounts on her ankles with the incline, but the tempered lust beneath her belly propels her forward. Once she reaches the top, she sees the bedroom door is open, but Bombei is not there. She sashays into the sunlit room, passes by the still made bed, and the blanket draped over the full-length mirror, and makes her way into the hall. Inside the massive walk in closet Bombei stands fully clothed, holding a square gift in his hand with a book on top of it as if he's mesmerized by the sight.

"I thought I'd be walking into something much different than this," Graigh says huskily.

"Me too."

"So why aren't you naked?"

"I realized I left your gift on the shelf."

"And?"

"My feelings changed."

"That's a downer," she tsks. "What is it?"

"Come see," he says gesturing his head for her to come his way.

Graigh slinks her way toward Bombei and wraps one arm around his lower back. She lays her head on his shoulder and lets her free hand rest on his chest covering his pounding heart. He brings her hand to his lips, kisses her knuckles, and hands her the book on top of the gift.

"What's this?" Graigh asks.

"Open it?" Bombei urges gently.

"If it's a gift, shouldn't I open it with everything else downstairs? Joy is ready for us to wrap this up . . . And so am I."

Depth returns to Graigh's voice as she misreads the moment.

Bombei says, "This is not a gift for everyone. It's a gift for you."

"And you want me to open it now?"

"I'm giving it to you now."

Graigh takes the brown, leather-bound book in her hands. The skin is smooth, not cracked, but she can tell it's old from the severe softness. Preserved for a purpose. She opens it and sees a woman she doesn't recognize smiling back at her. The woman is beautiful and radiant. Her hair is long, her smile wide, nose wider, and her belly is big in pregnancy. She reads the dated caption beneath the book. September 10, 1979.

"Is this . . .?" She starts the question and turns the page.

The same face, another smile, this time wider, belly bigger, nose even more spread, money in her hand, a paper plate flower on her head, joy in her eyes. Graigh reads the date: December 20, 1979. She turns the page to the handwritten letter. She squints to make out the fading blue ink and the hasty scrawl. She sees the words, *My dearest baby boy, Bombei.* Graigh slams the book shut. A shudder runs up her back and chills manifest on her arms.

"That's Mama," Bombei says.

"How long have you had this?" She asks, handing the book back to him.

He pushes it to stay in her hands, "Since I was ten," he answers. "Daddy gave it to me when I turned ten. On her day."

"Why didn't you show me this before? I thought you didn't have anything of hers."

"I always planned to give it to you when you got pregnant. I just never thought it would take us ten years to get here."

"I guess that's my fault," Graigh says defensively.

"It's no one's fault. Everything happens in its own time."

Thank you.

Graigh nods her head opening the book again. She lingers on the picture on the first page, and then looks at the image on the second. She flips back and forth between the two staring into the eyes of his mother he never knew, the Mother-in-Law she could never meet, never ask for advice, and never complain to about her hard-headed son.

"Do you have any more pictures of her?"

"Those are the only two I have. Daddy still has their wedding pictures. He has the whole album, but he doesn't take it out often. Not for a long time."

"Especially, not with that new lady coming around," Graigh says.

"He's finally moving on. It took him forty years, but I'm happy for him."

"Me too," Graigh says.

"That's not your only gift," Bombei says handing her the wrapped package."

Graigh places his baby book beneath the package and gently tears the blue balloon paper open at the seam he created with tape. Out of the wrapping she pulls another book; navy blue and leather bound. It's nearly identical to the one in her hand save for the color.

"Is this the reason you kept taking the baby book off the registry at all the stores."

"Yes," he says sheepishly.

"I was so mad at you."

"I know. But we weren't going to find this in Buy Buy Baby, Walmart, or Target. And this is the one I wanted us to have."

"Us?"

"I'm going to do what Daddy did for me. There's enough space in the book for us both to write notes and take pictures with our boy until he's five. My book is one sided after page three. His won't be, the Lord willing."

"I'm going to be fine," Graigh reassures.

"Mama thought the same thing too. Now my birthday reminds me of what I took from myself."

"It wasn't your fault."

"You can't tell me it was God's will though."

"I wasn't going to say that either. I'm just saying you can't carry the weight of your mother's death on your shoulders forever. Put it down."

"I didn't pick it up until I got this book. Until I read her words. Until I believed in her faith. Her Jesus. And failed to find comfort in anything she left behind outside of her smile. Daddy tolerated me as a child because he promised her, and I learned to tolerate myself."

"Do you think I just tolerate you?" Graigh steers the conversation away from his self-loathing.

"No. I know you love me."

"How do you know that?"

"You're having my baby. On purpose."

"You damn right," she laughs.

Her levity breaks his trance into the past. She sees the switch in his eye and the hold of his jaw. His feelings are safely tucked back on the inside of his body in the feet of his soul, in the pocket of his heart. She squeezes her rounded body between him and the rack of clothes and hugs him. Breathing into his neck, her fingers travel up the solid weight of his body, over his chest to his beard. She pulls through the curls of his chin with her freshly manicured nails. Graigh finger combs through his neat trim until her talons pull smoothly through the hair. Grabbing his chin, she moves his face toward her own and plants a kiss on his lips. Their skin touches. Open eyes reassure their enduring level of trust. He sighs into her mouth releasing the burden from his open wound. Graigh tongues away his pain, laps away his hurt, and leaves him a promise of their happiness. Their wordless conversation continues in a new connection.

I have pain, too.

So do I.

I have ghosts, too.

So do I.

Bombei engages with her. Graigh breaks the kiss and steps away breathlessly. She opens her eyes as she brushes the backs of her hands against his cheeks drying the tears that appeared at the corners of his eyes. She presses another quick kiss against his lips and then steps away.

"Let's go," she says grabbing both baby books.

"You have one more gift."

"What is it?"

"When Daddy first gave me the book, it was wrapped in a receiving blanket. One Mama picked out. The one I was wrapped in after she died. The one I stayed wrapped in while I was in the hospital."

"Hold on to it," Graigh says, dabbing at her own eyes.

"I want you to have it."

"It doesn't belong to me. It's his," she says looking down at her belly. "Leave it up here."

"You're leaving the books too? Right?"

"Just yours. I want to show off the one you bought. No one will know."

"Daddy will."

"That's okay."

"I guess," Bombei shrugs.

He smooths his black polo against his body and makes sure the hem lays flat against his slacks. They interlace hands and fingers in the doorway and walk step by step through the loft, down the stairs, through the kitchen and dining room, and into the living room where guests chatter, nibbling at crumbs, over empty plates.

"Let's open the gifts," Joy announces.

"I'd like to say something first," Graigh says.

"Go ahead, Mama, it's your party."

Grabbing Bombei's hand, she begins, "We want to thank everyone for coming out. Friends we've known forever, and new friends who have made an impact on our lives in such a short time. And to the family that's known us longer than we've known ourselves, we want to thank you for being here and sharing this next phase of our journey with us. Thank you."

Teddy and Shandra start a clap that erupts around the room. Bombei kisses Graph's temple then helps her sit back on the throne ordered specifically for his queen.

"Now, let's open the gifts," Joy says in a choked voice.

"I'll start with this one. It's our new baby book," she says holding up the leather-bound book for the room to see.

"Who got it, so I can write it down for when you send your thank you cards."

"Bombei got this one. And a thank you card won't be necessary," she says sliding her eyes to look at him.

"That's what got y'all in this mess in the first place," Teddy says aloud.

"Says the man with three kids," Graigh retorts.

"I hope he got you something more than that baby book," Shandra says. "Brother-in-law you need to step your game up for the push present."

"Shandra chill," Graigh admonishes. "I've got a baby boy coming and a baby book to share all the memories. Bombei's gotten me plenty."

"If you say so."

"I do." Graigh glances at Mr. Charles.

He tips his head toward her with a knowing look and raises his cup in her direction.

She mouths, "Thank you" as Joy hands her the next gift.

Thirty-Six

August 15—36 Weeks

The moon shines over the city as Bombei and Graigh walk through the raucous French Quarter. They walk down the middle of Bourbon street with the rest of the summer revelers stepping clear of spilled booze, vomit, and excrement from the saddled donkeys that take well-meaning tourists on trips through an area best seen and felt on foot. Hand in hand, they walk through the crowd holding tight to each other to keep from being separated by those tipping tipsily through the street. They pass bars and restaurants with doors wide open, music loud, and patrons even louder. Boutique hotels, stores carrying an array of beads and masks, daiquiri shops, and strip clubs where the bass from bounce and trap music compete for the aural attention of passersby with itchy hands ready to make it rain all over twerking asses. They make a right onto Conti passing the Royal Sonesta Hotel and immediately they're confronted by a line snaking outside the doors in front of Oceana Grill. At the front of the line, they let the hostess know they want in before they make their way to the back to wait with the hangry and hungover.

Bombei leans the back of his blue square striped shirt against the dusty red brick of the building Oceana shares with the Olde N'awlins Cookery and the Copper Monkey Grill. Graigh leans into him. He caresses her bare back in the peach halter maternity dress. The rounded gold bar of the dress's neckline gleams against her brown, moisturized skin, shining in the fading evening sun. Graigh extends her legs far out in front of her reclining against his chest to alleviate the pressure on her swollen ankles. The pressure doesn't dissipate despite the fact she opted for her gold, ankle cuff sandals buckled loosely in the first hole of the clasp, instead of the gold pumps she planned to wear to mark their eleventh wedding anniversary.

Laying against him with her eyes shut and their hands intertwined and wrapped around her belly, he hums along to one of the songs playing around them. Graigh bobs her head out of tune with the music from his mouth.

"Halvert. Party of two," a waitress yells down the line.

Graigh straightens her body and tugs Bombei's hand. They walk to meet the hostess waiting impatiently in the street.

"Is upstairs alright for y'all?" she asks, beholding the pregnant belly before her.

"That's fine," Graigh says, disliking the assumption of disability.

"Follow me," she says, turning toward the restaurant's door.

They follow her through the narrow door of the slim restaurant, where space was only found by building up instead of out. She grabs two menus and leads them up steep stairs. They follow her wagging booty in black polyester pants to the third floor. She leads them to a small brown wooden table against a wall beneath a blaring TV.

The hostess places the menu on the tables and says, "Your server will be right with you. Enjoy."

"Thanks," Bombei says.

He pulls out Graigh's chair and helps her into her seat, before taking his own across from her. Scanning the menu options for an appetizer, entree, and dessert to be ready when the server comes, Graigh rubs her bouncing belly where the baby kicks from inside announcing hunger pains of his own.

"I guess we're really hungry," she laughs, putting the menu down on the table.

"So now you're eating for two?" Bombei raises a surprised eyebrow.

"I'm still eating for one. He's not here yet. When I start nursing then I'll be eating for two. But he kicked me when I opened the menu, so I guess he's hungry too."

"Whatever," Bombei smirks. "Do you know what you want, Greedy? I mean, Graigh."

She steels her face toward his for a second longer than he expects before she lets her smile slowly spread from cheek to cheek. She laughs aloud as his eyes tell he worried he'd spoiled her mood and ruined the night with a joke she didn't appreciate.

"Gotcha," she laughs throwing her head back.

"Eleven years. I oughta be used to your moody ass."

"You should, but you're not. It's good to keep you guessing."

"You've kept me guessing alright. After our first date I never thought we'd be here."

"It wasn't a date," She says earnestly. "It was just lunch. A meeting really. To talk about you fixing my house for a fee."

"I never charged you."

"I believe you still got paid for your services," she says slyly.

"I still am," he says grabbing her leg beneath the table.

"And that's why I'm knocked up now." She jerks away from his creeping hand.

"Has it really been that bad?" Bombei asks. "Carrying our baby?"

Why would he ask me that?

"Good Evening. My name is William and I will be your server tonight. May I start you guys off with drinks? An appetizer?" he asks, his accent thick and charming.

"We'll have the Oceana's Famous Oysters for an appetizer," Graigh says, "and I'd like a Virgin Strawberry Daiquiri."

"Virgin?" William questions with a smirk and a side eye.

"He can't have it," Graigh says smoothing her dress tightly to show off her distended belly.

"Congratulations. I didn't notice. You don't even look pregnant."

Graigh laughs. "Don't say stuff you know isn't true just to work on your tip. We'll treat you right."

"Alright, alright. But you do carry it very well," William says.

"Alright now, Man; that's a married woman you talking to. My married woman."

"I got you, Baby. No disrespect. You're a lucky man."

"Sometimes," Bombei says, smirking at Graigh.

"Excuse me. Don't let this eleventh year be the last year."

"Eleven years, that's a long time," William says, awe in his voice.

Bombei says, "We've actually been together fourteen years. Married eleven."

"People don't stay together that long anymore. Not dating, not married. Not even these crazy-ass situation-ships. Two maybe three years tops. I hardly ever see anybody in here been together as long as you guys have."

"This is the Quarter," Bombei says. "Not exactly a place for long lasting relationships to survive."

"Especially not at night," Graigh adds with a knowing chuckle.

"Tonight, is our anniversary," Bombei says. Fourteen years ago, today, we went on our first date."

"Lunch," Graigh insists.

"And eleven years ago, today, we said, 'I do,' not too far from here in front of the Cathedral."

"And now we're having a baby," Graigh closes the story.

"First baby?" William asks.

"First one," Bombei confirms.

"Something else that's rare. You two are just unicorns in here tonight. I'll have to get you something on me to celebrate. Whatcha drinkin', my man?"

"Let me have a Jack and Coke. And add another appetizer. I want the atchafalaya."

"You got it. One virgin strawberry daiquiri. One jack and coke. And an order of our famous oysters and the gator sausage. I'll put those in for you and give y'all some time to look at our dinner options."

"My man," Bombei says, nodding William away.

"He was nice," Graigh says, once they're alone.

"He better be nice. He's living on tips. Nice is the name of the game."

"True. But he wasn't running game."

"Maybe. You gotta have the gift of gab to make working in the Quarter work for you."

"I guess."

Graigh looks up at the framed pictures on the wall. She gazes longingly at the black and white and sepia prints hung with care on the exposed red brick that matches the outside facade of the building. The prints depict scenes of a New Orleans past. Pictures of life before Katrina, before Betsy, before billion-dollar storms were the norm and pictures were lost to flooding, cleaning up, and starting over.

Graigh's glances run all the way up the wall to the exposed ducts and vents of the massive HVAC system. The cooling unit along with the brick, and wood support beams, add a rustic charm to the Cajun restaurant. The construction of convenience and probable austerity makes the three-floor restaurant appear more like an inner-city dive bar than a five-star eatery.

"What're you thinking about?" Bombei interrupts from across the table.

"Just looking at the pictures. How old they are?"

"You know those aren't originals though."

"So, what? It's starting to become a novelty to have really old stuff in this city if it's not on high ground."

"Eventually, everything will be in the cloud and then you can just Google it from the microchip implanted in your hand."

"We're not that far ahead yet."

"It's coming," Bombei nods assuredly. "By the time that boy's grown the internet age that even we had to catch up with will look nothing like what we know now."

"Hopefully, he won't grow up too fast."

"Time flies when you're having fun."

"That it does."

"So, has it?" Bombei asks.

"Has what?"

"Has it been fun being pregnant. Has it been as hard as you've made it seem?"

I thought he would forget. I should have known better.

Graigh bows her chin to her chest to look at her love on top before responding. She gives thought to the question that turns her quick "hell no" into an "it's different."

"Different how?"

"Physically it hasn't been as hard as I expected. Aside from my coughing and irregular breathing, which is kind of normal for me now anyway, physically I've been okay. It's all the other shit being pregnant has brought up that drains me."

Bombei nods, discerning without needing to probe for more understanding. He reaches for her hand across the table. She grabs his quickly without thinking. They sit in a comfortable silence, fingers intertwined, exchanging energy between the two of them in what they know will be one of their last times as a couple instead of the impending trio.

"Can you believe?" Bombei asks, breaking the silence. "That we've been together since you deserted me at the Gazebo?"

"I didn't desert you. I told you I had errands to run. It was just a meeting. I don't know why you're still so butt hurt about it."

"It was more than a meeting and you know it."

"It was just a meeting. Our first date was in October, after the house was raised."

"No, that was the second date."

"No, it wasn't"

"Let's ask William," Bombei says, turning to their smiling server, approaching with drinks and appetizers.

"Ask William what?" He grins, setting down their orders in front of them.

"We've been fighting about when our first date actually happened for the last fourteen years," Graigh begins.

"Uh-uh. Let me tell the story," Bombei interrupts. "So, we met on the 14th, right. We talk. We exchange numbers. We go to the Gazebo on the 15th for lunch. That's a date?"

"Did you pay?" William asks seriously.

"Damn sure did," Bombei says excitedly.

"Then, Baby, it was a date."

"No, it wasn't. He's leaving out all the important details."

"Okay, so tell me your side."

"So, we met after the storm. I was outside working on the house and he was sightseeing through the ninth being nosy; door poppin' by the time he got to me. He volunteered to help me rebuild. Of course, I don't turn down help. So, I agreed to meet with him about the plans for my home at the Gazebo. It was a meeting. A lunch meeting, not a date," Graigh insists.

"My man, are you in construction or something?"

"Nope. I play the trumpet."

"But he said he was good with his hands," Graigh defends.

"Baby, that was just to get into your pants," William says with a smirk. "It was a date."

"I don't even know why I expected you take my side. You men always stick together. You better hope your new friend here isn't in a chintzy mood or you can forget about your good tip. I'm the generous one."

"Don't be like that, Baby."

"It's alright, Bruh, I got you," Bombei says, slapping William's empty hand. "She's just mad because she knows I'm right."

"If it makes you feel any better," William begins, "it doesn't matter if it was a date or not because you guys are still together now."

"Don't try to make it up to me now," Graigh says waving her hand dismissively.

"Don't pay her no mind," Bombei says.

"No worries. Y'all know what you want for dinner?"

"I'll have the Redfish Oceana," Bombei says.

"Good choice. The chef's specialty."

"There you go taking his side again." Graigh pouts.

"Now, Miss Lady," William says with good-humored fluster.

"I'm just playing with you. I'd like the jazzy crab cake platter, and for a dessert I'd like the bananas foster ice cream cake."

"Another awesome choice." William smiles graciously.

"That's more like it," Graigh smiles widely.

"I'll put those selections in for you. Do you need anything else?"

"I'd like some water," Graigh says.

"Not a problem," William says as he walks away from the table.

"Now it's settled," Bombei says. "Fourteen years ago, today, we went on our first date."

"Whatever. I still say it was October."

"It couldn't have been the October date because we were celebrating two months together then."

"We weren't even together," Graigh protests. "And we argued that day."

"You argued about all the comparisons between Katrina and 9/11. I just listened," Bombei says.

"Whatever. All these alternative facts gon' get you a one-way trip to hell in a gasoline suit."

"No, it won't. God knows my heart."

Graigh rolls her eyes then raises her empty glass. "I propose a toast."

"To what?" Bombei asks lifting his as well.

"To us. Fourteen years together. Eleven years married. And thirty-six weeks pregnant."

"Here's to another fourteen. Another eleven. And another thirty-six. Not necessarily in that order." He winks.

"Slow down. Let's get him here first," Graigh cautions.

Bombei grins as they clink their glasses. William reappears with water for both. They sip the drinks in honor of themselves. They survived the storm, the tropical and emotional cyclones life swirled into their paths to destroy all they had, all they've rebuilt together, and all they've yet to deliver.

Thirty-Seven

Bombei and Graigh walk hand in hand up the steps of The Healing Center toward Doctor Grace's open door. The sound of her sandals with his flip flops are even and aligned. He waits for her on each step as she takes her time on the ascent. He pauses as she breathes in deeply with every move forward. At the top, Doctor Grace hands them each a bottle of water. It is her unspoken hello followed by an extended arm toward her chaise. They cross her threshold both draining the small bottles she gave them.

"You guys are almost parents." Doctor Grace says grabbing her clipboard behind her desk.

"We are," Bombei says helping Graigh ease onto the low seated sofa.

"Your hair is gorgeous," Graigh remarks.

"Thank you. I don't straighten it that often because all I can smell for weeks after is burnt hair."

"Smells of the Saturday before Christmas, Easter and Mother's Day," Graigh says.

"Ain't that the truth."

"Especially around our house," Graigh goes on. "Grandma Dottie would be booked for days leading up to the holidays, and that Saturday she barely had time to press my head. When I was old enough, she tried to teach me how to do it myself, but I was too afraid I'd burn my face that I never picked it up."

"I can't work a pressing comb," Doctor Grace says sitting across from the couple. "But my flat iron is an old friend. I don't pick her up often, but when I do it's like we've never been apart."

"For me it's natural or bust," Graigh says placing the empty water bottle at her feet. "If we were having a girl she'd be screwed, because this Mama is not the one for hair. I have three styles and these twists are a staple."

"They're pretty," Doctor Grace says.

"Pretty old. But I'm too tired, and too pregnant to take them down now. Baby boy will have to rock out with his mama looking rough around the head for at least a month or two after he gets here."

"Chile, don't worry about it," Doctor Grace says comfortably. "They can't see that well those first few weeks anyway. Eyes have to adjust to the new world around them."

Bombei clears his throat, "So are you guys going to talk about hair and my son for the whole appointment like I'm not here?"

"You feeling left out?" Graigh pokes him in his side with her elbow.

"No. I just know Doctor Grace doesn't believe in wasting time or money," he says, repeating her words from his last visit.

"I don't. You're right. So, what brings you two in today."

"We're here to check in," Graigh says tentatively. "The baby is due in three weeks. So here we are."

"You know that baby is going to come on his own time, right?"

"So I've been told."

"Just don't want you getting set on a date and freaking out if he comes before or after. Most first babies are late anyway."

"So I've been told," Graigh repeats.

"Well, you all seem to be doing better." Doctor Grace adjusts as she begins her sketch.

She outlines Bombei's long arm beside Graigh's body. The touch of their knees conjoining their legs and the hold of their hands.

"We are," Graigh affirms.

"So, why are you here?"

"To check in."

"About what?"

"There's the Doctor Grace I know," Bombei says, at the abrupt turn in the once playful conversation.

Graigh says, "I was watching the news a few weeks ago, and seeing all the crime and death, all the police shootings. All I could do was cry."

"I try to stay away from the news," Doctor Grace says. "Especially with Trump."

"Who doesn't?" Bombei humphs.

"How did you get over the stories?" Doctor Grace probes.

"I'm not sure she has," Bombei answers.

"On top of that it's hurricane season."

"And," Doctor Grace says, not following.

"I just wonder if after all this time was I right in making this my home. Our home," Graigh says, looking out the lone window on the back wall of the small office.

"And how do you feel?" Doctor Grace asks Bombei.

"I feel fine," he says. "This is the first I'm hearing about this. I'm learning just like you are right now."

"I watch the news every day," Graigh says. "Every day there's the same old death and destruction, and then the weather. All they can talk about now is what's brewing off the coast of Africa. Even if it's nothing coming, they want to talk about how there's still time for us to have an active hurricane season. They compare to last year or the last five years or ten years, and when none of that works they talk about Katrina. It's August now, so the Katrina talk is on steroids. I'm due on the fifth. Everyone keeps telling me don't get my hopes up that he'll be here then. And . . . It's just too much."

Graigh breaks down in the midst of her fears. Her held back tears echo through her hands.

"How long have you been holding this in?" Bombei asks, releasing her hand.

"I'm not holding anything in. It's just stuff I think about."

Doctor Grace inserts a blank card into her clipboard and starts a new drawing. This one shows Graigh and Bombei side by side, but with a slight space between them. Their thighs and knees no longer touch. They no longer hold hands. Bombei's face hardens and Graigh's eyes evoke a diffident sadness she tries to hide. Doctor Grace fills out their facial features first. The winsome looks from the first sketch give way to concerned glares, sidelong glances, and elongated visions of melancholy. Her black coal captures the raised position of foot taps, both of their tells of agitation. Bombei's beating hand, pummels his fist into the opposite palm, while Graigh opens and closes her fingers, flexing her wrist as if gripping a stress ball. Their bodies speak for them in the silent room. Their movements and gestures tell the story of questions all first-time parents ask. Her opening and closing hands, his fist pummeling, their foot taps, his accusing looks at the side of her face, and her evocative sadness all scream, "Are we doing this right?"

Doctor Grace puts her sketches to the side and stands up from her sofa chair. She adjusts the hem of her orange, Ankara print, circle skirt, pulling the back of the fabric from her legs where the two became stuck while she sat. She steps behind her desk, opens the refrigerator, and grabs three more water bottles. An offering to shift the conversation back to the present moment and what they need to see and say for themselves with her gentle nudging.

Bombei takes the water immediately. He takes both bottles nudging the cap of one into Graigh's bare shoulder. She turns to face him, startled, unable to hide the tears threatening to fall from her eyes. She drops the bottle between her legs and brings the back of her hands to her face. Graigh wipes the water that didn't fall in response to thoughts she keeps crowded in her bank of words left unsaid.

"Why are you crying?" Bombei asks.

"I don't know."

"Yes, you do," Doctor Grace says gently.

"Too much time to think about . . ." Graigh answers.

"About what?"

"We were talking about Grandma Dottie when I first walked in. Not on purpose. She just came up, which means she must be on my mind. That's what she used to say all the time. She used to fuss at me for talking about girls at school. She'd tell me 'Girl, when you talk about somebody as much as you do you must think a whole lot about 'em even if you don't like 'em.' Now here she is in the middle of my session, and I don't remember having her on my mind much lately."

"She's always with you," Bombei says. "You've never let her go. Never let her rest. You gotta stop blaming yourself for what you couldn't control or you're going to end up just like her."

"Why would you say that?" Graigh shrieks.

"I didn't mean it like that. You did the best you could to help after your grandfather passed, but she knew she wasn't long for this world without him, and you did too."

"I should have been here before he died."

"You were going through your own shit with . . ." Bombei trails avoiding the bubbling subject threatening to spill out of his mouth. "You couldn't have stopped or slowed his death. Just like you couldn't have stopped hers. You always said it was a blessing in disguise anyway."

Graigh turns her shattered face toward him. The tears she wiped away are now on full display falling quickly, and fatly, down her thick pregnant cheeks. Her bow lips tremble. They quiver with the want of shooting arrows with her words, to strike down the truth she's told herself. The truth he's repeated back to her to lift her from her sudden listlessness.

"Why was it a blessing?" Doctor Grace asks, bringing Graigh back to now.

She shakes her head refusing to say the words she admitted to herself long ago during the long slog to Tallahassee on a bumper to bumper I-10.

"Why was it a blessing?" Doctor Grace asks again.

"Tell her," Bombei says forcefully.

"Because if they had both been alive. Or even if just Grandma Dottie . . ." Graigh chokes on her tears falling faster than she can blink them away.

She finds her breath through the rain on her face. Closing and opening her fingers. Flexing her wrists, making a fist she continues, "If they'd both been alive we wouldn't have evacuated. All three of us would have been dead in that house. Twenty-three feet of water. Even if we would have been able to chop through the roof with the ax in the attic and sit up top until the Cajun navy or the national guard came by, we'd have probably still died in the heat. Or they would have. Ain't no way to get a bed ridden man into a crawl space let alone on top of a roof. She wouldn't have left his side and I wouldn't have left hers. We'd of all died."

"But you're here," Doctor Grace says.

"Yeah. I'm here in their house and they're not."

"Just because you don't like the blessing doesn't mean that it isn't one. Just because you didn't understand God's plan doesn't mean that it didn't work out for your good."

"And just because I feel guilty and I blame myself for what happened to them doesn't mean I should. And just because I made Bombei rebuild that house, and add a second story, doesn't mean we're going to be able to keep it, to live there, to raise our son there with the crime getting worse, the policing still corrupt, and the hurricanes getting bigger and stronger than Katrina ever was. I've done all these mental gymnastics, Doc. Doesn't mean I feel any better."

"You may never feel better," Doctor Grace says. "You may never get better. It for damn sure won't happen if you don't allow yourself to heal. Stop carrying around all the things you didn't do and can't control. Put those bags down."

"Join the chorus with everybody else in my life singing the same refrain."

"She's hardheaded," Bombei jokes with wry laughter. "You should know that by now."

"Obstinance will only get you a weekly, or monthly session right here on this chaise for the rest of your life. Time is money. And while I like making mine, I don't like making it off the same people who refuse to see the forest for the trees. Graigh you're better than this," Doctor Grace says, handing her the second sketch she completed.

She takes the note card with her twisted image raining tears and looking distraught beside a husband who looks aggravated and confused. Doctor Grace extends to her the first sketch. She takes the drawing and hides it behind the first one she received.

"Don't do that," Doctor Grace snaps. "Look at them both."

Graigh places each note card on a knee. The tears to her right. The smiles on her left. She glances at the image she knows and the one she doesn't recognize. Her sorrow and her joy apparent in each. Bombei looks at her visage in both, at his depiction in both. He sees the severe changes from left to right. The tension manifested in a matter of minutes. The sudden change from happy to sad, relaxed to stressed, overcome with external love to overwhelmed by internal doubt.

"Right now, both of these sketches are you. But the you on the right is who you choose to be on most of your days."

"I don't choose to be sad and crying every day," Graigh snaps.

"Don't you?" Doctor Grace challenges.

"No, I don't."

"Then prove it."

"I don't have shit to prove to you."

"I didn't say you had to prove it to me," Doctor Grace says gently. "But you do need to prove it to yourself. You owe yourself, your baby, and Bombei that much."

Graigh sighs longingly through her nose still running scenarios that have never or have yet to happen in her mind.

All of the what ifs of her adult life. She comes to one conclusion.

If I didn't go through all the bad from Jamal on, I probably wouldn't be here right now, married and pregnant with Bombei. We would have never met.

Graigh picks up the card on her left knee and brings it close to her face. She studies the incline of her head toward his. The detail on their entwined fingers. The flair of the sparkle from her engagement ring and wedding band. The two knees and one leg from their touching thighs to the feet on her floor.

"I choose this," Graigh says in a voice still full of cried tears and old emotions. "But for some reason I still can't let this go," she says holding up both sketches.

"As long as you choose joy, you can drop everything else little by little every day until it's all gone."

"You got it, Doc."

"Don't say it to placate me. I told you there's no need for me to take your money, while you waste both of our time delaying doing what you know you need to."

"I got it, Doctor Grace, damn," Graigh says more forcefully.

"That's all I need to hear." She stands up.

Bombei stands and then helps Graigh. They walk behind the diminutive Doctor whose height is diminished in her sandals.

"Hold on to those," she says, opening the door for them to pass through. "Compare them with your other notes."

"I will," Graigh says sullenly.

"You too, Bombei."

"Yup."

"Come back any time, and feel free to bring the baby once you're ready to have him outside."

"I will."

"You too, Bombei."

"I'm good. I'll leave the rest of these appointments for you and her."

"That's fine with me," Doctor Grace says lowering her voice. "I'm only here for people who are ready to tell the truth and do their work."

"Yup," Bombei says, casually walking down the stairs behind Graigh.

Graigh exits the doors of The Healing Center first, pulling and tugging at the waist band of her black yoga pants, adjusting for room she doesn't have in athleisure wear she refuses to admit is too small for the front load she's carrying. A final adjustment of her thin, oversized, off the shoulder sweatshirt, then she leans dissatisfied against the orange brick facade of the holistic health building.

"You feel better now?" Bombei asks.

"Not really. I never feel better after a session with her."

"So why do you keep on coming?"

"The same reason people run or work out hard all the time. You don't do it because it feels good while you're in it. You do it because it's good for you."

"Yeah, but from what I'm told runners say they feel amazing right after they've finished running."

"Yeah, well, the good juju from therapy takes a little longer to kick in."

"Are you sure?"

"I don't have any other choice but to believe that's true. Otherwise all of this," she gestures toward the office, "has been a waste of time."

"And you know Doctor Grace doesn't like anybody wasting time," Bombei mimics in her voice.

"Especially not hers."

"Time is money," Bombei imitates again. "How many times is she going to say that?"

"I take it you don't like her?" Graigh asks.

"She's alright. You picked her."

"I did. Yet you saw her on your own and then came back with me today, so I'd say you like her as well."

"I'm doing this for you."

"I could say the same, but truth is, at this point I'm doing it for myself. She forces me to be honest in a way you and Joy haven't been able to." Graigh shrugs.

"I guess," Bombei says uneasily.

"There's a blessing in everything though."

"I don't follow."

"It's like what Will Smith said on Oprah a long time ago. Greatness lives on the edge of destruction."

"Don't think I saw that episode," Bombei says dragging his hands through his scruff.

"You didn't need to. It's just a truth in life. For us. Hell, for the city. New Orleans after Katrina will be the greatest city ever, and us after all my drama will be the greatest family ever."

"If we don't self-destruct first," Bombei tempers.

"Yeah, I guess there's that," Graigh ponders leaning against the building with her eyes closed. "I never considered self-destruction as a permanent side effect on the road to greatness."

"Many people never do."

"We're not under that much pressure?" she asks, opening her eyes to look at his face.

"Aren't we?"

The question is both rhetorical and inquisitive, demanding an answer and none at all. She watches as he scratches the back of his neck in the space between his hairline and the collar of his T-shirt. The space that rarely itches. The space he uses as a decoy to lower his head, avert his eyes and not have a difficult conversation. She watches him move from scratching to preening. He tugs at the waistband of his dark wash jeans, pulling them over his butt where they won't stay without the belt he's not wearing. Bombei pulls at the sleeves of his salmon T-shirt adjusting them over the toned definition of muscles used to being held up through endless rounds of band practice, and his new-found zeal for playing in the home studio. His hands run over his hair in need of a cut after his ministrations with his clothes are complete. He finally resorts to rolling his feet back and forth on his ankles, anxious to leave the center of healing and the conversation they had within.

"What do you want to do now?" Graigh asks bemused.

"My horn is in the trunk."

"I know." Graigh smirks.

"Then if you knew what I wanted to do why didn't you just go along with the plan."

"Because I wanted to see if you had come out your feelings. Wasn't sure if you were mad at me, Doctor Grace or somebody else."

"I'm not mad at anybody. She's just intense."

"I prefer the word effective."

"Whatever. Are we going out or naw? As my students say."

"You tell me."

"Let's go," Bombei says grabbing her hand. "Some of my students apparently formed a band over the summer. They emailed me to tell me they were playing out in the Quarter."

"So, you just plan to be down in the Quarter all weekend huh?"

"We," Bombei emphasizes. "We plan to be down in the Quarter all weekend."

"As long as you feed me and find me somewhere to sit, I'm good."

"I got the chairs in the trunk right next to my horn."

"I didn't see you put those in."

"I did it last night while you were asleep because you too damn nosy."

"Watch your mouth now."

"Whatchu gon' do about it?" Bombei pulls Graigh away from the building's outer wall.

They walk hand in hand, step for step to the car parked around the corner on Roch Avenue along the side of Café Istanbul. It's the third colorful building in the set with Wild Lotus Yoga and The Healing Center. The loud hues are indicative of parties and fun, the cafe's vibrant purple specifically reminiscent of Mardi Gras. They walk as Bombei hums John Boutté's most popular song thanks to HBO. Graigh bounces in step with the beat of his mouth humming along with the tune she knows well.

"I thought you said you wanted to sit down?" Bombei asks with raised eyebrows as he opens her door.

"I want to have the option to sit when I'm not dancing."

"Yeah, mmhmm. You know good and well you won't be sitting for very long, and you're gonna have me dragging these chairs for no damn reason."

"As long as we both know, then it's not a surprise." Graigh slams her door shut on his face.

She continues humming the tune of the *Tremé* theme song moving into the verse and deviating away from the catchy chorus. Bombei is still humming when he gets in the car as well. A broad smile shows off his appreciation as they harmonize their hums in the stillness of the car until they get back to the steady rhythm of the refrain. They hum it twice before he ends his musical stylings and turns the ignition. The car ignites against the melody drowning out her hums but rocking ever so slightly to the steady taps of her feet patting out the second verse.

Thirty-Eight

August 21—37 Weeks

They pass the red gates of MLK coming up from Caffin and Claiborne. The opposite direction than they came on their first walk to the old pharmacy. They walk silently pass the school where Bombei teaches music and directs the band. They walk the grassy neutral ground step for step beneath the shade of the leaves from the massive trees that did not die despite being inundated with water.

Bombei walks in the quiet contemplation of his unspoken thoughts tapping his fingers against the thighs of his basketball shorts. Graigh counts as many houses as she can, arming herself with visual information for the argument she's prepared to have. They pass the two-story yellow house with a front porch, a second-floor balcony and side porch. They pass another home with solar panels, a few empty house lots on their side of the street, and two or three grassy fields where a whole row of neighbors didn't return between Prieur, Johnson, and Galvez. The church before Burnell's and the pharmacy slab still gleams. It beckons to all who pass by it, as a beacon of hope is supposed to. The reflective glass doors invite those who see themselves on the outside to come take a closer look, as perhaps God sees them from inside His house.

Graigh jaywalks across the street to the former pharmacy, until she's standing in front of the slab; her feet apart, squared and planted, her hands are on her hips, and her belly bigger than before. Bombei takes his time crossing to where she is. He looks both ways for traffic that isn't there, before coming to stand by her side, in support of a fantasy he doesn't want to be his reality.

"It still looks the same," Bombei says unenthused.

"Why would it look any different?"

"Why are we here?"

"Because I think it could be a good opportunity for us."

"I don't see it. The last people who ran this pharmacy. The Henry's. They didn't even come back after the storm. They opened out in the East and have a location on the Westbank. And technically the East had more damage than the Lower Ninth Ward, but nobody really talks about that."

"Because we're not playing the disaster Olympics. Everybody had damage over here."

"Anyway," Bombei continues. "I looked up the pharmacy after you brought me by here the first time. I knew you weren't gon' let it go."

"Because this pharmacy is what I know. What I know I and the community needs. Just like you were so gung-ho about school reopening because what's a neighborhood without a house of education," Graigh mimics. "I feel the same way. What's a community without a pharmacy and small convenience store."

"That's what the new CVS is for on Claiborne."

"And if CVS is the only option on this side of the bridge, they can jack up the prices more than Martin Shkreli if they feel like it. Or choose to only carry brand name drugs instead of generics. Or overprescribe because they're getting paid, instead of telling people that most of the things they take are making the bugs they catch smarter and more adept to dodging the potent effects of medicine that's no longer effective in this germ conscious, heal me now culture."

"And so here you swoop in to become Captain Save-a-Hood? Is that what this is? Take the woke cape off. "

"This has nothing to do with being woke," she says sarcastically. "I live in the ninth and work on Canal, basically in the Quarter. I'm cut from the same cloth as the generations of domestics and service workers before me who lived here and worked there."

"What's your point?" Bombei interrupts.

"My point is, if now is not the time to work where I live, to put all that I've learned and applied out of the ninth, back in, I don't know what is?"

"As usual it's all about Graigh. What Graigh wants."

"This isn't all about me. It's about us. Making money for us, leaving a legacy for the three or four of us. Me still doing what I do closer to home and helping people who need help. It's not like we don't have the money to get this going and I don't have the knowledge to keep it running"

"Graigh, this isn't about money or knowledge and you know it. It's about practicality. And don't try to persuade me by saying it's about legacy for the three or four of us. You know damn well this is your first and last baby. That's what you tell Joy on the phone all the time ain't it."

"I thought my first baby was my first and last baby, but you had a way of persuading me into this one now didn't you."

"Here we go." Bombei walks away from Graigh toward the barbershop on the other corner.

"There's nowhere to go, Bombei." Graigh waddles to catch up with him. "We're already here. This is our future."

"No. This is your past. Our future. *Our future* is around the corner. That's where *our* future is."

"Around the corner is also my past just like this, but we made that *our future*. I'm asking why we can't do the same with this pharmacy?"

"Because I don't have another eleven years to waste and a bunch of sessions with Doctor Grace for us to get the shit right. We've done that once. Let's get out of the clouds and finally enjoy the sunshine after the rain."

His exasperated honesty silences her response. The tears well up in her eyes from her gut and fall with the force of a river emptying into the ocean. She walks away from the corner and Bombei to stand back in front of the slab that used to be a pharmacy. The pharmacy Grandma Dottie sent her to when she was young. The pharmacy she walked to, ran to, and eventually drove to when she came back. The pharmacy she visited daily for the eight months between Poppy's death and Grandma Dottie's own passing. The career she aspired to and accomplished because of all of her errands. Visits where she watched the men behind the counter with fascination as they made sense of random symptoms, without a doctor's diagnosis, that led them to fill a bottle with the magic combination for patients to take two to four times a day to be well in two to four days.

Graigh cries with the overwhelming grief of Poppy and Grandma Dottie's death, Katrina's scourge on the neighborhood, and Bombei's unwillingness to reason. Fists pressed to her belly, legs bent into a squat, Graigh hovers above the hot concrete ground, and cries lonely tears no one and nothing has been able to cure.

"I don't see why you can't let the past stay in the past," Bombei says offering his hand.

She takes it and stands unsteadily on drained legs overwhelmed by the sudden demand to support a body of extra weight. The backs of her hands wipe snotty tears away from her face and on to the white, lace, peplum tank top she wore over another pair of yoga pants. Graigh hyperventilates to catch her breath—trying and losing—to keep her cough at bay. Serial, bronchial, asthmatic hacks erupt from her throat. Long and drawn out coughs bring fresh tears to her eyes for an entirely different reason. Bombei holds her waist while she's doubled over again trying to regain her composure.

Minutes pass before she is upright, tear and snot free. Graigh sighs her air and takes another longing look at the former pharmacy she imagines is still there.

"We learn from our past," Graigh says quietly. "Whatever lessons we don't learn we are destined to make again. I will not make the same mistake twice. Especially when I don't have to."

"What mistake is that?"

"Closing the door on opportunities you know are meant for you."

"I don't follow." Bombei reaches for Graigh's face and turns it toward him.

"Mr. Henry offered me a job here when I was fourteen when I first told him I wanted to be a pharmacist. Back then I was more concerned with boys than looking through his books, so I said no. He offered me a job when I was 18 and I left for school. I told him then I wasn't ever coming back to New Orleans so don't worry about saving me a spot. When I did come back, he mentioned it on one of my daily trips. Most times I would come to get something for Grandma Dottie, but he and I both knew she didn't need that much medicine. He knew I was coming to get out of the house once she fell asleep. He didn't pry about my return, just said he was happy to see me, and told me he could use my help if I felt up to it. I told him I had my hands full with my Dottie, and then after she was gone, I couldn't bear to go to the place she made familiar. Katrina came and went. Mr. Henry moved. I met you. We built a house. Now I'm pregnant and thinking about life in an entirely different way. I want everything that reminds me of what home meant for me, for him, and you want no parts."

"I never said that."

"You said it's not practical."

"Graigh, without knowing all you just told me . . . This little business venture of yours is not practical."

"And now that you know the entire back story?"

"To me?" Bombei stalls turning his head from side to side. "It's still not practical. It's emotional. Businesses, pharmacies, mom and pop shops don't run off emotions."

"All I am and all I have are my emotions. What feels sensible over what you think actually makes sense. I'm on a sensory journey right now and logic is irrelevant."

"Says the pharmacist who uses logic to deduce the proper prescription to treat the right condition. Okay."

"Just because I use logic to do my job doesn't mean I'm not ruled by emotion and passion. You Mr. Musician should understand that better than anyone else."

"I do, but passion and emotions don't make money. Passion and emotions don't buy diapers, wipes, clothes, and food."

"I will *make* money. Houses are here. Families are here. The need is here. I already have one client lined up for when I open."

"Who?"

"Janay."

"Who is that?"

"The pregnant girl who came to the baby shower with her boyfriend I met in the pharmacy."

"Oh yeah," Bombei sneers. "The couple you said reminded you of you and Jamal."

"That's what you remember about them."

"Yeah. That's what I remember about them."

Graigh sees the steely grip of Bombei's jaw that tells her don't press the issue.

She nods and goes on, "I saw them earlier today when I was shopping. I told her about the idea one time, when she came to get her prenatals and she says when I open, she'll be my first client."

"We'll see."

"What does that mean?" Graigh asks.

"It means you don't even know who owns the property and how much they want for it. You need to find out if we have to buy the land or rent it.. Then we have to actually build the goddamn pharmacy from the ground up, since ain't shit here but beams. It's not the right time, but your head is hard, and your ass is soft so if you fall, you'll bounce back."

"I thought that was one of the things you loved about me."

"For an entirely different reason, yes."

"That part makes this all the more better," Graigh smiles widely.

"Sometimes," Bombei grimaces, taking her hand.

"What the hell do you mean sometimes?"

Bombei looks both ways for them before crossing onto the neutral ground and then back to the other side of the street from which they came.

He says, "Sometimes, because you're stubborn to a fault. But you were that way when I met you. I don't know why I'd expect you to change now."

"Whatever," Graigh shrugs. "You can't always let other people discourage you from doing what you know in your heart is best. Sometimes the world needs more defiance."

"You don't have to keep convincing me," Bombei says as they walk down Galvez.

"I'm not trying to convince anybody. I'm just saying that after the painful past I've had, you've had, and this city's had somebody has to fight for it with more than the love of tourists, the hopes of people who didn't return, and the pride we show out with in a parade. Sometimes you just need pure and blatant defiance to get shit done."

"You talk like you're reading lines in a movie about your life."

"If my life were a movie it'd be the greatest story ever told."

"That's already the name of a movie about Jesus," Bombei says.

"And a TED Talk," Graigh adds.

"So, you need a new title."

"For what?"

"For the movie about your life."

"I don't know," Graigh muses.

"How about . . . The Defiant Ones?" Bombei suggests.

"Doctor Dre and Jimmy Iovine already took that title."

"I knew it sounded too good for a reason. Okay. How about . . . Defiantly Beautiful?"

"You think I'm beautiful?"

"I didn't say that." Bombei rolls his eyes.

"It's okay. I know you do. I like that. Defiantly Beautiful," Graigh whispers the name to herself. "Defiantly Beautiful," she says again as they turn on Charbonnet. "Just like the city."

Thirty-Nine

August 27—38 Weeks

"Your delivery could be weeks or days away," Doctor Marcella says to an anxious Graigh, sitting up on her exam table.

"So, what does that mean?"

"That means we're on his time. At least to a certain point."

"What point is that?" Bombei asks from his chair in the corner.

"Delivering too late can be just as bad as delivering too early. We don't want anything to happen to him in there because he's too comfortable to come out."

"So now what?" Graigh asks.

"It means go home and wait. Or go home and do all the things you can think of to try and get him here?"

"Like what?" Bombei asks with a knowing smile.

"From your smile I assume you've already looked up some of the most popular methods."

"Perhaps," he smiles again.

"What is he talking about and why is he smiling like that?" Graigh asks crossing her arms against her chest. "Why were you looking up ways to induce pregnancy anyway?" She turns her sharpened eyes toward Bombei.

"Because one of the most popular ways is sex," Doctor Marcella says. "Another one is nipple stimulation."

"Uh-uh," Graigh protests. "These boobs are off limits. They ache so bad right now."

"That's probably your milk production kicking into gear."

"Well, he needs to hurry up and get here so he can drink it then."

"Bae, calm down. Listen to Doctor Marcella and see what else she has to say about how to help me, help you."

"Perv."

"You like it though."

"Anyway," Doctor Marcella interrupts. "Other possible natural methods include eating spicy food, which we've got plenty of. We could strip your membranes here in the office. Or you can try working out and see if that doesn't help. Just don't overdo it."

"That means no sex," Graigh says staring at Bombei. "Because he likes to overdo it."

"I'm trying to get all I can before my son gets here and cock blocks me for six weeks."

"So damn selfish." Graigh rolls her eyes.

"All men are," Doctor Marcella says. "They get used to sloppy, wet pregnant sex with fat vaginas and forget that's only because their child is being grown. By the time the baby gets here, and they're cut off for six weeks, *or longer*, they get jealous and stupid."

"Wait, what do you mean *or longer*?" Bombei asks scratching the back of his head.

"I mean, if for some reason your wife can't deliver vaginally, and she has to be induced and have an emergency C-section, her recovery time goes from six to eight weeks."

"Let's not do that, okay," he says looking from Graigh to Doctor Marcella.

"Quite frankly, My Dear, you don't get to decide." Graigh smiles satisfactorily.

"She's got you there," Doctor Marcella says.

"But I don't want to be induced or have a C-section," Graigh says with a serious tone.

"Don't worry. Schedule your appointment for next week, like you normally would, and we'll talk then."

"Thank you," Graigh says.

"Thanks, Doc," Bombei says as Doctor Marcella leaves the room.

"Help me down," Graigh demands.

"C'mon," Bombei says, extending his hand. "I don't want you tripping and falling down one step because you're trying to be independent knowing good and well you can't see your feet."

"Nobody asked you for all that extra commentary."

"I don't care. I'm giving it to you anyway."

"Keep it up and you'll see what I don't give you when we get home."

"Whatever. You know you love it just as much as I do. Maybe even more."

"I don't know what you're talking about."

"The way you stalked me out at the baby shower. Yes, you do."

"I don't recall. This baby was an immaculate conception."

"And I bet Joseph still tapped that ass."

"You're going straight to hell in a hand basket."

"God knows my heart."

They laugh their way out of the exam room and through the labyrinthian hallways they've come to navigate without having to look for every exit sign. At the checkout counter they wait behind a mom standing with a stroller her belly still rounded with extra weight. Graigh makes faces at the chubby infant. A gurgle and a smile emerge from the rear facing car seat mounted on the stroller. The woman turns around to see what's caused her baby girl to smile. Graigh nods at the toffee skinned woman wearing a loose navy-blue T-shirt with a stain on the shoulder, and gray joggers. She observes the new mom's thin hair line despite the overgrown braid extensions hanging down her back. Her wide, baggy eyes tell of sleep deprivation, and her ashen skin belies that she hasn't seen lotion in days; maybe weeks, or months. Graigh crosses her eyes and sticks out her tongue at the mocha brown baby girl outfitted in hot pink everything; booties, pants with ruffled ankles, a onesie that says "Hot Stuff" with a flame for an exclamation point, and a flower headband pushing back the kinky curls of a thick, baby afro.

Graigh looks from mother to daughter. The fresh faced, chocolate cherub to the disheveled and exhausted mother standing in front of her. She sees a future she hopes doesn't come true.

"No matter what you must always make sure I shower and lotion and put on clean clothes once he gets here," Graigh whispers to Bombei standing behind her.

"Huh? What?"

"Nothing." She shakes her head. "How old is she?" Graigh asks the mother stepping away from the reception desk.

"Six months. And this one here is three months," the woman says placing a hand at her belly.

"Oh wow! Congratulations."

"Believe me this wasn't the plan. I told that man of mine to buy condoms but 'no,' his 'pullout game was strong'," she mocks.

Graigh nods. "Congratulations again. Your daughter is precious."

"Thank you. You look like you're about to pop."

"Due date is in a couple weeks, but I'm done. I'm going to try to walk him down and see if he can't get here sooner."

"That's good. Anything else makes these men crazy after you deliver."

"You see that," Graigh turns around to Bombei.

"Trust me. This was not the plan," the woman says pushing the stroller back and forth. "I wasn't sure I wanted her let alone two."

"I see," Graigh nods again. "Have a good one."

"You too," the woman says walking quickly toward the door.

She uses one hand to turn the doorknob behind her then bumps her butt against the wood and backs out of the doctor's office waiting room. Graigh watches the woman maneuver herself, the baby in the stroller, and the door expertly, without any help, accepting her new normal for the next few years.

"No sex," Graigh whispers to Bombei as she steps up to the receptionist. "One week please."

"You're almost there," the receptionist says inputting the information into the computer. "How about the twenty-eighth at nine in the morning?"

"That's fine. I'll see you then?"

Graigh walks away from the counter without another word. She follows the path the pregnant, new mommy forged out of office and into the cold sterile hallway. The rubber soles of her flip flops squeak against the linoleum floor. So do the soles of Bombei's sneakers. She walks past the elevator to the emergency stairwell. The door shuts completely closed behind her before she hears the loud bustle of it opening again. Bombei catches up to her on their walk to the parking lot.

He says beside her, "Did you think you were going to go into labor with that march you made down the stairs just now?"

"Any way I can get him here I will get him here?"

"Then let's go," Bombei says running ahead of her.

"No sex," Graigh says shaking her head with a smile. "I'm not about to be pushing out nobody's ladder babies. I don't care how much I love you."

"You can't get pregnant when you're already pregnant. I don't see the problem. You let that lady get in your head and you don't even know her."

"You just want to get your dick wet."

"What man doesn't and I love my wife. It's a win, win."

"Whatever?"

"You know you love it too."

He stares her down, daring her to call him a liar. Graigh averts her eyes.

He says, "You know there are ways this can work without being all traditional about it."

"Oh, yeah?" Graigh asks. "What's that?"

"She said something about nipple stimulation. Expand that to all over."

"I see how I win, but how do you?"

"There are five senses. We'll use them all in some alternative sex acts and see if we can't get you off and get him out."

"Let's try it," Graigh agrees. "But if it doesn't work, we're going for a walk."

"Walking where?"

Hopefully not that damn slab she calls a pharmacy.

Bombei's eyebrows leap into the topmost wrinkle of his still smooth forehead. He looks at her smiling eyes and unsmiling mouth knowing he's being set up; pressured into something he doesn't want. He knows she's tossing up her tennis ball ready to serve it into his court. He clicks the remote to unlock the car door and opens her side.

"You know where," Graigh says getting in.

Unfortunately.

Bombei closes the car door without a response. His knowingness heightens the awareness of his senses; the churn in his stomach, the grit in his teeth, the rub of his palms against his blue jean clad legs, and the tug of his beard. He fidgets with himself outside the driver's side door before getting in. Inside the car, Graigh reaches over to pop his door handle. Intuiting his delay, she forces him to confront her. Sitting together side by side, the engine purring, the air conditioning running, she angles her body toward his. She sits in such a way that if there were no middle console their knees would touch.

"Where do you want to walk, Elaine?"

"Don't be like that."

"Answer the question."

"Our pharmacy."

"We don't have a pharmacy."

"Why can't you give me a hard yes instead of a quick no."

"You're not God asking me to do something."

"And you're not Jonah."

"I don't get it."

"C'mon let's take a walk to our future and discuss a business plan I've come up with."

"A business plan?"

Bombei's eyebrows meet his non-existent wrinkles. He lowers his head and shakes it side to side. "I can't believe I'm doing this," he mumbles. "What's the name of your business."

"Pop and Dottie's Pharmacy and Food Store."

"You have been thinking about this." Bombei looks up at Graigh.

"I told you I have a plan."

I'm going to regret this.

Bombei nods his head. Graigh's smile spreads across her thick face showing off her teeth. He sees joy in her face where he's mostly seen worry. Hope and happiness on display instead of reserved behind her healthy skepticism. The person she probably used to be before him. He nods more and more, affirming her dream still in disbelief of his own acquiescence.

Bombei says, "We'll walk over there again. You'll tell me your business plan, and if I have any questions you can't answer, any ideas, thoughts, or concerns you didn't think of we're walking back and getting my son down my way."

"I told you, you just wanted to get your dick wet."

"I'm okay with that. Are you okay with the terms of our deal, Mrs. Halvert?"

She shakes his hand grinning her "yes."

Bombei pulls the car forward through the empty, adjacent parking space and slides one hand over to her thighs inclined toward him. He parts her legs with his hands and brings them to rest at the top of her lap beneath the warmth of her belly. His hands rock back and forth in her lap as he turns onto St. Claude Avenue.

"What are you doing?" Graigh asks.

"Getting you ready," Bombei says focusing his eyes on the road while his hand takes on a life of its own.

"You keep telling yourself that."

Graigh reclines her seat back and pulls her legs into her body cutting off circulation to his hand, forcing him to snatch it back. She laughs laying on her side looking at the rear facing car seat they installed as soon as she made thirty-six weeks. The moment made the weight of her pregnancy real for her. She realized then as they buckled the base of the seat in place that she would walk into the hospital one whole person and leave from it with a piece of her in her arms.

They installed the car seat in the evening when the blaze of the sun had begun to decline with the star's descent in the western sky. She supervised, reading the directions, and adding ones she thought were better than the ones left by the manufacturer. Standing in the same grass she had stood in when they met, she used the paper to hide the happy tears falling down her face. The ones she couldn't explain then and can't explain now as she lays next to the car seat that will be filled with the life she helped create sooner, than later.

"Drive to the pharmacy," Graigh directs.

"I thought we were going home first, and then walking over there." Bombei says. "It'd be easier to get what I want to do out of the way."

"And then what? We don't go by Pop and Dottie's because we have to turn around and come back to the hospital because I'm in labor?"

"You know it doesn't happen that fast right?"

"How would you know? This is your first kid too." Graigh says. "We're going to the pharmacy first."

He moves his hand up her prostrate legs. She catches him by the fingers.

"Let me help you," Bombei says, lust dripping from his cool baritone. "Help us."

Graigh detects the fear behind his confidence. She releases his hand and closes her eyes understanding he is trying to have one more moment with her . . . just in case . . .

She doesn't allow her mind to complete the thought, just as Bombei doesn't explain his insistence on his crave for connection he knows is more emotional and mental need than physical want. Graigh allows her body to succumb to the sensations he wants her to feel. The pleasure he wants her to be prepared for. The means to their only happy ending.

"Drive by the pharmacy first," Graigh says with her eyes closed, still reclined, facing the car seat. "I can tell you my business plan in the car before we get home. We have to pass Caffin anyway."

"That's what I'm talking about."

She smiles. "As long as he gets here. That's all that matters."

And you make it, Bombei thinks to himself as he maneuvers their car toward their new future.

Forty

August 28—39 Weeks

"What's the matter?" Doctor Grace asks, from the top step outside her office.

"He's almost here," Graigh says, running up the stairs as much as she can.

She reaches the top step panting and out of breath. She bends over and leans her arms against her legs. Unable to support the weight she falls to her hands and knees and catches her breath on all fours.

"Get up before you send yourself into an attack, or labor" Doctor Grace says, shoving water at Graigh. "Drink this."

The preventive measure is too late. Graigh is already wheezing. Panting and coughing. Her eyes water as she struggles for breath. She feels her face flush red as she tries to take the deep breaths she's been taught to moan and sigh during the yoga classes on the second floor. She sits back on her haunches releasing the tight grip from her maxi skirt. Extending her hand, Doctor Grace places the open bottle of water into her grip. It spills over Graigh's fingers as she coughs and wheezes. She takes sip after sip as her wheezes deescalate. In her version of Virasana, the pose of the hero,

Graigh sits between her heels, until her brown skin returns to its normal hue, her heartbeat slows down, and she can drink the rest of her water without stopping.

The crushed plastic is the sign to Doctor Grace that she's okay. She bends down beside Graigh and takes her hand. They stand up together. Graigh smooths her charcoal skirt she's wearing as a tube dress around her body. She walks into Doctor Grace's office in silence tossing the water bottle in the small black trash can beside the desk. The ocean blue chaise is familiar for Graigh who slips out of her sandals and makes herself comfortable against the cushions placing her hands atop her belly.

Doctor Grace closes the door to the office quietly. In liquid leggings, a pink linen tunic, and straight, blonde highlighted hair, she moves soundlessly across her space grabbing items she knows she needs; index cards and charcoal pencil sticks, two more bottles of water, and her clip board. She kicks off her baby pink Converse, hands Graigh another bottle of water, and scoots back into the plush cushions of her black sofa chair.

"I hadn't scheduled anyone for today. Wanted to find my way out to somebody's beach, but you sounded so badly on the phone. What's going on?"

Graigh sips her water and nods appreciating Doctor Grace's informal tone.

"He's almost here," she begins. "I went to the doctor this morning. I'm due in a week, but the baby could come any day now . . . or later. They're asking me about being induced. I don't want that and we both don't want a C-section.

"Who both?"

"Bombei and I."

"That's good you two made the decision together."

"He made the decision and I agreed," Graigh admits. "That's the other thing. Every day he sees me still pregnant the more distant and weird he starts to act."

"What do you think has caused that?"

"He's caught up thinking I'm going to end up like his mom?"

"What happened to her?"

"She died minutes, or maybe a couple hours, I don't remember which, after giving birth to him."

Doctor Grace nods her understanding. She uses the pause in the conversation to outline her subject. She starts with Graigh's face quickly sketching the pinched worry in her T-zone, her hair pulled up into a loose bun of kinky twists, and her pursed mouth.

"I've never thought much about his mom until he gave me the book at the baby shower," Graigh continues. "Now all I can think about is making sure he gets here, and I can do more than hold him. I can do more than write him a love letter I never get to fulfill."

"Book?" Doctor Grace asks, looking from her sketch card to Graigh.

"His mom started a baby book for him before he was born. There are a couple pictures of her in there and then this handwritten letter she wrote to him before he was born . . ."

"Before she died," Doctor Grace finishes.

"You think she knew?" Graigh blurts out.

"Who knew what?"

"His mom. That she was going to die?"

"That's not something I can answer," Doctor Grace says calmly. "What does he think?"

"I can't bring myself to ask him the question."

I could ask Mr. Charles, Graigh thinks to herself.

Doctor Grace puts her sketch tools aside. She says, "It's something you've been thinking about. So, think about it and answer the question for yourself. Do you think his mom knew she was about to die?"

Graigh takes her time before answering. She examines her own emotions and feelings for this, her second pregnancy.

I knew when I went to the hospital after Jamal, I would not walk out still pregnant. I knew before I got there, and when I left . . .empty was all I felt. If I knew I was going to lose my baby, she had to know she was going to lose her life.

"I do." Graigh says slowly.

"That was definitive. Why do you think she knew?" Doctor Grace asks.

"Because of what she says at the end of her note. She includes the scripture 'They that wait on the Lord.' It's like she was preparing him for her passing even though he's only come to understand his loss since becoming an adult."

"Do you think you're about to die?"

"No."

Nobody my age thinks they're about to die.

"So, why are you worried? Let that baby do what he needs to do, and you worry about keeping yourself calm."

"I'm trying. But the closer we get the more freaked out I get."

I can't take another loss.

"We've tried walking, I've been to yoga, we even had sex, nothing is getting him here."

"He sounds like his parents," Doctor Grace says.

"What's that supposed to mean?" Graigh cracks her first smile since her arrival.

"It means both of you are strong-willed and stubborn. Your son is an amalgam of both of you."

"So, basically he's hardheaded and will get here when he gets here."

"Basically," Doctor Grace nods.

"Everybody keeps telling me the same thing. Even my best friend Joy."

"I'll tell you what I told my daughter Naomi, you're not the first new mom to freak out before having a baby. You won't be the last. You're not the first woman ever to have a baby, and you won't be the last. He'll be here soon enough and then you'll wish you hadn't rushed him when you're walking around tired, trying to get him to eat, and go back to sleep."

Graigh blows air through her nose and crosses her arms at her chest. She rocks her splayed legs from side to side. Doctor Grace goes back to her sketch. She fills out the rest of her patient's body; the low hung pregnant belly telling her birth is imminent, and the long shapely legs parted to create a cool space for comfort. Doctor Grace sketches Graigh's tapping foot beating against the air like the wing of a butterfly pressing against the wind. She shades in contour and contrast in her face from the late morning light shining in the office. The drawing comes to life in their pondering silence. Graigh, wrapped in thoughts left unspoken, allows Doctor Grace to sketch in details she normally leaves out. The veins in her hands, the brilliance of her wedding and engagement rings, the swelling in her ankles and breasts.

"I was so focused on coping with the pregnancy I don't know if I ever really enjoyed it," Graigh says aloud. "Now he's almost here and all I can think of is everything that can go wrong."

"That's normal," Doctor Grace says setting her sketch materials to the side. "Your maternal instincts are kicking in. All you want to do is to protect your child and part of that is getting him here safely."

"You know . . . I never thought I'd be able to have a baby after what happened to me last time. I thought my uterus was broken . . . Incapable of sustaining life."

"Now you see it's not."

"That's still to be determined?"

"Do you really think both of you won't make it out of the delivery room?"

"I don't know . . . I don't know what I think. Bombei and I . . . We've both seen so much bad from birth it's hard not to imagine the worst happening to us again . . . To our own child. What if I'm not around because I either end up like his mother, or my own. What if he leaves like my father? There are too many unknowns from here on out."

"Every day of life is an unknown because no day is guaranteed. You and Bombei will do the best you know how to do. That's what parenting is."

"And that's how you get fucked up kids in the world. Everyone's best is not always good enough."

"Okay, and? You can only do the best you can do. The both of you. You know this. So, what's really going on here?"

"I was wondering how long it would take before the real Doctor Grace showed up." Graigh smirks as she stands.

At the window, Graigh looks out through the back of The Healing Center to the people in the parking lot below. The ones patronizing the food co-op. She watches the incessant activity as people walk in with their own grocery bags and walk out with packages of meat triple wrapped and held together with brown duct tape, while the tops of green vegetables overrun the bags still not big enough to contain them. The cars are as numerous on Roch and Rampart as the people out and about on rented bikes or choosing to walk despite the muggy heat.

"I just want him to be happy," Graigh says staring at the bustle of people.

"Happiness is fleeting, especially in babies."

"You know what I mean."

"I do, but you also have to be as optimistic as you are realistic. Babies don't come into this world happy. They come in kicking and screaming, fighting, and crying. They exude the happiness they see reflected around them."

Graigh nods her head, heading back to the chaise. She sits on the edge, her feet planted on the ground. "I just want him here. In my arms. Safe, nursing . . . Uh oh."

"What is it?"

"You're going to need a new couch. I think my water just broke."

"Oh shit," Doctor Grace says standing quickly. "We've got to get you to the hospital."

"I have to call Bombei. He's in class."

"Come on. I'll take you." Doctor Grace swings open the door to her office. "My car is in the back. Have you been having contractions?"

"Doctor Marcella said I was two centimeters when I saw her this morning. She said I was having contractions, but I wasn't feeling them. I still don't."

"Then you have time."

"Should I drive myself then? My go-bag is in the truck."

"It's up to you."

"Oh. Oooh."

"Contraction."

"It was something."

"Real labor contractions are nothing like the practice ones you've been feeling."

"I see," Graigh says, holding on to the wall. "You drive."

Doctor Grace locks her office door. She takes Graigh's hand and guides her down the stairs. Step by step they make their way out of The Healing Center down St. Claude to Roch to Rampart without Graigh having another contraction. At the door to Doctor Grace's red Kia Rio, Graigh lets loose a moan.

"You need to start timing. They seem to be every five to seven minutes, but they could be faster."

"I have the app."

"Get in," Doctor Grace says clicking the remote to the car door. "What hospital are you at?"

"UMC on Canal street."

Forty-One

Inside a private room in the maternity wing of the University Medical Center Graigh lays in the hospital bed, gown falling off her shoulders, sweating and thrashing her back against the upright mattress. Her eyes watch the monitor beside her tracking her contractions. She grits her teeth as she sees the beginning of the next one before she feels it. She squeezes Bombei's hand, presses her back and her butt into the bed, and pushes through the pain. She takes a deep breath and watches the monitor for the next one.

"How are you doing?" Bombei asks.

Graigh doesn't answer. Her eyes are daggers focused on the monitor. She's waiting to see what's coming next; a big one or a small one. One that will make her scream or one that she can remember to moan through. After eleven hours of small talk, minor jokes, not eating, and going to the bathroom every ten minutes she watches the monitor in subsumed silence for the contractions coming one minute apart. Bombei is silent with her. He stands beside her in his gray work slacks and short sleeved undershirt. His button-down dress shirt he wore to school was discarded two hours ago, tossed on the back of the sofa that doubles as a futon.

"How are we doing? Are we ready to bring this boy into the world?"

The question is from Doctor Marcella who breezes into the room with her typically cool stride. Instead of dressed in her normal feminine business attire she is wearing green scrubs and a white face mask. Graigh smiles slightly at the face of the Doctor she hadn't seen since she arrived hours ago with Doctor Grace.

"How far am I?" Graigh ekes out before the start of the next contraction.

Doctor Marcella looks from Graigh's face to the monitor and back again until the wave of intense pain passes.

"Nine centimeters," she answers. "I can see his head, but you're not quite crowning just yet."

"Okay?"

"It's time to push. Right when you feel the contraction coming, I want you to bare down and push from your butt."

Graigh nods her understanding that devolves into a scream. The shriek resounds in the room and through the open door leading out into the hospital maternity wing.

"Your blood pressure is too high." Doctor Marcella says.

"What does that mean?" Bombei asks.

"It means she needs to push to get him here before we have to have a change of plans."

"Push, Baby," Bombei encourages as Graigh emits another scream.

"Bare down and push," Doctor Marcella urges.

"I'm pushing," Graigh screams through bared teeth.

"Push harder."

She utters a low moan. Calling on her brief yoga study, she "oms" her way through the next contraction. Pressing down and back into the bed she "oms" and pushes through her abs and her ass until she has to stop and take a breath.

"Almost there," Doctor Marcella says.

"Come on, Graigh," Bombei urges through gritted teeth. "Bring him home."

She pushes. Oming. Screaming. She squeezes Bombei's hand and grips the bed rail pushing everything from her breasts down.

"Dad, can I talk to you for a moment?" Doctor Marcella asks, standing up from her stool in front of Graigh's propped up legs.

Bombei follows Doctor Marcella out of the room; just on the other side of the threshold from Graigh in front of the nurses' station.

"Her pressure is too high. We need to get her to the operating room to do a C-section."

"Why? You just said he was almost here."

"Almost doesn't count. Her labor is slowing down when it should be speeding up and she's not on any pain killers that would force the baby to get lethargic during his transition."

"How long before she has to have a C-section? How long can we hold off?"

"I'm ready to do it now but that's a decision between the two of you."

No C-section. She can do it.

Bombei walks away from Doctor Marcella without announcing his decision. Back into the room. Back beside Graigh. He takes her hand. Her wild eyes stare wide at the monitor showing another contraction is coming. He stares at her with his own determination, wishing he could trade places with her. He stares at her, willing his own power and might into her body as she screams, squeezes, grips, and pushes, spending all her breath and energy. Again, Graigh screams, squeezes, grips and pushes. The minute apart contractions come in triplets wracking Graigh's unrested body.

"What . . ." she begins through one contraction. "Did . . . She . . .Want?"

Graigh lays her head back against the hospital bed as the contraction counter on the monitor goes flat.

"You've got to bring him here now or she will," Bombei says.

"What . . . Oooooommmmmmmmmmm . . . Does . . . That . . . Mean?"

"It means I can't lose you too," Bombei says. "Push him out or emergency C-section."

"No . . ." Graigh says, screaming and moaning her answer into Bombei's ear.

He drops her hand and goes to the door where Doctor Marcella is standing, talking to nurses, making arrangements, for what they don't want.

"We'll wait a little longer," he says.

"Not much," Doctor Marcella says, coming into the room again.

She takes her seat in front of Graigh's opened legs. Latex gloves on. Mask covering everything but her bespectacled face.

"Push."

It is a command Graigh follows on cue. In the contraction, out of the contraction she pushes.

"There you go. Push."

Squeezing, gritting, gripping, baring, pushing. Graigh forces the pressure of the pain out of her body.

"We have a head," Doctor Marcella says looking up at Graigh's sweaty face. "Push."

Graigh squeezes. She grips. She bares down. She pushes until she feels everything inside escape. She pushes through staggered, wheezing breaths, gasping for waves of hot air. She pushes until she sees Bombei leave her side to stand by the Doctor.

Sound evaporates from the room. White noise is in her ears. She watches Bombei brandish the special scissors Doctor Marcella gives him to cut the umbilical cord. His hand dives beneath her spread legs to separate her from the baby he brings back up in his arms. Her baby she can barely see around the blue and red striped hospital receiving blanket. Her eyes preen to see what's still hidden from her. What the nurses surround with suction bubbles and other instruments as they pass him between themselves until they get to her. A nurse's cradled arms place the blanket wrapped baby in her own awaiting arms. Sound returns to Graigh's ears. She hears the splitting scream of her son jarred from his ten-month slumber to life.

"Don't cry, Baby, I'm here," Graigh coos.

Pressed against her skin she looks down on his face. His light skin obscured by the thick, creamy cottage cheese like substance still overlaid on his freshly born body. Graigh takes her thumb and wipes the blood and vernix from his forehead. Gently rocking her arms side to side to settle his cry she nuzzles her face close to his.

The nurse appears by her side to take him once again. Graigh watches as her baby is lifted from her arms and placed under heated lamps. She hears them yell out his height, twenty-two inches, and weight, eight pounds, five ounces.

"What time was he born?" Graigh asks.

"August twenty-ninth, 3:37 a.m." Bombei answers from in front of the incubator.

She watches as her newborn is wiped clean, put into his first diaper, and the navy blue, knit, bear eared cap she packed for him is placed on his head. A nurse double swaddles him in two hospital blankets and carries him back to her arms. Graigh looks on his face again. His clean light brown face with the reddish tint. Unblemished, not a scratch or scar in sight. The smooth skin just exposed to the elements of the world.

"Are you going to breast or bottle feed?" a nurse asks from the foot of the hospital bed.

"I'm going to try nursing and see how this works."

"Go ahead and try now. Both sides."

Graigh lowers the baby to her breast, cradling his head and holding out her nipple for him to learn to latch. The immediate power of his suction causes her to wince before she relaxes.

"You did it," Bombei says standing beside her.

"He's here," Graigh exhales.

He's really here.

"He is," Bombei says breathless.

"And he's healthy?"

"He is."

Graigh looks down on her feeding baby. His eyes are closed as his jaws work to draw in nutrients for the very first time. Bombei sits on the side of the bed and leans over to stroke the top of the baby's face. His thumb is the entire size of the baby's forehead. In their trio they breathe as one as the baby eats.

"You're beautiful," Bombei whispers to Graigh.

"I feel anything but beautiful right now," Graigh says. "He's the beautiful one."

"Handsome."

"Same difference. Ooh. Uh oh."

"What?"

"He unlatched. I guess we'll try the other side."

Graigh turns the baby from one side to the other and repeats the process of bringing his head close and extending her nipple. The awkward pain of successful acceptance comes and goes as he begins to eat from the other side. She smiles down at him proud of them both. Laying her head back against the slight recline of the bed she closes her eyes.

"Don't go to sleep and start bad habits early."

"Leave me alone," she says.

"How are you doing?"

The questioning voice belongs to Doctor Marcella.

"I'm good. We're good," Graigh says opening her eyes.

"It got a little dicey there for a second. I knew for sure we were heading to the operating room."

"I told you I didn't want a C-section," Graigh quips.

"Yeah, but what's on the birth plan and what actually happens rarely match up. Whatever he told you after we talked worked."

"It did," Graigh says nodding her head.

"I'll let you three get acquainted. We just need one more thing from you."

"What's that?" Bombei asks?

"His name. It's not on your paperwork you filled out for registration. Do you have one?"

"We do." Graigh says, looking at Bombei."

"What is it and we'll get it over to the office of vital records."

Graigh looks from the baby in her arms to Bombei's face and back again.

"Go ahead, Baby," Bombei urges.

"Good morning, Karter," Graigh whispers to the baby.

"Carter," Doctor Marcella repeats. "That's a nice name."

"Thank you," Graigh says still looking at her son. "It's Karter, with a 'K.'"

"Got it," Doctor Marcella says, scribbling on the paperwork she brought into the hospital room.

"Karter Robert Halvert."

Epilogue

Bombei maneuvers their car down Robertson to head across the bridge. He looks in his rearview mirror as he goes and smiles at his sleeping son he cannot see—strapped in the rear-facing car seat—and at his wife whose serene face is inclined toward their new creation. Graigh doesn't look up to meet Bombei's gaze, and she doesn't cross her body. Instead, her heart quickens as they cross the bridge. It beats rapaciously as they descend into the lower Ninth Ward.

To her left she sees Brad Pitt's handiwork. The brightly colored, modernly constructed houses, meant to stand the next test of water, wind, and heat. The one hundred or so homes spread around Jordan Avenue and Deslonde are in direct contrast to what Graigh knows is on her right. Homes, some of which have not been retouched, renovated, or modernized. Homes where the people were left to fend for themselves.

Graigh nods knowingly to her sleeping son. She knows that as he ages and his eyes adjust he, too, may see what she sees. Homes where the water lines have been replaced by mildew because it's been too long. Homes where the wooden siding has buckled under the weight of the humid mornings that turn in to humid days and humid nights. She knows that as he grows, water will be his constant. The lake she will take him to, the river he will walk along, the canals he will cross, and the Gulf he will swim in.

Bombei turns onto Charbonnet as Graigh muses in her mind. She sees the wooden frames of the few houses on her block that bear the marks of a history long forgotten. The homes painted in bright colors echoing the French, Spanish, and African influences that became American. Graigh knows his life, Karter's life, will be a mix of all of these influences. Influences in an upbringing Graigh is determined he have.

Sitting beside her sleeping baby, she is determined he know the chaos of convergence that happens on Decatur Street in the French market, where tourists clog the street jetting from Jackson Park to the St. Louis Cathedral in their drunken mania; or inhaling the sweet confections that are the city's famed beignets, from Café du Monde on Decatur and St. Ann. She is determined that he see Armstrong Park and do more than take the guided tour of Congo Square, where the once enslaved population could gather to be free—if only for a moment, if only for a day. Graigh is determined to raise Karter to understand that in that square that became a staple of the Vieux Carré his people, his history, and his ancestors played music that moved them, and sold the goods they grew or made to eventually buy their freedom.

Graigh knows one day Karter will grow to realize that freedom is elusive; and bondage, be it physically or mentally, is still bondage. But she hopes that what he eventually learns in the world will always stand in direct dissonance to what he understands at home. What he comes to understand at Pop and Dottie's Pharmacy and Food Store, where he will grow up seeing his mother unbought, unbossed, and unbothered.

As Bombei pulls into their carport and they are surrounded by the sparse population of their block, their neighborhood, and their community, Graigh hopes she can endow to Karter the freedom of his imagination. It is the freedom of her own imagination. To see the things that are not, as though they were. To call something out of the surrounding nothingness that for now—fifteen years after the storm—is a constant reminder of pain, anguish, and death, even though she has brought life.

Graigh looks up, from Karter's sleeping countenance to meet Bombei's gaze in the rearview mirror. He smiles his knowing smile, as she lets the joy emanate across her face. They share a similar, and unspoken sentiment as Graigh loosens the buckles of her nestled baby beside her in the back seat. In picking him up, bringing him to her chest, and easing out of the car door Bombei opened for her, she hopes she is endowing him with the spark of what she began. The lighted splint of what the families around her who returned and rebuilt began. That he—clutched close to her body as she moves up the steps, only days old—maybe he can finish what they all began; until it is restored and more beautiful and more Black than what it was before. That he may see himself reflected everywhere he goes beginning in his home.

"We're here," Bombei says, opening the front door.

Graigh breathes into Karter's body and seals her endowments with a kiss on his forehead.

She looks at Bombei in his eyes and says, "We're home."

Acknowledgements

We've made it to the end of another adventure. This time in a new city. Yes, Doctor Grace is Naomi's mom from *Adulting*. No, I still don't know who the father is for Naomi's daughter. But hey, you know she had a daughter. Now that we've gotten that out of the way . . . Let's talk about *Beyond Bourbon Street*.

This book has been about thirteen to fifteen years in the making. I am from Chicago and I live in Jacksonville, Florida, however, both my mother and father are from New Orleans, hence the setting. New Orleans served as a second home for me and my brother. Our holidays and summers were spent in the Big Easy from my earliest remembrances. The house where this book is set on Charbonnet Street in the Lower Ninth Ward was my grandmother's home. Her house is the one on the cover of this book and what it looked like after the storm. It has since been demolished.

When Hurricane Katrina hit New Orleans, I was in my second year of undergrad at FSU. Watching the coverage on my 13-inch TV in my dorm, not being able to get in touch with my family was sickening. They all evacuated and were safe, but phone lines were shoddy, and I couldn't reach anyone. All I could do was watch. Author Sarah M. Broom says in her memoir, *The Yellow House*, that after the storm something in her burst open. I identify with that sentiment on a cellular level. And so, the journey to *Beyond Bourbon Street* began.

In a final project for my undergrad speech class I performed an obituary for my grandmother's house. My English honors thesis was a novella entitled, *From Pillar to Post*, where the characters of Graigh and Bombei were first conceived and brought to life.

The only people who read that work were three of my teachers who served on the board for my thesis defense, my mother, and three roommates. My roommate, Indira Goodwine, said upon reaching the end, "I need a sequel." (I know. Me and endings.) In 2008, I didn't know what the future would hold for Graigh and Bombei but I knew their story wasn't complete.

As life would have it, they began to return to my consciousness after the birth of my son. However, I didn't have the time or the energy to expend on their story because I was chest deep on my journey to bring *Four Women* to life. In the two years' time between the completion of *Four Women* (2015) and its publication (2017) *Beyond Bourbon Street* was born.

After the birth of my son I began to think of the couple I had written about so long ago and wonder what their lives would look like in the present. In my novella, they had just met and were repairing Graigh's home. Chapter four of the book you're holding was chapter one of my novella word for word.

I began *Beyond Bourbon Street* in October 2016 and finished it in August 2017 just months before *Four Women* was released. I knew I wouldn't release it until 2020 as part of my own personal commemoration of the fifteenth anniversary of Hurricane Katrina.

This novel, while fiction, is steeped in my personal memories and my own life journey. Since its completion and the release, it has gone through six drafts. It was originally forty-eight chapters. Now it is forty-one with an epilogue that was added around draft three or four. I am nervous and anxious about the release of this novel as I am taking a story that is only partly mine and giving voice to experiences I have only heard second hand.

For the research of this novel much thanks is owed to Gary Rivlin's phenomenal mapping of the conditions of New Orleans immediately after the storm in his book, *Katrina: After the Flood*. After reading Sarah M. Broom's, *The Yellow House*, I had a deeper understanding of the emotional journey of New Orleanians post-Katrina. My mother, Jacqueline Leeper, answered every call for every question and my family shared with me their stories when they didn't have to. A shout out to my cousin LMaun Morris for the line "If the city ain't got time to come fix the street, you think they got time to cut grass?"

Thank you, God, for the gift that has brought me to this moment. Thank you to my incredible team Roy Glenn and Arvita Roberts-Glenn for editing and Gisette Gomez of Zodiac Studios Co. for yet another cover design. (GG, this is six!) And last but certainly not least, thank you, the reader for rocking with me these last few years. I truly appreciate all the love and support. And if you have questions, concerns, want to chop it up or shoot the sh** hit me up at *www.newwrites.com* or on the socials @Nikesha_Elise basically everywhere.

Until next time . . .
Peace, Blessings, and Abundance,

CPSIA information can be obtained
at www.ICGtesting.com
Printed in the USA
BVHW030607091020
590668BV00002B/4/J